U0144380

2011 不求人文化

2009 懶鬼子英日語

我識出版集團
I'm Publishing Group
www.17buy.com.tw

2005 意識文化

2005 易富文化

2003 我識地球村

2001 我識出版社

2011 不求人文化

2009 懶鬼子英日語

2005 意識文化

2005 易富文化

2003 我識地球村

2001 我識出版社

午休5分鐘的英文閱讀

Spending Five Minutes in Lunch Break to Learn English Reading

本書適用時機

早上配早餐使用｜一日之計在於晨，搭配早餐，補充身體與腦袋的能量。

消夜泡泡麵使用｜書放在泡麵上，邊學習，邊等泡麵熟，一舉兩得。

通勤裝文青使用｜收起手機，拿出書本，知識力、文青力迅速提升。

等人發呆時使用｜把握等人的空檔，多看幾句會話，等等聊天就能現學現賣。

睡前 5 分鐘使用｜睡前學的內容更容易被大腦吸收，黃金學習時間一定要把握。

本書使用方式

★ 獨家講述閱讀技巧，就算只有 5 分鐘，就算面對不同情境、不同長度的文章，也能馬上掌握文意關鍵。

★ 除了「閱讀」，更補充撰寫文章的寫作技巧，全書文章、單字更請專業美籍老師錄製 MP3，同時加強「寫作力」與「聽說力」。

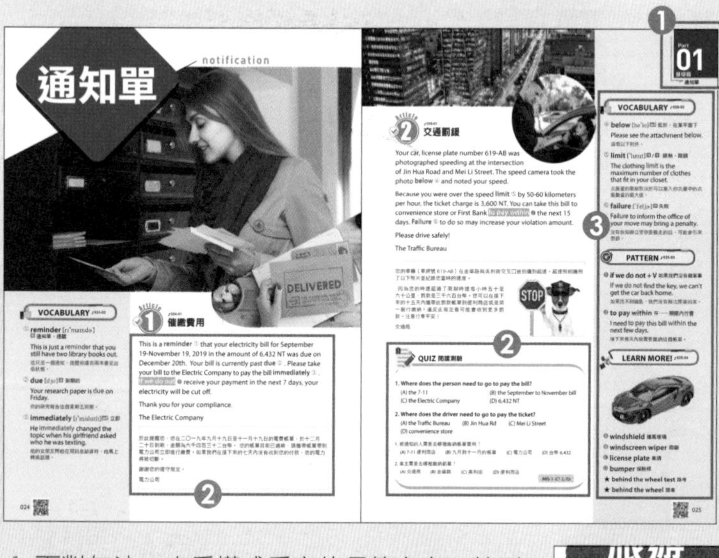

1. 全書分為：生活化的「基礎篇」＋主題豐富的「進階篇」＋學了就會用的「應用篇」，保證最豐富、最實用。

2. 每篇文章皆提供中英文，搭配閱讀測驗，即時檢測學習成效。

3. 補充豐富的單字、句型與例句，能夠一次學到多種用法。

4. 面對無法一次看懂或看完的長篇文章，特別將文章以一個段落為單位，提供中英文與單字解說，既能分段學習，也方便對照。

5. 除了使用 CD 片，也可下載隨書附贈的虛擬點讀筆 App，只要事先下載好音檔，就能隨掃隨聽、離線也能聽。（虛擬點讀筆說明，請見下一頁）

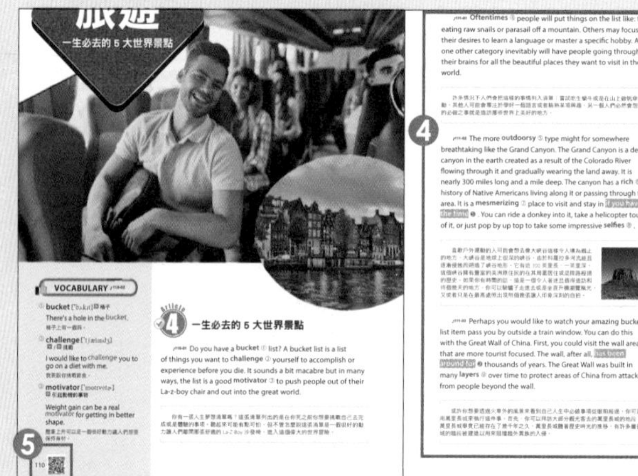

[FREE!!]

免費附贈 2,000 單字電子書，符合全民英檢初級程度，就算沒有帶書出門，也能隨時隨地背單字。

線上下載「VRP 虛擬點讀筆」App

為了幫助讀者更方便使用本書，特別領先全世界開發「VRP 虛擬點讀筆」App（Virtual Reading Pen），安裝此 App 後，將可以更有效率地利用本書學習。讀者只要將本書結合已安裝「VRP 虛擬點讀筆」App 的手機，就能利用手機隨時掃描書中的 QR Code 立即聽取本書的中英文單字、英語會話。就像是使用「點讀筆」一樣方便，但卻不用花錢再另外購買「點讀筆」和「點讀書」。

虛擬點讀筆介紹

「VRP 虛擬點讀筆」App 就是這麼方便！

❶ 讀者只要掃描右側 QR Code 連結，就能立即免費下載「VRP 虛擬點讀筆」App。（僅限 iPhone 和 Android 兩種系統手機）或是在 App Store 及 Google Play 搜尋「VRP 虛擬點讀筆」即可下載。

★ 若一開始沒有安裝「VRP虛擬點讀筆」App，掃描書中的QR Code將會導引至App Store或Google Play商店，請點選下載App後即可使用。

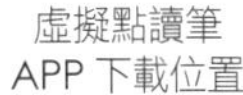
虛擬點讀筆
APP 下載位置

❷ 打開「VRP 虛擬點讀筆」後登入，若無帳號請先點選「加入會員」，完成註冊會員後即可登入。

❸「VRP 虛擬點讀筆」App 下載完成後，可至 App 目錄中搜尋需要的音檔或直接掃描內頁 QR Code 一次下載至手機使用。（若以正常網速下載，所需時間約四至六分鐘；請盡量在優良網速環境下下載）。

❹ 當音檔已完成下載後，讀者只要拿出手機並開啟「VRP 虛擬點讀筆」App，就能隨時掃描書中頁面的 QR Code 立即播放音檔（平均 1 秒內），且不需要開啟上網功能。

❺「VRP 虛擬點讀筆」App 就像是點讀筆一樣好用，還可以調整播放速度（0.8-1.2 倍速），配合學習步調。

❻ 如果讀者擔心音檔下載後太佔手機空間，也可以隨時刪除音檔下次需要使用時再下載。購買本公司書籍的讀者等於有一個雲端的 CD 櫃可隨時使用。

★「VRP虛擬點讀筆」App僅支援Android 4.3以上、iOS 9以上版本。

★ 雖然我們努力做到完美，但也有可能因為手機的系統版本和「VRP虛擬點讀筆」App不相容導致無法安裝，在此必須和讀者說聲抱歉，若無法正常使用，請讀者使用隨書附贈的CD。

利用「零碎時間」學習更有效率！

「每次看到一堆英文，我的頭就好痛。」

「看到超過 5 句的英文文章，注意力就開始渙散了。」

「想在國外網站買東西，但完全不知道該如何操作。」

這些話，是不是有說中你的心聲？或是，踩到你的痛處？

英文閱讀一直是大家想要加強，卻又不知道如何開始學習的能力，多數人都還能掌握「單字＋單字」或是「單句＋單句」的意思，但只要單字超過 100 字以上，或是句子超過 5 句以上，腦中就會呈現一片空白，甚至拒絕思考。

面對這樣的問題，有些人會選擇去補習班上課。但每個人一天只有二十四小時，要做的事情很多，想擠出一個完整的時間來學習英文，可以說是天方夜譚。「時間不夠用」是現代人碰到的共通問題，學生有念不完的書、準備不完的考試；上班族有做不完的工作、吃不完的飯局⋯⋯。

與其每週擠出完整的 50 分鐘去上英文課，還不如蒐集每段零碎的 5 分鐘，積少成多；妥善運用每段零碎的 5 分鐘，每天看一點《午休 5 分鐘的英文閱讀：利用「零碎時間」，學習更有效率！》的內容，聚沙成塔，就會發現不知不覺中，你的英文閱讀力增長了不少。

這本《午休 5 分鐘的英文閱讀：利用「零碎時間」，學習更有效率！》並不會教你如何考好多益、準備升學考試，而是希望透過生活化的主題，引起你的學習興趣。書中分成基礎、進階、應用篇，從短篇的廣告單、公告、活動通知、社群媒體貼文，到稍微長篇一點的文章、或者是網路商店購物的實際應用，提供給你最生活化的情境、最實用的內容，讓你學到真正用得到的英文，提升你的英文閱讀力。

而這本書的每一頁都是完整的學習內容，你可以跳著學、挑著學，翻到哪頁就看哪頁，5 分鐘看一頁，沒有太大的學習壓力，又能學習很有效率。除此之外，這本書也免費附贈虛擬點讀筆 App、2,000 單字電子書，讓你能在任何地點、任何時間用喜歡的方式學英文。

最後，要跟大家分享，運用零碎時間學習所帶來的另一個好處是「能夠訓練自己，迅速集中注意力，並進入學習或是工作狀況」，每天花 5 分鐘學英文，不僅學好英文，還可以培養專注力，一舉兩得！

不求人文化編輯群

目錄

Contents

02

基礎篇

03
進階篇

04
應用篇

01 Chatting Time
每段零碎時間，都能學英文

大家都知道要把握零碎時間學習，但到底哪些是零碎時間？要用什麼方式學習呢？在這裡為大家推薦幾個免費的英文學習資源，想要學英文，不需要花大錢上補習班，網路上就有很多資源可以輔助學習！以下按照不同用途，介紹背單字、看影片、逛網站的免費學習資源，但請注意，有些網站與 App 在初期使用時不需要收費，但如果想要使用更多功能或是做更深入的學習，可能會被收取部分費用（依網站、App 提供者規定）。

零碎時間，來背背單字！

Vocabulazy

專為懶人設計，方便使用者在零碎時間背單字，收錄 7,000 單字、多益、托福等不同主題的單字表，可以直接加強較弱的單字分類，且有搭配測驗功能，有助於了解英文程度。

English4Formosa

比較偏向用字根、字首、字首的學習法，單字較偏向托福、GRE 的難度，對於想要出國留學的朋友非常實用。

英漢字典 VoiceTube Dictionary 影音字典

每個單字都有美國、英國的發音，並提供豐富實用的例句，也可以運用 App 功能來建立專屬自己的單字本，且可以連結到 Voicetube 用影片學單字。

Biscuit

可以讓使用者在瀏覽英文網頁時，即時翻譯不懂的單字，並把該單字加入到個人專屬單字本中。另外也有功能可以讓 App 定時提醒自己要背單字。

不想背單字，就來看影片！

Voicetube

https://tw.voicetube.com/

主打「看影片學英文」的概念，主題豐富多元。影片有標示級數、腔調，並搭配可切換的中英文字幕，而單字也有即時字典可做查詢，並提供筆記、錄音等功能，部落格專區也有收錄許多句子跟文法講解。

★ 也有提供 App 喔！

Ted

https://www.ted.com/

由美國 TED Conference LLC. 經營，收錄 TED 著名的 15 分鐘演講影片，由各界專業的人士進行演講，主題涵蓋生活、人文、商業、科學、藝術、設計等主題。影片亦有提供腳本，甚至標示影片秒數，非常方便學習。演講內容用字精闢、內容豐富，不僅可訓練聽力，也能豐富英文書寫力。

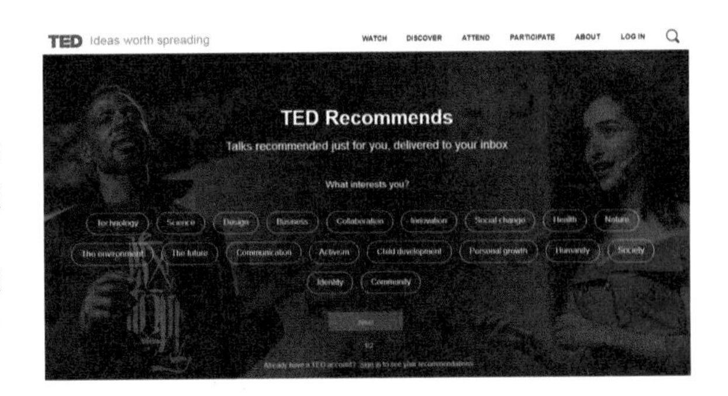

不要逛網拍，來逛逛英文網站吧！

Mental Floss

http://mentalfloss.com/

網站中收錄許多與自然、動物、歷史有關的文章和冷知識，淺顯易懂、容易閱讀。

★
新 聞

NPR

https://www.npr.org/

美國國家公共廣播電台的網站，內容涵蓋時事、文化、藝術和音樂，雖然有些文章比較艱深，但許多文章也會提供影片跟語音的文字稿，很適合同時訓練英文聽力與閱讀。

A Beautiful Mess

https://abeautifulmess.com/

由一對姊妹經營的部落格，分享她們喜歡的工藝品、居家裝潢、烹飪等等，文章輕鬆易讀，用字活潑俏皮，閱讀起來沒有負擔。

Nomadic Matt

https://www.nomadicmatt.com/

裡面充滿部落格格主分享的旅行經驗與注意事項，文章使用簡單易懂的英文，不僅可以了解其他國家的文化、如何規劃旅行，還有許多旅遊愛好者會有興趣的話題。

Refinery29

https://www.refinery29.com/en-us

內容主要是流行時尚、娛樂、時事評論，要注意的是這個網站沒有使用正式的寫作風格，也會使用網路俚語。

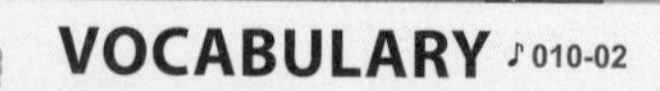

VOCABULARY ♪010-02

① **repairman** [rɪ`pɛrmən] n 修理工

The repairman looked at the refrigerator and said it wasn't worth fixing.

修理人員看了冰箱之後說這個問題不值得花錢修理。

② **fix** [fɪks] v 修理

It took James two minutes to fix the light switch.

詹姆士只花了兩分鐘修理燈的開關。

③ **apologize** [ə`pɑləˌdʒaɪz] v 致歉，道歉

I apologize for being so rude to you.

我很抱歉對你這麼沒禮貌。

Article 1

♪010-01

公告停電

Dear residents:

We are having problems ❶ with the building's electrical wiring. A **repairman** ① will come tomorrow to **fix** ② the problem. The electricity in the building will be turned off from 8 am to 5 pm.

We **apologize** ③ for any inconvenience.

Sincerely,
Building Management

親愛的住戶：

目前住宅建築物內的電線出了些問題。明天會有修理人員前來解決這個問題。明天早上八點到下午五點這段時間電力將會被關閉。

如有造成您任何不便，我們深感抱歉。

住戶管理委員會 敬啟

Article

2 公告停水

♪011-01

To Whom It May Concern:

A water **leak** ④ is causing damage to the second floor stairway area. This Thursday and Friday, the Water Company will **send someone** ❷ over to take a look at the problem. Please be informed that the building water will be turned off **during** ⑤ the day on those two days.

Please make sure to prepare **buckets** ⑥ of water on Wednesday.

Thank you for your understanding.
Building Management

敬啟者：

漏水導致二樓樓梯區域受損。本週四與週五自來水公司將會派人前來查看此問題。請注意這兩天的白天時間自來水將會暫時被關閉。請確保您在星期三的時候事先儲備幾桶水。謝謝您的理解。

住戶管理委員會

QUIZ 閱讀測驗

1. What time will the repairman start working?
   (A) tomorrow (B) 5 pm
   (C) The electrical wiring (D) 8 am

2. Who is likely to fix the leak problem?
   (A) Mr. Wednesday (B) the building guard
   (C) a water company repairman (D) a specially hired repairman

1. 修理人員何時會開始進行工作？
   (A) 明天 (B) 下午五點 (C) 電線 (D) 早上八點

2. 誰可能會修理漏水問題？
   (A) 溫斯德先生 (B) 大樓管理員
   (C) 自來水公司的修理人員 (D) 特別雇用的修理人員

ANS: 1. (A) 2. (C)

VOCABULARY ♪011-02

④ **leak** [lik] n 漏洞 v 滲漏

There is a leak in the swimming pool!
這個游泳池會漏水！

⑤ **during** [ˋdjurɪŋ] prep 在……期間

During the day, he is just an office worker, but at night, he's a superhero.
白天的時候他是一名辦公室員工，但晚上的時候他是一位超級英雄。

⑥ **bucket** [ˋbʌkɪt] n 水桶 v 下傾盆大雨

It took twenty buckets of water to fill up the bathtub.
需要二十桶水才能夠填滿這個浴缸。

PATTERN ♪011-03

❶ **having problems V-ing + in N**
某事物有……的問題

Joey and Catherine are having problems in their marriage.
喬伊跟凱薩琳的婚姻中有一些問題。

❷ **V + someone** ……人

Please tell someone to come and help me.
請叫人過來幫忙我。

GRAMMAR

英文句子的架構主要可分為這 5 大句型

1. **主詞＋動詞**
   例 **Nothing happens.** 什麼事都沒發生。
2. **主詞＋動詞＋受詞**
   例 **I like cats.** 我喜歡貓。
3. **主詞＋動詞＋補語**
   例 **She is pretty.** 她很漂亮。
4. **主詞＋動詞＋受詞＋受詞**
   例 **He gives you a rose.**
   他給你一朵玫瑰花。
5. **主詞＋動詞＋受詞＋補語**
   例 **I think he is handsome.**
   我覺得他很帥。

Article 3

♪012-01

公告管理費調漲

VOCABULARY ♪012-02

⑦ **fee** [fi] n 費用

The school fees are due by the end of the month.

這個月底學費繳納的期限就會到期了。

⑧ **bill** [bɪl] n 帳單

The waiter brought the bill, but he gave it to the wrong person.

服務生拿了帳單過來，但是他給錯人了。

⑨ **leave** [liv] v 留下

You can leave your coat at the front desk.

你可以把你的外套留在前台。

MORE VOCABULARY ♪012-03

alter [`ɔltɚ] v 修改

revise [rɪ`vaɪz] v 修改、修正

recompose [ˌrikəm`poz] v 修改、改編

decline [dɪ`klaɪn] v 婉拒、謝絕

refuse [rɪ`fjuz] v 拒絕、不願
[`rɛfjus] n 廢物、垃圾 a 無用的

deny [dɪ`naɪ] v 拒絕、否定

clean [klin] v 清潔

volunteer [ˌvɑlən`tɪr] v 志願

maintenance 維修

Good Afternoon,

As you know, our building maintenance **fees** ⑦ have stayed the same for the last five years.

Starting next month, there will be a monthly increase of 300NT to each renter's **bill** ⑧. 200NT of this will go toward building maintenance expenses, and the remaining 100NT ❸ will be added to the building guard's salary.

If there are any questions, please **leave** ⑨ them with the building guard.

Thank you.

大家下午好：

如各位住戶所知，我們大樓的管理費在過去五年中沒有漲價。但從下個月開始，每位承租人的帳單每個月將增加三百台幣的費用。其中的兩百台幣將用於大樓管理費，剩下的一百台幣則會納入大樓管理員的薪資支出上。

如果您有任何疑問，請與大樓管理員詢問。

謝謝你。

LEARN MORE! ♪012-04

有時候你的心聲會告訴你不認同或不想要，就別為難自己了，勇敢說不吧！

- **I disagree with you about this.** 我不認同你說的這一點。
- **I don't think so.** 我不這麼認為。
- **I beg to differ.** 恕難苟同。
- **That's not always the case.** 並不總是這樣的。
- **It's not as simple as it seems.** 並沒有像看起來的那麼簡單。
- **I'm not sure about that.** 我不確定是那樣。

Article 4 社區管委會開會

♪013-01

Dear Residents:

The **bimonthly** ⑩ Building Administrative Meeting will take place this Saturday at 10 am. At this meeting, we will discuss the need to replace the central cooling system. There will also be some communication on the current building rules.

Several residents have complained that not everyone is following the building rules **regarding** ⑪ the separation of recycling and respecting the quiet hours of 10 pm to 6 am.

If anyone would like to ❹ attend, please sign up at the front desk to let us know how many seats to **prepare** ⑫.

Thank you.

親愛的住戶：

每兩個月舉行一次的社區行政會議將於本週六上午十點舉行。 在這次會議上，我們將討論更換中央冷卻系統的必要性， 也會討論目前現有的住宅規定。

有一些住戶抱怨有其他住戶不遵守回收規定，以及不尊重晚上十點到隔天早上六點的噪音防制規定。

如果您希望參加此次會議，請在管理室前台登記以利我們知道需要準備多少座位。

謝謝你。

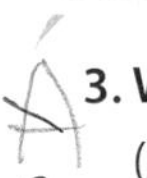

QUIZ 閱讀測驗

3. Where will most of the money go to?

(A) to the renters　(B) to the building expenses
(C) to the bills　(D) to the guard's salary

4. What will not be talked about at the meeting?

(A) when to have elections　(B) building rules
(C) cooling the building　(D) respecting quiet hours

3. 大部分增加的費用會用在哪？
(A) 給住戶用　(B) 納入大樓管理費用　(C) 增加到帳單中　(D) 納入管理員薪資中

4. 會議中什麼項目不會被討論？
(A) 何時舉行選舉　(B) 住宅規定
(C) 大樓冷卻系統　(D) 尊重噪音防治規定

ANS: 1. (B) 2. (A)

VOCABULARY ♪013-02

⑩ **bimonthly** [ˋbaɪˋmʌnθlɪ] a 兩月一次的

I think a bimonthly meeting is necessary to keep everyone on the same page.

為了確保每個人知道的資訊對等，我認為兩個月一次的會議是必要的。

⑪ **regarding** [rɪˋgardɪŋ] prep 關於

This is a letter regarding the company's business plans.

這封信是關於公司的商務計畫。

⑫ **prepare** [prɪˋpɛr] V 準備，起草

We'd like to prepare the table especially for this dinner, so please be sure to RSVP.

為了這次的晚餐我們要準備餐桌座位，所以請回覆確認是否參加。

PATTERN ♪013-03

❸ **the remaining + (amount of money or time)** 剩餘的……多少錢（或時間）

The remaining 500NT should be enough to pay for our dinner.

剩下的五百台幣應該可以支付我們的晚餐錢。

❹ **if anyone would like to V** 如果有人想要做……（某事）

If anyone would like to visit, please write a letter to the school first.

如果有人想要拜訪，請事先寫信給學校。

公告

announcement

VOCABULARY ♪014-02

① **annual** [ˋænjʊəl] a 年度的

Our annual meeting is going to be held this Friday.

我們的年度會議將於本週五舉行。

② **answer** [ˋænsɚ] v 回答、回覆

I have been answering emails all morning long.

整個早上我都在回覆電子郵件。

③ **normal** [ˋnɔrml̩] a 正常的

Normal work hours are from 9 am to 6 pm Monday to Saturday.

正常上下班時間是從星期一到星期六的早上九點到下午六點。

Article 1

♪014-01

放假通知

Dear valued clients,

Our offices will be closed from October 7th to 17th for the company's **annual** ① employee trip. Any email or phone messages received during that time will be **answered** ② as soon as we return to ❶ **normal** ③ business hours on October 18th .

We apologize for any inconvenience.

Andrew and Matheson Brothers Law Firm

我們親愛的客戶：

因為公司年度員工之旅的緣故，我們的辦公室將於十月七日到十七日這段期間關閉。所有的電子郵件跟電話語音留言都將於十月十八日回歸正常上班時間後立即回覆。

如有造成任何不便，我們誠摯於此致歉。

安德魯和馬西森兄弟律師事務所

♪ 015-01

中午休息時間調整

Attention all employees:

June will be the last month that the midday break will be from 12:30-1:30 for all employees. This is not **beneficial** ④ to our customers that need assistance during the midday hours. Hence, **we are changing to a** ❷ shift-style midday break.

Starting on July 1, Group A will take a break from 11:45 am to 12:45 pm. Group B will take a break from 12:45 pm to 1:45 pm. For anyone wishing to select a **specific** ⑤ group, there will be a signup sheet in the **breakroom** ⑥.

We thank you for your cooperation.

Myers Industry Office Management

所有員工請注意：

六月將是我們實施員工午休時間從中午十二點半到下午一點半的最後一個月。在這段時間午休對需要我們幫助的客戶來說無益。因此，我們將會把原本的模式修改成換班模式的午休。

從七月一日開始，A 組會從中午十一點四十五分到十二點四十五分這段時間休息，B 組會從中午十二點四十五分到下午一點四十五分這段時間休息。希望可以選組的人可以去休息室登記。感謝您的合作。

麥爾斯工業辦公室管理部

VOCABULARY ♪ 015-02

④ **beneficial** [ˌbɛnəˋfɪʃəl] a 有利的

They say it is beneficial to take probiotics when you take antibiotics.

他們說如果你有在服用抗生素，這時候吃益生菌是有幫助的。

⑤ **specific** [spɪˋsɪfɪk] a 特定的、明確的

Please let us know if you have any specific needs for the meeting.

會議上有任何特別需求的話請讓我們知道。

⑥ **breakroom** [brek][rum] n 休息室

It seems like Annie's spends all of her time in the breakroom.

安妮似乎整天待在休息室裡。

PATTERN ♪ 015-03

❶ **as soon as we return to** 我們一回到……

I'll get out those orders as soon as we return to regular business hours.

我們一回到原本的上班時間，我就會把這些訂單弄出去。

❷ **we are changing to a** 改變為……

We are changing to a more modern service-style at our restaurant.

我們的餐廳正在轉換成一種比較現代的自助用餐模式。

QUIZ 閱讀測驗

1. Who might be affected by this company trip?

(A) the building janitor (B) someone needing a lawyer's help
(C) a patient (D) a travel company

2. Who is likely to be in Group A?

(A) Employees with last names starting with A-M.
(B) Employees with last names starting with N-Z.
(C) Employees that sign up for Group A.
(D) Employees that sign up for Group B.

1. 誰可能會被這個員工旅行影響到？
(A) 大樓清潔員 (B) 需要律師幫助的人 (C) 病人 (D) 旅行社

2. 誰比較有可能在 A 組？
(A) 姓氏開頭為字母 A 到 M 的員工 (B) 姓氏開頭為字母 N 到 Z 的員工
(C) 登記 A 組的員工 (D) 登記 B 組的員工

ANS: 1. (B) 2. (C)

LEARN MORE! ♪ 015-04

café 咖啡

tea 茶

snack 點心

biscuit 小餅乾

sandwich 三明治

waffle 華夫餅／鬆餅

VOCABULARY ♪016-02

⑦ **companywide**
[ˋkʌmpənɪ͵ɚaɪd] a 全公司的

The companywide picnic is a great place to get to know people from other departments.

全公司的野餐活動是一個認識其他部門同事的好場合。

⑧ **showcase** [ˋʃo͵kes]
v 展示……優點、充分展示

We hope this art exhibition will help Mary showcase her talent.

我們希望這次的藝術展，可以幫助瑪麗展現她的天份。

⑨ **compete** [kəmˋpit] v 競爭

If you want to compete, you have to be ready to practice.

你如果想要參與競爭，你必須做好開始練習的準備。

⑩ **developed** [dɪˋvɛləpt] a 發展的

Our research department has developed a new use for this headache medication.

我們的研發部已經針對這個頭痛藥研發了一種新用法。

⑪ **enjoy** [ɪnˋdʒɔɪ] v 享受

We hope you will enjoy your dinner.

我們希望你們享受晚餐。

⑫ **deeply** [ˋdiplɪ]
ad 非常、極其、深深地

I cannot tell you the number of times I have been deeply hurt by people I thought were my friends.

我已經數不出來我有多少次，被自己認為是朋友的人深深地傷害。

Article 3

♪016-01

比賽報名

Dear employees,

As the year is winding down ❸, and we are getting ready for the New Year break, don't forget that it's time once again for our **companywide** ⑦ talent competition! Can you play the piano? Can you sing well? Do you have any other talents that you would like to **showcase** ⑧? Everyone that **competes** ⑨ is a winner as we have lots of great prizes. The top prizes include a three-day trip to Kenting for two, a 10,000 NT bonus, and a 5,000 NT bonus.

What are you waiting for? Sign up with the president's secretary by November 30, and get to practicing!

親愛的員工們：

隨著年底的到來，我們都在準備迎接新年的假期，但別忘了還有為全公司舉辦的才藝競賽！你會彈鋼琴嗎？你唱歌好聽嗎？你有什麼想要「炫」的才藝嗎？每個參與競賽的人都可以是贏家，因為我們準備了許多很棒的獎品。首獎是為期三天的兩人墾丁之旅、也有一萬元台幣跟五千元台幣的獎金項目。

還在等什麼？在十一月三十日之前，趕緊跟董事長的祕書報名登記並開始練習吧！

QUIZ 閱讀測驗

3. Which is not the mentioned prize?

(A) a promotion from the president (B) a trip to Kenting
(C) a three-day holiday trip for two (D) a money bonus

3. 哪一個項目不是提及的獎品內容？

(A) 董事長的提拔 (B) 墾丁之旅 (C) 為期三天的兩人之旅 (D) 獎金

ANS: 3. (A)

♪ 017-01

活動通知

General Announcement for all Newsom Employees:

Our company has recently **developed** ⑩ a business partnership with Yogatime!, a yoga play space in downtown Taipei. As part of this ❹ cooperation, Yogatime! has provided a limited-time offer where all Newsom employees are able to **enjoy** ⑪ one month of free yoga classes. After that time, Newsom employees may get a Yogatime! membership at a **deeply** ⑫ discounted price.

If you are interested, please attend the official cooperation celebration event on Wednesday at 8pm. At the event, you can tour the facilities and pick up your free one-month access card.

We hope to see you there!

Newsom Management

請所有 Newsom 員工注意：

最近我司跟台北市中心一家名為「Yogatime!」的瑜伽機構建立商業合作關係。其中一部分的合作項目包括 Yogatime! 提供我司全部員工限時的免費優惠，每位員工可以上為期一個月的免費瑜伽課。免費課程結束後，Newsom 的員工可以用極其優惠的折扣價格加入 Yogatime! 的會員。

如果你對此活動感興趣，請參加星期三晚上八點舉辦的正式合作慶祝活動。活動中你可以參觀各項設施並且領取免費一個月的課程卡。

希望我們可以在活動中看到你喔！

Newsom 管理部

QUIZ 閱讀測驗

4. Who will enjoy one month of Yoga classes?

(A) Yogatime! employees (B) Newsom employees
(C) Newsom clients (D) new Yogatime! members

4. 誰可以享有一個月的免費瑜伽課程？

(A) Yogatime! 的員工 (B) Newsom 的員工 (C) Newsom 的客戶
(D) 新加入 Yogatime! 的員工

ANS: 4. (B)

PATTERN ♪ 017-02

❸ **the (time) is winding down**
（逐漸）進入休息／結束狀態

The week is winding down, so why don't we go out for a drink?

這個星期快結束了，我們一起出去喝一杯吧？

❹ **as part of this + N** 是……的一部分

As part of this business deal, we plan to join together both departments.

如這份商業協議的一部分所言，我們計畫合併這兩個部門。

MORE VOCABULARY ♪ 017-03

reliable [rɪˋlaɪəbḷ] a 可靠的
responsible [rɪˋspansəbḷ] a 有責任感的
welfare [ˋwɛl͵fɛr] n 福利
reward [rɪˋwɔrd] n 獎金、獎品
bonus [ˋbonəs] n 獎金、津貼
afternoon tea ph 下午茶

LEARN MORE!

一般公司常見的福利有：年終獎金、績效獎金、生日聚餐、員工聚餐、免費下午茶、員工旅遊、員購優惠、休閒設施……等，根據媒體調查報告顯示，比起金錢上的福利，員工更偏好能夠有改善工作環境、提供休閒活動……等，更精神層面的福利。

♪ 018-01

開會通知

To All Human Resources Department Employees:

The Deputy Head of Human Resources has decided there will be a meeting this Friday afternoon at 3:30pm. This is a **mandatory** ⑬ meeting for all **members** ⑭ of the Human Resources Department.

Mr. Simmons said the **topics** ⑮ of the meeting will be resolving issues with office staff leaving early on Fridays and discussing ways to improve office efficiency. He **expects the meeting to take** ❺ two hours, but if it goes over, dinner boxes will be prepared for everyone.

See everyone on Friday.

致所有人力資源部員工：

人力資源部副理決定本部門將於這星期五下午三點半舉辦會議。這是強制性的會議，每一位人力資源部的員工都必須參加。

賽門斯先生說明此次會議的主題是解決辦公室人員星期五早退的問題，以及討論如何可以增進辦公室效率。他估計此次會議會進行兩個小時左右，但如果時間超過的話，會幫每個人準備好晚餐盒。

大家星期五見。

QUIZ 閱讀測驗

5. What will they talk about at the meeting?

(A) dinner boxes (B) staying late (C) leaving early
(D) mandatory meetings

5. 會議上他們將會討論什麼？

(A) 晚餐盒 (B) 在公司待到很晚 (C) 早退 (D) 強制性會議

ANS: 5. (C)

VOCABULARY ♪ 018-02

⑬ **mandatory** [ˋmændə͵torɪ]
a 強制的、必須履行的

There was a mandatory fire drill last week.

上個星期有強制性的防災演習。

⑭ **member** [ˋmɛmbɚ] n 成員

All of the band members agreed to go on tour.

全部的團員同意巡迴。

⑮ **topic** [ˋtɑpɪk] n 主題

Tonight's topic of conversation will be on when to allow a child to have a mobile phone.

今天的對話主題是關於什麼時候可以允許小孩擁有手機。

PATTERN ♪ 018-03

❺ **expect (something) to take**
預期（某事物）……花費（時間）

Joe expects the interview to take about an hour.

喬認為面試會花費大概一小時。

LEARN MORE! ♪ 018-04

在會議中可能說到的話。

- I can explain it to you.
  我可以解說給你聽。
- For more information, please refer to our official website.
  有關詳細資訊，請參考我們的官網。
- It's quicker to make a phone call.
  用打電話的方式比較快。

Skill!!
閱讀公告、通知單的技巧

公告單、廣告單、通知單……等這類型的文章，通常篇幅較短，訊息內容也不複雜，它們的目的在於將訊息清楚地傳達給接收者，所以只要掌握四大重點，就能夠掌握文章想要傳達的訊息。

Point 1 to whom 給誰的

- To: All Affected Residents 此致所有受影響的住戶
- Dear Sir 敬啟者 您好
- Dear Readers 讀者，您好

Point 2 by / from whom 誰寫的

- XXX City Council's Public Hearing XXX 市議會公聽會
- Please take note that our company will conduct a vote for...
  請注意我們的公司將舉辦……選舉
- ABC Magazine is writing to you with an update on...
  ABC 雜誌寫信要跟您更新……

Point 3 what / why 內容／原因

- Your water service will be temporarily shut off... 您的自來水服務將暫停……
- We would like to hear your comments on... 我們希望聽取您對……的意見
- We wish to inform you that a notice is being sent to cardholders...
  我們要通知您已經寄給持卡人通知……

Point 4 when and where 時間和地點

- from 8:00 a.m. to 6:00 p.m. 早上八點到下午六點
- Wednesday, January 30, 2019 二〇一九年一月三十日星期三
- between Tuesday, May 1 and Thursday, May 3 五月一日星期二到五月三日星期四
- at Forest Gary Hote 在佛瑞斯特蓋瑞飯店

尋人／物

someone / something is missing

VOCABULARY ♪ 020-02

① **news** [njuz] n 新聞、消息

Have you heard any news about when the construction will start?

你有聽聞任何關於動工時間的消息嗎？

② **whereabouts** [ˋhwɛrəˋbauts] n 行蹤、下落

The whereabouts of my other shoe are a great mystery to me.

我另一隻鞋子到底在哪裡，真的讓我摸不透。

③ **contact** [kənˋtækt] v 聯繫、聯絡
[ˋkantækt] n 接觸、聯繫

We will contact you when we make a decision.

我們做好決定後會聯繫你。

Article 1

♪ 020-01

小孩走失

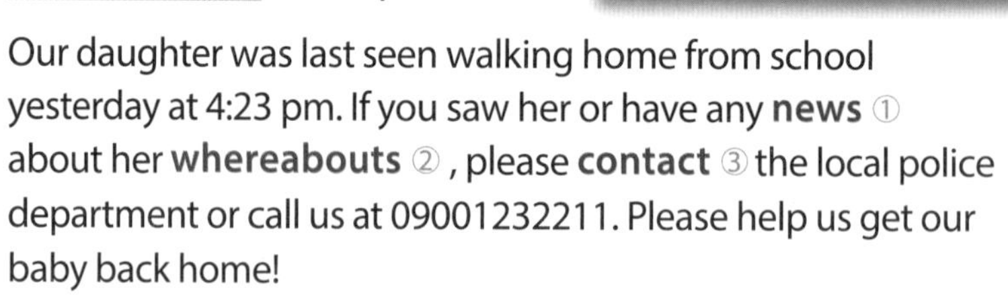

Missing!

 Have you seen ❶ this person?

Our daughter was last seen walking home from school yesterday at 4:23 pm. If you saw her or have any **news** ① about her **whereabouts** ② , please **contact** ③ the local police department or call us at 09001232211. Please help us get our baby back home!

尋人啟事！

你有見到這個人嗎？

我們的女兒最後一次被看到是昨天下午四點二十三分從學校回家的時候。如果你有看見她或是任何跟她行蹤有關的消息，請跟當地警察局聯繫或是打給我們，我們的號碼是 09001232211。請幫助我們的寶貝女兒回家！

♪ 021-01

老人走失

Jolene Jo went missing yesterday near Veteran's Hospital. She was in the hospital visiting her husband, but then she **disappeared** ④ before her son could ❷ pick her up.

Jolene has early stages of dementia and may not know who she is or where she lives. We have **attached** ⑤ a picture of her.

If you do see her, please take her to the **nearest** ⑥ police station as they have been alerted to her being missing. Any help is appreciated and please also share this information on Facebook. Thank you for all assistance!

Annabelle Lin

喬蕾．喬昨天榮民總醫院附近失蹤了。她當時在醫院探望她先生，但在她兒子來到醫院接到她之前她就消失了。

喬蕾有老年癡呆的初期症狀，有可能不知道自己是誰或她住哪裡。我們附有一張她的照片。

你如果有見到她，請將她帶到離你最近的警察局，全部的警察局都已經接獲她失蹤的通報。我們感謝您任何一滴點的幫助，請協助我們將此則貼文分享到臉書上。感謝大家幫忙！

安娜貝爾．林

VOCABULARY ♪ 021-02

④ **disappeared** [ˌdɪsəˋpɪrɪd] a 消失的

The kitten disappeared before I could give it some food.

在我能給小貓一些食物之前牠就消失了。

⑤ **attached** [əˋtætʃt] a 附件的

Attached, please find all information about the property that is for sale.

全部代售資產的資訊請見附件檔案。

⑥ **nearest** [ˋnɪrlɪst] a 最近的

When the kids were little, we always took them to the nearest playground to run around.

孩子們還小的時候，我們總是帶他們去最近的公園跑跑。

PATTERN ♪ 021-03

❶ **Have you (seen / heard / noticed / felt / wondered / wished)**

你有看到／聽過／注意到／感到／想過／希望……

Have you noticed how long the line is for the ride?

你有注意到排隊搭乘的隊伍有多長嗎？

❷ **before someone could**

在某人能夠做……之前

Before I could speak, he kissed me and took my breath away.

我都還來不及回話他就吻了我，讓我頓時反應不過來。

QUIZ 閱讀測驗

1. Where is the little girl?

(A) at home (B) no one knows (C) at the police department (D) on the way home from school

2. Why didn't Jolene get into her son's car?

(A) She was mad at him. (B) She went missing.
(C) She wanted to go to Annabelle Lin's house
(D) She wanted to visit her husband.

1. 小女孩在哪裡？
(A) 在家 (B) 沒人知道 (C) 在警察局 (D) 在從學校回家的路上

2. 為什麼喬蕾沒有搭到她兒子的車？
(A) 她在生她兒子的氣。 (B) 她走失。 (C) 她想要去安娜貝爾林的房子。 (D) 她想要拜訪她丈夫。

ANS: 1. (B) 2. (B)

MORE VOCABULARY ♪ 021-04

student [ˋstjudn̩t] n 學生
freshman [ˋfrɛʃmən] n 大一生
sophomore [ˋsafmor] n 大二生
junior [ˋdʒunjɚ] n 大三生
senior [ˋsinjɚ] n 大四生
graduate student ph 研究生
exchange student ph 交換學生

Article 3

♪022-01

尋找失物

Stolen!

One large-sized street bicycle with helmet, speedometer, and special **edition** ⑦ Kiri water bottle.

Please help me find my bike. It went missing last night while I went in to order a late-night snack. The bike is green with white **stripes** ⑧ and is for riders 185-195 cm tall.

If you have seen my bike, **feel free to** ❸ text me at 0912-345-678 to give me any information. If your information helps me to find the bike, I will pay a 5,000 NT **reward** ⑨ .Thank you for all of your help.

Ian

失物協尋！

我的一台大型街頭自行車，附帶著自行車安全帽、計速器以及特別版的 Kiri 水瓶被偷了。

請大家協尋我的腳踏車。昨天晚上我進去點宵夜的時候，它就被偷了。車身是綠色搭配白色條紋，適合身高大概 185-195 公分的騎士。

如果你有看到我的腳踏車，請傳訊息給我到這支電話號碼：0912-345-678 跟我說任何你知道的消息。如果你的消息幫助我找到腳踏車的話，我會用台幣五千元作為報答。感謝各位的幫助！

伊恩

♪022-02

尋找寵物

Please help me **find** ⑩ my puppy Mr. Bumpkins,

He's a two-year-old toy poodle, and he went missing three days ago as we were out for a walk. He does not have an ID chip, but he has a distinctive brown fur **patch** ⑪ over his right ear. He **goes by** ❹ the names: Mr. Bumpkins, Bumpy, Little Bump, and Biddle Bumps. He is not afraid of strangers and will **approach** ⑫ you if you call his name.

If you see him, please call Joan at 09992343212. Thank you!

請幫忙尋找我的小狗，牠的名字是邦博金斯先生。

牠是一隻兩歲大的玩具貴賓犬，三天前我們外出散步時走失了。牠沒有註冊晶片，但牠右耳上有一小區塊辨識度滿高的棕色毛髮。這些名字都可以叫得動牠：邦博金斯先生、邦皮、小邦跟小小邦。牠不怕陌生人，如果你叫牠的名字牠會向你靠過來。

如果你有看到牠，請打這隻電話號碼給喬安：09992343212，謝謝你！

VOCABULARY ♪023-01

⑦ **edition** [ɪˋdɪʃən] n 版本

The latest edition of this board game has real wooden pieces!

這款桌遊的最新版本有真正木製的棋子。

⑧ **stripe** [straɪp] n 條紋

The number of stripes down a skunk's back tells you if it's a male or female.

臭鼬背上的條紋數量，可以讓你知道牠們是公的還是母的。

⑨ **reward** [rɪˋwɔrd] n 獎賞、報答

All the reward I want is to spend some time with you

我想要的獎賞是跟你一起相處。

⑩ **find** [faɪnd] v 尋找

I am hoping to find my missing ring.

希望我能找到我遺失的戒指。

⑪ **patch** [pætʃ] n 塊、小塊

I have a patch of dry skin on my elbow.

我手肘上有一塊乾燥的皮膚。

⑫ **approach** [əˋprotʃ] v 接近

Never approach a strange animal too quickly.

不要太快接近奇怪的動物。

PATTERN ♪023-02

❸ **feel free to** 感到自在做……某事

You should feel free to call me if you want to get together.

你想見面的話就直接打給我。

❹ **goes by** 以……為名字

My name is James, but I go by Jimmy.

我的名字是詹姆士，但叫我吉姆就行。

QUIZ 閱讀測驗

3. **Why does Ian think his bike was stolen?**
   (A) It's for large riders. (B) It was gone after he bought his snack.
   (C) It has white stripes. (D) It has a special edition Kiri bottle.

4. **Which is not the name for the poodle?**
   (A) Biddle bits (B) Biddle Bumps (C) Bumpy (D) Mr. Bumpkins

3. 為什麼伊恩認為他的腳踏車被偷了？
   (A) 因為他的腳踏車是給身高高的騎士。 (B) 他買完他的宵夜後腳踏車就不見了。
   (C) 腳踏車有白色條紋。 (D) 腳踏車有特別版的 Kiri 水瓶。

4. 以下哪一個不是這隻貴賓狗的名字？
   (A) 小小塊 (B) 小小邦 (C) 邦皮 (D) 邦博金斯先生

ANS: 3. (B) 4. (A)

通知單

notification

VOCABULARY ♪024-02

① **reminder** [rɪˋmaɪndɚ]
n 通知單、提醒

This is just a reminder that you still have two library books out.

這只是一個通知，提醒你還有兩本書是出借狀態。

② **due** [dju] a 到期的

Your research paper is due on Friday.

你的研究報告這個星期五到期。

③ **immediately** [ɪˋmidɪɪtlɪ] ad 立即

He immediately changed the topic when his girlfriend asked who he was texting.

他的女朋友問他在寫訊息給誰時，他馬上轉換話題。

Article 1

♪024-01

催繳費用

This is a **reminder** ① that your electricity bill for September 19-November 19, 2019 in the amount of 6,432 NT was due on December 20th . Your bill is currently past **due** ② . Please take your bill to the Electric Company to pay the bill **immediately** ③ . If we do not ❶ receive your payment in the next 7 days, your electricity will be cut off.

Thank you for your compliance.

The Electric Company

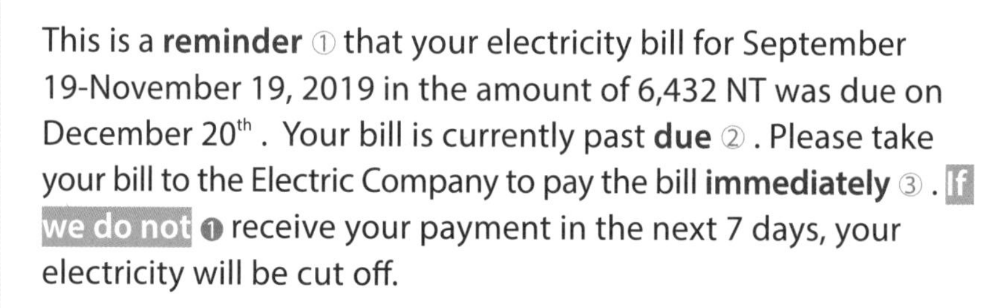

於此提醒您，您在二〇一九年九月十九日至十一月十九日的電費帳單，於十二月二十日到期，金額為六千四百三十二台幣。 您的帳單目前已過期，請攜帶帳單到電力公司立即進行繳費。如果我們在接下來的七天內沒有收到您的付款，您的電力將被切斷。

謝謝您遵守規定。

電力公司

Article 2 ♪ 025-01

交通罰鍰

Your car, license plate number 619-AB was photographed speeding at the intersection of Jin Hua Road and Mei Li Street. The speed camera took the photo **below** ④ and noted your speed.

Because you were over the speed **limit** ⑤ by 50-60 kilometers per hour, the ticket charge is 3,600 NT. You can take this bill to a convenience store or First Bank **to pay within** ❷ the next 15 days. **Failure** ⑥ to do so may increase your violation amount.

Please drive safely!

The Traffic Bureau

您的車輛（車牌號 619-AB）在金華路與美利街交叉口被拍攝到超速。超速照相機照了以下照片並紀錄您當時的速度。

因為您的時速超過了限制時速每小時五十至六十公里，罰款是三千六百台幣。您可以在接下來的十五天內攜帶此罰款帳單到便利商店或是第一銀行繳納。違反此規定者可能會收到更多罰款。注意行車平安！

交通局

QUIZ 閱讀測驗

1. Where does the notified person need to go to pay the bill?

(A) the 7-11 (B) the September to November bill
(C) the Electric Company (D) 6,432 NT

2. Where does the driver need to go to pay the ticket?

(A) the Traffic Bureau (B) Jin Hua Road (C) Mei Li Street
(D) convenience store

1. 被通知的人需要去哪裡繳納帳單費用？
(A) 7-11 便利商店 (B) 九月到十一月的帳單 (C) 電力公司 (D) 台幣 6,432

2. 車主需要去哪裡繳納罰單？
(A) 交通局 (B) 金華路 (C) 美利街 (D) 便利商店

ANS: 1. (C) 2. (D)

VOCABULARY ♪ 025-02

④ **below** [bəˋlo] ad 低於、在某平面下

Please see the attachment below.
請看以下附件。

⑤ **limit** [ˋlɪmɪt] n / v 限制、限額

The clothing limit is the maximum number of clothes that fit in your closet.
衣服量的限制取決於可以塞入你衣櫃中的衣服數量的最大值。

⑥ **failure** [ˋfeljɚ] n 失敗

Failure to inform the office of your move may bring a penalty.
沒有告知辦公室你要搬走的話，可能會引來懲罰。

PATTERN ♪ 025-03

❶ **if we do not + V** 如果我們沒有做某事

If we do not find the key, we can't get the car back home.
如果找不到鑰匙，我們沒有辦法開車回家。

❷ **to pay within** 在……期限內付費

I need to pay this bill within the next few days.
接下來幾天內我需要繳納這個帳單。

LEARN MORE! ♪ 025-04

Ⓐ **windshield** 擋風玻璃
Ⓑ **windscreen wiper** 雨刷
Ⓒ **license plate** 車牌
Ⓓ **bumper** 保險桿
★ **behind-the-wheel test** 路考
★ **behind the wheel** 開車

VOCABULARY ♪026-02

⑦ **attempt** [ə`tɛmpt] v 嘗試、努力

The attempt to steal second base ended in an out.

偷盜二壘的嘗試最終以出局收場。

⑧ **return** [rɪ`tɝn] v 歸還

I have returned your letter because I told you not to write to me anymore.

我已經把你寄的信退回，因為我已經跟你說過不要再寫信給我。

⑨ **pleasant** [`plɛzənt] a 令人愉快的、親切有好的

I had a pleasant night of sleep last night.

昨晚我睡得很好。

LEARN MORE!

根據寄送方式，郵件可分成平信（ordinary mail）、掛號（registered mail）、快捷（express mail）、航空郵件（airmail）。如果郵差在投遞掛號信時失敗的話，會在信箱留下招領掛號信（registered mail claim），收件者須自行去郵局領取。

除了郵局，也可選擇快遞或貨運業者寄送，有些業者也會提供貨到付款（cash-on delivery / collect-on delivery）的服務。而不管是用什麼方式寄送，都一定要填寫寄件人、收件人的郵遞區號、地址、電話與姓名，貼上郵票（stamp）或支付郵資（postage），如此才能順利送達。

Article 3 ♪026-01 郵件招領

Dear Mr. Shi,

We attempted to deliver you package at 10:35 am today, but there was no one home. This was our second **attempt** ⑦ to deliver your package. Now you will need to take this notice and a photo ID and go to your nearest post office to pick up the package.

Please note that ❸ the post office will only hold your package for two weeks from today and then it will be **returned** ⑧ .

Take care and have a **pleasant** ⑨ day.

The Post Office

親愛的施先生：

我們今天上午十點三十五分嘗試投遞您的包裹，但沒有人在家。 這是我們第二次嘗試投遞您的包裹。現在您需要攜帶此通知和有照片的證件到離您最近的郵局領取包裹。

請注意：郵局從今天起將保留您的包裹兩週，之後它將被退回寄件者。

保重並祝您度過愉快的一天。

郵局

QUIZ 閱讀測驗

3. What does Mr. Shi need to get the package?

(A) a ride to the post office (B) a photo ID
(C) a copy of the package contents (D) some money to pay for the package

3. 施先生需要用什麼來領取包裹？

(A) 跑一趟郵局 (B) 有照片的證件 (C) 包裹內容物的文件副本
(D) 用來支付包裹的一些現金

ANS: 3. (B)

♪027-01
法院傳票

This is a summons for you to **appear** ⑩ in court on February 17th for case number 45434. On this day, a judge will **make a decision as to** ❹ your guilt or innocence in the case of drunk driving from January 31st. Please come to courtroom 234 at 9:45 am. If you are not **present** ⑪, the judge will still decide your case, and you will not be able to **challenge** ⑫ the judge's decision.

Staying Fair and Square.

The District Court

此傳票於此通知您必須於二月十七日當日出庭案件號碼 45434 的案件。當天法官將會判決您於一月三十一日犯下的酒駕是否有罪。當日請於早上九點四十五分到 234 號法庭。如果當日沒有出席，法官仍會進行判決，您屆時並無法對法官的判決提出辯駁。

保持公正與光明。

地方法院

QUIZ 閱讀測驗

4. What is the case number?
(A) 31st (B) 45434 (C) 234 (D) 945

4. 案件號碼為何？
(A) 31 號 (B) 45434 號 (C) 234 號 (D) 945 號

ANS: 4. (B)

VOCABULARY ♪027-02

⑩ **appear** [ə`pɪr] v 出現

After my father left, I always looked out the window thinking he would appear.

我父親離開後，我總是從窗戶往外看，想著他可能會再出現。

⑪ **present** [`prɛzn̩t] a 出席的、在場的

Kim wasn't present at school today because she was sick.

金今天沒有來學校因為她生病了。

⑫ **challenge** [`tʃælɪndʒ] n / v 挑戰

Larry decided to challenge Joe for first chair trombone.

賴瑞決定跟喬挑戰首席長號的位置。

PATTERN ♪027-03

❸ **please note that** 請注意／留意……

Please note that John said he will be late for dinner tonight.

請注意到約翰說的，他今天晚餐時間會晚點到。

❹ **make a decision as to** 做……有關的決定

Sometime next week I need to make a decision as to where to move to in December.

下星期有空的時候，我必須決定十二月時我要搬去哪裡。

LEARN MORE! ♪027-04

bank 銀行

post 郵政

jail 監獄

government 政府

police 警察

fire fighting 消防

♪ 028-01

- two-way traffic 雙向行駛
- overtaking prohibited 禁止超車
- winding road left ahead 前方彎曲道路
- lane reduction right lane ends 前方右道縮減
- handicapped accessible facility 無障礙設施
- radar 測速雷達

NO U TURN
禁止迴轉

NO ENTRY
禁止進入

NO LARGE TRUCKS
禁止大卡車

SLIPPERY WHEN WET
小心地滑

FALLING ROCKS
小心落石

INTERSECTION AHEAD
前方行交叉路口

RIGHT CURVE AHEAD
前方右彎道

RIGHT TURN AHEAD
前方右轉

PARK
停車

30 km/HIGH SPEED LIMIT
速限 30

LEARN MORE! ♪ 028-02

和交通有關的句子：

- Be careful not to knock down the pedestrian. 小心不要撞到行人。
- Here is your ticket. 這是你的罰單。
- Show me your driving license. 讓我看你的駕照。
- Did you run through the traffic light? 你闖紅燈了嗎？
- The brakes are out of order. 剎車失靈了。
- Let's detour to avoid the traffic jam. 讓我們繞道避免堵車。
- The crackup was due to the driver's drunk driving. 這起車禍起因於司機酒後駕車。

PATTERN

♪029-01 ❶ **I have a terrible pain in...** 我……很痛

A: I have a terrible pain in my back. I guess it's because of bad posture.
我的背很痛。我猜是坐姿不良的緣故。

B: My waist is very sore. Let's go for a massage!
我的腰很痠。一起去按摩吧！

♪029-02 ❷ **How long...?** ……多久？

A: How long will this meeting take?
這個會議要開多久？

B: It will take about an hour.
大概一小時。

♪029-03 ❸ **Are you ready to...?** 你準備好……了嗎？

A: Are you ready to improve your life?
你準備好改善你的生活了嗎？

B: Yes, I'm ready!
是的，我準備好了！

♪029-04 ❹ **I can't stand...** 我無法忍受……

A: I can't stand their noisy conversation.
我無法忍受他們嘈雜的交談。

B: Put on your headphones!
戴上耳機吧！

♪029-05 ❺ **it seems that...** 看來……

A: It seems that Nicole is always busy working.
看來妮可總是忙於工作。

B: Yeah, she's a workaholic.
對呀，她是工作狂。

♪029-06 ❻ **I don't feel like...** 我不想……

A: I don't feel like talking right now.
我現在不想說話。

B: I'll talk to you when you are in a better mood.
等你心情好一點，我再找你談。

♪029-07 ❼ **I can tell you how to...** 我可以告訴你如何……

A: I can tell you how to solve the problem.
我可以告訴你如何解決這個問題。

B: That would be great.
太好了。

廣告

advertisement

VOCABULARY ♪030-02

① **throughout** [θru`aʊt]
ad 在各處、自始自終

Throughout the year, we have deep discounts on clothing that hasn't sold.

我們一整年都有針對未銷售出去的服飾的大幅折扣。

② **giveaway** [`gɪvə͵we] n 贈品

I love to go to fashion shows for the great giveaways.

我喜歡參加時裝秀拿免費贈品。

③ **coupon** [`kupɑn] n 折價卷

Mommy, I made you a book of coupons for free hugs!

媽媽，我做了一本免費擁抱的折價卷給你！

♪030-01

新店開幕

Grand Opening!

On Sunday, May 12th , Kelly's Killer Tacos will have its Grand Opening! Make sure you ❶ come down to see us.

We'll be open all day from 9:30 am to 9:30 pm and **throughout** ① the day, we will have all sorts of **giveaways** ② , including **coupons** ③ for free tacos and discounts on T-shirts and baseball caps. Also, if you buy five tacos, we'll give you two free.

Come on over to Kelly's Killer Tacos to help us open our store!

盛大開幕！

五月十二日星期日當天，凱莉的殺手鋼墨西哥捲餅店將盛大開幕！請一定要來共襄盛舉！

當天營業時間從早上九點半到晚上九點半，我們也將於此時段中送出一些禮物，其中包括墨西哥捲餅的免費折價卷、T 恤以及棒球帽的折扣。當天也有買五送二的活動。

趕緊來凱莉的殺手鐧墨西哥捲餅店大快朵頤，一起慶祝開幕吧！

Article 2

♪ 031-01

周年慶活動

Don't miss ❷ this weekend's Annual Sale!

Starting at 8 am Saturday, we'll open our doors with rock-bottom prices.

Every hour on the hour, there will be new items that will be on **deep** ④ discount. There will be free balloons for the kids and a lucky **draw** ⑤ for an 8,888 NT free shopping spree. Anyone that buys something can **enter** ⑥ to win.

Don't forget, even if you don't catch the deepest discounted items, almost everything in the store will still be discounted at least 25%!

不要錯過這個週末的年度促銷活動！

從星期六早上八點開始，我們將以最低價格開啟營業的一天。

每小時整點都會有新商品的超值折扣推出。小孩可以有免費氣球拿，還有價值台幣八千八百八十八元的幸運抽獎血拼活動。只要有買東西的人都可以參加抽獎。

別忘了，就算你沒有搶購到最低折扣的商品，幾乎商店裡的每樣商品都打了至少 75 折！

VOCABULARY ♪ 031-02

④ **deep** [dip] a 深的

The deep end of the pool is scary for little kids.

游泳池的深處對小孩來說很可怕。

⑤ **draw** [drɔ] n 抽籤、抽獎

There will be a draw tonight to see who will take home the prize.

今晚有一個抽獎活動，看誰可以把獎項抱回家。

⑥ **enter** [ˋɛntɚ] v 進入

If you enter the race, you should try to do your best.

如果你進入比賽，你就要試著做到最好。

PATTERN ♪ 031-03

❶ **make sure you** 確保你……

Make sure you tie your shoelaces.

確保你鞋帶繫好了。

❷ **don't miss** 不要錯過……

Don't miss out on the chance to go with your friends this weekend.

不要錯過這個週末跟你朋友出去的機會。

QUIZ 閱讀測驗

1. What can't you get by going to the Grand Opening?

(A) free T-shirts (B) lots of tacos (C) coupons for free tacos (D) discounted baseball caps

2. How much is most stuff in the store discounted?

(A) rock-bottom (B) 25% (C) 8,888 NT (D) deep discount

1. 如果你參加開幕，你拿不到什麼東西？

(A) 免費 T 恤 (B) 許多墨西哥捲餅 (C) 免費墨西哥捲餅的折價卷 (D) 折扣過的棒球帽

2. 商店裡大部分的商品都是打幾折？

(A) 最低價 (B) 75 折 (C) 折價台幣 8,888 (D) 大折扣

ANS: 1. (A) 2. (B)

♪ 032-01

母親節特賣

Have you bought something special for your mother **yet** ⑦ ? If not, look no further.

This **whole** ⑧ week, we are having a giant Mother's Day Sale. Kitchen appliances, makeup, women's clothing, bed linens, plates and silverware, pots and pans, and jewelry are all on sale. If that's not enough, be sure to say "Mama sent me" , and you'll get to **take advantage of** ❸ our extra special **secret** ⑨ discount.

Also, just for moms, we're giving out carnations and coupon booklets valued at $100.

Make your way to Allen's Wares now!

你有為媽媽買一些特別的禮物了嗎？ 如果沒有，請不要再找了。

整整一周，我們有大規模的母親節特賣會活動。廚房用具、化妝品、女士服裝、床單、盤子、銀器、鍋碗瓢盆和珠寶都是在架商品。如果這還不夠，請務必說「媽媽要我來的」，你就可以享有我們額外的祕密折扣優惠。

此外，只是為了母親們的福利，我們將會贈送康乃馨和價值一百美金的優惠券小冊子。

現在就動身前往「艾倫的店」吧！

QUIZ 閱讀測驗

3. What is not mentioned as something that can be bought at Allen's Wares?

(A) Jewelry (B) Silverware
(C) Makeup (D) Exercise equipment

3. 可以在艾倫的店中買到的東西中，哪項沒有被提及？

(A) 珠寶 (B) 銀器
(C) 化妝品 (D) 運動器材

ANS: 3. (D)

母親節（Mother's Day）是個為了感謝母親而慶祝的節日。世界各地的母親節時間不大一樣，但相同的是，孩子們會在這天向母親表示感謝，而康乃馨被視為母親節的代表鮮花。

阿富汗的母親節定在 3 月 8 日；英國則是在大齋其中的第四個星期天慶祝母親節；韓國和阿爾巴尼亞會在 5 月 8 日舉辦父母節；墨西哥是 5 月 10 日；波蘭是 5 月 26 日。而大多數的國家都是將母親節定在 5 月的第二個星期天，例如：美國、加拿大、丹麥、德國、冰島、瑞士、澳洲、日本、新加坡與馬來西亞。

美國的母親節是由安娜．賈維斯（Anna Jarvis）發起，她提出設立紀念日來紀念默默做出奉獻的母親們，經過多年的請願，美國國會於 1913 年確定將每年 5 月的第二個星期日作為法定母親節。

VOCABULARY ♪033-01

⑦ **yet** [jɛt] ad 尚未

Have you bought your tickets to the dance yet?

你買去舞會的票了嗎？

⑧ **whole** [hol] a 全部的、整體的

I was so hungry that I ate a whole chicken.

我太餓了，吃了一整隻雞。

⑨ **secret** [ˋsikrɪt] a 祕密的

This secret passageway will take you to the hidden treasure.

這條祕密通道將引領你到隱藏寶藏的所在地。

PATTERN ♪033-02

❸ **take advantage of** 利用

I hope you will take advantage of the free massage coupons I got last week.

希望你會利用我上個禮拜拿到的免費按摩折價卷。

LEARN MORE! ♪033-03

和媽媽說母親節快樂！

· You are the one that I love the most. Have a happy Mother's Day.
  您是我最愛的人。祝您有一個快樂的母親節。

· I may not often say it, but I do love you.
  我也許並不常掛在嘴上，但我真正愛您。

· To the world's number one mom!
  給世界上最好的媽媽！

· Thanks for being there, Mom. Happy Mother's Day.
  謝謝您不斷地扶持我。祝您母親節快樂。

· Thank you for being you.
  謝謝您的一切。

· You are the best mom that a daughter ever had.
  你是女兒心中最好的媽媽。

VOCABULARY ♪034-02

⑩ **serving** [ˋsɝvɪŋ]
n 提供（食物）、提供服務

I have been serving food at this restaurant for ten years.
我已經在這個餐廳提供餐點服務十年了。

⑪ **bargain** [ˋbɑrgɪn]
n 便宜貨、好價格的商品

At 90 NT, this is a real bargain.
以 90 台幣來說，這真的是一個好交易。

⑫ **reasonable** [ˋriznəbl̩]
a 合理的、可以接受的

I think you are asking for a very reasonable price for this Mustang.
我認為你針對這台福特野馬要求的是一個非常合理的價格。

PATTERN ♪034-03

❹ **that means** 這意味著……

Well, that means I won't have to work on the farm anymore.
這麼說的話，這代表我再也不用在農場工作了。

Article 4 ♪034-01 關店特賣

Final Closeout Sale!

After thirty years of **serving** ⑩ the Fairmont community, we are closing our doors. And that means ❹ every last item needs to go. Come and find those **bargains** ⑪ you've been looking for. If you need it, we have it. We have always sold top quality items for **reasonable** ⑫ prices, and now we want you to take home some great deals.

Help us say goodbye by coming by!

最後的特賣會！

在為費爾蒙社區服務三十年後，我們現在要結束營業了。這意味著店裡的每個商品都要售出。快來我們店裡尋找你一直希望得到的超值商品。你要的我們全部都有。我們一直以來都用合理的價格銷售高品質的商品，現在我們希望您帶一些超值商品回家。

過來說聲再見吧！

QUIZ 閱讀測驗

4. Why is the shop closing down?

(A) They don't say.
(B) They are tired after thirty years.
(C) They can't find good bargains anymore.
(D) They want to move to a new town.

4. 為什麼商店會結束營業？

(A) 他們沒有說。
(B) 開店三十年後感到疲勞。
(C) 他們找不到更好的交易。
(D) 他們想要搬到一個新的城鎮。

ANS: 4. (A)

PATTERN

♪035-01 ❶ **Are there any other...for...?** ……有沒有其他……呢？

A: Are there any other requirements for the position?
這個職位有沒有其他條件呢？

B: Candidates must also have relevant experience.
求職者還必須具有相關經驗。

♪035-02 ❷ **I guess...** 我想應該是……

A: I guess it will take about three weeks to see her happy face.
我想大概要三個星期才能看到她的笑臉。

B: I couldn't wait that long.
我可能無法等那麼久。

♪035-03 ❸ **What is...used for?** ……有什麼用途呢？

A: What is the presentation used for?
這個簡報有什麼用途呢？

B: That's for promoting our company's products.
為了宣傳我們公司的產品。

♪035-04 ❹ **in my opinion,...** 依我所見，……

A: In my opinion, there is no better way to protect the homeless children from sadness.
依我所見，沒有更好的方法能保護無家可歸的孩子免於悲傷。

B: Don't be so pessimistic. It'll work out all right.
別那麼悲觀。總會有辦法的。

♪035-05 ❺ **I heard that...** 我聽說……

A: I heard that Jack's resignation was related to his early retirement.
我聽說傑克的離職與他提早退休有關。

B: Really? Amy told me that he resigned because of health problems.
真的嗎？艾咪跟我說他是因為健康問題而離職。

♪035-06 ❻ **I'm not sure if...** 我不確定……

A: I'm not sure if the washing machine works well.
我不確定這台洗衣機是否好用。

B: If you don't want to use this old washing machine, you can go to the next building to use a newer one.
如果你不想用這台老舊的洗衣機，可以去隔壁棟使用較新的洗衣機。

租屋廣告

rental advertisement

Article 1

♪ 036-01

房東租屋

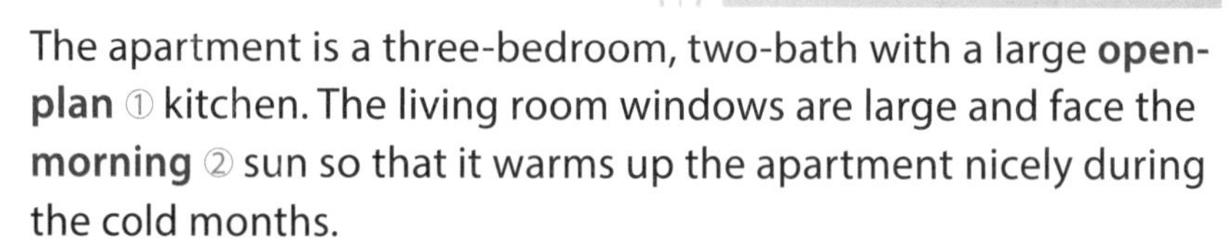

Apartment for Rent

The apartment is a three-bedroom, two-bath with a large **open-plan** ① kitchen. The living room windows are large and face the **morning** ② sun so that it warms up the apartment nicely during the cold months.

There are central heating and cooling, a full-size oven, and a large refrigerator. Other appliances will need to be provided by the renter. The rent is 47,000 a month, **plus** ③ 3000 for guard fees. There is a parking space included, but all utilities are paid by the renter. Looking for a longer lease of 2 or more ❶ years.

If interested, please call Mrs. Wang at 0521-331-2271

公寓出租

此公寓的格局包含三間臥室、兩間衛浴，以及一開放式廚房。客廳的窗戶很大，並且面朝早晨的陽光，因此在寒冷的月份中也可以讓室內暖和起來。

公寓中附有中央暖氣和空調、一台一般規格的烤箱，以及一台大型冰箱。其他電器用品須由承租人自行添購。租金是一個月四萬七千台幣，加上三千台幣的管理費。也附有停車格，但是所有的公共設施的費用均由承租人支付。目前正在尋找至少將會承租兩年或是以上的房客。

如果您對此公寓感興趣，請致電 0521-331-2271 與王女士聯繫。

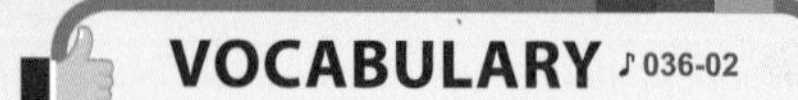

VOCABULARY ♪ 036-02

① **open-plan** [ˋopənˋplæn] a 開放式的

I love the open-plan layout of this apartment.

我喜歡這間公寓的開放式格局。

② **morning** [ˋmɔrnɪŋ] n 早晨、上午

I always find it difficult to get up for my morning classes.

早上要特地起床去上課對我來說很困難。

③ **plus** [plʌs] prep 加上

The total is $9.59, plus 41 cents for tax; so $10 in total.

金額是九點五九美金，加上四十一美分的稅金，所以總金額是十美金。

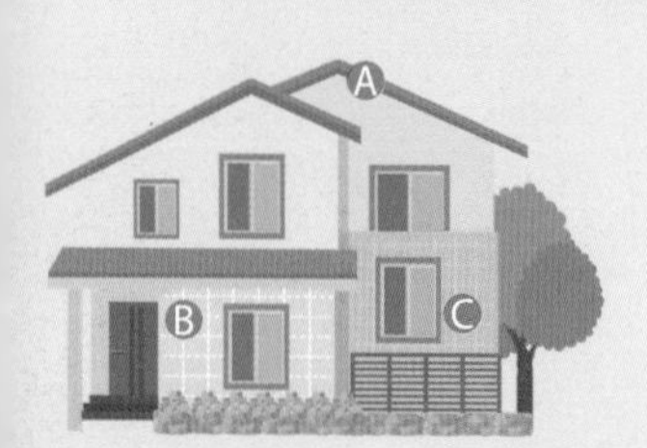

Ⓐ **roof** 屋頂

Ⓑ **front door** 大門

Ⓒ **fence** 柵欄

♪ 037-01

找人合租

Hi! We're looking for someone to share our **awesome** ④ apartment.

Who we are: two 24-year-old female college graduates working in the city.

Who we are looking for: someone 21-30 that is **neat** ⑤, isn't scared of cleaning, likes to hang out, enjoys having friends over from time to time, and likes **to share** the cooking **duties** ⑥ **with** ❷ us.

We are also very sporty, and you are welcome to join us in activities. Prefer a female, but males can also respond.

Our place has 4 bedrooms and 3 baths, a large kitchen, great living space, and an awesome outdoor patio.

No smokers and no pets, please.

Write to emmandjemma@yahoo.com to let us know you are interested!

嗨！ 我們正在尋找一個人一起合租我們超棒的公寓。

我們是誰？兩個在市中心工作的二十四歲女大學生。

我們尋找的房客必須符合以下特質：二十一到三十歲之間、愛乾淨、不嫌打掃麻煩、喜歡一起出去玩、可以接受偶爾邀請朋友來家裡，以及一起分擔煮飯責任的人。

我們兩個都是熱愛運動的人，所以也很歡迎你加入我們的活動。我們希望找的是女生室友，但男生也可以試試看。

我們住的地方有四間臥室、三間衛浴、一個大廚房、極佳的生活空間，以及一個很棒的露天平臺。

我們不接受吸煙者跟有養寵物的人，謝謝。

有興趣的話，請寫信至此電郵地址：emmandjemma@yahoo.com

QUIZ 閱讀測驗

1. What is something the renter will need to buy?
(A) a refrigerator (B) an oven (C) an air conditioner (D) a microwave

2. Who is writing the roommate search info?
(A) the landlord (B) a male (C) a 30-year-old female
(D) two 24-year-old females

1. 承租人必須自行購買哪些東西？
(A) 冰箱 (B) 烤箱 (C) 冷氣機 (D) 微波爐

2. 誰寫了這個尋找租屋室友的訊息？
(A) 房東 (B) 某男性 (C) 某三十歲女性 (D) 兩名二十四歲的女性

ANS: 1. (D) 2. (D)

VOCABULARY ♪ 037-02

④ **awesome** [ˋɔsəm] a 很棒的

He's an awesome teacher; I love his class.
他是個很棒的老師，我很喜歡他的課。

⑤ **neat** [nit] a 乾淨的

I try to keep my room neat, but sometimes, it's a struggle.
我試著保持我的房間乾淨，但有時候真的很難。

⑥ **duty** [ˋdjutɪ] n 責任

Kitchen duties include doing dishes and sweeping and mopping.
廚房的責任包括洗碗、掃地跟拖地。

PATTERN ♪ 037-03

❶ **or more + N** 或是更多……

It will take the cleaning crew 5 or more days to finish.
清潔隊會花五天或是更多天來完成。

❷ **to share with** 與……分享

I could only marry someone that is willing to share the household chores with me.
我只能跟願意分擔家事的人結婚。

LEARN MORE!

書房 study room ♪038-01
- **bookshelf** 書架、書櫃
- **bookend** 書擋
- **desk** 辦公桌、書桌
- **stationery** 文具
- **reading lamp** 檯燈

臥室 bedroom ♪038-02
- **bedding** 寢具
- **wardrobe** 衣櫃
- **dressing table** 梳妝檯
- **sleepy** 想睡的
- **dreamland** 夢鄉、睡覺

餐廳 dining room ♪038-03
- **tableware** 餐具
- **dining table** 餐桌
- **delicious** 美味的
- **dining** 用餐
- **gathering** 聚會

廚房 kitchen ♪038-04
- **kitchenware** 廚房用具
- **cookbook** 食譜
- **counter** 流理臺
- **cuisine** 菜餚、烹飪
- **kitchen waste** 廚餘

MORE VOCABULARY ♪039-01

living room [ˋlɪvɪŋ][rum] ph 客廳
bedroom [ˋbɛdˏrum] n 臥室
bathroom [ˋbæθˏrum] n 浴室
kitchen [ˋkɪtʃɪn] n 廚房
basement [ˋbesmənt] n 地下室
laundry room [ˋlɔndrɪ][rum] ph 洗衣間

MORE VOCABULARY ♪039-02

pillow [ˋpɪlo] n 枕頭
sheet [ʃit] n 床單
bed [bɛd] n 床
quilt [kwɪlt] n 棉被
duvet [djuˋve] n 羽絨被
mattress [ˋmætrɪs] n 床墊

MORE VOCABULARY ♪039-03

carpet [ˋkarpɪt] n 地毯
bathtub [ˋbæθˏtʌb] n 浴缸
sofa [ˋsofə] n 沙發
French window [frɛntʃ][ˋwɪndo] ph 落地窗
lounge chair [laundʒ] tʃɛr] ph 躺椅
bedside table [ˋbɛdˏsaɪd][ˋtebḷ] ph 床頭櫃

GRAMMAR

英文的疑問句有以下兩種問法：

1. Yes / No 疑問句

用 be 動詞作為開頭，問話者希望答話者能夠回答是（Yes）或不是（No）。

例 **Are you coming soon?** 你快來了嗎？
Can he join us tonight? 他今晚可以加入我們嗎？
Did you pass the final exam? 你通過期末考了嗎？

2. 5W1H 疑問句

以 Who（誰）、What（什麼）、Which（哪個）、Where（哪裡）、When（何時）、Why（為什麼）、How（如何）起頭的問句。

例 **Who is the girl in red skirt?** 穿紅裙子的女孩是誰？
What are you doing? 你在做什麼？
Which one is your favorite? 哪一個是你的最愛？
Where is my true love? 我的真愛在哪裡？
When do you go to the airport? 你什麼時候去機場？
Why did he say that? 他為什麼那麼說？
How do you do? 你好嗎？

活動通知

activity

VOCABULARY ♪040-02

① **wow** [waʊ] int 使印象深刻、使叫絕

The dancers wowed the audience with their wonderful routine.

舞者們完美的舞蹈動作，讓評審們印象非常深刻。

② **tune** [tjun] n 旋律、曲子

I remember that tune from when I was a little boy.

我記得這個旋律來自我還是個小男孩的時候。

③ **round** [raʊnd] n 一輪、一局

The winner of this round gets all the money!

這局的贏家可以拿到全部的錢！

Article 1 ♪040-01 歌唱比賽

Singing Competition this Monday Morning!

Do you think you've got what it takes to ❶ **wow** ① the judges? Are you somebody that has to sing in the shower?

Come on down to Mercy Community Mall this Monday morning at 9 am to belt out a few **tunes** ② and see if you have what it takes to sing on live TV!

The charge to participate is just $5, and the top ten competitors will make it to the next **round** ③ , the state competition, at the end of the month.

週一早晨歌喉賽！

你覺得你的歌喉能讓評審們大感驚艷嗎？ 你是淋浴時一定要唱歌的人嗎？

這個星期一早上九點來到仁慈社區購物中心哼個幾句吧，看看自己有多少能耐，說不定你就是下個能夠在電視上現場演唱的明日之星。

參賽費用僅僅需要五美元，前十名參賽者將在本月底進入下一輪的全州歌唱比賽。

♪ 041-01

演講比賽

The **topic** ④ of this year's speech contest is: How I Learned From My Hero.

We're looking for ❷ speeches that really move the audience or that do a good job bringing your hero to light. Please don't forget that people need the help of heroes every day. Some heroes **rescue** ⑤ cats from trees. Some heroes teach children to read. Still others help to plant a community garden.

A hero knows how to make a difference, and now, it's your turn to let us know what makes a hero in your eyes.

Your speech should be no longer than five minutes, and if you **mention** ⑥ a person by name, please make sure the person is OK with that. The top three speeches will be presented to the mayor at the county fair, and the winners will receive a $75 dollar check.

今年演講比賽的題目是：如何跟我的英雄學習。

我們正在尋找能夠真正感動觀眾或者能夠讓你的英雄亮相的演講內容。請不要忘記，人們每天都需要英雄的幫助。一些英雄從樹上救貓。一些英雄教孩子們閱讀。還有一些人幫忙種植社區花園。

英雄知道如何創造改變讓事物更美好，而現在是你絕佳的時機讓我們知道怎樣的人在你眼中是一名英雄。

演講時間不應超過五分鐘，如果你有提到人名，請確保這個人同意自己的名字在演講中被提及。前三名的演講內容將在縣博覽會上呈現給市長，獲獎者們將會得到價值七十五美元的支票。

QUIZ 閱讀測驗

1. Where is the competition?

(A) on TV (B) on Monday morning (C) in the state
(D) at the community mall

2. What is not mentioned as something a hero does?

(A) help with your homework (B) get cats out of trees
(C) plant vegetables (D) teach someone to read

1. 比賽在哪裡舉辦？

(A) 電視上 (B) 星期一早上 (C) 州內 (D) 仁慈社區購物中心

2. 就英雄做的事來說，哪一項沒有被提及？

(A) 幫你寫作業 (B) 把貓從樹上救下來 (C) 種蔬菜 (D) 教人閱讀

ANS: 1. (D) 2. (A)

VOCABULARY ♪ 041-02

④ **topic** [ˋtapɪk] n 主題

The topic of my paper is written in bold letters.

我論文的主題是用粗體字寫。

⑤ **rescue** [ˋrɛskju] v 救援、解救

My mom had to rescue our cat from a tree.

我媽必須把貓從樹上救下來。

⑥ **mention** [ˋmɛnʃən] v 提及

I'm going to mention you to my friend on the phone tonight.

今晚我跟我朋友講電話時我會提到你。

PATTERN ♪ 041-03

❶ **get what it takes to** 有做……的能耐

It seems like she's really get what it takes to be a star.

看來她真的有當明星的能耐。

❷ **we're looking for** 我們正在找……

We're looking for someone to work night shifts five days a week.

我們在找可以一星期做五天夜班的人。

♪ 042-01

Article 3 舞蹈表演

Dance into Spring!

We love dancing, and we'd like to **share** ⑦ that with you.

This spring we will hold a Dance Into Spring activity for **seniors** ⑧ to get you up on your feet ❸ and moving.

You can choose if you'd like to slow dance to golden oldies music, learn easy hip hop moves that won't cause you to put out a hip, do salsa dances to **flirt** ⑨ with the other seniors in your community, or just watch us dance.

舞進春天！

我們喜歡跳舞而且我們也想和你們分享。

今年春天，我們將為老年人舉辦一場「舞進春天」活動，讓你舞動起來。

你可以選擇是否想要隨著黃金老歌跳起慢舞、學習簡單無害的嘻哈舞蹈動作，或是用騷莎舞跟社區內的其他老年人調情，又或者你可以看我們跳舞就好。

QUIZ 閱讀測驗

3. Where are you most likely to see this flier?

(A) in a museum (B) at an old folks' home (C) in a park (D) at a kindergarten

3. 在哪裡最有可能看到這個廣告？

(A) 博物館 (B) 老人之家 (C) 公園 (D) 幼稚園

ANS: 3. (B)

VOCABULARY ♪ 042-02

⑦ **share** [ʃɛr] v / n 分享

I need to share my thoughts with you about your performance.

我需要跟你分享我對你表演的想法。

⑧ **senior** [ˋsinjɚ] n 年長者、年邁人士

Seniors may be older, but they still have a lot to teach the world.

年長者雖然年紀較大，但是他們還是可以帶給這個世界許多東西。

⑨ **flirt** [flɝt] v 調情

That boy just winked at me; is he flirting with me?

那個男孩對我眨眼，他是在跟我調情嗎？

PATTERN ♪ 042-03

❸ **get you up on your feet** 起身

This music is guaranteed to get you up on your feet.

這音樂保證讓你起身動起來。

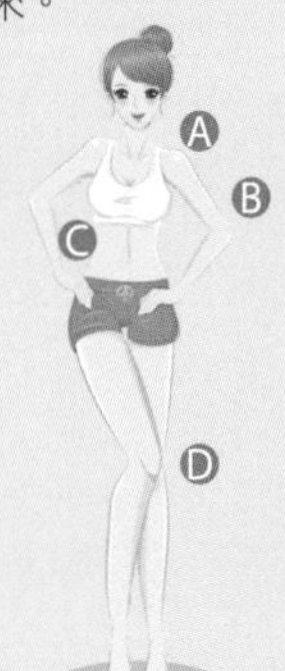

Ⓐ **shoulder** 肩膀

Ⓑ **elbow** 手肘

Ⓒ **waist** 腰

Ⓓ **knee** 膝蓋

LEARN MORE! ♪043-07

一般常說的國際標準舞（international standard，簡稱：國標舞）包含：華爾茲（Waltz）、探戈（Tango）、狐步（ Foxtrot）、快步（Quick Step）。
而國際拉丁舞（international Latin）則包含：倫巴（ Rumba）、鬥牛舞（ Paso Doble）、恰恰恰（ Cha-cha-cha）、桑巴（ Samba）、捷舞（ Jive）。
跟跳舞有關的句子有：

- May I dance with you? 我可以和你跳舞嗎？
- Never criticize your dance partner. 永遠不要挑剔你的舞伴。
- Dance; it's where your heart is. 舞蹈是心之所至。
- Dance fills our lives with hopes and dreams. 舞蹈讓我們的生命充滿希望和夢想。
- Life isn't about waiting for the storm to pass; it's about learning to dance in the rain. 生活不是等待暴風雨過去，而是要學會在雨中跳舞。

♪ 044-01

登山活動

Join us in a class hike to Mount Andrew. Percy High School classes of '85-'95 are meeting this Saturday for an **easy** ⑩ hike up Mount Andrew.

The hike is suitable for ④ all ages and all fitness levels. When we reach the top, there will be a **picnic** ⑪ laid out for us to enjoy. We can spend a lovely day **socializing** ⑫ with our long-lost high school buddies.

If you decide that you really don't want to do the hike, the picnic is going to be set up right next to the main parking area on Mount Andrew, so you can just park and come and join in.

Go Percy High, Go Team Go!

加入我們的徒步旅行到安德魯山。伯希高中 '85-'95 年的班級將於本週六來個安德魯山輕旅行。

此次的徒步旅行適合所有年齡層和所有體能水平的人。當我們抵達山頂時，將會有準備好的野餐等著我們享用。屆時我們可以和我們失散多年的高中夥伴們交流並度過愉快的一天。

如果你確定真的不想要徒步旅行到山頂，野餐將會事先在安德魯山的主要停車場的隔壁安排好，所以你可以直接在停車場停車後並加入我們。

伯希高中衝衝衝！

VOCABULARY ♪ 044-02

⑩ **easy** [ˋizɪ] a 簡單的

I barely did any work in this class because it was an easy A.

在這堂課我幾乎沒有什麼讀書，A 很輕易拿到。

⑪ **picnic** [ˋpɪknɪk] n 野餐

My favorite part of family get-togethers is the picnic.

家庭聚會中我最喜歡的部份就是野餐。

⑫ **socialize** [ˋsoʃə͵laɪz] v 交際

My parents love socializing with other parents from my school.

我的父母喜歡跟學校其他的父母交流。

⑬ **competitor** [kəmˋpɛtətɚ] n 競爭者、參賽者

The competitors lined up at the starting line.

參賽者在起跑線排隊。

⑭ **support** [səˋport] v 支持

I support you in everything that you do.

我支持你做的任何事。

⑮ **fee** [fi] n 費用 v 付費

The fee for entry is $15.

入場費是十五美元。

QUIZ 閱讀測驗

4. Who is this event for?

(A) Percy High School seniors
(B) Percy kindergartners
(C) Percy school parents
(D) Percy High School graduates from the past

4. 這個活動是為了誰而舉辦？

(A) 伯希高中的畢業班學生　(B) 伯希高中的幼稚園生
(C) 伯希高中的父母　(D) 伯希高中的過往的畢業生／校友

ANS: 4. (D)

♪ 045-01

運動會

Our town is having a track and field family get-together **to bring the community together** ❺ . Come and join us on June 12th to celebrate our community.

We're going to have sack races, three-legged man races, bobbing for apples, and so much more. For our real **competitors** ⑬ , the day will start off with a 5K run to **support** ⑭ breast cancer.

Get out and get your tennis shoes on to make a difference.

The entry **fee** ⑮ is ten dollars, which includes a T-shirt and a $5 donation to our community breast cancer awareness foundation.

我們的小鎮將會舉行家庭田徑運動，以凝聚社區向心力。請在六月十二日一起加入我們並共同慶祝我們的社區。

我們將舉辦麻袋賽、兩人三腳男子比賽和水中咬蘋果等等競賽。對我們正式的競賽者，當天先從五公里路跑展開，此活動是用來支持乳癌相關議題。

動身起來，穿上你的網球鞋，並開始創造改變！

入場費是十美元，其中包括一件 T 恤，以及五美元將會捐給我們的社區提高乳癌意識基金會。

QUIZ 閱讀測驗

5. Who is likely to be at this event?

(A) people wanting to watch a rock concert (B) families
(C) people that want to start a motorcycle gang
(D) people that just got out of prison

5. 誰最有可能參加此活動？
(A) 想看搖滾演唱會的人 (B) 家庭 (C) 想要組織摩托車團的人 (D) 剛出獄的人

ANS: 5. (B)

PATTERN ♪ 045-02

❹ is suitable for 對……適合

This movie is suitable for audiences of all ages.
這部電影適合所有年齡層的人。

❺ to bring (something) together 使……聚集

We are having a reunion this summer to bring the family together.
今年夏天我們有一個家族聚會，凝聚家庭成員。

LEARN MORE! ♪045-03

人活著就是要動，多動多健康！

bicycle 腳踏車

golf 高爾夫球

boxing 拳擊

ice hockey 冰上曲棍球

tennis 網球

badminton 羽毛球

pole vault 撐竿跳

long jump 跳遠

VOCABULARY ♪ 046-02

⑯ **visit** [ˋvɪzɪt] v 拜訪

I visited my aunt last weekend, and she made me my favorite dessert.

上個週末我拜訪了我的阿姨，她做了我最喜歡的點心。

⑰ **antique** [ænˋtik] n 古董 a 古代的

These antiques would look amazing in my living room.

這些古董擺在我的客廳的話，看起來一定很棒。

⑱ **treasure** [ˋtrɛʒɚ] n 寶藏

One man's trash is another man's treasure!

某人的垃圾可能是另一個人的寶藏！

LEARN MORE!

在美國幾乎天天都有車庫拍賣（garage sale），又稱為庭院拍賣（yard sale），它是一種私人舉辦的活動，通常是屋主為了清理家中的舊物，將物品擺在私人車道或是院子供人挑選。販賣的內容琳瑯滿目，只要仔細尋找容易挖到寶。

而如果是自己想要舉辦車庫拍賣的話，也不難，可以自製牌子（賣場也有賣）、發布廣告，廣告內容記得寫清楚舉辦的時間、地點。而拍賣當天要準備商品清單、計算機、價格標籤等等，商品清單能夠讓你很清楚知道哪些是要賣的，哪些物品是不小心被拿出來的，不然像《玩具總動員》一樣，胡迪和巴斯光年不小心被拿出來賣就不好了。

Article 6 ♪ 046-01 車庫拍賣

We're having a garage sale, so please come and **visit** ⑯.

We have so much to **get rid of** ⑥. We have children's clothing, men's and women's formal wear, a ton of toys in top condition, and a great collection of **antiques** ⑰ and knick-knacks. Some of the stuff for sale belonged to my great-grandma, so you know it must be worth a lot.

Come and pick through everything to take home your **treasures** ⑱ and help us clear everything out!

2311 Cedar Drive, 11 am-6 pm April 7th.

我們現在有一個車庫舊物拍賣，請來參觀選購。

我們有很多東西需要清除。我們有兒童服裝、男士和女士的正式服裝、大量狀態良好的玩具，以及大量的古董收藏和裝飾用的小玩意兒。一些待售的東西曾屬於我的曾祖母，所以你知道它們其實很有價值。

快來挑選屬於你的寶藏，也幫助我們清空一切！

位於雪松路二三一一號，四月七日上午十一點至下午六點。

QUIZ 閱讀測驗

6. What is something you probably won't find at a garage sale?

(A) second-hand roller skates (B) antique furniture
(C) kids' clothing (D) tickets to the upcoming NBA game

6. 哪項是你在車庫舊物拍賣中可能不會找到的商品？

(A) 二手溜冰鞋 (B) 古董傢俱 (C) 小孩的衣物 (D) 即將到來的 NBA 籃球賽門票

ANS: 6. (D)

♪ 047-01

捐血活動

Got a pint? Give a pint!

Please donate blood. Our bloodmobile is going to be **parked** ⑲ outside of SOGO Mall all week to get blood donations.

Did you know your blood donations help save lives?

When there's an **accident** ⑳ , blood is needed.

If someone **loses a lot of blood** ❼ , blood is needed.

If someone is a hemophiliac and can't stop bleeding, blood is needed!

Blood saves lives. Be a **hero** ㉑ and make a difference—give blood today.

喝了一品脫？ 就給一品脫！

請捐血。我們的捐血車將於整週停靠在 SOGO 購物中心外面等您到來。

您知道您的捐血有助於挽救生命嗎？

當事故發生時，我們非常需要血液。

如果有人失去大量血液，我們非常需要血液。

如果某人是血友病患者且無法止血，這時則非常需要輸血！

鮮血拯救生命。成為英雄並創造改變——從今天開始捐血。

QUIZ 閱讀測驗

7. Why would someone want to donate blood?

(A) because he is a hemophilia
(B) because he lost a lot of blood
(C) because he wants to drive the bloodmobile
(D) because he wants to help out

7. 為什麼有人會想要捐血？

(A) 因為他是血友病患者 (B) 因為他失去許多血
(C) 因為他想要開捐血車 (D) 因為他想要幫助人

ANS: 7. (D)

VOCABULARY ♪ 047-02

⑲ **park** [park] v 停車

We parked outside the mall and waited for Jenny to get off work.

我們在百貨外面停車並且等待珍妮下班。

⑳ **accident** [ˋæksədənt] n 意外事故

Andy's accident left him with scars all over his knee.

發生在安迪身上的意外讓他整個膝蓋都留下疤痕。

㉑ **hero** [ˋhɪro] n 英雄

Henry was a real hero when he stood up to the bully hitting the little kid.

哈瑞是一個真正的英雄，他起身對抗毆打那個小孩的霸凌者。

PATTERN ♪ 047-03

❻ **get rid of** 擺脫

I have been trying to get rid of Johnny for hours, but he won't go away!

我已嘗試要擺脫強尼好幾個小時了，但他就是不走開！

❼ **lose a lot of blood** 失血過多

Yvonne lost a lot of blood and had to be rushed to the hospital.

伊凡失血過多且必須馬上被送去醫院。

MORE VOCABULARY ♪ 047-04

blood [blʌd] n 血液 v 抽血
blood type ph 血型
erythrocyte [ɪˋrɪθrə͵saɪt] n 紅血球
leukocyte [ˋlukə͵saɪt] n 白血球
platelet [ˋpletlɪt] n 血小板
blood transfusion ph 輸血
coma [ˋkomə] n 昏迷
immunity [ɪˋmjunətɪ] n 免疫力

Article 8

♪ 048-01

慈善拍賣會

Helping out the ⑧ community is done one step at a time.

This May, we are **holding** ㉒ a charity auction of famous paintings and sculptures by our local artists that have been so generous to **donate** ㉓ some lovely items. The auction is going to be a silent auction which means people can write down their **bids** ㉔ on a piece of paper near the item. The item will then be sold to the highest bid written down.

All proceeds go to help children with disabilities, so please, bid high!

幫助社區的進程是靠一步一腳印完成的。

今年五月，我們正在舉辦慈善拍賣會，其中包括我們當地藝術家熱心捐出的著名畫作與雕塑。這將是一場無聲拍賣，這意味著人們可以在藝術作品旁邊的一張紙上寫下他們的出價。該商品將以寫下的最高出價出售。

所有收益都將用於幫助殘疾兒童，所以請別吝嗇出高價！

VOCABULARY ♪ 048-02

㉒ **hold** [hold] v 舉辦

We are holding a dinner party this Friday if you are free.

你如果有空的話，我們這星期五會舉辦一個晚餐派對。

㉓ **donate** [ˋdonet] v / n 捐獻

I donated my time to help read to children in the library.

我貢獻我的時間幫助圖書館的小孩閱讀。

㉔ **bid** [bɪd] v 出價

We are going to bid on this piece, and the highest bidder wins.

我們將要針對這個作品出價，喊價最高的人可以得到此作品。

㉕ **provide** [prəˋvaɪd] v 提供

I hope you can provide us with a bed to sleep in tonight.

希望今晚你能夠提供我們一張床睡覺。

㉖ **available** [əˋveləbḷ] a 可用的、有空的

Is there any space available in your car for the ride home?

你的車上還有空位載人回家嗎？

㉗ **zone** [zon] n 區域

I feel like the Royal zone is the best place to go to find fabric.

我感覺皇家區是可以找到布料的最好地帶。

QUIZ 閱讀測驗

8. What is not something that will be auctioned?

(A) ceramic bowls (B) sculptures
(C) famous paintings (D) local paintings

8. 哪樣的東西不會被拍賣？

(A) 瓷碗 (B) 雕塑 (C) 名畫 (D) 當地畫家的畫作

ANS: 8. (A)

♪ 049-01

淨灘活動

Cleaning the Beach is Super Fun!

Join us this Sunday as we spend the whole day cleaning up the beach.

We'll meet at 8 am at Baishawan and get to work. We will **provide** ㉕ garbage and recycling bags, and we will have gloves **available** ㉖ if you have forgotten yours.

Our goal is to collect one hundred bags of garbage to really clean up the Baishawan beach **zone** ㉗ and make it **feel like home** ❾ .

清潔海灘可是非常有趣的！

這個星期天就加入我們，讓我們好好花上一整天淨灘。

我們將於上午八點在白沙灣見面並開始工作。我們將提供垃圾袋跟回收袋。如果您忘記帶自己的手套，我們也將會提供可用的手套給你。

我們的目標是收集一百袋垃圾，真正地清理白沙灣的海灘區，讓它感覺像家一樣。

QUIZ 閱讀測驗

9. What is something the group will not have?

(A) gloves (B) tongs to pick up garbage (C) garbage bags (D) recycling bags

9. 這個團隊不會有什麼東西？

(A) 手套 (B) 撿垃圾的夾子 (C) 垃圾袋 (D) 回收袋

ANS: 9. (B)

PATTERN ♪ 049-02

❽ help out the… 幫助……人

We work hard to help out the unfortunate people that live on the streets.

我們幫助那些不幸淪落街頭的人。

❾ feel like home 感覺像在家一樣

The smell of apple pie in the air really makes it feel like home.

空氣中蘋果派的香氣讓人感覺在家一樣。

LEARN MORE! ♪ 049-03

在海灘上會看到的生物有：

shell 貝殼

starfish 海星

hermit crab 寄居蟹

crab 螃蟹

spiral shell 螺

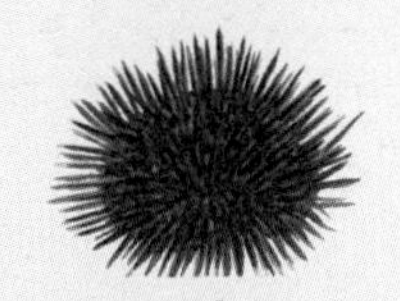

sea urchin 海膽

菜單

menu

VOCABULARY ♪ 050-01

① **maximum** [ˋmæksəməm]
n 最大值

The maximum parking time allowed here is 45 minutes.
這邊允許的最長停車時間是四十五分鐘。

② **accumulate** [əˋkjumjəˏlet]
v 累積

No matter how many times I give away clothes, I just keep accumulating them.
不管我把衣服送人多少次，我還是一直囤積。

③ **freebie** [ˋfribi] n 贈品

There are a lot of freebies in the hotel room, like shampoo, soap, and conditioner.
飯店房間裡有許多贈品，像是洗髮精、肥皂還有潤髮乳。

PATTERN ♪ 050-02

❶ **at an additional + (amount of money)** 需增加＋（某個額度）

At an additional cost of 140 NT, you can go into the Space Exhibition.
多加一百四十元台幣，你可以參加太空展。

Article 1 咖啡店

Coffee, Tea, or Dessert for Me

Americano	55NT
Cappuccino	95NT
Latte	95NT
Espresso	55NT
Herbal Tea	85NT
Mountain Black Tea	65NT
High-Antioxidant Green Tea	85NT
Desserts	45-95NT
Cappuccino + Dessert Set	120NT (Dessert max. 50NT value)

- 1-hour **maximum** ① stay during busy hours
- Almond milk, soy milk, and coconut milk available at an additional charge ❶
- 3NT discount for bringing your own cup
- Join our member's corner today to **accumulate** ② points and get **freebies** ③
- Buy ten coffees, get one free

來份咖啡、茶、點心？	
美式	55NT
卡布奇諾	95NT
拿鐵	95NT
義式濃縮	55NT
花草茶	85NT
高山紅茶	65NT
高抗氧綠茶	85NT
點心	45-95NT
卡布奇諾＋點心	120NT（搭配點心價格最高 50NT）

- 忙碌尖峰時刻至多只能坐一小時
- 也有杏仁奶、豆漿或是椰奶等選項，需加價
- 自備容器可折三塊
- 加入我們的集點會員並開始累積點數拿贈品
- 買十杯咖啡送一杯

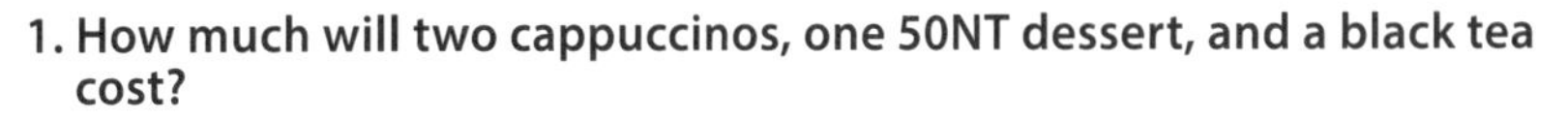

QUIZ 閱讀測驗

1. How much will two cappuccinos, one 50NT dessert, and a black tea cost?
(A) 300NT (B) 280NT (C) 305NT (D) 250NT

1. 兩杯卡布奇諾加上一份五十元的甜點，以及一杯紅茶，全部的費用為何？
(A) 台幣 300 元 (B) 台幣 280 元 (C) 台幣 305 元 (D) 台幣 250 元

ANS: 1. (B)

LEARN MORE!

走進咖啡店點咖啡的時候，你能夠分辨每個咖啡的差異嗎？

濃縮咖啡（espresso）

是義式咖啡，在短時間內萃取出的咖啡精華，上層覆蓋細緻的泡沫。

美式咖啡（Americano）

口味淡，製作快速，屬大眾化咖啡。

康寶藍（con panna）

在濃縮咖啡上覆蓋一層鮮奶油。

卡布奇諾（cappuccino）

濃縮咖啡、牛奶和奶泡的組合比例約為 1:1:1，口感以咖啡風味為主，隱約綻放奶香。

拿鐵咖啡（coffee latte）

濃縮咖啡、牛奶與奶泡的的組合比例約為 1:2:1，可同時品嚐到平衡的咖啡和牛奶風味。

摩卡（mocha）

具有巧克力風味；在卡布奇諾加上巧克力醬為摩卡奇諾，而拿鐵和巧克力的組成則為摩卡拿鐵。

VOCABULARY ♪052-01

④ **brownie** [ˋbraʊnɪ] n 布朗尼

My mom makes the best caramel brownies.

我媽媽做的焦糖布朗尼是最棒的。

⑤ **truffle** [ˋtrʌfl̩] n 軟糖

Chocolate truffles come in all different shapes and flavors.

巧克力軟糖有各種形狀跟口味。

⑥ **gianduja** 巧克力榛果醬

Creamy gianduja is an amazing filling for a pastry dessert.

濃郁的巧克力榛果醬是做酥餅類點心的極佳內餡。

PATTERN ♪052-02

❷ **except for** 除……之外

Everyone is available to work except for Billy.

除了比利之外，其他人都可以工作。

LEARN MORE! ♪052-03

❶ **What would you like for...?** 你想要什麼……？

What would you like for your breakfast?

你想吃什麼早餐？

❷ **I'd like to have...** 我想要點……

I'd like to have a plate of French fries.

我想要點一盤薯條。

❸ **What... do you recommend?** 你推薦什麼……？

What dessert do you recommend?

你推薦什麼甜點呢？

Article 2 甜點店

Charlie's Chocolates

Chocolate Cake

Black Forest Cake

Deep Chocolate **Brownies** ④

Hot Fudge Sundae
+ brownie pieces
+ fruit
+ pound cake
+ nuts
+ whipped cream

Chocolate Mousse

Chocolate Tart

Chocolate Shake

Chocolate **Truffles** ⑤, assorted
+ raspberry
+ coffee
+ ginger
+bourbon cream
+**gianduja** ⑥

If you like chocolate, we've got it. All of our desserts are priced by the 100 grams **except for** ❷ truffles which are priced by the piece. Come and get your chocolate on!

查理的巧克力店

巧克力蛋糕

黑森林蛋糕

雙倍布朗尼

熱奶油軟糖霜淇淋聖代
+ 布朗尼碎片
+ 水果
+ 磅蛋糕
+ 堅果
+ 奶油

巧克力慕斯

巧克力塔

巧克力奶昔

巧克力軟糖（各種口味）
+ 覆盆子
+ 咖啡
+ 薑
+ 波本威士忌奶油
+ 巧克力榛果醬

如果你喜歡巧克力，我們什麼品項都有。除了巧克力軟糖是用顆數計算外，其餘的點心都是以一百克為單位來計算價格。快來選購你的巧克力吧！

LEARN MORE!

蛋糕 ♪053-01

chiffon cake 戚風蛋糕
white chocolate cake 白巧克力蛋糕
cheese cake 乳酪蛋糕
fruit cake 水果蛋糕
mango mousse cake 芒果慕斯蛋糕
sponge cake 海綿蛋糕
caramelized plum cake 焦糖蜜棗蛋糕
lava cake 熔岩蛋糕

甜點菜單 ♪053-02

matcha roll cake 抹茶生乳捲
lemon tart 檸檬塔
coconut milk pudding 椰奶布丁
chocolate mousse with cherry 巧克力櫻桃慕斯
white chocolate 白巧克力
peanut brittle 花生糖
succade 蜜餞

烘焙材料 ♪053-03

cornstarch 玉米澱粉
sweet potato flour 地瓜粉
vanilla powder 香草粉
caramel 焦糖
glucose syrup 葡萄糖漿
food coloring 食用色素

QUIZ 閱讀測驗

2. How is the price of a chocolate tart figured?

(A) by the 100 grams
(B) by the slice
(C) by the piece
(D) buy one get one free

2. 巧克力塔的價格是如何計算的？

(A) 以一百克為單位來計算
(B) 以片數計算
(C) 以塊數計算
(D) 買一送一

ANS: 2. (A)

Article 3 西餐廳

Surf and Turf

Pasta (Choose one)	170NT
Bolognese	
Carbonara	
Pesto	

Entrées

Steak

Ribeye	450NT
Sirloin	595NT
Fillet	799NT

* Comes with two free **sides** ⑦ , your choice of: **baked** ⑧ potato, fries, mashed potatoes, sweet potato, corn, coleslaw, fried mushrooms, side salad

Fish

Fried Cod	375NT
Salmon with Orange Sauce	425NT

* Comes with two free sides, **your choice of** ❸ : baked potato, fries, mashed potatoes, sweet potato, corn, coleslaw, **fried** ⑨ mushrooms, side salad
* Enjoy a plate of pasta with a nice entrée for 20% off.

VOCABULARY ♪054-01

⑦ **side** [saɪd] n 配菜

I'd like to get a side of mashed potatoes, please.

我想要用馬鈴薯泥當我的配菜，謝謝。

⑧ **bake** [bek] v 烤

We baked the ham in the oven for two hours.

我們用烤箱烤了火腿兩小時。

⑨ **fried** [fraɪd] a 炸的

The fried chicken was loved by everyone.

每個人都愛這道炸雞。

PATTERN ♪054-02

❸ **choice of** ……的選擇

For tonight's movie, you have a choice of *Yes* and *Alexander's Day*.

今晚的電影選項中，你可以選《是的》或是《亞歷山大的一天》。

MORE VOCABULARY ♪054-03

red wine glass 紅酒杯
white wine glass 白酒杯
chopsticks 筷子
water glass 水杯
bowl 碗
napkin 餐巾
tablecloth 桌布

QUIZ 閱讀測驗

3. Which is NOT a side listed?

(A) mashed potatoes (B) corn (C) sweet potato fries (D) coleslaw

3. 哪一個不是配菜的選項？

(A) 馬鈴薯泥 (B) 玉米 (C) 炸蕃薯條 (D) 涼拌菜絲

ANS: 3. (C)

衝浪好手

義大利麵（擇一）	170NT
肉醬義大利麵	
培根蛋義大利麵	
香蒜義大利麵	

主菜

牛排

肋眼牛排	450NT
沙朗牛排	595NT
菲力牛排	799NT

＊皆搭配兩份自選的免費配菜：烤馬鈴薯、炸薯條、馬鈴薯泥、蕃薯、玉米、涼拌菜絲、炸香菇、沙拉

魚排

炸鱈魚排	375NT
鮭魚排佐橘子醬	425NT

＊皆搭配兩份自選的免費配菜：烤馬鈴薯、炸薯條、馬鈴薯泥、蕃薯、玉米、涼拌菜絲、炸香菇、沙拉

＊以八折優惠享有您的義大利麵搭配一份主餐。

MORE VOCABULARY ♪055-01

- A cake fork 甜點叉
- B dessert spoon 甜點匙
- C salad fork 沙拉叉
- D dinner fork 餐叉
- E service plate 服務盤
- F plate 盤子
- G dinner knife 餐刀
- H spoon 湯匙

VOCABULARY ♪056-01

⑩ **speedy** [ˋspidɪ] a 快速的

He was a speedy taxi driver and got me home quickly.

他是開很快的計程車司機，而且很快把我送到家。

⑪ **set** [sɛt] n 套餐

The meal set was cheaper than ordering the items separately.

點套餐比單點便宜。

⑫ **bigger** [bɪgɚ] a 較大的

It is going to take a bigger bag for us to put in all the groceries.

我們需要更大的袋子來裝入所有買的食品雜貨。

PATTERN ♪056-02

④ **add a...for** 為了……加入……

Can I add salami to the pizza for 30NT?

我可以用台幣 30 元加購薩拉米香腸到我的披薩中嗎？

LEARN MORE!

去到美國，不要再只吃麥當勞、肯德基、漢堡王了，來試試看其他人氣漢堡吧！

★ **In-N-Out Burger**

薯條是整顆馬鈴薯現切炸的！

★ **Five Guys**

幾乎每家店都有整箱花生任你吃！

★ **Shake Shack**

使用安格斯牛肉，還有被評比為業界最棒的奶昔！

★ **Habit Burger Grill**

除了經典漢堡，還有日式照燒、聖塔芭芭拉風味！

★ **Super Duper**

保證使用天然、有機的食材！

Article 4 速食店

Speedy ⑩ Eats and Treats

Hamburger		59NT	French Fries	small	25NT
Cheeseburger		69NT		medium	40NT
Bacon Cheeseburger		95NT		large	50NT
Grilled Chicken Burger		85NT	Salad		65NT
Fried Chicken Burger		89NT	Drink	small	15NT
Chicken Fingers	3 piece	45NT		medium	25NT
	6 piece	65NT		large	35NT
	9 piece	85NT			

☐ Burger **set** ⑪ meal (+medium set Fries and Drink) 100NT

☐ Get a **bigger** ⑫ size (Large set) 110NT

☐ **Add a** vanilla ice cream to a set **for** ④ 10NT

快速小吃與享受

漢堡		59NT	炸薯條	小份	25NT
起司漢堡		69NT		中份	40NT
培根漢堡		95NT		大份	50NT
烤雞漢堡		85NT	沙拉		65NT
炸雞漢堡		89NT	飲料	小杯	15NT
炸雞柳	三塊	45NT		中杯	25NT
	六塊	65NT		大杯	35NT
	九塊	85NT			

☐ 漢堡套餐（加上中份薯條與飲料） 100NT

☐ 加大（大份套餐）110NT ☐ 加上香草冰淇淋 10NT

QUIZ 閱讀測驗

4. How much would it cost to buy a large meal set with an ice cream?

(A) 95NT (B) 110NT (C) 120NT (D) 145NT

4. 如果買大份的套餐加上一支冰淇淋，價格會是多少？

(A) 台幣 95 元 (B) 台幣 110 元 (C) 台幣 120 元 (D) 台幣 145 元

ANS: 4. (C)

LEARN MORE!

♪057-01 ❶ **Does the...taste⋯?** ……嚐起來……嗎？

A: Does the cake taste salty?
這個蛋糕嚐起來會鹹嗎？

B: Nope. It's very sweet.
不，它很甜。

♪057-02 ❷ **please reserve...for...** 請預訂……人的……

A: Hello. Rilakkuma Cafe. How may I help you?
拉拉熊咖啡廳你好，能為你效勞嗎？

B: Please reserve a table for two at 8:30 tonight.
請預訂今晚八點半兩人的桌位。

♪057-03 ❸ **we're expecting to...** 我們期待……

A: We're expecting to move to New York.
我們期待搬到紐約。

B: I hope you'll come back to visit us once in a while after moving to New York.
希望你們搬到紐約後，偶爾會回來探望我們。

♪057-04 ❹ **that's...dollars altogether** 一共是……元

A: How much in total?
總共多少錢呢？

B: That's one thousand dollars altogether.
一共是一千元。

♪057-05 ❺ **Could you tell me where a...is?** 可以請你告訴我……在哪裡嗎？

A: Could you tell me where a flower shop is?
可以請你告訴我花店在哪裡嗎？

B: Go down this street and turn left.
沿著這條街走，然後左轉。

♪057-06 ❻ **...doesn't shut until...** ……直到……才打烊

A: The supermarket doesn't shut until 8 p.m.
那家超市直到晚上八點才打烊。

B: Let's set out at six this evening!
那我們今晚六點出發吧！

♪057-07 ❼ **here is...** 這是……

A: Here is the bottle of body lotion for you.
這就是要給你的身體乳液。

B: Thank you so much! I like body lotion made in Japan.
非常謝謝你！我喜歡日本製的身體乳液。

♪057-08 ❽ **thanks for...** 謝謝你……

A: Thanks for your useful advice.
謝謝你的實用建言。

B: If you have other questions, you can consult me.
如果你還有疑問，可以請教我。

LEARN MORE!

在歐美有許多食物專賣店，有時候逛街累了可以進去坐著休息，也是多數人聚餐、續攤的選擇之地。

甜甜圈店

披薩店

炸雞店

杯子蛋糕店

蘇打飲料店

熱狗店

冰淇淋店

塔可店

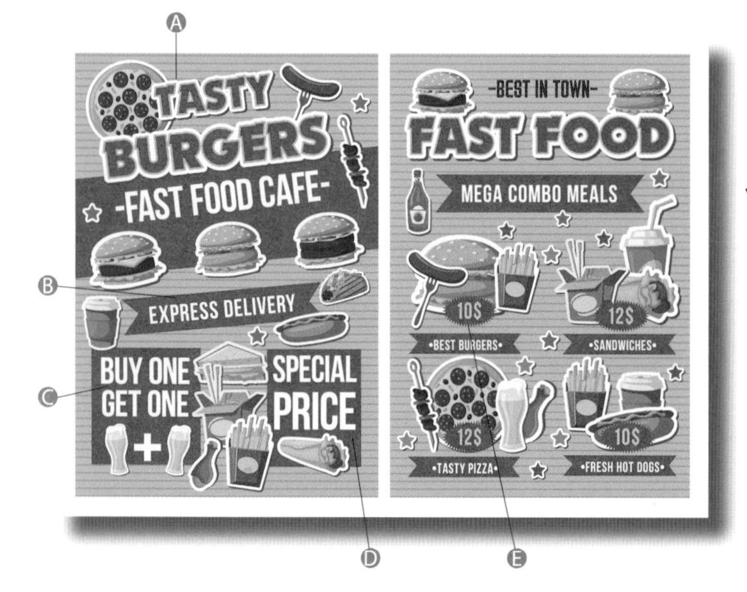

LEARN MORE!

在看餐廳的廣告傳單的時候，可以從以下幾點掌握傳單的關鍵訊息。

Ⓐ 餐廳、食物類別

Ⓑ 特色：express delivery 是「快速送達」的意思，也可以解釋為「快速出餐」。

Ⓒ 優惠：buy one get one 就是「買一送一」。

Ⓓ 特價：special price 就是「特惠價」的意思。

Ⓔ 特餐的價錢、名稱，可從圖片中看到套餐的內容。

披薩店

Pamela's Pizza Pies

Base includes pizza dough ⑬ and marinara sauce

8″	thin crust	60NT	deep dish	90NT
10″	thin crust	90NT	deep dish	120NT
12″	thin crust	120NT	deep dish	150NT
Calzone		130NT		

Add ingredients 20NT per topping⑭ :

mozzarella	onions	mushrooms
olives	garlic	jalapenos

30NT per topping❺ :

anchovies	bacon	spinach
pepperoni	pineapple	Canadian ham

50NT per topping:

artichoke	parma ham

Add three toppings and get a 10NT **discount** ⑮

帕美拉的披薩派

披薩餅皮加上義式蕃茄醬

8 寸	薄皮	60NT	厚片	90NT
10 寸	薄皮	90NT	厚片	120NT
12 寸	薄皮	120NT	厚片	150NT
披薩餃		130NT		

【加料】20 元配料項目	莫薩里拉起司	洋蔥	蘑菇
	橄欖	大蒜	墨西哥辣椒
30 元配料項目	鯷魚	培根	菠菜
	義大利辣香腸	鳳梨	加拿大香腸
50 元配料項目	洋薊	巴馬火腿	

加三種配料可享有 10 元折價

QUIZ 閱讀測驗

5. How much would it cost to add pepperoni, spinach, and artichoke?

(A) 90 NT (B) 100 NT (C) 110 NT (D) 135NT

5. 如果加上義大利辣香腸、菠菜跟洋薊，價格會是多少？

(A) 台幣 90 元 (B) 台幣 100 元 (C) 台幣 110 元 (D) 台幣 135 元

ANS: 5. (B)

VOCABULARY ♪059-01

⑬ **dough** [do] n 麵團

The pie dough took no time to prep up, but it needed to chill in the freezer.

準備派的麵團不用花什麼時間，但是它必須在冰箱中冷卻。

⑭ **topping** [`tapɪŋ] a （淋在食物上的）配料

My favorite sundae topping is caramel sauce.

我最喜歡用焦糖醬來當霜淇淋的配醬。

⑮ **discount** [`dɪskaunt] n 折扣 [ˌdɪs`kaunt] v 打折

I'm looking for a discount on the items I've got.

我在找我選的東西還有沒有折扣。

PATTERN ♪059-02

❺ **per (+ N)** 每……（項目）

Warren paid $80 per day for his hotel room.

沃藍的飯店房間每天的費用是八十美金。

酒吧

Wood's

- Well Drinks 90 NT (these include standard vodka, tequila, gin, and rum drinks)
- Top **Shelf** ⑯ Drinks 150NT
- Beer 100NT
- Mixed drinks **starting at** ❻ 180NT
- Pina Colada, Long Island Iced Tea, Bloody Mary, Cosmopolitan, and Screwdrivers 180NT
- Frozen Drinks: Daiquiris and Margaritas 200NT
- Fruit Frozens: Strawberry, Mango, Tropical Fruit Daiquiris and Margaritas 220NT

* Happy Hour is from 6-8PM and that's buy-one-get-one-free on all drinks!
* Ladies drink for free on Wednesday nights—that's Ladies' Night!
* We do **card** ⑰ , so have a form of ID on you because we will not serve **underage** ⑱ drinkers.

叢林酒吧

- 吧台現有酒精飲品 90 NT（包括標準伏特加、龍舌蘭酒、杜松子酒和朗姆酒）
- 頂級酒精飲品 150NT
- 啤酒 100NT
- 調酒價位從 180NT 開始
- 椰林飄香、長島冰茶、血腥瑪麗、柯夢波丹和螺絲起子 180NT
- 冰鎮調酒：戴綺麗和瑪格麗特 200NT
- 冷凍水果調酒：草莓、芒果、熱帶水果的戴綺麗和瑪格麗特 220NT

* 歡樂時光（優惠時間）是從晚上六點到八點，所有飲料都是買一送一！
* 女士們在周三晚上可免費暢飲 - 當天是我們的女士之夜！
* 我們會確認身份，所以請攜帶你的證件，因為我們不會提供未成年者酒精飲品。

VOCABULARY ♪060-01

⑯ **shelf** [ʃɛlf] n 層架

The books on the top shelf are impossible to reach.

書櫃最上層的書根本不可能拿得到。

⑰ **card** [kɑrd] n 卡 v 出示證件

They carded my brother after he was pulled over.

我弟路邊停靠後他們要求他示出證件。

⑱ **underage** [ˋʌndɚˋedʒ] a 未滿法定年齡的

The underage student tried unsuccessfully to sneak into the bar.

那個未成年學生沒有成功混入酒吧。

PATTERN ♪060-02

❻ **starting at (+ price, time)** 價格、時間從……開始計算

Starting at noon, we will go on a juice fast.

從中午開始我們會只用喝果汁禁食。

LEARN MORE!

到酒吧，酒單上常見的調酒有以下幾種：

1. 血腥瑪麗 **Bloody Mary**
2. 柯夢波丹 **Cosmopolitan**
3. 螺絲起子 **Screwdriver**
4. 摩西多 **Mojito**
5. 瑪格莉特 **Margarita**
6. 性感海灘 **Sex on the beach**
7. 長島冰茶 **Long Island Iced Tea**

調酒雖然喝起來甜甜的，很容易順口地一杯接著一杯入肚，但其實調酒的酒精濃度不低，以長島冰茶為例，它的酒精濃度可以高達 35%！

QUIZ 閱讀測驗

6. Which drinks are the most expensive?

(A) Long Island Iced Tea (B) Well drinks
(C) Strawberry Daiquiris (D) Margaritas

6. 哪些飲品最貴？

(A) 長島冰茶 (B) 吧台現有的酒精飲品 (C) 草莓戴綺麗 (D) 瑪格麗特

ANS: 6. (D)

MORE VOCABULARY ♪ 061-01

kiss [kɪs] v 親吻
hug [hʌg] v 擁抱
caress [kə`rɛs] v 撫摸
pat [pæt] v 輕拍
romantic [rə`mæntɪk] a 浪漫的
couple [`kʌpḷ] n 情侶
affair [ə`fɛr] n 風流韻事

LEARN MORE! ♪ 061-02

· How nice to meet you again! 能再次見到你真好！
· You look more handsome. 你變得更帥氣了。
· I'd like to, but I have an appointment tonight.
我很想去，但今晚有約了。
· I'd like to invite you to the special occasion.
我想邀請你參加這個特別的場合。
· I cordially invite you to dinner at the restaurant.
我誠摯邀請你去那家餐廳享用晚餐。

MORE VOCABULARY ♪ 061-03

beer [bɪr] n 啤酒
drunk [drʌŋk] a 喝醉的
tipsy [`tɪpsɪ] a 微醉的
hangover [`hæŋˌovɚ] n 宿醉
shit-faced [`ʃɪtˌfesɪd] a 爛醉的
bottoms up 乾杯
blacked out 喝掛

MORE VOCABULARY ♪ 061-04

whiskey [`hwɪskɪ] n 威士忌酒
vodka [`vadkə] n 伏特加酒
gin [dʒɪn] n 琴酒
rum [rʌm] n 蘭姆酒
brandy [`brændɪ] n 白蘭地酒
cocktail [`kakˌtel] n 雞尾酒
rock [rak] n 冰塊

Article 7 uber eats

Your favorites:

Juice ⑲ Bar
$ Juice and Smoothies
10-20 Minutes 4.8 stars 30TWD Fee

You **last ordered here** ⑦ on February 7

People who **ordered** ⑳ A Dao's Cut Noodles also **enjoyed** ㉑

Fang's
$$ Chinese
25-30 min 4.9 stars 25TWD Fee

Recommended Dishes
Under 25 Minutes
New on Uber Eats

你的最愛：

果汁吧
$ 果汁和果昔
10 到 20 分鐘 4.8 顆星 費用 30TWD

最後訂購紀錄於二月七日

在阿道刀削麵消費的人也喜歡

阿凡的店
$$ 中式餐點
25 到 30 分鐘 4.9 顆星 費用 25TWD

推薦餐點
低於二十五分鐘
在 Uber Eats 的最新推薦

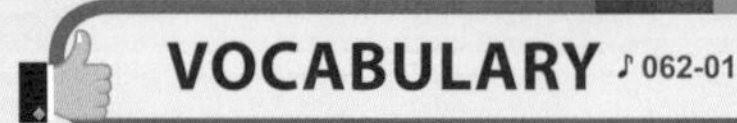

VOCABULARY ♪ 062-01

⑲ **juice** [dʒus] n 果汁

I love to start my day with fresh-squeezed juice.

我喜歡用新鮮的現榨果汁開啟我的一天。

⑳ **order** [ˋɔrdɚ] v 點餐

They ordered dinner and sat down at the table to wait.

他們點了晚餐後坐在位子上等待來餐。

㉑ **enjoy** [ɪnˋdʒɔɪ] v 享受

I really enjoyed our date last night.

我真的很享受我們昨晚的約會時光。

㉒ **preheat** [priˋhit] v 事先預熱

Preheat the oven before baking the cookies.

烤餅乾前要預熱烤箱。

㉓ **blend** [blɛnd] v 混合

Blend the fruit, ice, and fruit juice in the blender to make a smoothie.

把水果、冰塊、果汁放在果汁機裡打成果昔。

㉔ **tray** [tre] n 托盤

The server used his tray to carry drinks around the party.

服務生用他的托盤承裝飲品，穿梭在派對上。

食譜

Chocolate Chip Cookies

¾ cup sugar	2¼ cups flour	¾ cup brown sugar
1 tsp baking soda	1 cup butter	1 tsp baking powder
1 tsp vanilla	a pinch of salt	2 eggs
1½ cup chocolate chips		

Directions:

1. **Preheat** the ㉒ oven to 375 degrees
2. Mix together dry ingredients—flour, baking soda, baking powder, and salt. **Put aside** ⑧ .
3. Add sugars in cream butter and **blend** ㉓ until creamy. Add eggs and mix well.
4. Add vanilla. Incorporate the dry ingredients just until well mixed.
5. Add chocolate chips in the end.
6. Place in balls on a cookie **tray** ㉔ and bake for 10 to 12 minutes.

巧克力碎片餅乾

¾ 杯糖	2¼ 杯麵粉	¾ 杯黑糖
一茶匙小蘇打粉	一杯奶油	一茶匙發酵粉
一茶匙香草香料	一搓鹽	兩顆蛋
1½ 杯巧克力碎片		

準備方式：

1. 預熱烤箱到三百七十五度。
2. 將乾的材料攪和在一起——麵粉、小蘇打粉、發酵粉以及鹽巴。先放置一邊。
3. 把奶油加入糖之後開始攪拌至呈現糊狀，再加入雞蛋後拌勻。
4. 加入香草，之後再把放置一邊的乾狀材料也一併攪合均勻。
5. 最後加入巧克力碎片。
6. 將成品以球狀放置在餅乾烤盤上，烘培十至十二分鐘。

QUIZ 閱讀測驗

7. Which location is likely to deliver the fastest based on what is seen?
(A) Fangs (B) A Dao's Cut Noodles (C) New on Uber Eats (D) Juice Bar

8. What is not a dry ingredient?
(A) flour (B) baking powder (C) salt (D) butter

7. 根據顯示資訊，哪一個地點可以用最快的速度外送？
(A) 阿凡的店 (B) 阿道刀削麵 (C) Uber Eats 的最新推薦 (D) 果汁吧

8. 哪一項不是乾的材料？
(A) 麵粉 (B) 發酵粉 (C) 鹽巴 (D) 奶油

ANS: 7. (D) 8. (D)

PATTERN ♪063-01

⑦ **last ordered here** 最後訂購商品

You last ordered here a week ago; did you want the usual?

上週的最後訂購項目於此，你想要再次選購一樣商品嗎？

⑧ **put aside** 放置一旁

We should put aside our differences and work together.

我們應該撇開分歧並一起工作。

LEARN MORE! ♪063-02

麵包通常是以黑麥（rye）、小麥（wheat）、大麥（barley）、玉米（corn）、米（rice）等作物為基本材料，磨成粉後再加入水、鹽、酵母（yeast）等和麵（knead dough），之後再以烘焙（bake）或蒸的方式加熱製作。麵包有時候也會加入牛奶、雞蛋、穀物（grain）、堅果（nut）、燕麥（oat）等，做出各種不同變化。

麵包的種類繁多，一般常見的有以下幾種，有些人會將麵包作為主餐，也些人是作為趕時間果腹食用。

- **bagel** 貝果
- **bun** 餐包
- **multi-grain bread** 雜糧麵包
- **wheat bread** 小麥麵包
- **rye bread** 黑麥麵包
- **croissant** 可頌麵包
- **garlic bread** 大蒜麵包

社群媒體

social media

VOCABULARY ♪ 064-02

① **totes** [tots] ad 完全、徹底

This bag is totes amazing!

這個包包真的超級棒！

② **summer** [ˋsʌmɚ] n 夏天

I am not going to make any plans at all this summer.

這個夏天我不打算計畫任何事。

③ **super** [ˋsupɚ] a 超級的

She is super shy, but we get along great.

她超級害羞，但我們處得很來。

Article 1

♪ 064-01

facebook

Annaliese **is with** ❶ Eric Jo, Carol PZ, Adam Z, and 3 others

OMG, we are **totes** ① adorbs! I hope we can get together again next **summer** ②! You guys are so **super** ③ smart and amazing. Don't ever change!

艾娜雷斯目前跟艾力克・周、卡羅・PZ、亞當・Z 以及其他三個人在一起。

我的老天爺，我們根本就超可愛！希望下個夏天我們能夠再次相聚！你們大夥真的是超級聰明又棒的朋友。希望這永遠不會改變！

QUIZ 閱讀測驗

1. What does Annaliese mean by "Don't ever change"?

(A) She doesn't think people should change their uniforms.
(B) She wants everyone to stand in the same position for the next picture.
(C) She wants everyone to keep the same hairstyle.
(D) She wants everyone to keep being the same great people.

1. 安娜雷斯説「Don't ever change?」指的是什麼意思？

(A) 她認為人們不該改變他們的制服。
(B) 她想要每個人下次拍照都要用一樣的姿勢。
(C) 她想要每個人都保持一樣的髮型。
(D) 他想要每個人都保持一樣，繼續當很棒的人。

ANS: 1. (D)

♪065-01

Instagram

miss_palmieri **just** ④ me and Fluffs trying to wake up #needmy**coffee** ⑤ #don'teventhinkabouttalkingtomeyet

Fluffs **for life** ❷ !

miss_palmieri I know, right?

miss_palmieri 就只是我跟毛球嘗試起床 # 我需要我的咖啡 # 休想跟我說話 這輩子只要毛球！
miss_palmieri 就是說啊，對吧？

♪065-02

twitter

UT Chica: I'm a **weirdo** ⑥ . I'm a clown. I graduated in 1995! #Hook'EmHorns #UT**Forever** ⑦

Alabama_J: **Girl** ⑧ , you **are the biggest** ❸ longhorn fan I know #Bama'sBest

UT Chica：我是一個怪咖。我是一個小丑。我一九九五年的時候畢業！# 德州加油 # 永遠的 UT

Alabama_J：女孩，我真的沒有看過比你還要支持長角牛（longhorn）的！# 阿拉巴馬最棒

QUIZ 閱讀測驗

2. What does miss_palmieri mean by "I know, right"?
(A) I don't know. (B) That's so true. (C) That's so weird. (D) You're weird to not know.

3. Which hashtag is not shown above?
(A) #Bama'sBest (B) #YouTeeNo1 (C) #德州加油 (D) #UTForever

2. miss_palmieri 回覆的「I know, right?」是什麼意思？
(A) 我不知道。 (B) 講得對極了。 (C) 那真的超怪。 (D) 你不知道的話就太奇怪了。

3. 哪一個井字符號的內容沒有在上面寫出來？
(A) #Bama'sBest (B) #YouTee 第一 (C) #Hook'EmHorns (D) #永遠的 UT

ANS: 2. (B) 3. (B)

VOCABULARY ♪065-03

④ **just** [dʒʌst] ad 就是
Just let me have a few minutes to wake up.
再多給我幾分鐘起床。

★ **type** [taɪp] v 打字
I'm typing an email as we speak.
我們講話的時候我也在寫郵件。

⑤ **coffee** [`kɔfɪ] n 咖啡
Let's get together tomorrow for a coffee.
明天去喝杯咖啡聚一下。

⑥ **weirdo** [`wɪrdo] n 奇怪的人、怪咖
Henry is a total weirdo and not in a good way.
亨利完全是個怪咖，而且不是正面的那種怪。

⑦ **forever** [fɚ`ɛvɚ] ad 永遠
I am forever on your side.
我永遠站在你這邊。

⑧ **girl** [gɝl] n 女孩
Girl, you ate my last piece of pizza!
女孩，你吃了我最後一片披薩！

PATTERN ♪065-04

❶ **is with** 某人和……在一起
Annie is with Alex and Carl in this picture.
這張照片裡安尼跟艾力克斯還有卡羅在一起。

❷ **for life** 一生
You and I are going to be friends for life!
你跟我將是一輩子的朋友！

❸ **are the biggest...** 是最大的……
Angel is the biggest adventure seeker I know.
安琪拉是我認識的人中最熱衷於冒險的。

Skill!!
使用社群媒體的技巧！

在使用社群媒體、通訊軟體時，不管是 FB、Line 、Twitter 或 Instagram，大家都在 po 訊息，而發表個人訊息、閱讀他人訊息的技巧就是……「使用關鍵字（keywords）」！在社群媒體上回覆的技巧主要有三個：

1. 使用貼圖或表情符號（Emoji）
2. 對貼文按個讚（Give a Like!）
3. 使用關鍵字做回應。

Annoying Relatives 煩人的親戚 **回應** We are lucky to choose our friends. 我們很幸運可以選擇朋友。	Home grown organic apples 自家栽種有機蘋果 **回應** They look tasty and healthy. 看起來美味又健康。	It is with a heavy heart that we announce the peaceful passing of our cat. 我們心情沉重地宣佈我們的貓安詳地離開了。 **回應** R.I.P. (Rest in Peace) 願它安息。

在較長篇的社群媒體上的對話，也可以同樣使用關鍵字：

A: Hi, message me when you arrive. 嗨，到了傳訊息給我

B: I am downstairs. 我在樓下了

C: Me, too. Let's meet at the entrance. 我也是，入口見

A: How did it go? 還好嗎？

B: Something was wrong with the equipment. 設備出了問題

A: Did the engineer come to fix it? 工程師有來修嗎？

B: Yes, the on-site service was provided, and the problem was solved. 有提供現場服務，問題解決了

A: That's a relief. 真是鬆了一口氣

看懂關鍵字，可以讓你立即進入並了解主題，更能迅速即立即回覆。

♪ 067-01

認識新朋友

Hi there,

My name is Harriet. Our friend Charles said you and I should **get in touch** ❹ because he thinks we'd be great friends. It's kind of hard in this day and age to reach out to people and try to make new friends, but I think it's kind of important to try because it gets us off the computer **screen** ⑨.

Anyway, he thought we'd get along well because we both like to paint. I've been painting for about 5 years, and that's **primarily** ⑩ what I do in my free time. My other big thing is to get outdoors and go hiking, which Charles also said you are into. So, I was thinking, maybe we could meet up and go for a little hike with some painting **gear** ⑪. If you're interested, drop me a line at this email.

你好：

我叫哈麗特。我們的共同朋友查爾斯說我們應該互相認識看看，因為他認為我們可以成為好朋友。在這個時代，與人們接觸並嘗試結交新朋友是很困難的一件事，但我認為嘗試這一點仍非常重要，因為這樣可以讓我們離開看電腦螢幕的世界。

總而言之，他認為我們可以相處得很好，因為我們都喜歡畫畫。我已經畫畫大約五年了，這主要是我在空閒時間做的事情。我的另一個喜好就是到戶外走走跟健行，查爾斯也說你對這方面感興趣。 所以，我就在想或許我們可以見個面，然後帶著一些繪畫用具去遠足。如果你感到有興趣，就以這封電子郵件回覆給我吧。

QUIZ 閱讀測驗

4. What kind of activity are the two likely to do together?

(A) sailing (B) hiking (C) swimming (D) skating

4. 這兩個人有可能共同進行哪項活動？

(A) 划船 (B) 健行 (C) 游泳 (D) 溜冰

ANS: 4. (B)

VOCABULARY ♪ 067-02

⑨ **screen** [skrin] n 螢幕

I have been staring at my computer screen all day!

我今天一整天都盯著我的電腦螢幕看。

⑩ **primarily** [praɪˋmɛrəlɪ] ad 主要地

She is primarily interested in finding a better job.

她目前主要感興趣的事，是找到一個更好的工作。

⑪ **gear** [gɪr] n 裝備、用具

What kind of ski gear did you bring with you?

你帶了怎樣的滑雪裝備？

PATTERN ♪ 067-03

❹ **get in touch** 聯繫

I was hoping we could get in touch and talk about the problem.

我本來希望我們可以聯繫並討論這個問題。

LEARN MORE! ♪ 067-04

如果要討論個人、事物的優缺點，可以用下列的單字：

優點

advantage 優勢

benefit 好處

positive 積極的

缺點

disadvantage 劣勢

drawback 缺點

negative 負面的

Article 5 好友聊天

♪068-01

Janna, I have to tell you the news. Andy popped the question last night! OMG, I am over-the-moon **excited** ⑫ . I can't believe that after **dating** ⑬ for five years, we're finally going to get married.

Will you be my Maid of Honor? You know I wouldn't ask anyone else. We're talking about a spring wedding. I already have all these **details** ⑭ running through my head. I need to set up a venue and caterer, get invitations, taste cakes, and get a dress. It's insane to think of all the things that have to be decided.

I can't wait until you read this; I know you are going to **flip out** ❺ !

Kisses

喬娜，我得告訴妳這個消息。安迪昨晚突然提出這個問題！天哪，我真的超級興奮。我不敢相信，在約會交往五年之後，我們終於要結婚了。

妳願意當我的伴娘嗎？妳知道我不會考慮別人的。我們在討論春天的時候結婚。我現在腦中已經都考量了全部的細節。我需要確定場地跟宴客餐廳、籌備邀請函、試吃婚禮蛋糕還有挑選禮服。要決定全部的細節用想的就感到瘋狂。

我等不及妳讀到我的訊息了，我知道妳一定也會感到很驚喜！

親親！

QUIZ 閱讀測驗

5. What is something the bride-to-be does not have to plan?

(A) the seating arrangements (B) the location for the wedding
(C) who will make the food (D) invitations

5. 哪些是準新娘不用計畫的事？

(A) 座位的安排 (B) 結婚的場地 (C) 決定誰會準備婚宴的食物 (D) 邀請函

ANS: 5. (A)

PATTERN ♪068-02

❺ **flip out** （因為驚訝或是震驚）而失去控制

Alistair flipped out when he heard his favorite band was coming to town.

艾莉絲塔爾一聽到她最喜愛的樂團要來小鎮上表演整個人都樂瘋了。

❻ **where would (somebody) be without (+ V, N)** 沒有……的話……會在哪

Where would Josie be without Aaron's help changing her tire?

如果沒有艾倫幫喬西換輪胎的話，根本都不知道她現在人在哪 / 會怎樣。

MORE VOCABULARY ♪068-03

- **bride** [braɪd] n 新娘
- **bridegroom** [ˋbraɪd͵grum] n 新郎
- **propose** [prəˋpoz] v 求婚
- **engagement** [ɪnˋgedʒmənt] n 訂婚
- **marriage** [ˋmærɪdʒ] n 婚姻
- **maid of honour** ph 伴娘
- **best man** ph 伴郎
- **flower girls** ph 花童
- **bridal bouquet** ph 新娘捧花

Article 6

♪ 069-01

加入新群組聊天

Greetings, I'm new to this group. Thanks for **accepting** ⑮ me! I'm a big movie nerd and love sci-fi movies. I mean, *Bladerunner, The Fifth Element, 12 Monkeys,* **where would we be without** ⑥ these movies, right? I'm interested in meeting other people that like to talk about anything sci-fi **related** ⑯ .

I'm not really into **gaming** ⑰ because that is a time sucker. But I would love to meet up at a sci-fi con somewhere and even see if someone wants to do something crazy and make our own costumes! Why don't you guys tell me about your favorite sci-fi movies?

大家好，我是這個群組新加入的人。感謝同意接受我的加入！我是超級電影迷，熱愛科幻電影。我的意思是，像是《銀翼殺手》、《第五元素》跟《未來總動員》這些電影，如果沒有它們，我們現在會在哪裡，對吧？ 我有興趣與其他也喜歡談論科幻相關電影的人見面。

我真的沒有喜歡玩遊戲，因為會浪費很多時間。但我真的滿希望可以跟你們在科幻大會上見面，說不定有人想要一起做些瘋狂的事，之後我們也可以一起做我們的服裝！大夥們不如告訴我你們喜歡怎樣的科幻電影吧？

QUIZ 閱讀測驗

6. Which movie is not mentioned?

(A) *Bladerunner* (B) *The Fifth Element*
(C) *12 Monkeys* (D) *Ready Player One*

6. 哪一部電影沒有被提到？

(A)《銀翼殺手》 (B)《第五元素》 (C)《未來總動員》 (D)《一級玩家》

ANS: 6. (D)

VOCABULARY ♪ 069-02

⑫ **excited** [ɪkˋsaɪtɪd] a 興奮的

Anthony was so excited when he heard he got the part in the play.
安東尼得知他在戲中佔有一席時非常興奮。

⑬ **date** [det] v / n 約會

Joe and Hannah have been dating for about 6 months.
喬跟漢娜已經約會六個月了。

⑭ **detail** [ˋditel] n 細節

Do you have any details on when the client will be arriving?
你知道客人什麼時候會抵達的細節嗎？

⑮ **accept** [əkˋsɛpt] v 接受

I was accepted into five of the universities I applied to.
我被我申請大學中的五間率取。

⑯ **related** [rɪˋletɪd] a 跟……相關

This is a business-related question, so I might need a few minutes of your time.
這是跟生意相關的問題，所以我可能會需要你幾分鐘的時間。

⑰ **game** [gem] v 玩遊戲

Jay spent the whole night gaming.
傑整晚都在打電動。

LEARN MORE!

世界知名的電影獎有以下幾個：

奧斯卡金像獎（Academy Awards）
美國為表彰電影業者所頒發的年度獎項。

金球獎（Golden Globe Awards）
由美國舉辦與頒發，與電影與電視有關的獎項。

金熊獎（Goldener Bär）
柏林國際電影節的最高榮譽。

金獅獎（Leone d'oro）
威尼斯國際電影節的最高榮譽。

金棕櫚獎（Palme d'Or）
法國坎城國際電影節的最高獎項。

其中，金獅獎與金棕櫚獎、金熊獎，並稱為電影節三大最高榮譽象徵。

流行

popular

紅髮艾德（Ed Sheeran）演唱會

VOCABULARY ♪070-02

① **idea** [aɪˋdiə] n 點子

I had no idea he was so into playing Pokémon.

我都不知道他這麼喜歡玩寶可夢。

② **besotted** [bɪˋsɑtɪd] a 迷戀的

Joe was besotted with Janie because of her beautiful smile.

喬非常迷戀潔妮，因為她美麗的微笑。

③ **shy** [ʃaɪ] a 害羞的

I used to be really shy back when I was in high school.

我高中的時候非常害羞。

④ **younger** [ˋjʌŋgɚ] a 比較年輕的

When she was younger, she used to hang out with a pretty rough crowd.

她年輕一點的時候，她習慣跟一大群人出去瞎混。

Article 1 紅髮艾德（Ed Sheeran）演唱會

♪070-01 We went to an Ed Sheeran concert last week. I had no **idea** ① I was going to become such a super fan, but I am afraid I am **besotted** ②. He was incredible! I think it's something about how he grew up being really **shy** ③ and bullied because that is exactly like me. When I was **younger** ④, people always picked on me because I was so quiet when I talked. What they didn't know was when I would be at home, I would sing all the songs I loved **at the top of my lungs** ❶!

我們上週參加了 Ed Sheeran 的演唱會。我不知道我會成為這樣一個超級粉絲，但我恐怕就是如此迷戀他。他真的是很不可思議地棒！我覺得我會這麼喜歡他是因為他成長過程中是多麼的害羞和被霸凌，這跟我是完全一樣的成長經驗。當我年少的時候，人們總是找我麻煩，因為我說話的時候很小聲。他們不知道的是，當我在家時，我會高聲唱出所有我喜歡的歌曲！

♪071-01 Anyway, back to the show. The band that played before him, Japanese One OK Rock, did a great job, and they really put the **audience** ⑤ **in the right mood** ❷ for Ed Sheeran because they were really **upbeat** ⑥ and rocky, and the drive in their music was very powerful. But they weren't Ed Sheeran! When One OK Rock went off the **stage** ⑦, it was so crazy to see the stagehands get ready for Ed to go on.

無論如何，回到討論演唱會本身。在他之前演奏的是一個日本樂團 One OK Rock，他們表現極佳，他們那種歡樂跟搖滾風格強烈的驅動力把現場氣氛炒得非常熱，讓現場的觀眾更可以用極佳的心情迎接 Ed Sheeran。但他們仍然不是 Ed Sheeran！當 One OK Rock 離場後，當你看到舞台工作人員正在準備讓 Ed Sheeran 上台的時刻真的非常讓人興奮。

♪071-02 Normally, there's going to be a lot of equipment on stage, and they will need to bring in a lot of stuff for the band; but with an Ed Sheeran concert, it's the **total** ⑧ opposite. One OK Rock has four band members, so the stagehand took all this stuff off the stage until all that was really left was the **microphone** ⑨. It was crazy. It was like things were getting put away for the night.

一般來說，舞台上會有很多設備，他們需要為樂團準備很多東西，但是在 Ed Sheeran 音樂會上，這是完全相反的。One OK Rock 有四個樂團成員，因此舞台工作人員將所有設備從舞台上移走，直到留下來的東西只剩一支麥克風。真的很瘋狂。就好像今晚什麼東西都要被收光了一樣。

♪071-03 And then Ed Sheeran runs out onto the stage. Everyone's so excited and yelling their brains out. And he didn't even talk. He just smiled at the audience and started playing. I was **trying to figure out** ❸ how he could make such a big sound with no one up there with him, so I looked it up online. He has this **machine** ⑩ called a looper with about six different pedals that he can step on. Each of the pedals has different stuff saved in it and he can add that on when he's playing and it feels like a whole band is there. I guess that was something he started doing when he was just making music on YouTube.

然後 Ed Sheeran 跑到舞台上。每個人都超級興奮且瘋狂大叫到腦袋炸裂的程度。他甚至一句話都還沒說，他只是對著觀眾微笑然後就開始演奏。我一直想要知道他為什麼有辦法可以獨自在舞台上演奏地這麼大聲，所以我就上網查了一下。他有一台叫做 Loop 的機器，上面有六種不同可以踩的踏板。每個踏板都有存取不同的內容物，他在演奏的時候可以同時加入這些元素，這樣感覺起來就像他是跟整個樂團在表演。我猜這是他一開始還在 Youtube 上創作音樂時就開始在做的事。

VOCABULARY ♪071-04

⑤ **audience** [ˋɔdɪəns] n 觀眾

The audience gave the performer a standing ovation.

觀眾們給這名表演者起立鼓掌。

⑥ **upbeat** [ˋʌpˏbit] a 樂觀的、積極向上的

Annie is so upbeat; I don't think I have ever seen her sad.

安妮很積極向上，我不認為我有看過她難過的時候。

⑦ **stage** [stedʒ] n 舞台

After Alex went up on the stage, he sat down at the piano and began to play.

艾力克斯上了舞台後，他坐在鋼琴前然後開始演奏。

⑧ **total** [ˋtotl̩] a 全部的、徹底的

I was a total nerd last year, but it paid off with my good grades.

我去年完全就是個書呆子，但好成績讓一切都值得。

⑨ **microphone** [ˋmaɪkrəˏfon] n 麥克風

The microphone isn't on right now.

麥克風現在沒有聲音。

⑩ **machine** [məˋʃin] n 機器

I bought my daughter a drum machine, and she loved it.

我買給我女兒一個整合式鼓機，她很喜歡！

PATTERN ♪071-05

❶ **at the top of my lungs** 特別大聲地

Crystal screamed at the top of her lungs, but no one came.

克里斯蒂扯破喉嚨地尖叫，但沒有人過來。

❷ **in the right mood** 心情好

I have to be in the right mood to focus on studying.

我要心情好才能夠專注於讀書。

❸ **trying to figure out** 嘗試明白某事

I'm trying to figure out where we should go this summer.

我正在想我們這個夏天要去哪裡。

♪072-01 Anyway, he played so many of his famous songs, like "The A Team", which he said he has played at every concert since he was 18. That's crazy! He's about 28 now and has played **all over the world** ④, and he still plays that song, and it's an awesome song. Everybody in the audience was holding up little lights that made it look like lighters, and the crowd was **immense** ⑪.

不管怎樣，他當天演奏了很多他的著名歌曲，例如《The A Team》，他說他從18 歲起就在每場演唱會上表演這首歌，這真的很瘋狂！他現在大約 28 歲，已經在世界各地演出過，他仍然演奏那首歌，而這也真的是一首很棒的歌。觀眾席裡的每一個人都拿著小燈具，看起來就像許多打火機照亮現場，而且現場人多到爆。

♪072-02 He also played "Don't" and after a while talked to the audience about how he was glad to be in Taipei and how he knew that 98% of the people loved the show and wanted to be there dancing and singing, but that there's 2% that don't want to be there. 1% are the boyfriends that are not into the music, and the other 1% are the dads who are there to make **sure** ⑫ the kids are safe. He was so funny! Then he played Justin Bieber's "Love Yourself", and the audience loved it. At the end, he **finished** ⑬ up with his **massive** ⑭ hit, "Shape of You" and a song where he was rapping.

他也表演了《Don't》這首歌，過了一會後他跟觀眾說很開心能夠在台北演出，他還說他知道有百分之九十八的人喜歡這次的表演，而且想要隨歌起舞，另外的百分之二的人不想在這。其中百分之一的人是根本不喜歡音樂的男朋友，剩下百分之一是爸爸那類的，在這邊確保自己的孩子安全。他真的很好笑！之後他又演奏了 Justin Bieber 的《Love yourself》，觀眾很愛這首。最後他用他最受歡迎的《Shape of you》結束表演，這也是他用說唱風格呈現的一首歌。

VOCABULARY ♪072-03

⑪ **immense** [ɪˋmɛns] a 巨大的

I was an immense relief to pay off my school debt.

還清學貸後我真的感到巨大的解脫感。

⑫ **sure** [ʃur] a 確認的

He was sure that he had seen the thief before.

他很確定他之前有看到小偷。

⑬ **finished** [ˋfɪnɪʃt] a 結束、完成

We finished packing the car and were ready to head out.

我們剛打包完，可以準備出發了。

⑭ **massive** [ˋmæsɪv] a 巨大的、大量的

A massive explosion rocked the building and caused many injuries.

巨大的爆炸動搖的建築物，造成許多人受傷。

⑮ **scene** [sin] n 景象

The party scene was a lot of fun back in college.

大學時候的派對光景真的充滿樂趣。

♪073-01 It was a crazy **scene** ⑮ that one person could keep a whole audience entertained with just a guitar and a mike; I mean, even Bob Dylan plays with his whole band. But that's what amazed me so much and made me a full-blooded Sheerrio (Ed Sheeran fan). My next big goal is to work **to save up some money** ❺ and go and catch Ed Sheeran somewhere else live on tour!

一個人單單用一把吉他跟一支麥克風就可以讓全場神魂顛倒，這真的是很瘋狂的一個景象。我的意思是，甚至連 Bob Dylan 都是跟整個樂團演出的。這也是為什麼他這麼讓我感到驚艷，這也讓我成為一個死忠粉絲 Sheerrio（Ed Sheeran 的鐵粉）。我下一個目標是工作存錢以參加 Ed Sheeran 之後在別的地方的巡迴現場演出。

QUIZ 閱讀測驗

1. Why does the author feel a connection to Ed Sheeran?

(A) because they are both redheads
(B) because they both play the guitar
(C) because they were both bullied as kids
(D) they both like to go to music concerts

2. How did the author feel about One OK Rock?

(A) She thought they were average.
(B) She loved that she got to meet them.
(C) She thought they played too long.
(D) She thought they set the right mood for Ed Sheeran.

3. How did the author feel about Ed Sheeran's equipment that he needed?

(A) She was glad One OK Rock lent theirs to him.
(B) She was surprised there wasn't any.
(C) She felt like he had way too much.
(D) She wished he had a microphone.

4. What is the author's next big goal?

(A) She wants to play on stage with Ed.
(B) She wants to meet the guys in OK One Rock.
(C) She wants to buy a guitar and start making her own music.
(D) She wants to save money to see another Sheeran show.

1. 為什麼作者感到與 Ed Sheeran 有某種連結感？

(A) 因為他們兩個都是紅髮 (B) 因為他們兩個都彈吉他
(C) 因為他們小時候都被霸凌過 (D) 他們兩個都喜歡去音樂會

2. 作者認為 One OK Rock 如何？

(A) 她認為很普通。 (B) 可以見到他們讓她感到很開心。 (C) 她認為他們表演太久。
(D) 她認為他們的表演為 Ed Sheeran 接下來的演出鋪陳了很好的情緒。

3. 作者覺得 Ed Sheeran 所需使用的設備怎麼樣？

(A) 她很高興 One OK Rock 留給他用。 (B) 她很驚訝沒有其他設備。
(C) 她覺得他用得太多。 (D) 她希望他當時有用麥克風。

4. 作者的下一個重要目標是什麼？

(A) 她想和 Ed 一起登台演出。 (B) 她想和 OK One Rock 樂團見面。
(C) 她想買一把吉他並開始製作自己的音樂。
(D) 她想存錢去看另一場 Sheeran 的表演。

ANS: 1. (C) 2. (D) 3. (B) 4.(D)

PATTERN ♪073-02

❹ all over the world 全世界

Her novel was popular all over the world.

她的小說在世界各地都很受歡迎。

❺ to save up some money 存下一些錢

Hopefully I can save up some money by working a summer job.

希望這個夏天我可以打工存下一些錢。

流行

popular

巴黎時裝

VOCABULARY ♪074-02

① **top** [tɑp] a 最好的、最高的

It's impossible to get reservations at the top restaurant in town.

要訂到鎮上最好的餐廳根本不可能。

② **extravagant** [ɪkˋstrævəgənt] a 奢侈的、鋪張的

His extravagant dress makes him stand out from the crowd.

他奢華的服裝讓他從人群中脫穎而出。

③ **live** [laɪv] a 活的

Live fish take a lot of special care.

活魚需要許多特別照顧。

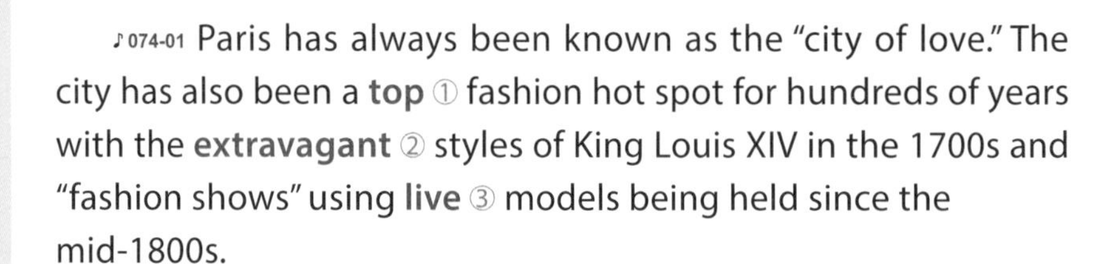

Article 2 巴黎時裝

♪074-01 Paris has always been known as the "city of love." The city has also been a **top** ① fashion hot spot for hundreds of years with the **extravagant** ② styles of King Louis XIV in the 1700s and "fashion shows" using **live** ③ models being held since the mid-1800s.

巴黎一直以來都以「愛情之城」為名。這個城市也是數百年來最熱門的時尚熱點，擁有十八世紀國王路易十四的奢華風格，以及從十九世紀中期開始使用現場模特兒的「時裝秀」。

♪075-01 **The best times to** ❶ visit Paris are in the spring and the fall. And the best reason to visit Paris is for the Paris Fashion Week, of course! Paris Fashion Week is held twice a year, **rolling out** ❷ the Spring / Summer and Fall / Winter top fashion **collections** ④ for the season. It is the grand finale of the Big Four fashion shows that start in New York, London, and Milan and **finish** ⑤ in Paris. Officially known as Semaine de la mode de Paris, the Paris Fashion Week is considered by many to be the most **prestigious** ⑥ of the four.

拜訪巴黎的最佳時機是春天和秋天。當然，參觀巴黎的最佳理由就是巴黎時裝週！巴黎時裝週每年舉辦兩次，推出春夏季和秋冬季的頂級時裝系列。這是四大時裝秀的最後一站，從紐約開始，然後是倫敦和米蘭，最後在巴黎落幕。巴黎時裝週在官方的法文名稱為 Semaine de la mode de Paris，被許多人認為巴黎時裝週是四大時裝秀中最負盛名的。

♪075-02 While New York Fashion Week is the **original** ⑦ fashion week starting in 1943, Paris Fashion Week, which started in 1973, is purported to be the chicest of the four. During the week of over 100 events, it is not only the collections of major international designers, such as Elie Saab, Issey Miyake, Mui Mui, and Alexander McQueen that are on display. French designers Chanel, Givenchy, Céline, Christian Dior, and Louis Vuitton also have their brands highlighted in **main** ⑧ locations such as the Carrousel du Louvre, Grand Palais or the Espace Eiffel.

雖然紐約時裝週是一九四三年就開始的時裝週起源地，但一九七三年才開始的巴黎時裝週據稱是四個時裝週中最時尚的。一週內就有一百多個活動，展出的不只是國際知名設計師的作品，像艾莉．沙巴（Elie Saab）、以薩．米亞卡（Issey Miyake）、謬謬（Mui Mui）跟亞歷山大．麥奎因（Alexander McQueen），也有在像是在羅浮宮（Carrousel du Louvre）、巴黎大皇宮（Grand Palais）跟艾菲爾藝術工作空間（Espace Eiffel）等主要位置展出的法國設計師的品牌，像是香奈兒（Chanel）、紀梵希（Givenchy）、賽琳（Céline）、克里斯汀迪奧（Christian Dior）跟路易威登（Louis Vuitton）。

VOCABULARY ♪075-03

④ **collection** [kəˋlɛkʃən]
n 收藏品、收集物

Jerry's stamp collection was something he kept for years.
傑瑞的集郵冊是他保留多年的東西。

⑤ **finish** [ˋfɪnɪʃ] v 結束

After the opening band, the main act finished the concert.
樂團開場表演之後，主要的演出結束了這場演唱會。

⑥ **prestigious** [prɛsˋtɪdʒɪəs]
a 有威望的

The prestigious school admitted very few students.
這所富有盛名的學校每年收很少的學生。

⑦ **original** [əˋrɪdʒənḷ]
a 起初的、原先的

Kelly Products is the original maker of staplers.
凱莉商品是釘書機的原始製造者。

⑧ **main** [men] a 主要的

The main exhibit at the museum has been on display for months.
博物館的主要展出已經進行好幾個月了。

PATTERN ♪075-04

❶ **the best times to** 做……最佳時機

The best times to visit the park are during the spring.
拜訪這個公園的最佳時機是春天的時候。

❷ **rolling out** 推出（新產品、服務）

They are rolling out a new program for computer technicians.
他們為電腦技術人員推出了新的程式。

♪076-01 Each of the global fashion shows has its **unique** ⑨ features. For the Paris show, the collections on display are Men's Fashion, prêt-à-porter, and haute couture. Prêt-à-porter refers to ❸ finished, off-the-rack products that are factory made and sold in finished condition, and that are ready to wear. Haute couture is something a little more **special** ⑩ .

每個全球時裝秀都有其獨特的地方。在巴黎的時裝秀展出的系列包括男士時裝、成衣和高級時裝。Prêt-à-porter 指的是在工廠生產而且以成品方式販售並已經有其標準碼的衣物，可以馬上買來穿的衣物。高級時裝則比較特別一點。

♪076-02 For a fashion house to hold the label of haute couture, they must **produce** ⑪ clothing that has been custom-made and fitted for the wearer, and all of the elements such as the beading and embroidery and piping must be hand-sewn by skilled artisans. Only the finest quality of materials may be used. Haute couture is a French-protected word, so just as only brandy produced in the Armagnac region can hold the label of Armagnac, true haute couture is only found in ❹ France.

對於一個擁有高級時裝品牌的時裝屋來說，他們必須生產專門為客人量身訂製的服裝，而且所有使用的元素，像是珠飾、刺繡和滾邊都必須由熟練的裁縫師傅手工縫製。只有最優質的材料用在高級時裝上。法文高級時裝這兩個字 Haute couture 是只有法文裡獨享的字，就像只有在雅文邑地區（Armagnac）生產的白蘭地可以使用雅文邑的標籤，真正的高級時裝只能在巴黎找到。

VOCABULARY ♪076-03

⑨ **unique** [ju`nik] a 獨特的

He has a unique perspective when it comes to morality.
論及道德觀，他有很特別的看法。

⑩ **special** [`spɛʃəl] a 特別的

There's something about the grilled cheese sandwiches that she makes that is really special.
她做的烤起司三明治有很獨特的地方。

⑪ **produce** [prə`djus] v 生產

The farmers produce large quantities of vegetables every year.
這些農夫們每年產出大量的蔬菜。

PATTERN ♪076-04

❸ **refers to** 意指……

Christianity refers to a kind of religion.
基督教指的是一種宗教。

❹ **is only found in**
某事物只有在……可找到

Ginseng is mostly only found in forests.
人參主要只在森林裡可以找到。

♪077-01 This haute couture exclusivity and the **mass** ⑫ variety of events held during Paris Fashion Week create a huge **boost** ⑬ to the economy of hundreds of millions of dollars in Paris. Celebrities, top models, wealthy and **influential** ⑭ people, fashion designers, fashion wholesalers, and fashion journalists all converge together.

享有高級時裝盛名的獨特性與時裝週舉辦的各種時尚活動，為巴黎帶來數億美元的經濟成長與價值。像是名人、超模、有錢人跟具有社會影響力的人、時尚設計師、時裝批發商和時尚記者全部齊聚一堂。

♪077-02 It is the perfect opportunity for designers to see what everyone else is putting on the runway, critique their own collections to look for areas for improvement, decide which models best showcase their designs, and take a bow for the hard work they've put in.

對設計師來說這是一個絕佳的機會看到其他設計師呈現在伸展台上的成品，批評自己的創作成品來尋找進步的空間，或是決定哪些時裝模特兒更可以把他們的設計理念完整呈現，並且向他們在伸展台上一切的努力致敬。

VOCABULARY ♪077-03

⑫ **mass** [mæs] a 大量的、大規模的

The mass popularity of this new ice cream brand is insane.

這個新的冰淇淋牌子受歡迎的巨大程度很扯。

⑬ **boost** [bust] v 增強、推動

The economic boost provided by the sale helped the company immensely.

透過銷售帶來的經濟推動對這個公司的幫助極大。

⑭ **influential** [͵ɪnflʊˋɛnʃəl] a 具有影響力的

Our influential friend got us into the club last night.

我們那個有影響力的朋友，昨晚把我們弄進俱樂部。

♪078-01 It's an opportunity for models to stand out from the crowd, make a healthy paycheck, be seen, own the runway, and become famous as they run between the different events they are walking for.

在不同的活動中走秀也是一個讓模特兒從人群中脫穎而出的機會，得到優渥的酬勞、被世界看見、稱霸伸展台並且聲名大噪的好時機。

♪078-02 And as the events in Paris wrap up the fashion season, the designers have finished their jobs and the focus goes over to the newspapers and magazines, such as Elle, Vogue, Marie Claire, and InStyle to analyze, describe, and accessorize all of the fashion season's events and bring the styles to the public.

隨著巴黎時裝週各項活動來到季度的尾聲，設計師們的工作已經差不多結束，現在重心轉移到報章雜誌上，像是 Elle、Vogue、Marie Claire 和 InStyle 等雜誌來分析、描述跟添飾時尚季中的各種活動內容，並讓大眾知道這些最新時尚風格。

♪078-03 If you have an eye for ⑤ fashion, and you want to figure out what's "hot" to wear and what's "not" for the upcoming fashion season, it should probably be on your bucket list to make your way into Paris Fashion Week. You are **likely** ⑮ to walk away never looking at fashion the same way again.

如果你對時尚有鑑賞眼光，並且想要了解穿著什麼是「走在潮流尖端」以及下個季度什麼「不該穿」，那去一趟巴黎時裝週肯定是人生必做事情之一。去一趟之後你就會發現你再也不會用一樣的眼光看待時尚。

VOCABULARY ♪078-04

⑮ **likely** [ˋlaɪklɪ] a 有可能的

We're likely to need more time to figure this out.

我們可能需要更多時間來釐清這件事。

PATTERN ♪078-05

⑤ **have an eye for** 對⋯⋯有鑑賞眼光

Carla has an eye for fashion.

卡拉對時尚很有鑑賞眼光。

QUIZ 閱讀測驗

1. What is NOT mentioned as Paris being known as?

(A) the city of love
(B) the city of fashion
(C) the city of Paris Fashion Week
(D) the city Napoleon lived in.

2. How often is Paris Fashion Week held?

(A) once a month
(B) twice a year
(C) once a year
(D) twice in ten years

3. What is NOT mentioned as a unique feature of Paris Fashion Week?

(A) It's open to the public.
(B) It is the last of the Big Four.
(C) It shows haute couture.
(D) Prêt-à-porter and Menswear feature in the shows.

4. What is the term to describe ready-off-the-rack, factory-made clothing??

(A) haute couture
(B) a la mode
(C) semaine
(D) prêt-à-porter

1. 巴黎沒有以什麼樣的事物有名？

(A) 愛情之城
(B) 時尚之城
(C) 舉辦巴黎時裝週的城市
(D) 拿破崙住在這個城市。

2. 巴黎時裝週多久辦一次？

(A) 一個月一次
(B) 一年兩次
(C) 一年一次
(D) 十年兩次

3. 哪一個不是巴黎時裝週所提及的特色？

(A) 它向公眾開放。
(B) 它是四大時裝秀的最後一個。
(C) 它展示了高級時裝。
(D) 時裝秀中包括成衣跟男裝的展示。

4. 哪一個專門的詞是用來描述有標準碼且在工廠生產的衣服？

(A) 高級時裝
(B) 流行的
(C) 週
(D) 成衣

ANS: 1. (D) 2. (B) 3. (A) 4.(D)

世界知名流行品牌

Louis Vuitton VALENTINO GIORGIO ARMANI

Coco Chanel 曾說：「時尚會過去，只有風格才能屹立不搖。」時尚品牌有很多，重點不在於跟風、穿著豪奢，而是要穿出自己的風格。

Louis Vuitton

1854 年成立，法國的時尚品牌。LV 交織的圖案具有強大的識別性，是時尚界的經典。

GUCCI

1821 年成立，義大利時裝品牌，簡單設計的風格，深受商業人士喜愛。

Dior

1946 年成立，法國品牌，使用上等質料、作工精細，不會使用較大的 LOGO 在衣服或飾設計上，是華麗女裝的代名詞。

CHANEL

1910 年成立，法國女性知名時裝品牌，高雅、簡潔、精美的風格，是上流社會的愛用品牌。「Chanel No 5」香水也是經典中的經典。

PRADA

1913 年成立，義大利品牌，其製作的皮製商品是世界公認的頂尖產品。

HERMÈS

1837 年成立，法國知名品牌，宗旨在展現產品的精美到無可挑剔地步，產品內斂又不譁眾取寵。

VALENTINO

1960 年成立，義大利品牌，特色為富麗華貴、美艷動人，是豪奢生活的象徵。

GIORGIO ARMANI

1975 年成立，義大利時裝品牌，除了流行時裝之外，也跨足到家居用品、飯店和餐廳。

流行

popular

電動車

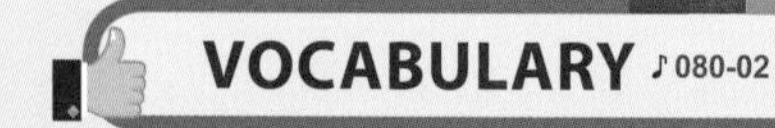

VOCABULARY ♪080-02

① **continually** [kənˋtɪnjʊəlɪ]
ad 頻繁地

I am continually amazing at how you can get all your clothes so dirty.

我常常被你可以把你全部的衣物用得有多髒感到驚奇。

② **emission** [ɪˋmɪʃən] n 排放物

The man's noxious emissions grossed out the people sitting behind him.

那個男人放的屁，讓坐在他後面的人們感到很噁心。

Article 3 電動車

♪080-01 The world as we know it is **continually** ① dealing with pollution assaults to the environment. One of the biggest problems comes from greenhouse gas **emissions** ② that are causing the planet to warm and water levels to rise. One greenhouse gas increaser that everyone knows is the standard car. With an estimated more than 1.25 billion cars out on the road today increasing the world's pollution, it's no wonder that ❶ people are looking for a way to do things better.

我們所知道的世界正在不斷處理對環境造成污染的攻擊。其中一個最大的問題來自溫室氣體排放導致地球暖化和海水水位上升。其中一項眾所皆知的溫室氣體排放來源便是一般的標準小客車。現今估計有超過 12.5 億輛汽車在路上行駛，這提升了對地球的污染。這也難怪人們正在尋找更好的方法兼顧便利與環境保護。

♪081-01 That's where electric cars come in ❷ . For a little **background** ③ , conventional cars are those that still run like the first cars produced by Henry Ford. Ford developed the **internal** ④ combustion engine, where gasoline goes in, creates a reaction that powers the car and propels it forward.

這就是電動汽車的用武之地。簡單介紹一下背景：傳統汽車指的就是那些福特汽車公司第一批生產的車子。福特開發了內燃機，汽油進入後會產生一種驅動汽車前進的動力。

♪081-02 The ability to move like this is **wondrous** ⑤ , but the problem comes down to the gasoline that is used. Gasoline is not a clean energy source. Its use causes health problems and environmental problems and **requires** ⑥ people to rely on fossil fuels.

可以像這樣子推動汽車是很棒的，但是問題來自使用的汽油燃料。汽油不是一種乾淨的驅動原料。使用汽油會導致健康的問題跟環境的問題，而且這也讓人們依賴化石燃料。

VOCABULARY ♪081-03

③ **background** [ˋbækˏgraʊnd]
n （事件的）背景

I'm going to need a little background into why you two are fighting.

我需要知道你們為什麼打架的背後原因。

④ **internal** [ɪnˋtɝnḷ] a 內部的

Internal bleeding was determined to be the cause of death.

內部出血被判定為是死亡原因。

⑤ **wondrous** [ˋwʌndrəs]
a 極棒的、絕妙的

We had a wondrous time sitting on the beach for a week.

我們有在海邊度過的完美一週。

⑥ **require** [rɪˋkwaɪr] v 需要

His work requires that he travel 20 weeks of the year.

他的工作需要他一年出差二十週。

PATTERN ♪081-04

❶ **it's no wonder that** 難怪……

It's no wonder that Megan and John got married.

難怪梅根跟約翰結婚了。

❷ **that's where (+N) comes in**
這是某事物從……介入／進入／發生

I'm exhausted, and that's where your help is going to come in.

我累壞了，這時候就是你可以幫忙的時候。

LEARN MORE! ♪081-05

近幾年來對於博愛座的使用規範，大家爭議不斷，有些人為了避免讓座產生的麻煩，而不選擇不坐博愛座，但其實每個位置都可以是博愛座，面對有需要的人，都應該主動讓座才是美德，那需要讓座的人有哪些呢？

- **elder** 年長者
- **pregnant woman** 孕婦
- **the disabled** 殘障人士
- **baby-holding passenger** 抱小孩的乘客
- **the injured** 負傷者
- **patient** 病患

VOCABULARY ♪082-03

⑦ **major** [ˋmedʒɚ] a 主要的

One major problem I have with Chloe is that she never tells the truth.

我跟克柔伊的主要問題在於她從來不說真話。

⑧ **mode** [mod] n 模式

This game has a single-player mode and a competitive mode.

這個遊戲有單人模式跟競賽模式。

PATTERN ♪082-04

❸ **needs to be plugged in**
需要被插入（充電）

This equipment needs to be plugged in to that outlet over there.

這個設備需要用那個電源插座來充電。

道路施工的時候，會在工地附近看到這個立牌，有些工程時間較長的施工，還會公告施工的時間、單位、項目。

- The alley is under construction.
  這條巷子正在施工。
- The new overpass is still under construction.
  新天橋還在建造中。

♪082-01 Electric cars are quiet; electricity is cheaper than gasoline, and they are easier overall on the environment. There are three **major** ⑦ types of electric cars. The first type is the hybrid. The plug-in hybrid still has a gasoline engine for unleaded or diesel gas, but it also has an electric motor that **needs to be plugged in** ❸ to recharge. Because electric power is seen as being a cleaner energy source than gasoline and because electric cars need less gas than a standard car, they are cleaner for the environment than a standard car.

電動汽車行駛起來很安靜，使用的電力也比汽油便宜，而且對整體環境而言更友善。電動車主要有三種類型。第一種是混合動力車。插電式混合動力車仍有使用無鉛汽油或是柴油的汽油發動機，但它同時也有一個電動馬達必須充電。因為電力被視為比汽油更環保的能源，同時電動汽車所需要的汽油量比標準汽車更少，它們跟一般汽車比起來對環境更環保友善。

♪082-02 Most of these cars have two major **modes** ⑧ : all-electric and hybrid. All-electric means that the car is traveling completely on electricity, so the motor and the battery are providing all the energy. Hybrid means both electricity and gasoline are used. This mode means there is a backup in case the car runs out of electricity, but it is still incredibly fuel efficient so that it is pretty much like the car is getting a hundred miles to the gallon.

這些汽車大多數有兩種主要模式：全電動和混合動力。全電動的意思是指汽車完全只靠電力行駛，所以是靠馬達跟電池來提供所有的動力。混合動力則意味著使用電力和汽油。這種汽車種類代表當汽車用完電力之後還會有備用的燃料，但仍然非常節省燃料的使用，就好像只有一加侖的汽油但卻可以開到一百英里遠。

♪083-01 Another type of electric car is the battery-electric. These cars use no gas, only battery power to make their way around. They can be some of the **cleanest** ⑨ cars around, environmentally speaking, because there are no emissions from the tailpipe, and gasoline is swapped out for electricity. They are perfect for ❹ getting around in **local** ⑩ communities but can not be easily used for long-distance travel.

另一種類型的電動汽車是靠電池驅動的。這些汽車不使用汽油，只需要給電池充電。從環保的角度來看，它們是最環境友善的汽車，因為沒有任何氣體從排氣管排出，而且汽油完全被電力取代。它們非常適合在居住的當地社區使用，但如果是長途旅行就沒有那麼方便。

♪083-02 The newer styles of the full electric car are those that use hydrogen fuel cells. These cars can go further and refuel faster, but they rely on hydrogen refueling **stations** ⑪ that are not yet easy to find. Therefore, this can limit the car's travel **range** ⑫ .

最新的全電動汽車是那些使用氫氣燃料電池的汽車。這些汽車可以跑得更遠而且補充燃料更快速，但它們倚靠氫氣加氣站來補充燃料，氫氣加氣站不是那麼容易找到，因此限制了汽車可以行駛的範圍。

VOCABULARY ♪083-03

⑨ **cleanest** [klinɪst] a 最乾淨的

This is the cleanest I have seen the kitchen in months.

這是我幾個月來看到廚房最乾淨的一次。

⑩ **local** [`lok!] a 當地的

It's best to eat the local food when traveling to new countries.

旅行到新國家時最棒的事情就是吃當地的食物。

⑪ **station** [`steʃən] n 站

Is there a gas station anywhere near here?

這附近有任何加油站嗎？

⑫ **range** [rendʒ] n 範疇、範圍

The cell phone doesn't have a very long range when out of the city.

出了城市之後這支手機沒有很大的通訊範圍。

PATTERN ♪083-04

❹ **they are perfect for**
某事物……適合……

I love these shoes; they are perfect for hiking.

我很愛這些鞋子，它們用來健行非常適合。

VOCABULARY ♪084-04

⑬ **assist** [əˋsɪst] V 協助

Joe, could you assist me with carrying this desk?

喬，你可以協助我搬一下這張桌子嗎？

⑭ **compensate** [ˋkampən͵set] V 補償、彌補

Can you compensate me for the baseball glove I bought you last week?

你可以補償我上星期為了你才買的棒球手套的錢嗎？

⑮ **generation** [͵dʒɛnəˋreʃən] n 世代

This generation of students seems to not know what to do with their lives.

這個世代的學生似乎不知道他們的人生要幹嘛。

PATTERN ♪084-05

❺ **we are moving toward** 我們正在向……前進

With this sale, we are moving toward a profitable year.

隨著這項銷售，我們正朝向有盈利的一年。

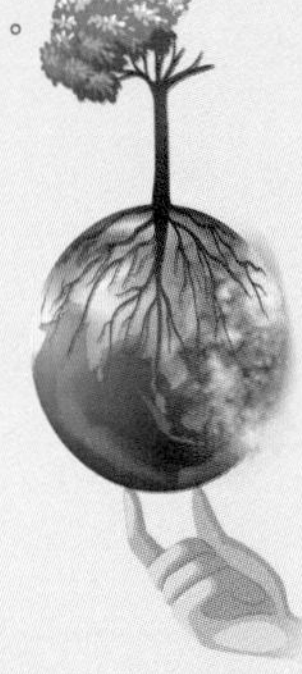

♪084-01 The last of the three types is known as the convention hybrid. These cars are not the top energy savers like the full electric car, but they still do have an impact on greenhouse gas emissions. When the vehicle is stopped, the engine idles-off to save fuel, and the conventional engine can take over at any time to make sure the vehicle is running smoothly.

這三種類型中的最後一種被稱為常規混合車。這類型汽車不像全電動汽車那樣最節省能源，而且它們仍會對溫室氣體排放產生影響。當車輛停止行駛時，引擎會空轉以節省燃料，傳統引擎仍可以隨時啟用以確保車輛平穩行駛。

♪084-02 The accessories and air conditioner are battery powered and the car's battery **assist** ⑬ or power assist function works to efficiently lower need for the gasoline engine. While the gasoline engine does produce less power in this model, the electric motors **compensate** ⑭ for this to make the car as powerful as or even more powerful than a conventional car.

汽車內的配置設備和空調採用電池供電，汽車的電池輔助或助力功能可有效降低引擎使用汽油的需求。雖然汽油引擎確實在這種類型的汽車中產生較少的動力，但電動馬達彌補了這部分，且使它們跟一般傳統汽車比起來一樣或甚至更強大。

♪084-03 The little steps we take to think about our environment today can have powerful effects on the world of our future. By moving away from the conventional automobile, **we are moving toward** ❺ a better world for our future **generations** ⑮ .

我們今天考慮環境因素的一小步可以對我們未來的世界產生強大的影響。藉由逐漸淘汰傳統汽車，我們正在為我們的後代邁向一個更好的世界。

QUIZ 閱讀測驗

1. What causes temperatures and water levels to rise?

(A) a lot of rain
(B) typhoons
(C) an increase in greenhouse gases
(D) volcanic activity

2. Which cars run like the ones made by Henry Ford?

(A) greenhouse cars
(B) hybrid cars
(C) hydrogen cell cars
(D) conventional cars

3. Which is not a part of the internal combustion process?

(A) The car is propelled forward.
(B) The brakes are pressed on the car.
(C) The gasoline goes into the engine.
(D) There is a reaction.

4. Which is NOT a problem of using gasoline?

(A) People rely on fossil fuels.
(B) People can't drive long distances.
(C) People have health problems.
(D) There are environmental problems.

1. 是什麼導致溫度和水位上升？
(A) 多雨
(B) 颱風
(C) 溫室氣體增加
(D) 火山活動

2. 哪些汽車像福特製造的汽車一樣來發動？
(A) 溫室汽車
(B) 混合動力汽車
(C) 氫動力汽車
(D) 傳統汽車

3. 哪個部分不是內燃過程的一部分？
(A) 汽車被向前推進。
(B) 汽車煞車。
(C) 汽油進入引擎。
(D) 會有反應產生。

4. 哪個不是使用汽油會產生的問題？
(A) 人們依賴化石燃料。
(B) 人們不能開車長途旅行。
(C) 人們有健康問題。
(D) 會造成環境問題。

ANS: 1. (C) 2. (D) 3. (B) 4.(B)

LEARN MORE!

♪085-01 ❶ **I can't get the car to start.**
我無法發動車子。

A: Why haven't you gone out yet?
你怎麼還沒出門呢？

B: I can't get the car to start, and it has a flat tire.
我無法發動車子。我的車爆胎了。

♪085-02 ❷ **I'm almost out of gas.**
我的汽油快用完了。

A: I'm almost out of gas. Is there a gas station near here?
我的汽油快用完了。這附近有加油站嗎？

B: There's one just up ahead.
前面就有一家。

♪085-03 ❸ **Please fill my car up.**
請幫我的車子加滿油。

A: Please fill my car up. Do you take credit cards?
請幫我的車子加滿油。你們收信用卡嗎？

B: No. I'm sorry. We accept cash only.
沒有，抱歉，我們只收現金。

♪085-04 ❹ **Can you show me...?**
我……？

A: Can you show me which road to take?
你可以告訴我應該走哪條路嗎？

B: Sorry, but I have no idea.
抱歉，我不知道。

流行

年輕人創業風潮

popular

VOCABULARY ♪086-02

① **expression** [ɪk`sprɛʃən]
n 表示、表達、神情

Her pained expression showed how unhappy she was with the situation.
她痛苦的神情表現了她對於此狀況有多不開心。

② **impressive** [ɪm`prɛsɪv]
a 有印象的、令人印象深刻的

This sculpture is an impressive artwork.
這個雕像是令人印象的藝術品。

年輕人創業風潮

♪086-01 The **expression** ① entrepreneurial whiz kids sounds like something out of a science fiction novel or a video game, but there are a lot of **impressive** ② business minds out there that are not very long in the tooth.

創業神童這樣的描述聽起來是在科幻小說或是電玩裡面才會有的角色，但實際上，的確有許多年輕且富有令人欽佩生意頭腦的聰明人。

♪087-01 Most people imagine that it takes years of studying and decades of work experience to get higher up on the work ladder till you are at the point where you are calling the shots. Yet, there are a lot of young people out there that never chose to follow that long and **difficult** ③ path to the top and instead decided to jump into the stratosphere right away with their crazy and successful business ideas.

大部分的人都可以想像得到的，為了在工作崗位上晉升並且到達可以做出決策的地位，需要多年的學習和數十年的工作經驗才可以有此成就。然而有許多年輕人從未選擇這樣又長又辛苦的道路來一步步晉升，他們反而決定直接用自己瘋狂跟成功的商業點子跳入商業中最高階層的位置。

♪087-02 Take, for example, one of this generation's business whiz kids, Bill Gates. Gates started writing computer programs at the age of 13. By 20, he had **bucked** ④ the conventional route, dropped out of Harvard University and formed Microsoft, which is one of the biggest technology companies in history. Gates left the company as the world's highest-earning billionaire, so one could say that his youthful **endeavor** ⑤ paid off for him.

用這個世代其中一位商業神童比爾．蓋茲為例，蓋茲於十三歲開始寫電腦程式，二十歲前他就走上一條違背傳統的路，從哈佛大學輟學並創立了微軟公司，此公司是歷史上最大的科技公司。蓋茲離開微軟時是世界上最富有的億萬富翁，你可以說他年輕時的努力都得到了回報。

VOCABULARY ♪087-03

③ **difficult** [ˋdɪfə͵kəlt] a 困難的

It is very difficult for me to buy all the presents for others at Christmas.

對我來說要在聖誕節買全部的禮物給別人很困難。

④ **buck** [bʌk] v 反抗

I bucked society's norms and created my own company.

我對抗社會的常規並創建了自己的公司。

⑤ **endeavor** [ɪnˋdɛvɚ] v 努力、奮力

Diane endeavored to form a friendship with her direct boss.

黛安努力想跟她的直屬上司發展友誼。

VOCABULARY ♪088-03

⑥ **launch** [lɔntʃ] v 發起、發行

Our company is going to launch a new product next week.

我們的公司下個星期要發行一個新產品。

⑦ **individual** [ˌɪndəˋvɪdʒuəl] n 個人

The individual that stole my purse was caught last night.

偷我錢包的那個人昨晚被抓到了。

⑧ **original** [əˋrɪdʒənḷ] a 原始的、原創的

The original TV show is much better than the recent remake.

原本的電視劇比最近翻拍的版本更好看。

⑨ **know-how** [ˋnoˏhaʊ] n 技術、技能

Andre's know-how helped the repairman to fix the machine.

安德烈的技術幫助了那位修理工修理機器。

PATTERN ♪088-04

❶ **another example of** 另一個……的例子

Paula's crying is another example of why she shouldn't go to bed too late.

寶拉哭了這件事就是另一個為什麼她不該太晚睡覺的例子。

❷ **by the age of** 從幾歲開始

By the age of twelve, children need to buy an adult plane ticket.

從十二歲開始，小孩必須購買成人機票的價格。

★ 「by the age of ＋ 年紀」的意思會跟著文意改變

♪088-01 Just **another example of** ❶ an entrepreneurial whiz kid would be Mark Zuckerberg. You probably know him better as the mastermind behind Facebook. Much like Bill Gates, Zuckerberg started writing computer programs in middle school. On a similar path to that of Bill Gates, Zuckerberg was also a Harvard student. Mark used part of his time in college to create and **launch** ⑥ Facebook, and like Gates dropped out of Harvard, and the rest is history. In 2018, he was the only **individual** ⑦ in the Forbes ten richest people list to be under 50 years of age.

另一個創業奇才的例子則是馬克．祖克伯，會知道他大概是因為他是臉書經營背後的決策者。就像比爾蓋茲一樣，祖克伯從中學開始就在寫電腦程式。也像比爾．蓋茲一樣，祖克伯也是哈佛大學的學生。他在大學唸書時用他一部分的時間創建並發起臉書，也像蓋茲一樣從哈佛輟學，後來的事是人盡皆知的。他也是二〇一八年的富比士雜誌十大富豪榜單上唯一年紀低於五十歲的人。

♪088-02 These two **original** ⑧ whiz kids had better watch out, though, because there's a new generation of smart out there that knows how to turn their **know-how** ⑨ into big bucks. Take Mark Bao for example, Mark started programming when he was still in elementary school. **By the age of** ❷ 18, he had already launched 11 web-based businesses and sold three, two of which made him a significant amount of money.

但這兩個最早的神童可要注意了，因為新一世代的聰明人也知道如何把他們的知識與技術變成賺大錢的工具。以包馬克為例子，他小學時就開始寫程式，十八歲前他就已經發起了十一個以網站經營的生意，並且賣了三個網站，其中兩個就為他帶來可觀的財富。

♪089-01 This new generation technology entrepreneur is also interested in **giving back to** ❸ the **community** ⑩ and has started two nonprofit organizations. He was asked about his attitude toward business, "When you're young, don't fear failing," he said. "Whether you succeed or fail, the things you learn will be incredibly valuable for your future endeavors."

這位新世代的科技企業家對於回饋社會也感到興趣，並創辦了兩個非營利組織。當被問到他對於經商的態度時，他說：「當你還年輕的時候，不要怕失敗。」「不論你成功或是失敗，你學到的事情對你未來的努力來說都是無比珍貴的。」

♪089-02 While the young talents mentioned above all seemed to make their through the development of technology, a lot of today's young **shining** ⑪ business stars are making their way in a lot of different areas. Adora Svitak is a writer and public speaker. By the age of 12 she had published two books and spoken at over 400 schools with an interest in how young people use technology in the modern world.

雖然上面提到的年輕才子似乎全部都是靠科技發展來達到他們的成功，但現今也是有很多年輕的商業之星在不同的領域中發光發熱。鄒奇奇（英文名 Adora Svitak）是一名作家也是一名演說家。在十二歲前她就出版了兩本書並且在超過四百家學校發表年輕人如何在現代社會中使用科技的演講。

♪089-03 Philip Hartman, as a 15-year old inventor, had created a new **method** ⑫ for fusing optical fibers and came up with a new system that changed the windshield business. In 2008, he was named the Young Inventor of the Year.

菲力普．哈特曼（Philip Hartman），作為一名十五歲的發明家，創造了一種融合光纖的新方法，並提出一種改變擋風玻璃產業的新系統，二〇〇八年時他被評為年度少年發明家。

♪089-04 For the majority of these brilliant minds, one thing stands out. Instead of saying the world will figure out the problems that need to be fixed and **sitting by the wayside** ❹, they jumped in. They looked for **something that needed fixing** ❺ or improving and went about making it better.

對這些大部分的天才來說，有一件事情是特別突出的。他們不是坐著空等並說世界會自行想出那些需要解決的問題，相反地，他們是直接一頭栽入。他們尋找那些需要被解決跟改善的問題，並著手開始改善。

VOCABULARY ♪089-05

⑩ **community** [kəˋmjunətɪ] n 社區

Our community is throwing a small benefit next weekend.

我們的社區下個週末會舉辦一個小型義賣。

⑪ **shine** [ʃaɪn] v 閃耀

The moon was shining in the night sky.

月亮在夜晚中閃閃發光。

⑫ **method** [ˋmɛθəd] n 方法

Jumping on a trampoline is my method for relieving stress.

我釋放壓力的方式是跳蹦床。

PATTERN ♪089-06

❸ **giving back to** 回饋給……

Fiona believes in giving back to society by helping out in different associations.

費歐納相信她可以藉由在不同的機構幫忙來回饋社會。

❹ **V by the wayside** 半途而廢

Being super busy, Thomas let a lot of things fall by the wayside.

超級忙的關係，湯瑪斯讓許多事情都半途而廢了。

❺ **something that needed fixing** 某事物需要修理

Cole's car has something that needs fixing.

克柔伊的車有一些問題需要修理。

VOCABULARY ♪090-02

⑬ **notice** [ˋnotɪs] v / n 注意

I hope no one will notice my eye infection.

我希望沒有人會注意到我眼睛有感染。

⑭ **genius** [ˋdʒinjəs] n 天才

Albert is a crazy genius and can solve any math problem.

艾伯特是一個超級天才而且可以解決任何數學問題。

⑮ **benefit** [ˋbɛnəfɪt] n 利益、好處

For the benefit of the audience, the singer came out for an encore.

為了觀眾們的好處，歌手再次出現唱安可曲。

♪090-01 They **noticed** ⑬ something that people would want and that was missing, and they created something to satisfy that lack. It just goes to show that, while we may not be all young **geniuses** ⑭ , with a good idea, we can all **benefit** ⑮ society and make a difference.

他們注意到什麼是人們想要但卻沒有的東西，他們進而創造出些什麼來滿足這個缺口。這說明了就算我們可能不全是年輕的天才，但有好主意的話，我們仍然可以使社會受益並創造改變。

QUIZ 閱讀測驗

1. Who is not mentioned as a whiz kid?

(A) Ajit Nayak (B) Mark Zuckerberg
(C) Philip Hartman (D) Bill Gates

2. Who was the only under-50-year-old Top 10 listed in Forbes?

(A) Hartman (B) Gates
(C) Bao (D) Zuckerberg

3. Who is mentioned as being interested in giving back to the community?

(A) Hartman (B) Gates
(C) Bao (D) Zuckerberg

1. 誰不是文中提到的神童？

(A) 阿吉特．那亞克 (B) 馬克．祖克伯
(C) 菲利普．哈特曼 (D) 比爾．蓋茲

2. 誰是富比士十大富豪排行榜上唯一不到五十歲的人？

(A) 哈特曼 (B) 蓋茲
(C) 包 (D) 祖克伯

3. 哪位被提及的人有興趣回饋給社群？

(A) 哈特曼 (B) 蓋茨
(C) 包 (D) 祖克伯

ANS: 1. (A) 2. (D) 3. (C)

Skill!!
閱讀中長篇文章的技巧

700 是個神奇的數字，它是中英文作文要求的長度，更是美國大學短論文要求的字數。一般而言，700 字的文章在段落安排上會有四到五段，功能分別為起、承、轉、合，也就是引言（introduction）、內文（body）和結論（conclusion）。

從邏輯的「點」出發，串聯成「線」，再從「面」來通盤了解。我們就以大數據（big data）為主題，來學看懂 700 字左右文章應具備的技巧。

引言（introduction）

在引言部分，我們要看懂的是最重要的主題句（Topic Sentence），包括：

- What is big data? 大數據是什麼？
- Big data grows exponentially with time. 大數據隨著時間而倍增。
- Big data becomes so important these days. 現在大數據變得很重要。

內文（body）

在內文的部分，則要根據主題句，找出論點陳述，這些句子就變得很重要：

- Big data is large and complicated. 大數據又大、又複雜。
- Data is oil of this century. 資料是本世紀的石油。
- We all know when data grows faster, it gets bigger. 我們都知道資料成長得愈快、數量就愈多。

衍伸和申論（further support and argument）

下一個段落，當然是進一步的衍伸和申論：

- To come out of a big data solution, one engineer needs to know about at least ten technologies.
  要發展出大數據解決方案，工程師必須知道至少十種以上的技術。
- Each day, on average, there are 3.5 billion searchers on Google.
  每一天平均有 35 億人會使用 Google 做搜尋。
- Big data makes individuals and companies more efficient and productive.
  大數據讓個人和公司更有效率、更具生產力。

結論（conclusion）

結論段落中會使用的句子：

- After all, big data is just data. 畢竟大數據也只是資料。
- In short, big data affects every aspect of our life. 簡而言之，大數據影響了我們的各個生活面。
- To sum up, big data makes the world better. 總之，大數據讓我們的世界變得更好。

旅遊

海島潛水

travel

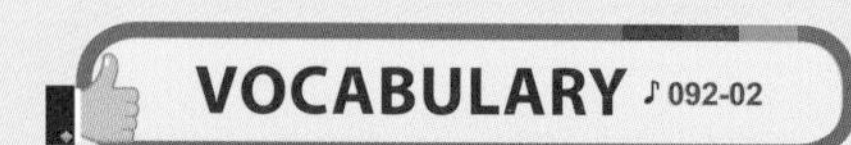

VOCABULARY ♪092-02

① **romantic** [rə`mæntɪk] a 浪漫的

Her romantic gesture left Abel grinning ear to ear.

她浪漫的表現讓阿貝爾笑得合不攏嘴。

② **expense** [ɪk`spɛns] n 花費

The expense to fix the car is just not worth it.

修車要花的錢根本不值得。

③ **track** [træk] n 痕跡、軌跡

The tracks on the road show that it was a jeep that drove through the area.

路上的痕跡顯示，駛過這區域的是一台吉普車。

Article 1

海島潛水

♪092-01 There's something so **romantic** ① about putting on diving gear and explore the deep blue seas while holding your partner's hand. The idea of getting up close to nature that most people in the world will never see is alluring. However, for most people, the **expense** ② of buying diving gear like oxygen tanks, wet suits, diving masks, flippers and more must stop a lot of would-be divers ❶ in their **tracks** ③ .

穿上潛水裝備探索深藍色的海洋世界，同時握著你另一伴的手，是多麼浪漫的事。可以一窺大部分的人從不會見到的大自然面貌的想法是很誘人的。然而對於大多數人來說，購買潛水裝備（如氧氣罐、潛水服、潛水面罩和蛙鞋等等）的費用讓許多想要嘗試潛水的人卻步。

♪093-01 That's why it's so **intriguing** ④ to go on an island diving holiday. Normally, it's possible to buy a multi-day package that includes boat rides out to excellent diving areas, and an instructor who provides instruction on how to use all the gear, gear rental, and sometimes lodging or additional **transportation** ⑤ for groups of people wanting to experience diving.

這就是為什麼去海島潛水度假會是這麼有趣的事。正常來說你可以買到多天的套裝行程，其中包括搭乘快艇到極佳的潛水區域、教你如何使用全部裝備的教練、裝備租借費用，有時候也會提供住宿跟額外的交通服務給想要體驗潛水的團體遊客。

♪093-02 People put it on their bucket lists to make sure they **get the chance to** ❷ give diving a try. Island diving can be amazing, too, as a boat drops you off at an island area for the day. Some places that are top areas for diving trips include the Great Barrier Reef in Australia, Micronesia, Boracay, Hawaii, Belize, Thailand, and Indonesia, to name a few.

人們把潛水列在人生必做之事的清單上，確保有生之年一定要嘗試潛水看看。在海島上的潛水也很棒，船會把你載到一個島上待一整天。有些國家是極佳的潛水地點，像是澳大利亞的大堡礁、密克羅尼西亞聯邦、長灘島、夏威夷、貝里斯、泰國、印尼……等等。

VOCABULARY ♪093-03

④ **intriguing** [ɪnˋtrigɪŋ]
a 非常有趣的、引人入勝的、神祕的

It is intriguing how sad a person can be when her life is doing so well.

她日子過得這麼好，想像她可能還會有什麼難過的事是滿神祕的。

⑤ **transportation**
[͵trænspɚˋteʃən] n 交通

Public transportation is a great way to travel around a city.

使用大眾交通工具是在城市裡移動的好方法。

❶ **would-be (V+er)**
想要做……的、試圖成為……的

Helen is a would-be teacher; she never finished her studies.

海倫想當老師，但她從沒有完成她的學業。

❷ **get the chance to V**
有做……的機會

Albert wanted to get the chance to talk to Fern about his worries.

艾伯特想要有機會跟凡恩說他的擔憂。

海洋保育工作

海洋的面積占地球表面積的71%，其含水量則佔地球總水量的97%，海洋不僅是地球大部分的組成成分，更能夠平衡氣候、供應氧氣，對地球很重要，甚至有80%的生物都以海洋為家，但人類無止盡的利用，破壞了海洋生態，前陣子流出的兩張照片——「海龜鼻孔中插有吸管」、「海馬勾著棉花棒」，引發社會大眾的震驚與討論，也因此開始重視了海洋生態的保育。

在環境保育方面，最重要的就如同左圖，少用塑膠製品，不僅是因為生物誤食到塑膠製品後，會導致不能消化而死，更因為塑膠製品難以分解，會造成地球永續的汙染。

除此之外，海洋的永續經營也是很重要的，漁業的濫捕可能會導致幼苗還沒辦法長大就被吃掉了，久而久之會導致生物的數量縮減、繁衍趨緩，也影響到整個海洋生物鏈的存亡。所以時時注意「吃進了什麼」也是很重要的，不要購買與食用已經過度捕撈的魚類。

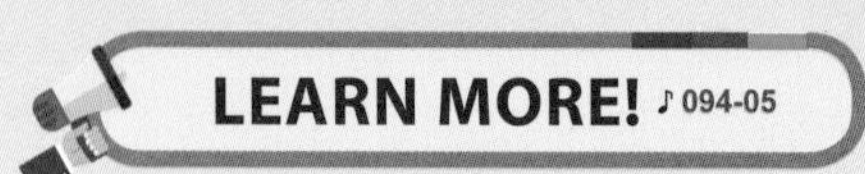

LEARN MORE! ♪094-05

tuna 鮪魚

salmon 鮭魚

octopus 章魚

squid 魷魚

flying fish 飛魚

clam 蛤

♪094-01 Every area has its unique **marine** ⑥ ecosystem, so naturally folks that make it to one of the above dive spots will probably fall in love with the world of diving and **make it their goal to** ❸ hit some of the other spots as well.

每個海域都有它們自己獨特的海洋生態，所以最常發生的就是當人們去了其中一個上述的國家潛水後就愛上潛水世界，之後便將其他潛水地點也列為目的地之一。

♪094-02 People getting the opportunity to experience the underwater panorama would probably be interested in helping the environment. After all, who would want to throw their plastic bags into the water after seeing a sea turtle swim by with a bag stuck around its neck? It sometimes takes seeing the damage we humans do up close to understand why not to do it.

有機會體驗海底世界全景的人或許會對幫助環境感興趣。畢竟，在看到游過你身邊的海龜脖子上卡了一個塑膠袋之後，誰還會想要再把塑膠袋丟入海中？有時候是需要人類親眼看到我們所造成的傷害，進而理解為什麼我們不該這樣做。

VOCABULARY ♪094-03

⑥ **marine** [mə`rin] a 海洋的

The marine water park was filled with incredible exhibits.

海洋公園內有許多驚奇的展覽。

PATTERN ♪094-04

❸ **make it their goal to**
使……成為目標

Parents make it their goal to take care of their children.

父母把照顧他們的孩子設為目標。

♪095-01 Polluting the oceans kills the wildlife and destroys the beautiful living coral. Over-tourism does a lot of damage to the coral and marine ecosystem as well. Being a diver must make you **appreciate** ⑦ the importance of the delicate **balance** ⑧ of the world around us.

海洋污染殺死野生動物，也毀了美麗的珊瑚礁。過度的觀光活動也對珊瑚礁還有海洋生態造成許多傷害。作為一名潛水者也會讓你更重視我們脆弱世界現有平衡的重要性。

♪095-02 **Naturally** ⑨ , people that spend some time underwater will see some incredible views. It's logical to see why these folks might get into underwater photography. After all, **normally** ⑩ when one is diving, you're spending all your time searching around for wonders to catch your eye. If you have an underwater camera with you, you can capture those wonders for all **eternity** ⑪ .

可想而知的，有在海底潛水過的人在看到很多美妙的景象。可以明白為什麼潛水者進而想要進行水中攝影。畢竟當你一個人在潛水時，所花費的時間就是在用來尋找海底奇觀。如果你有一台水下照相機，你便可以讓把捕捉到的畫面化為永恆。

VOCABULARY ♪095-03

⑦ **appreciate** [ə`priʃɪˌet]
v 感謝、欣賞

Paul would really appreciate your input on this problem.

保羅會很感謝你對這問題的付出。

⑧ **balance** [`bæləns] n / v 平衡

The single father worked hard to balance his private life and work life.

這位單親爸爸努力平衡他的私人生活跟工作生活。

⑨ **naturally** [`nætʃərəlɪ]
ad 自然地、天生的、當然

Alex is naturally confused by Wren's need for more time.

艾力克斯自然對於沃倫需要更多時間這件事感困惑。

⑩ **normally** [`nɔrmḷɪ] ad 正常來說

Normally I would be scared, but I actually enjoyed the horror movie.

正常來說我會感到害怕，但我實際上滿享受看恐怖片。

⑪ **eternity** [ɪ`tɝnətɪ] n 永遠

It's going to take us an eternity to pick up all the beans that spilled on the floor.

我們將要花一輩子的時間，才能把撒在地上的豆子全部撿起來。

VOCABULARY ♪096-04

⑫ **novice** [ˋnɑvɪs] n 新手

The skater was a novice, so he spent more time falling off his board than riding.

這個溜滑板的人是個新手，所以他實際上從滑板上跌下來時間比溜滑板更多。

⑬ **creature** [ˋkritʃɚ] n 生物

The stone creatures that line the church walls keep the water off of them.

教堂牆上排列的石狀生物讓水跟它們分離。

⑭ **wreck** [rɛk]

n（交通工具的）殘骸、沈船的殘骸

The wrecks of the ships were brought up from underwater.

沈船的殘骸從水底被打撈起來。

PATTERN ♪096-05

❹ **truth be told**

真相是……、說實話

Lois, truth be told, is a beautiful woman.

老實說，洛伊斯是個美麗的女人。

♪096-01 A basic underwater camera is probably fine for the first-time, or **novice** ⑫, divers. However, it is understandable that those who take to diving and start to make it a dedicated hobby would be willing to shell out some money to take top-quality photos. After all, if the diver gets really good at underwater photography, he can probably make a living off of selling his photos.

一台基本的水下照相機對一個新手潛水者來說應該是夠用的，但對於那些很投入潛水並且開始把水下攝影培養成一專門興趣的人來說，他們願意花更多錢來拍到更高品質的照片也是可以理解的。畢竟，如果潛水時可以拍到極佳的水中景象，說不定也可以透過賣這些照片來賺錢謀生。

♪096-02 Some people, though, are not into getting completely geared out and swimming in the vast ocean where who knows what kinds of **creatures** ⑬ might pop out and scare the living daylights out of them. These folks might be content to put on a dive mask and grab a snorkel to do some more surface level exploration.

但是也有人對於全副武裝在浩瀚海洋中潛水不太感興趣，誰知道潛水的時候會不會遇到什麼奇怪生物之後把自己嚇得半死。這樣的潛水者可能只要戴上潛水鏡跟用水下呼吸管探索海洋表層，就感到很滿足。

♪096-03 **Truth be told** ❹, a lot can be seen dive with no tank. In the Philippines, for example, there's an area in the southwest where you can free dive(Dive with no tank) about 5 meters and see the **wrecks** ⑭ of Japanese ships destroyed during World War II. This is probably more than enough adventure for the diving squeamish.

事實上也是真的，不戴氧氣筒就可以看到很多東西。舉例來說，你可以在菲律賓西南方的某個海域自由潛水（不攜帶氣瓶）到五公尺深的地方，就可以看到當初第二次世界大戰被摧毀日本船艦的殘骸。這樣子的體驗應該對神經緊張的潛水者來說就很足夠了。

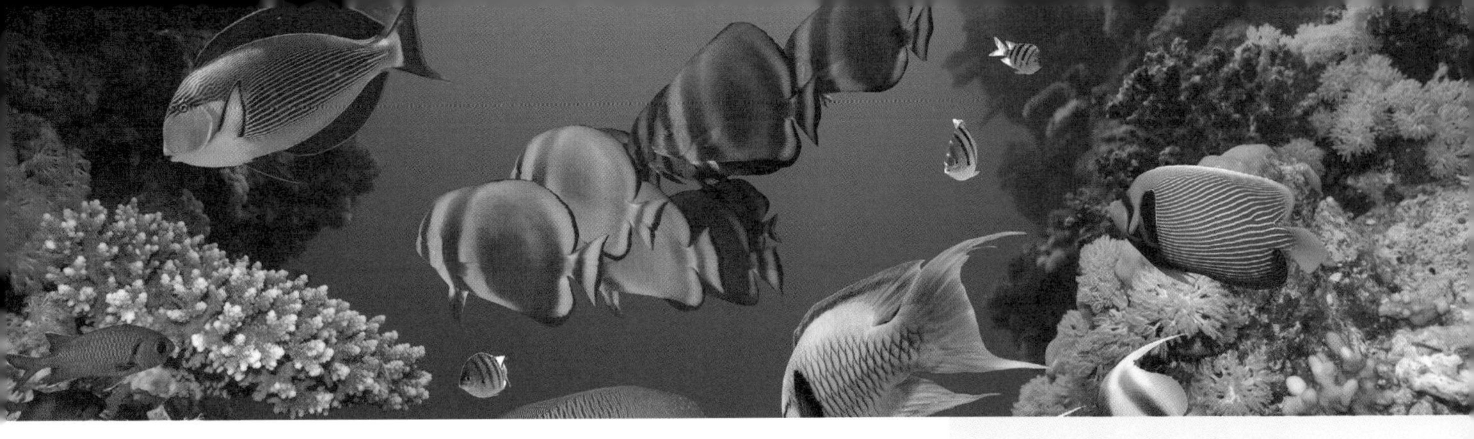

♪097-01 Going diving can **literally** ⑮ open up a whole new world for people. Exploration of the deep blue sea is exciting and **a must-do for** ❺ many adventurous spirits of the world.

潛水可以為人們開啟一個全新的世界。探索深藍色大海是很令人感到興奮的，對世界上具有冒險精神的人來說也是必做之事。

QUIZ 閱讀測驗

1. What stops a lot of people from getting into diving?

(A) cost
(B) the need to do it with other people
(C) the thought of sharks
(D) the coral reef

2. What is an easy way to go diving?

(A) Buy a boat
(B) Buy a diving package
(C) Get married to an instructor
(D) Start a club

3. Where is not mentioned as a good place to go diving?

(A) Great Barrier Reef
(B) Florida
(C) Hawaii
(D) Thailand

4. Why would someone get interested in underwater photography?

(A) It's easier than photography on land.
(B) There's no light down there, so it's cool to see what happens with the flash.
(C) They have a desire for danger.
(D) They hope to make a living off of it.

1. 什麼阻止了許多人進行潛水活動？
(A) 成本（所需花費）
(B) 需要與其他人一起做
(C) 想到海底有鯊魚
(D) 珊瑚礁

2. 進行潛水的簡單方法是什麼？
(A) 買船 (B) 買一個潛水套裝行程 (C) 與潛水教練結婚 (D) 創辦俱樂部

3. 哪裡沒有被提及是去潛水的好地方？
(A) 大堡礁 (B) 佛羅里達 (C) 夏威夷 (D) 泰國

4. 為什麼有人會對水下攝影感興趣？
(A) 它比陸地上的攝影更容易。
(B) 海底沒有光線，所以用閃光捕捉海底世界很酷。
(C) 他們渴望危險的事物。
(D) 他們希望以此賺錢謀生。

ANS: 1. (A) 2. (B) 3. (B) 4.(D)

VOCABULARY ♪097-02

⑮ **literally** [ˋlɪtərəlɪ]
ad 確實地、名副其實地

Angela is literally the first person to find out that Joe quit.
安琪拉的確是第一個發現喬離職的人。

PATTERN ♪097-03

❺ **a must-do for**
某事對……是必須要做的事

Surfing is a must-do for people that like to snowboard.
喜歡滑雪板的人一定要嘗試衝浪。

旅遊

登山健行

travel

VOCABULARY ♪098-02

① **habit** [ˋhæbɪt] n 習慣

His gambling habit has caused his family a lot of pain.

他嗜賭的習性已經造成他家人許多痛苦。

② **intimidating** [ɪnˋtɪmə͵detɪŋ] a 令人緊張的、嚇人的

Her expression was very intimidating and left everyone scared.

她的表情非常嚇人，並且讓每個人感到害怕。

Article 2

登山健行

♪098-01 Much like playing golf and camping out, the **habit** ① of hiking is one that people can pick up ❶ at any time in their lifetimes. While it can be **intimidating** ② to think of going on a long hike, once you get on the path, you'd be surprised at how very pleasant your day in nature will be.

就像打高爾夫球和露營一樣，徒步旅行是人們在一生中隨時可以發展的興趣。想到長途跋涉的健行過程可能會讓你感到害怕和不安，但一旦你踏上這條健行之路，你會對被自然包圍的一整天下來有多愉快感到驚訝。

♪099-01 One of the first things you need to consider before heading outdoors is how long you plan to stay out. You want to think this through for **several** ③ reasons. For one, if you plan to be out most of the day, you will want to make sure you put on a layer of sunscreen and bring a bottle with you.

朝戶外出發之前需要考慮的第一件事，就是你計劃在野外待多長時間，而為什麼要仔細想這件事情有幾個原因。首先，如果你計畫一天的時間內都在戶外，你會想要確保自己有塗上防曬乳跟隨身攜帶水瓶。

♪099-02 You will also definitely want to plan ahead for snacks and water. Trail mix is a great snack to have with you when hiking. It's a combination of nuts and ❷ **dried** ④ fruit and gives you a real pick-me-up when **hunger** ⑤ hits. If you plan to stay out even longer, you might want to prepare a barbeque meal that you can cook on a fire. A lot of trails provide grills and fire pits for hikers to make meals.

你也會想要先計畫好帶多少補充體力的點心跟水。什錦果乾是健行時的點心好選擇，它包括各種堅果跟果乾，在你餓的時候可以快速幫你補充體力與精神。如果你計畫在戶外待更長的時間，你可能會想要準備一些可以讓你用火燒烤的烤肉食材。很多健行步道提供健行者烤架跟烤爐來烤肉。

♪099-03 An absolute must is water. You need to have plenty of water with you to keep you hydrated, and you need to keep your eye out while hiking for places to top up your water so you don't run out.

還有一定要帶的東西就是水，你要確保有足夠的水，讓你隨時保持水分充足，健行的時候，也要隨時注意哪裡可以讓你把水補滿，以確保可飲用的水一直是足夠的。

VOCABULARY ♪099-04

③ **several** [ˋsɛvərəl] a 許多的

There are several places we need to clean out today.

今天我們有許多地方需要清理。

④ **dried** [draɪd] a 乾燥的

The dried fruit in the cereal made it very flavorful.

燕麥片裡的果乾讓燕麥吃起來風味十足。

⑤ **hunger** [ˋhʌŋgɚ]
n 飢餓感、渴望、盼望

Alli's hunger for knowledge was satisfied by evening college classes.

透過上夜間大學的課，阿里滿足了自己求知的慾望。

PATTERN ♪099-05

❶ **can pick up** 開始做……

Maybe we can pick up a new pastime of watching movies together.

或許我們可以一起看電影來作為我們休閒時光的活動。

❷ **a combination of...and...**
……跟……的結合

This drink is a combination of vodka and orange juice.

這個調酒是伏特加跟柳橙汁的綜合。

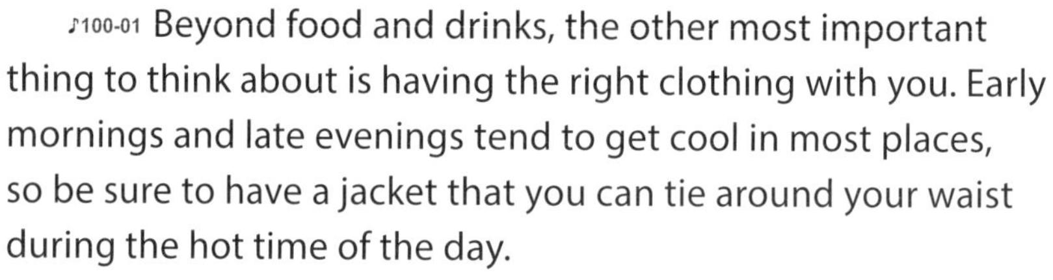

♪100-01 Beyond food and drinks, the other most important thing to think about is having the right clothing with you. Early mornings and late evenings tend to get cool in most places, so be sure to have a jacket that you can tie around your waist during the hot time of the day.

除了食物和飲料，另一個最重要需要考量的點就是穿著合適的服裝。在大多數的地方的清晨跟晚上天氣都比較涼爽，所以確保你有一件在日間氣溫較高時，可以繫在腰間的夾克。

♪100-02 A sunhat or baseball cap makes all the difference for **keeping the** sun **off** ❸ your face. And, if you are **planning** ⑥ a multi-day hike, don't forget your tent and a sleeping bag to keep you warm at night.

一頂遮陽帽或是棒球帽可以讓陽光不要直射你的臉，會有很大的幫助。如果你計畫的是多天的健行行程，別忘了你的帳篷跟睡袋，讓你晚上可以保暖。

♪100-03 Once you've considered these things, it's time to figure out what kind of hike you want to go on. If you are traveling to a great hiking area for the holidays, you may plan **multiple** ⑦ hikes over a period of several days.

一旦你考慮完這些事情，現在就是思考你想要進行怎樣的徒步旅行的時候了。如果你想要在假日時前往一個規模較大的健行區域，你可以在一段時間內規劃數個健行路段。

VOCABULARY ♪100-04

⑥ **planning** [ˋplænɪŋ] n 計畫

Alec spent weeks planning a surprise party for her sister.

艾蕾克花了幾週的時間，為她姊姊規劃一個驚喜派對。

⑦ **multiple** [ˋmʌltəpḷ] a 許多的

We've had multiple problems with our neighbor last month.

上個月我們跟鄰居有許多問題。

PATTERN ♪100-05

❸ **keeping the (+N) off** 使……離開

Ken is keeping the pressure off by exercising.

肯透過運動來擺脫壓力。

♪101-01 You might want to start with a warm-up hike. This is a hike that lasts about 2 to 3 hours and may go up around 300 to 500 meters. This kind of hike lets you get used to the area, **challenge** ⑧ yourself a little bit with going up some in altitude, but it won't completely exhaust you.

你可能會想要從熱身的健行路段開始，這樣的健行路段通常需要二到三小時完成，高度至多從三百到五百海拔公尺。這樣的健行路線讓你先熟悉環境，隨著海拔高度上升來挑戰自己的耐受度，但這樣的高度也不會完全讓你累倒。

♪101-02 Planning a two-day hike should be based on how you feel after one day of hiking. If you wake up the next day really **sore** ⑨ and worn out, then your second day of hiking should stay pretty **level** ⑩ , maybe going up 100 meters or so, and take two hours but not much more than that. That's called a rest and **recharge** ⑪ hike.

計畫兩天的健行，應該根據你第一天健行後的狀況決定。如果你起床的時候感到全身痠痛跟疲勞，那麼你第二天的健行最好保持在跟第一天相當的程度，或許你可以上升約一百公尺跟走兩小時，但不用比這更多。把它視為一個放鬆跟充電模式的健行。

VOCABULARY ♪101-03

⑧ **challenge** [ˋtʃælɪndʒ] v / n 挑戰

I challenge you to a game of chess.

我要挑戰你下棋。

⑨ **sore** [sor] n 痠痛 a 疼痛的

Getting back into the gym last week left me terribly sore.

上週回歸健身房運動後讓我全身痠痛。

⑩ **level** [ˋlɛvl] n 程度

Be sure you stay on a level surface when you first start skateboarding.

你一開始溜滑板的時候，確保你是保持在平面上。

⑪ **recharge** [riˋtʃardʒ] v 充電、恢復體力、恢復精力

We need to recharge the battery so that we can use the drill again.

我們必須幫電池充電，這樣我們才可以繼續用這個鑽機。

VOCABULARY ♪102-04

⑫ **perhaps** [pɚ`hæps] ad 或許

Perhaps you know how to build a birdhouse.

或許你知道怎麼蓋個鳥屋。

⑬ **challenging** [`tʃælɪndʒɪŋ] a 具有挑戰性的、考驗人的

It has been a challenging time for us since my grandmother died.

自從奶奶過世後這段時間我們過得很艱辛。

⑭ **view** [vju] n 視野、景觀

The views from the top of the mountain were incredible.

山頂的風景非常動人。

⑮ **flat** [flæt] n 平面

Anna started walking down a flat path for endurance training.

為了耐力訓練，安娜開始進行平地健走。

PATTERN ♪102-05

❹ **curl up with**
與……蜷縮起來（做某事）

Tonight, I just want to curl up with a good book and relax.

今晚我只想要好好地蜷曲起來看書跟放鬆。

♪102-01 **Perhaps** ⑫ you wake up after your one-day hike, and you are raring to go. That means your day 2 hike should be **challenging** ⑬ . It's time to think of going up about 1000 meters and turning the hike into something that lasts 4 to 5 hours.

也或許你第二天醒來時感到躍躍欲試，想趕緊動身。那這就代表你第二天的健行可以更具有挑戰性。這時候可以讓自己爬到一千公尺海拔的高度，之後讓時間長度增為四到五小時左右。

♪102-02 This is a hike that is likely to tire you out and let you get some great **views** ⑭ while you're out. Make sure to pack a pair of binoculars or a camera and be prepared to be exhausted the next day.

這樣子的健行程度大概已經可以讓你感到疲累，同時也可以享受到戶外的好景色。記得要帶望遠鏡或是相機，之後要有心理準備隔天可能會非常疲憊。

♪102-03 Don't forget: if you're foot sore, you can still get out there and hike. Just stay flat ⑮ and make it short. It will be a good day to spend the rest of the afternoon curled up with ❹ a good book.

別忘了，如果你的腳很痠痛，你還是可以繼續健行的，只要確保你走的路段平坦且時間不要太長。健行後好好蜷縮起來讀本好書，來度過你美好的下午休息時光。

QUIZ 閱讀測驗

1. When should people start hiking?

(A) when they are young
(B) when they start playing golf
(C) whenever they want to
(D) when their children are adults

2. Why should you consider how long you want to stay out?

(A) You might get lost.
(B) You might not have enough phone battery.
(C) You might need to tell a friend.
(D) You might need to pack a snack.

3. What is not something mentioned to bring with you hiking?

(A) Ice cream to cool down
(B) Water to keep hydrated
(C) A sunhat to keep sun off
(D) Snacks to keep energy up

4. What is considered a challenging hike?

(A) One that takes 1 to 2 hours.
(B) One that is on level ground.
(C) One that goes up 1000 meters.
(D) One that is a recharge hike.

1. 人們應該什麼時候開始徒步旅行？

(A) 他們年輕的時候
(B) 當他們開始打高爾夫球時
(C) 他們隨時想要的時候
(D) 當他們的孩子成為成年人的時候

2. 你為什麼需要考慮你在戶外想待多久？

(A) 你可能會迷路。
(B) 您可能沒有足夠的手機電池。
(C) 你可能需要告訴一個朋友。
(D) 你可能需要打包點心。

3. 什麼不是健行中提及該帶的東西？

(A) 降暑的冰淇淋
(B) 讓自己隨時保持水分充足的水
(C) 阻擋陽光的遮陽帽
(D) 補充體力的點心

4. 怎樣是具有挑戰性的健行？

(A) 需要一到兩個小時的健行
(B) 在地平面高度的健行
(C) 海拔一千公尺高度的健行
(D) 恢復精力為主的健行

ANS: 1. (C) 2. (D) 3. (A) 4.(C)

世界著名山脈 Famous mountain

安地斯山脈（The Andes）

是陸地最長的山脈，位於南美洲西岸，長度約 7,500 公里，平均海拔 3,660 公尺。最高峰為阿空加瓜山，高度 6,962 公尺，是美洲第一高峰，也是世界第一高的火山。

阿爾卑斯山山脈（The Alpen）

位於歐洲，共有 128 座海拔超過 4,000 公尺的山峰，最高峰勃朗峰海拔 4,808 公尺，位於法國和義大利的交界處。

喜馬拉雅山山脈（藏語：Himalaya）

世界海拔最高的山脈，位於亞洲的中國與尼泊爾之間，全長約 2,400 公里，約有 70 多個山峰，主峰珠穆朗瑪峰（又稱聖母峰）海拔高度 8,844.43 公尺，是世界第一高峰。

旅遊

travel

米其林餐廳

米其林評鑑

《米其林指南（法語：Le Guide Michelin）》可以分成紅色和綠色兩種，紅色主要是以評鑑餐廳和旅館為主，綠色則包括旅遊的行程規劃、景點推薦等等。

近年來《米其林指南》在歐洲的影響力逐漸下滑，因此積極開拓海外市場，進軍亞洲和北美等地。雖然米其林是餐飲業者的指標評鑑，但也傳出有餐廳因為登上米其林，而被業主增加租金而不得不遷徙或結業的情況。

而除了米其林指南外，比利時的 Monde Selection、荷蘭的 A.A. Taste Awards、英國的 Great Taste，也是可供參考的美食評比指南。

Article 3 米其林餐廳

♪104-01 Where should you go out to eat to celebrate this year's special **occasion** ① ? Why, if you do not know, **why not ask** ❶ Bib, the Michelin Man? The Michelin Man is that amazing marshmallow-like shaped white **mascot** ② for Michelin Tire Company for over one hundred years. What would he have to do with finding a top-notch restaurant, you may ask?

今年的特殊節日你該去哪吃飯慶祝呢？如果你還不知道，為何不問問米其林寶寶必比登？白色棉花糖狀的必比登是米其林輪胎公司超過一百年來的吉祥物。你可能會想問為什麼他跟找到頂級餐廳之間有所關聯？

♪105-01 Well, it just so happens that the creators of the star rating system for **exceptional** ③ food are actually the tire company brothers Édouard and André Michelin. The two started the Michelin Guide in France in 1900 to encourage more cars to get out on the road (there were only 3000 in the country at the time).

事實上為了尋找美味食物的評比系統的創建者就是經營輪胎公司的兩兄弟，分別為安德烈．米其林跟安德華．米其林。這兩個人於一九〇〇年在法國發起了米其林指南，用來鼓勵更多駕駛上路（當時法國國內只有三千台汽車）。

♪105-02 By the 1920s, the guide **turned** its **focus from** ❷ useful tips for motorists to being more of a restaurant ranking guide, and the brother's started **charging** ④ for the guide for as André observed, "man only truly respects what he pays for."

到了一九二〇年代，米其林指南從提供駕駛者實用的建議轉變為比較像是餐廳的排名指引，米其林兄弟也開始針對指南收取費用，就像安德烈說的：「人們只會真心重視他們付錢得來的東西。」

♪105-03 The brothers hired anonymous inspectors to look for, patronize, and review appetizing restaurants. In 1930, the creation of the star categories, from zero to three was instituted, and later in that decade, the ranking system was released.

米其林兄弟雇用匿名的美食鑑賞家來尋找、光顧並給予餐廳評價。一九三〇年時，星等評價類別的創造，從一到三顆星開始啟用，接下來的十年時光中排名系統也跟著發佈。

VOCABULARY ♪105-04

① **occasion** [əˋkeʒən] n 場合

On which occasion will you be meeting with your family?

怎樣的場合下你會跟你的家人見面？

② **mascot** [ˋmæskət] n 吉祥物

The team mascot is the Cowboy.

這團隊的吉祥物是牛仔。

③ **exceptional** [ɪkˋsɛpʃənl̩] a 極佳的

The weather has been exceptional these last few weeks.

過去這幾週的天氣非常的棒。

④ **charge** [tʃɑrdʒ] v 充電

I am charging my phone at the moment.

我現在正在幫手機充電。

PATTERN ♪105-05

❶ **why not ask** 為何不問……

Why not ask your father if you can go to the park?

你為何不問問你爸你可不可以去公園？

❷ **turned focus from** 把注意力從……轉移

We turned all our focus away from the problems at home.

我們把所有注意力從家裡的問題轉移到別的事物上。

VOCABULARY ♪106-03

⑤ **category** [ˋkætə͵gorɪ] n 類別

There are three different categories that you can put things in.

有三種不同的類別你可以用來擺放東西。

⑥ **connoisseur** [͵kɑnəˋsɝ] n 鑑賞家

Albert is a real wine connoisseur.

艾伯特是一名真的葡萄酒鑑賞家。

⑦ **badge** [bædʒ] n 象徵、標誌

Jess won a badge of honor for his actions.

傑斯的行動贏得榮耀的象徵。

PATTERN ♪106-04

❸ **all of this is well and good, but**

一切都很好，但是……

All of this is well and good, but I need to figure out a better way to do this.

這一切都很不錯，但我需要想出一個更好的做法來做。

♪106-01 The stars art rated as follows: 1-star is "A very good restaurant in its **category** ⑤ ", 2-stars is "Excellent cooking, worth a detour" and 3-stars is "Exceptional cuisine, worth a special journey."

星等的評價方式如下述：一顆星代表在同等類別的餐廳中此餐廳是很好的一家餐廳；兩顆星代表極好的烹調，值得你繞道而行；三顆星代表不同凡響的料理，絕對值得你特別拜訪。

♪106-02 **All of this is well and good, but** ❸ who actually cares? As it turns out, many, many people, chefs, and restaurants do. The Michelin Guide over time has gained a respected reputation as being a solid **connoisseur** ⑥ of top establishments. Some people will plan trips just to try out 3-star restaurants. It is a **badge** ⑦ of honor as a chef or a restaurant to have a star and can lead to improved business or additional recognition.

這些指南的一切都很好，但誰真的在意？事實證明有許多人還有廚師跟餐廳在意。米其林指南多年來作為一個可信賴的美食與餐廳鑑賞家，已經贏得受到敬重的信譽。有些人會規劃行程就只是為了品嚐到三等星的餐廳美食。擁有一個星等對廚師或是餐廳來說是一個榮譽的象徵，而且這也帶來更多生意還有額外的認可。

♪107-01 So how is a star level determined? It turns out ❹ the **anonymous** ⑧ reviewers are not looking at interior or place settings. Instead, the main focus is on these five elements: the quality of the ingredients used, the chef's personality in his cuisine, the value for money, the mastery of flavor and the cooking techniques, and the **consistency** ⑨ between visits.

那麼星等是怎麼決定的呢？讓人意外的是，匿名評價者並非注重餐廳的室內裝潢或是空間設置，相反地，他們主要注重這五項元素：使用食材的品質、廚師在料理中展現的個人風格、價格是否值得、對於味道的掌控和烹調技巧，以及餐點品質在多次拜訪中的穩定性。

♪107-02 When a restaurant checks all of these boxes, the stars are coming. If a reviewer returns and some of these elements are lacking, however, a star once given can always be taken away. This keeps restaurants focusing on consistently producing quality dishes.

當一個餐廳符合以上這些條件，就會得到星等。如果評價者再次造訪並發現以上這些元素有遺漏的部分，曾被給予的星等就會被取消。這樣的機制讓餐廳們致力於提供品質穩定的好料理。

VOCABULARY ♪107-03

⑧ **anonymous** [əˋnanəməs]
a 匿名的

I received an anonymous phone call last night.
昨晚我接到一通匿名電話。

⑨ **consistency** [kənˋsɪstənsɪ]
n 持續性

The machine's consistency is extremely solid.
這台機器的持續性非常穩定

PATTERN ♪107-04

❹ **it turns out**
結果是（指出乎意料的結果）

It turns out that Steven didn't know how the machine works.
結果是史蒂芬不知道機器怎麼運作。

♪108-01 Over the years, the Michelin Guide has added another category for a "Bib Gourmand" rating (named after the Michelin Man). The Bib Gourmand establishments are recognized for being friendly locales that have moderate prices and good food. It is not a star but is still a sign of **quality** ⑩ .

這幾年來米其林指南也增加了一個叫做「超值餐廳（或稱必比登推薦）」的新類別。（主要根據米奇人的名字來命名的類別。）必比登推薦此類別中的餐廳讓人感到舒適且提供的食物好吃，價位也讓人可以接受。雖然不到一個星等，但這仍是代表餐廳品質的一個標誌。

♪108-02 Currently, there are red-covered Michelin Guides for over 23 countries or regions around the world. Besides long-standing guides for its **original** ⑪ country France and other European countries such as Italy, Switzerland, Belgium, and Germany, other areas of the world have gotten guides as well.

目前全球有超過二十三個國家或是區域享有米其林提供的紅色指南。除了沿用至今的創始法國米其林指南以及其他歐洲國家的米其林指南（像是義大利、瑞士、比利時跟德國）之外，世界上其他地區也都有米其林指南。

♪108-03 For example, multiple US cities have guides. In Asia, Guangzhou, Tokyo, Bangkok, Singapore, Seoul, Hong Kong, and Taipei are among the **locations** ⑫ that have Michelin recognition.

舉例來說，在美國有許多城市也有米其林指南。在亞洲，像是廣州、東京、曼谷、新加坡、首爾、香港和台北這些地方都是有米其林認可餐廳的地方。

♪108-04 Taipei, as of the Michelin Guide 2019 selection, currently has one 3-star restaurant, Le Palais, five 2-star locations including RAW and Taïrroir, and 18 one-star restaurants including Kitcho and Danny's Steakhouse. With those topnotch choices **aside** ⑬ , there are also 58 Bib Gourmand options in the big city.

目前根據二〇一九的米其林指南指出，台北有一家三等星的餐廳叫做頤宮中餐廳（Le Palais）；五家二等星的餐廳，其中包括 RAW 跟態芮（Taïrroir）；十八家一等星的餐廳，其中包括吉兆割烹壽司（Kitcho）跟教父牛排 Danny's Steakhouse。除了這些頂級的餐廳之外，在這個城市也另外有五十八家必比登推薦類別中的餐廳。

VOCABULARY ♪108-05

⑩ **quality** [ˋkwalətɪ] n 品質

Quality control in the company needs to be handled by specialists.

公司的品質管理必須讓專家來處理。

⑪ **original** [əˋrɪdʒən!]
a 原始的、原本的

The original plan is that he will arrive in Paris and attend that meeting this Sunday.

原始計畫是他這禮拜天會抵達巴黎，並參與那個會議。

⑫ **location** [loˋkeʃən] n 地點

Filming locations are not difficult to find.

要找拍攝地點不難。

⑬ **aside** [əˋsaɪd]
n 一旁、小聲說的話、離題的話
ad 在旁邊

As an aside, Bernie asked Danielle when she wanted to move.

伯尼小聲地問丹妮爾她什麼時候想要搬家。

LEARN MORE!

♪108-06 ❶ **How would you like...done?**
你想要怎麼做……？

A: How would you like the meal done?
你希望這頓餐點怎麼做？

B: I want to add lots of onions and tomatoes.
我想要加大量的洋蔥和番茄。

♪108-07 ❷ **How long do I have to wait for...?**
我需要等候……多久呢？

A: How long do I have to wait for my meal?
我需要等候餐點多久呢？

B: Yours is almost done. Please wait a second.
你的快要做好了，請稍待。

♪129-01 So, returning to the ⑤ question, where should we eat for this **extremely** ⑭ special meal? Just flip through the pages of the 2019 Guide, and you are sure to not be **disappointed** ⑮ .

讓我們回到問題本身：我們應該在哪裡品嚐極為特別的料理呢？就翻翻二〇一九年的米其林指南吧，你絕對不會感到失望的。

QUIZ 閱讀測驗

1. Who is the Michelin Man?

(A) Édouard Michelin (B) Andy Michelin
(C) a famous chef (D) a Michelin mascot

2. When did the Michelin Guide start to focus more on restaurants?

(A) 1900 (B) 1920 (C) 1950 (D) 2019

3. Which is not an area that is used to decide Michelin stars?

(A) the quality of the ingredients used
(B) the chef's personality in his cuisine
(C) the value for money
(D) the location of the restaurant

4. Which is not a place mentioned in Michelin Guides?

(A) Tokyo (B) Hong Kong (C) Switzerland (D) Nepal

1. 誰是米其林人？
(A) 愛德華．米其林 (B) 安迪．米其林
(C) 一位著名的廚師 (D) 米其林吉祥物

2. 米其林指南何時開始把重心放在餐廳？
(A) 1900 年 (B) 1920 年 (C) 1950 年 (D) 2019 年

3. 哪個不是用於決定米其林星等的元素？
(A) 使用食材的品質 (B) 廚師在料理中展現的個人風格
(C) 價格是否值得 (D) 餐廳的位置

4. 哪個不是米其林指南中提到的地方？
(A) 東京 (B) 香港 (C) 瑞士 (D) 尼泊爾

ANS: 1. (D) 2. (B) 3. (D) 4.(D)

VOCABULARY ♪109-02

⑭ **extremely** [ɪk`strimlɪ]
ad 極其的

I am extremely tired at the moment.
我現在真的超級累。

⑮ **disappointed** [ˏdɪsə`pɔɪntɪd]
a 失望的

We were deeply disappointed that you didn't call on her birthday.
我們對於你沒有在她生日當天打給她，感到非常失望。

PATTERN ♪109-03

⑤ **returning to the** 變回……

We are returning to the basics to start things fresh.
我們回到基礎以重新開始。

旅遊

一生必去的 5 大世界景點

travel

VOCABULARY ♪110-02

① **bucket** [ˋbʌkɪt] n 桶子

There's a hole in the bucket.

桶子上有一個洞。

② **challenge** [ˋtʃælɪndʒ] v / n 挑戰

I would like to challenge you to go on a diet with me.

我要跟你挑戰節食。

③ **motivator** [ˋmotɪvetɚ] n 引起動機的事物

Weight gain can be a real motivator for getting in better shape.

體重上升可以是一個很好動力，讓人們想要保持身材。

一生必去的 5 大世界景點

♪110-01 Do you have a **bucket** ① list? A bucket list is a list of things you want to **challenge** ② yourself to accomplish or experience before you die. It sounds a bit macabre, but in many ways, the list is a good **motivator** ③ to push people out of their La-z-boy chair and out into the great world.

你有一張人生夢想清單嗎？這張清單列出的是在你死之前你想要挑戰自己去完成或是體驗的事項。聽起來可能有點可怕，但不管怎麼説這張清單是一個很好的動力讓人們離開那張舒適的 La-Z-Boy 沙發椅，進入這個偉大的世界冒險。

♪111-01 **Oftentimes** ④ people will put things on the list like: try eating raw snails or parasail off a mountain. Others may focus on their desires to learn a language or master a specific hobby. And one other category inevitably will have people going through their brains for all the beautiful places they want to visit in the world.

許多情況下人們會把這樣的事情列入清單：嘗試吃生蝸牛或是在山上做帆傘運動，其他人可能會專注於學好一個語言或者精熟某項興趣。另一個人們必然會想到的必做之事就是造訪那些世界上美好的地方。

♪111-02 More **outdoorsy** ⑤ type might for somewhere breathtaking like the Grand Canyon. The Grand Canyon is a deep canyon in the earth created as a result of the Colorado River flowing through it and gradually wearing the land away. It is nearly 300 miles long and a mile deep. The canyon has a **rich** ⑥ history of Native Americans living along with it or passing through the area. It is a **mesmerizing** ⑦ place to visit and stay in **if you have the time** ❶. You can ride a donkey into it, take a helicopter tour of it, or just pop by up top to take some impressive **selfies** ⑧.

喜歡戶外運動的人可能會想去像大峽谷這樣令人嘆為觀止的地方，大峽谷是地球上很深的峽谷，由於科羅拉多河流經且逐漸侵蝕而朔造了峽谷地形。它有近三百英里長，一英里深。這個峽谷擁有豐富的美洲原住民的在其周圍居住或是陸路經過的歷史。如果你有時間的話，這是一個令人著迷且值得造訪和待個幾天的地方。你可以騎驢子走進去或是坐直升機瀏覽風光，又或者只是在最高處照出現照個幾張讓人印象深刻的自拍。

♪111-03 Perhaps you would like to watch your amazing bucket list item pass you by outside a train window. You can do this with the Great Wall of China. First, you could visit the wall areas that are more tourist-focused. The wall, after all, **has been around for** ❷ thousands years. The Great Wall was built in many **layers** ⑨ overtime to protect areas of China from attack from people beyond the wall.

或許你想要透過火車外的風景來看到自己人生中必做事項從眼前經過，你可以用萬里長城來執行這件事。首先，你可以拜訪大部分觀光客去的萬里長城的地段。萬里長城畢竟已經存在了幾千年之久，萬里長城隨著歷史時光的推移，有許多層長城的牆段被建造以用來阻擋牆外異族的入侵。

VOCABULARY ♪111-04

④ **oftentimes** [ˋɔfn̩ˏtaɪmz] ad 常常

Oftentimes, I wonder how we were able to finish on time.

我常常在想我們能夠如何準時完成。

⑤ **outdoorsy** [ˋautˋdɔrzɪ] a 戶外的、喜愛戶外的

The outdoorsy couple spent the summer camping out.

這對喜歡戶外活動的情侶在夏天的時候露營。

⑥ **rich** [rɪtʃ] a 豐富的

This area has a rich variety of flora and fauna.

這個區域有很多豐富種類的動植物。

⑦ **mesmerizing** [ˋmɛsməˏraɪzɪŋ] a 迷人的

Her crystal blue eyes were mesmerizing.

她水晶般透亮的藍色眼睛很迷人。

⑧ **selfies** [ˋsɛlfɪz] n 自拍

The two girls spent their night out taking selfies.

這兩個女生在外面的整晚都在自拍。

⑨ **layer** [ˋleɚ] n 層次

This onion has so many layers.

洋蔥有很多層次。

PATTERN ♪111-05

❶ **if you have the time** 你如果有時間

If you have the time, could you mow the lawn?

你如果有時間，可以除草嗎？

❷ **has been around for** 某事物一直都在

This pyramid has been around for centuries.

這座金字塔已經存在幾世紀。

♪112-01 If you **make your way onto** ❸ a train **heading** ⑩ north to Ulan Bator from Beijing, you will see areas of the wall built during the Warring States period, the Northern Wei Dynasty, the Han Dynasty, the Northern Qi, the Sui Dynasties, the Jin and Ming Dynasty. From your train window, successful **bits** ⑪ of the wall will appear in the distance, and you can **mark that** marvel **off** ❹ of your list.

如果你從北京搭火車往北前往烏蘭巴托，你可以看到在不同時期建造的長城區域，從戰國、北魏、漢朝、北齊、隋朝、晉朝一直到明朝。從火車的窗戶你可以看到遠方出現的那些城牆的一部分景象，這時候你就可以把這個項目從人生夢想清單中劃除啦。

♪112-02 If you are the kind of person that prefers to get right into nature instead, you can **organize** ⑫ a trip to go diving at the Great Barrier Reef in Australia. It is the world's largest coral reef system and stretches for over 2,300 kilometers and can be seen up in space. CNN has **labeled** ⑬ it one of the seven natural wonders of the world. And diving there, you are sure to see a **cornucopia** ⑭ of amazing marine life.

如果你是那種比較喜歡大自然的人，你可以規劃一趟去澳洲大堡礁潛水的旅程。這是世界上最大的珊瑚礁生態，綿延超過兩千三百公里長，甚至可以從外太空看到其景象。CNN 把它列為世界七大自然奇景之一。在那邊潛水，你可以看到許多豐富驚奇的海洋生物。

♪112-03 But maybe that's not for you. Perhaps instead you prefer to observe the amazingness of nature from the **security** ⑮ of a boat. If you do, you can splash out and get on a boat to see Antarctica. Around 40-50,000 people make their way down south a year. Some make their way onto Antarctica proper while others sail along the coastline to see it up close. Any place that calls to mind "journey of a lifetime" when you think of doing it has a proper place on your bucket list.

但也有可能這不適合你，或許你偏好在船上安全地觀賞大自然的驚奇。如果是這樣的話，你可以花大錢乘船去南極，每年約莫有四到五萬人坐船去南極觀光。有些人只是去到南極洲，有些人則是沿著海岸線航行以看得更近。任何地方只要是你想到時覺得是「生命中的旅程」，在你的人生夢想清單上都佔有一席之地。

VOCABULARY ♪112-04

⑩ **head** [hɛd] v 前往

I am heading to bed unless you need me for anything.

除非你需要我幫你任何事，不然我要去睡覺了。

⑪ **bit** [bɪt] n 小片、小塊

There were bits of spinach stuck in her braces.

有一些菠菜的碎渣卡在她的牙套裡。

⑫ **organize** [ˋɔrgə͵naɪz] v 組織、安排

We need to organize the office into a guest room.

我們需要把辦公室重新佈置成會客室。

⑬ **label** [ˋlebḷ] v 貼標籤

We labeled all the boxes in the room.

我們把房間裡的每個箱子都貼了標籤。

⑭ **cornucopia** [͵kɔrnəˋkopɪə] n 豐盛、大量

There's a cornucopia of food on the table.

桌上有豐盛的食物。

⑮ **security** [sɪˋkjurətɪ] n 安全

The security camera was hooked up and transmitting images.

監視器被連接上並傳送畫面。

PATTERN ♪112-05

❸ **make your way onto** 移動到……

If you make your way onto the stage, we'll present you the award.

你如果來到舞台這，我們會頒獎給你。

❹ **mark that off** 劃除

We can mark that item off the list now.

我們現在可以把那個項目從清單中劃除了。

♪113-01 One last thing on your bucket list might be the farfetched. A perfect example of this is to want to visit the moon. Heck, **I'd put that one on** ❺ my bucket list. If it weren't too expensive, imagine being able to go out in 1/6 the gravity of Earth and walk around in a place that few other feet have ever touched. To me, that's an ideal end to my bucket list!

最後一件在你的人生夢想清單上的事可能是很牽強的，最好的例子就是拜訪月球這樣的事。糟糕了，我早已經把這件事放在我的清單上。如果不會太貴的話，想像我可以在一個只有地球六分之一引力的地方且沒有什麼人拜訪過的地方走走，對我來說，這就是我的人生夢想清單的理想結局！

PATTERN ♪113-02

❺ I'd put that one on
我已經增加那項在……

I'd put that one on the list to be handled next week.
我已經把那個項目列在下週要處理的事務清單上了。

QUIZ 閱讀測驗

1. Which is not a place mentioned to be put on a bucket list?
(A) Antarctica (B) Egypt (C) The Moon (D) Grand Canyon

2. How was the Grand Canyon created?
(A) Aliens (B) Cowboys (C) A river running through it (D) Earthquakes

3. What would be the best way to visit the Great Barrier Reef?
(A) On foot (B) By bus (C) Diving (D) Parasailing

4. What is not a dynasty mentioned with the Great Wall?
(A) Northern Wei Dynasty (B) Han Dynasty
(C) Ming Dynasty (D) Yuan Dynasty

1. 哪個不是提到要放在人生夢想清單上的地方？
(A) 南極洲 (B) 埃及 (C) 月亮 (D) 大峽谷

2. 大峽谷是如何形成的？
(A) 外星人 (B) 牛仔 (C) 一條河流經它 (D) 地震

3. 參觀大堡礁的最佳方式是什麼？
(A) 徒步 (B) 坐巴士 (C) 潛水 (D) 帆傘運動

4. 什麼不是提到跟長城有關的朝代？
(A) 北魏 (B) 漢朝 (C) 明朝 (D) 元朝

ANS: 1. (C) 2. (C) 3. (C) 4.(D)

LEARN MORE! ♪113-03

人生的路上充滿美景，有時候會錯過某些景色，有時候會想念曾經歷過的事物，而「miss」這個字有錯過的意思，也有思念的意思，可以用在許多日常生活中的情境喔！

- **miss out** 遺漏
- **miss the point** 不得要領
- **miss the boat** 錯失良機
- **miss the mark** 沒有達到目標
- **hit or miss** 無論成功與否
- **hit-and-miss** 碰巧的

人文

埃及金字塔傳說

humanities and cultures

VOCABULARY ♪114-02

① **revere** [rɪ`vɪr] v 尊敬

Alan was revered for his great writing skills.

艾倫因為他極佳的寫作技巧而受到敬重。

② **mystery** [`mɪstərɪ] n 神祕的事物

The mysteries of the universe keep scientists awake at night.

宇宙的神祕讓科學家們徹夜未眠。

PATTERN ♪114-03

❶ **appreciated for** 因為……被感謝

The scientist was appreciated for his contribution to the society.

這名科學家因他對社會的貢獻而被感謝。

Article 1 埃及金字塔傳說

♪114-01 The pyramids in Egypt are amazing feats of architecture that have been **revered** ① for the skill and manpower needed to create them and **appreciated for** ❶ their beauty. Yet, there is more than meets the eye with these wonderful creations as they hold all sorts of **mysteries** ② .

埃及的金字塔是令人驚嘆的建築傑作，建造它所需要的技術與人力贏得了世人的崇敬，它的美也大大地受到讚賞。然而不單單是視覺上感受金字塔的宏偉，它們也保有各種神祕的面紗。

♪115-01 One of the biggest mysteries surrounds how the pyramids were **actually** ③ built. The tallest of the pyramids, the Great Pyramid of Giza, stood at 146.5 meters tall. Block by block, the pyramids were built but just how did all those blocks get to the building site, and **how in the world could** ❷ they be stacked so high?

其中一個最大的謎團就是金字塔到底是如何建造的。吉薩金字塔是最高的金字塔，高達 146.5 公尺高。金字塔是一塊一塊建造成的，但是這些石塊到底是如何運送到金字塔的建造地點，而且這些石塊到底又是怎麼被堆疊地這麼高？

♪115-02 This has been a mystery to historians for centuries. Some people have even **speculated** ④ that aliens were involved in the creation of the pyramids. Realistically, the Pyramid of Giza has been standing for more than 4,000 years. No wheel and no pulley system had been **created** ⑤ yet, and no iron tools were being used at the time. So really, the alien idea seems like a real possibility.

幾個世紀以來對歷史學家來說這一直是一個謎團。有些人猜測這些金字塔的創建跟外星人有關。事實上金字塔已經存在四千多年之久，當時還沒有輪子跟滑輪系統，也沒有使用鐵器。這麼說起來，似乎外星人一說是真的有可能。

♪115-03 However through much research by a team of Dutch researchers, it was discovered that the massive stones, some weighing up to 90 tons, were moved on sled-like **contraptions** ⑥ . Based on written documents that were found, someone would pour water on the sand in front of the sled to **reduce** ⑦ friction and enable the weight of the stones to be carried along.

但透過荷蘭研究員團隊的大量研究發現，當時的的巨大石塊（有些甚至重達九十噸）是透過一種像是雪橇的裝置來移動。根據被發現的文獻指出，有人會在類雪橇裝置前面的沙子上倒水以減低摩擦力，好讓這些笨重的巨石可以被搬動。

VOCABULARY ♪115-04

③ **actually** [ˋæktʃuəlɪ] ad 實際上

I actually wanted to be an actor before I became a doctor.

我成為醫生之前其實想當的是演員。

④ **speculate** [ˋspɛkjəˌlet] v 猜測

He speculated on when Erica would come home.

他猜測艾瑞卡什麼時候會回家。

⑤ **create** [krɪˋet] v 創造

You created an amazing mobile app.

你創建了一個很棒的手機 APP。

⑥ **contraption** [kənˋtræpʃən] n（指笨拙、過時的）裝置

The exhibition comes up with the weirdest contraptions.

展覽提出了展出最奇怪的裝置的想法。

⑦ **reduce** [rɪˋdjus] v 減少

I go running twice a week to reduce stress.

我一個星期慢跑兩次來降低壓力。

PATTERN ♪115-05

❷ **how in the world +(do, could, would, should)**

到底／究竟怎麼⋯⋯（做／能夠／會／應該）

How in the world could you think that is true?

你到底怎麼能夠相信這是真的？

VOCABULARY ♪116-03

⑧ **belief** [bɪˋlif] n 相信

It is my belief that Santa Claus is real.

我相信聖誕老人是真的。

⑨ **impossible** [ɪmˋpɑsəbl̩] a 不可能的

It would be impossible for you to understand what happened to me.

對你來說，要相信發生在我身上的事情是不可能的。

⑩ **accuracy** [ˋækjərəsɪ] n 精確、精準

He shoots free throws with 87% accuracy.

他的罰球精準度高達百分之八十七。

⑪ **ramp** [ræmp] n （人造的）斜坡

The disabled ramps make it possible for wheelchairs to get into the building.

殘障坡道讓使用輪椅的人，可以進入這棟建築物。

⑫ **curse** [kɝs] n / v 詛咒

The witch's curse put the entire kingdom to sleep.

巫婆的詛咒讓整個王國陷入沈睡狀態。

♪116-01 This movement of the rock works very well. When you just need to move a stone down a hill, but there is **belief** ⑧ that some of the stone came from 500 miles away. This seems like an **impossible** ⑨ concept until it was noted that the Nile used to flow a lot closer to ❸ the current Pyramid of Giza, and there is evidence of a port near the building area, so boats could have transported the stones to the site. But once the stones got to the site, who moved them into place?

當你只是需要把石頭從山坡上往下移動，這樣搬運石頭的方式可以有效地運作。但也有一個看法是有些石頭原料是來自五百英里遠的地方，這似乎不是一個讓人可信的概念，直到有資料指出尼羅河曾經流經離吉薩金字塔非常近的地方，離金字塔建造地很近的地方也有港口曾經存在的證據，如此一來船隻便可以搬運這些石頭到金字塔的建造地。但是當這些巨石抵達建造地之後，誰負責搬運它們？

♪116-02 The Great Pyramid is built to an **accuracy** ⑩ that matches that of today's architecture, but really how did it get put together? It is believed that **ramps** ⑪ were put up and taken down to move the stones. But who moved the stones?

大金字塔在建築工藝上的精確程度可比擬現今的建築，但到底是怎麼組合在一起的呢？人們相信他們是透過架設斜坡跟移動其高度來移動石塊。但誰要負責移動石塊？

♪117-01 Speculation has always been that slaves had to do all of the work to complete this task. However, the more likely case is that skilled laborers were hired to place and work the stones. It is believed that up to 5000 people were hired and given places to live in communities that were located near the building site.

根據推測這些勞力活全都是由奴隸完成。然而，更有可能的是雇用熟練的勞工來挪動跟處置這些石塊。據信當時有至少有五千人被雇用並住在離金字塔建築地附近的社群裡。

PATTERN ♪117-03

❸ a lot closer to 更近

Jared is a lot closer to Ellen than I am.

傑瑞德跟我比起來與艾倫更親近得多。

♪117-02 Moving away from the building of the Great Pyramid, we come to the curse. There is a legend of a **curse** ⑫ of the mummies. Some say the sinking of the Titanic occurred because it was transporting a cursed mummy's coffin across the ocean to its new home in America.

除了大金字塔的建築謎團之外，跟它相關的詛咒也不絕於耳。有一個跟木乃伊詛咒有關的傳說是鐵達尼號的沈船事故，有人說是因為當時鐵達尼號運送了受詛咒木乃伊的棺材到美國。

VOCABULARY ♪118-03

⑬ **inscribe** [ɪnˋskraɪb]
V 題寫、雕、刻

The tattoo artist inscribed a heart-shaped tattoo onto the man's arm.

刺青師傅在那個男人的手臂上刻了一個心型的刺青。

⑭ **strain** [stren] n 壓力

The strain of coursework wore the teenager out.

課程的壓力讓這名青少年感到筋疲力盡。

⑮ **assistance** [əˋsɪstəns]
n 協助、幫助

I am looking for your assistance on this project.

針對這個計畫我尋求你的幫助。

PATTERN ♪118-04

❹ **the fact is that** 事實上是

The fact is that Eric is an incredible basketball player.

事實上艾瑞克是一位極佳的籃球選手。

❺ **may not be quite so**
或許不是這麼⋯⋯

This may not be quite so easy for us to talk about.

這或許對我們來說不是這麼容易談論。

♪118-01 **Inscribed** ⑬ on the walls of the tomb of Giza were threats that anyone that came to disturb or destroy the corpses should be met with death by crocodiles, scorpions, lions, or snakes. While these threats seemed to come true for a number of the people that opened the tombs, and while it has been shown that mummies can hold a mold **strain** ⑭ that can cause bleeding in the lungs, **the fact is that** ❹ there seems to be no actual curse. The inscribed threats served more as a security system to keep thieves away.

銘刻在吉薩金字塔陵墓牆上的是一些警告威脅的內容，讓入侵者知道如果你膽敢來打擾或者是破壞木乃伊，你將會遭受跟鱷魚、蠍子、獅子跟蛇有關的死亡詛咒。這些詛咒也隨著一些打開陵墓的人生病後應驗了，但實際上並不是什麼詛咒，而是那些木乃伊帶有會讓肺部感染出血的黴菌菌絲。那些刻寫的威脅文字比較像是保護作用，以防止盜墓者。

♪118-02 So, although there have been thousands of years of writings to tell us of curses and speculations on mysterious alien building **assistance** ⑮ , it seems that the mysteries of the Great Pyramid **may not be quite so** ❺ mysterious.

即使這些詛咒已經有幾千年的歷史，跟人們猜測金字塔可能是透過外星人的幫助建造的，似乎大金字塔的神祕已不如以往。

QUIZ 閱讀測驗

1. How were the stone blocks probably brought to the building site?
(A) By boat (B) By train (C) By plane (D) By aliens

2. How old are the pyramids?
(A) 200 years old (B) 2 million years old
(C) More than 8000 years old (D) More than 4000 years old

3. What impresses people today about the pyramids?
(A) how they were built to such precision
(B) how they have pretty pictures drawn inside them
(C) How small they actually are
(D) How the curse killed everybody around them

4. Who is believed to have built the pyramids?
(A) Aliens (B) Slaves (C) The pharaoh (D) Skilled workers

1. 石塊可能是怎麼樣被運到建築地？
(A) 透過船 (B) 透過火車 (C) 透過飛機 (D) 藉由外星人

2. 金字塔有幾年的歷史了？
(A) 200 年 (B) 200 萬年 (C) 已有 8000 多年的歷史 (D) 已有 4000 多年的歷史

3. 現今金字塔的什麼讓人們感到驚奇？
(A) 它們的建築是如此精確 (B) 它們內部的牆上畫有許多漂亮的圖像
(C) 它們實際上有多小 (D) 它的詛咒如何殺死周圍的人

4. 據信誰建造了金字塔？
(A) 外星人 (B) 奴隸 (C) 法老 (D) 熟練的工人

ANS: 1. (A) 2. (D) 3. (A) 4.(D)

古埃及法老 Egyptian Pharaoh

「法老」是古埃及國王的尊稱，他掌握全國的軍政、司法和宗教大權，是古埃及的最高統治者。法老被認為是太陽神之子，是神在地上的代理人和化身，而官員們以能親吻法老的腳而感到自豪。

而最著名的法老就是「圖坦卡門（Tutankhamun）」，他是古埃及新王國時期第十八王朝的一位法老。他年僅 18 歲便去世，其陵墓並未藏在金字塔中，而是建在地下，直到 1922 年才被英國的考古學家霍華德˙卡特發現。陵墓內充滿奇珍異寶，也有塊寫著「誰擾亂了這位法老的安寧，『死神之翼』將在他頭上降臨。」詛咒的匾額，而後只要敢進入法老墓穴的人，皆一一應證咒語而死，法老王的詛咒便逐漸傳散開來。

人文

達文西、拉斐爾、米開朗基羅

humanities and cultures

VOCABULARY ♪120-02

① **mutant** [ˋmjutənt] n 突變體

The mutant snake lived with two heads.

這條突變的蛇有兩個頭。

② **great** [gret] a 很棒的、偉大的、大的

The great man showed his kindness by donating money to the charity.

藉由捐錢給慈善機構，這名偉大的人展現了自己的善心。

達文西、拉斐爾、米開朗基羅

♪120-01 What do Michelangelo, Leonardo da Vinci, and Raphael **have in common** ❶ ? For you younger people out there, yes, they, along with Donatello, are names of the Teenage **Mutant** ① Ninja Turtles. But TMNT were given these names because these men were the greats of the Italian Renaissance. Leonardo da Vinci, Michelangelo, and Raphael are seen as the three **great** ② master artists of the time.

米開朗基羅、達文西和拉斐爾有什麼共同之處？對你們年輕人來說，沒錯，他們跟多納太羅一樣，是忍者龜卡通裡的人物名稱。但實際上忍者龜（TMNT）中的卡通人物被這樣命名是因為這些人是義大利文藝復興時期的偉大人物。李奧納多．達文西、米開朗基羅跟拉斐爾被視為當代的偉大藝術大師。

♪121-01 The Renaissance period was the period between the middle ages and modern times. Much of the ❷ focus of the Renaissance **period** ③ was on humanism and a return to an appreciation of Greek **philosophy** ④ .

文藝復興時期介於中世紀和現代之間。文藝復興時期的大部分焦點都聚集在人文主義以及回歸到對希臘哲學的崇尚。

♪121-02 Renaissance means "rebirth", so it was shown through a rebirth of interest in the human **emotion** ⑤ in art. During this period, much money went to supporting artists and creating historic art pieces, and many of the wealthy families **sponsored** ⑥ great artists and enabled them to live and create art.

文藝復興意味著「重生」，是透過對人類情感興趣的重生來表現在藝術中。在文藝復興時期，藝術家得以得到金援贊助並創造許多具有歷史性的藝術作品，也有許多富裕家庭願意支助藝術家，讓他們能夠同時生活和創作藝術。

♪121-03 The first of the three most famous Renaissance artists to be born was Leonardo da Vinci. An illegitimate child born in Florence, Italy, da Vinci is the actual **epitome** ⑦ of a renaissance man. A renaissance man is one who shows amazing talents in not just one field but in most areas they engage in.

這三位最著名的文藝復興時期的藝術家中第一位出生的是李奧納多．達文西。在義大利佛羅倫斯出生的非婚生子女達文西可稱作是文藝復興時期的典型人才。文藝復興時期的人才不僅僅只是在同一個領域中出類拔萃，而是在許多不同的領域都有優異的表現。

VOCABULARY ♪121-04

③ **period** [ˋpɪrɪəd] n 時期

This period in her life made her think a lot about what she wanted.

她生命中的這個階段讓她更知道自己要什麼。

④ **philosophy** [fəˋlɑsəfɪ] n 哲學

It's my philosophy to live and let live.

我的人生哲學是互相寬容。

⑤ **emotion** [ɪˋmoʃən] n 情緒

His emotion got the better of him when he got angry at his brother.

他生弟弟的氣的時候，情緒戰勝了他的理智。

⑥ **sponsor** [ˋspɑnsɚ] v 贊助

This concert has been graciously sponsored by Anne Freyte.

這場演唱會是由安娜．費宜特大方贊助。

⑦ **epitome** [ɪˋpɪtəmɪ] n 典型、典範

Eddie is the epitome of a good liar.

艾迪是善於說謊者的典型代表。

PATTERN ♪121-05

❶ **have in common** 有共通點

It was incredible to discover we had a lot in common.

發現我們彼此之間有許多共通點真的讓人感到驚奇。

❷ **much of the** 許多的……

Much of the time, we hang out together at my girlfriend's house.

大部分的時間我們一起在我女朋友家瞎混。

♪122-01 This was definitely the case for da Vinci, who was a talented inventor, mathematician, anatomist, scientist, engineer, sculptor, painter, architect, writer, botanist, and musician. You name it, he could do it. His **intricate** ⑧ engineering sketches are amazing **to behold** ❸, with helicopters and tanks and designs for focused solar power.

達文西絕對就是這樣的才子，他是一位才華洋溢的發明家、數學家、解剖家、科學家、工程師、雕塑家、畫家、建築師、作家、植物學家和音樂家。你說得出來的他都做得到。他精細繪製的直升機、坦克還有聚光太陽能設計的工程草稿圖也讓人目不轉睛。

♪122-02 He is **primarily** ⑨ remembered for his *Mona Lisa* and *The Last Supper*, where his focus on the human form, his layering of paints, and his awareness of light and shadow make him remarkable.

他最為人所知的作品就是《蒙娜麗莎的微笑》跟《最後的晚餐》兩幅畫，在這兩幅作品中他強調的人的形體、顏料的層次以及他對光影的捕捉使他聲名遠播。

達文西 Leonardo da Vinci

李奧納多．達文西
Leonardo da Vinci
1452.04.15 – 1519.05.02

他的畫作以寫實性聞名，而備受人們尊崇是因為他在技術上的獨創性，他曾探索機械上、土木工程、光學、流動力學，雖然多數的設計都未建造出來，但留下不少手稿筆記供後人研究。他也探索解剖學，其畫作《維特魯威人》就是一幅關於人體比例的作品。

PATTERN ♪122-03

❸ **to behold** 看見、注視

She was a sight to behold when she was totally soaked by walking in the rain.

當她全身濕透地走在雨中，讓每個人都目不轉睛地注視著她。

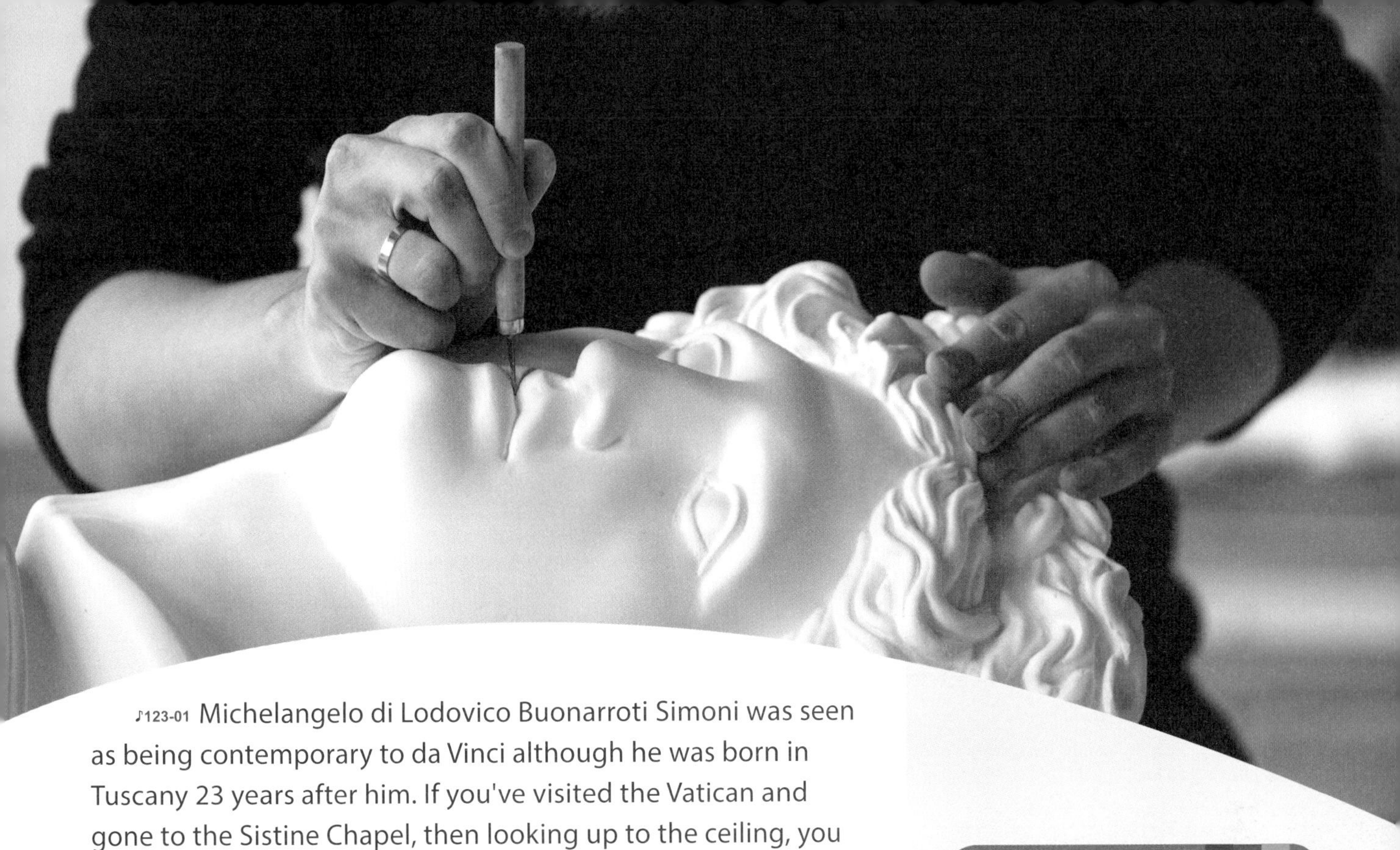

♪123-01 Michelangelo di Lodovico Buonarroti Simoni was seen as being contemporary to da Vinci although he was born in Tuscany 23 years after him. If you've visited the Vatican and gone to the Sistine Chapel, then looking up to the ceiling, you have gotten a sense of the impressiveness of Michelangelo's technical **skill** ⑩ and anatomical accuracy in painting.

米開朗基羅・迪・洛多維科・博納羅蒂・西蒙尼被視為跟達文西同時代的人，雖然他是在達文西出生後二十三年在托斯卡納出生的。如果你曾拜訪梵諦岡的西斯汀教堂，仰望教堂天花板時，你會被米開朗基羅在繪畫中展現的高超技藝與有如解剖學般的精準度所震懾。

♪123-02 Interestingly, though, Michelangelo saw himself more as a sculptor. And what an amazing sculptor he was. No one can look upon his *La Pieta* sculpture of Mary holding her dead son Jesus without **sensing** ⑪ the incredible skill needed to produce such a **piece** ⑫.

但有趣的是，米開朗基羅更將自己視為一名雕塑家。他是一名如此技藝精湛的雕塑家。沒有人可以看著他的作品《聖殤》（聖母瑪麗抱著死去兒子耶穌的雕像）而不感知到要完成這樣的一件作品所需要的是何等精湛技藝。

♪123-03 Other amazing pieces by Michelangelo are his *Moses* (with horns) sculpture and his *David*. Michelangelo lived to the age of 88 and was working up to six days before he passed away.

米開朗基羅其他的驚人作品包括《摩西像》（摩西頭上有長角）以及《大衛像》。米開朗基羅活到八十八歲，在他去世之前的六天他都仍還在工作。

VOCABULARY ♪123-04

⑧ **intricate** [ˋɪntrəkɪt] a 錯綜複雜的、難以理解的

The intricate design in the graffiti drew everyone's eye.

塗鴉中錯綜複雜的構圖設計，吸引了每個人的注意。

⑨ **primarily** [praɪˋmɛrəlɪ] ad 主要

I am primarily involved in researching new web design styles.

我主要參與的是研究網站設計的新風格。

⑩ **skill** [ˋskɪl] n 技巧

Her skill at playing video games is much better than her brother's.

她玩電動遊戲的技巧比她哥哥的更好。

⑪ **sense** [sɛns] v 意識到、感覺到

I'm sensing that you are angry at me right now.

我感覺到你現在很氣我。

⑫ **piece** [pis] n 作品

This piece was influenced by the artist's muse.

這幅作品受到藝術家的靈感影響。

♪124-01 The third of the three Renaissance greats was Raphael Sanzio da Urbino who only lived to the age of 37 but was able to **make his mark** ❹ on the Renaissance period during that short time. Born nearly a decade after Michelangelo in Urbino, Italy, Raphael was a master during the High Renaissance. He was influenced by the great da Vinci and was **disliked** ⑬ by Michelangelo and the two were seen as rivals.

文藝復興時期的第三位偉大藝術家則是拉斐爾．聖齊奧，他只活到三十七歲，但在他短暫人生旅途中他在文藝復興時期留下了自己的印記。在米開朗基羅出生後將近十年，在義大利烏爾比諾出生的拉斐爾是文藝復興全盛時期的大師。他受到偉大達文西的影響，同時也被米開朗基羅所厭惡，他們倆在當時是競爭對手。

♪124-02 Raphael is best known for his *School of Athens* where Plato and Aristotle make an appearance in great detail in the beautifully balanced fresco. Other great works attributed to Raphael are his *Disputo fresco* and his *Madonna del Prato*. He was well respected for his **smooth** ⑭ composition development and his **clarity** ⑮ of form in his works.

拉斐爾最為人所知的作品是《雅典學院》，在與美達到絕佳平衡的溼壁畫中清晰描繪著柏拉圖與亞里斯多德的形象。拉斐爾其他偉大的作品還有溼壁畫《聖禮的辯論》跟《草地上的聖母》。他最受人推崇且敬重的是他在作品中呈現的流暢構圖發展跟形態的清晰度。

VOCABULARY ♪124-03

⑬ **dislike** [dɪsˋlaɪk] v / n 不喜歡

Henry disliked talking to strangers.

哈瑞不喜歡跟陌生人說話。

⑭ **smooth** [smuð] a 光滑的、流暢的

Her smooth complexion was the envy of all her friends.

她光滑的皮膚是她所有朋友嫉妒的來源。

⑮ **clarity** [ˋklærətɪ] n 清楚、清晰

The speaker gave a speech that gave a lot of clarity to the topic.

這名講者的演講讓主題更清晰易懂。

PATTERN ♪124-04

❹ **make his mark** 留下他的痕跡

Milton hopes to make his mark on the dance world.

米爾敦希望在舞蹈界留下自己的足跡。

❺ **continued on for** 持續……（時間）

Their argument continued on for several weeks.

他們的爭論持續了幾週的時間。

♪125-01 After the time of these three, the Renaissance period continued on for ❺ another 150 years or so. Yet each of these gentlemen left their indelible mark on the period and no one can deny that the talent these three men displayed is some of the best in history. Heck, why else would the Teenage Mutant Ninja Turtles have been named after them!

在這三位偉大藝術家的存歿後，文藝復興又持續了一百五十年之久。這三位偉大的藝術家在文藝復興時期留下了不可抹滅的印記，沒人會否認他們所展現的藝術天份在歷史上無疑是最極致的。哎呀，這也難怪忍者龜會以他們的名字命名了呀！

QUIZ 閱讀測驗

1. Who was born in Florence?

(A) Leonardo (B) Raphael
(C) Michelangelo (D) The Teenage Mutant Ninja Turtles

2. Who is the youngest of the painters?

(A) Leonardo (B) Raphael
(C) Michelangelo (D) The Teenage Mutant Ninja Turtles

3. How did Raphael and Michelangelo get along?

(A) They were best friends. (B) They didn't know one another
(C) They liked the same woman (D) They had a rivalry.

4. Who lived the longest?

(A) Mona Lisa (B) Michelangelo
(C) Leonardo (D) Raphael

1. 誰出生在佛羅倫斯？
(A) 李奧納多 (B) 拉斐爾 (C) 米開朗基羅 (D) 忍者龜

2. 誰是畫家中最年輕的？
(A) 李奧納多 (B) 拉斐爾 (C) 米開朗基羅 (D) 忍者龜

3. 拉斐爾和米開朗基羅是如何相處的？
(A) 他們是最好的朋友。 (B) 他們不認識彼此。
(C) 他們喜歡同一個女人。 (D) 他們是競爭關係。

4. 誰活最久？
(A) 蒙娜麗莎 (B) 米開朗基羅 (C) 李奧納多 (D) 拉斐爾

ANS: 1. (A) 2. (B) 3. (D) 4.(B)

LEARN MORE!

♪125-02 ❶ **I need to change it to...**
我需要把它改成……

A: What do you want this model to look like?
你希望這個模型是什麼樣子的呢？

B: I need to change it to something like a mirage.
我需要把它改成像海市蜃樓的樣貌。

♪125-03 ❷ **Is it convenient for me to...?**
方便我……嗎？

A: Is it convenient for me to make a speech during the lecture?
方便我在講座中演講嗎？

B: Certainly! It's our pleasure that you are willing to make a speech.
當然！你願意演講是我們的榮幸。

米開朗基羅 Michelangelo

米開朗基羅
Michelangelo
1475.03.06 – 1564.02.18

他一生都在追求藝術的完美，堅持自己的藝術思路，著名的雕像作品為「大衛像」、最著名的繪畫作品是梵諦岡西斯汀禮拜堂的《創世紀》天頂畫、壁畫《最後的審判》。其風格影響了幾乎三個世紀的藝術家。

① **behind** [bɪˋhaɪnd]
ad 在（……的）後面

Watch out because there's a strange man behind you.
小心！你後面有一個奇怪的男子。

② **universe** [ˋjunə͵vɝs] n 宇宙

The universe works in mysterious ways.
宇宙用神祕的方式運作著。

③ **capture** [ˋkæptʃɚ] v 捕捉

I am trying to capture the moment they fell in love on film.
我嘗試用底片捕捉他們墜入愛河的時刻。

玩攝影

♪126-01 Lights, camera, action! When you get **behind** ① a camera lens, you are the master of the **universe** ②. With one shot, you can capture the delighted smile of a child or get the moment when a butterfly lands on someone's head. Being the person taking pictures is all about expressing your unique creativity through the images that you **capture** ③ and using one image to say a thousand words to the world.

燈光對了，相機準備，按下快門！當你透過相機鏡頭看世界，你主宰了整個宇宙。按下快門那刻，你可以捕捉孩子的燦爛笑容或是蝴蝶停靠在某人頭上的時刻。作為一個拍照的人，就是透過你捕捉的影像來表達你獨特的創造力，用一張影像向世界訴說千言萬語。

♪127-01 There are those that like to focus on landscape images. They will travel far and wide ❶ to find the most **breathtaking** ④ nature shots - forest full of trees with the sunlight pouring in or waves crashing against a rocky mountain cliff. Others may like to capture the human element and look for great images of natural action moments like people walking along a busy street or fireworks **whizzing** ⑤ around crowds of people at a temple celebration.

有些人喜歡專注於拍攝風景照，他們到處旅行以找尋最令人驚艷的自然美景來拍攝，像是陽光灑落樹群的森林或是海浪拍打陡峭山崖的畫面。有些人則可能喜歡捕捉有人物元素的影像，找尋人與人之間自然互動的瞬間，像是繁忙街道上的行人或是廟會慶典時煙火與人群熙熙攘攘交錯的畫面。

♪127-02 Portrait photographers look to capture the perfect expression of their subject, whether it's a couple saying their wedding vows or a child kicking the winning goal. Regardless of ❷ the photographer's **focus** ⑥ , most will make sure they incorporate some important techniques, like centering the shot correctly, making sure the lighting is correct or making sure the focus is sharp or fuzzy depending on the aim of the picture. **Mastering** ⑦ these techniques comes naturally to some but there are plenty of others that go to school to make sure they get all the techniques just right.

人像攝影師則是希望捕捉目標人物的完美的神情，無論是一對新婚伴侶在婚禮上宣誓時或是一個小孩成功進球瞬間的神情。無論攝影師著重是什麼，大部分的攝影師都會確保自己拍攝時有融入一些重要的拍攝技巧，像是確保畫面置中、光線正確，或是根據照片的目的來決定焦點是要清晰還是模糊。對有些攝影師來說這些技術很自然而然地就可以掌握，但也有許多人特別去學校學習以確保他們使用正確的拍攝技術。

VOCABULARY ♪127-03

④ **breathtaking** [ˋbrɛθ͵tekɪŋ] a 美得驚人的、驚人的

Her breathtaking performance amazed the crowds.

她驚人的表演讓群眾嘆為觀止。

⑤ **whiz** [hwɪz] v 快速移動

The car whizzing down the road was pulled over by police.

那台在路上快速前進的車被警察攔了下來。

⑥ **focus** [ˋfokəs] n 焦點、中心

The focus of today's class is "religions and why we choose them."

今日課程的焦點是「宗教以及為何我們選擇它們」。

⑦ **master** [ˋmæstɚ] v 精通、掌握

I spent two years mastering my photo techniques.

我花了兩年的時間來精通拍照技巧。

PATTERN ♪127-04

❶ **far and wide** 從四處、從各處

Compared with other runners from far and wide, Bianka is the best runner in the country.

跟各處來的跑者比起來，畢昂卡是國內最好的跑者。

❷ **regardless of** 無論如何

Regardless of what I said to Jasi, she still wouldn't clean up her dishes.

無論我跟潔西說什麼，她就是不肯清理她的盤子。

VOCABULARY ♪128-03

⑧ **option** [ˋɑpʃən] n 選項

We considered our options and decided not to go away on holiday.

我們考慮了我們的選項，並決定假日時不要離開。

⑨ **joy** [dʒɔɪ] n 喜悅

The joy Anders felt was lessened by Ella's refusal to meet him.

安德斯感受到的喜悅，因為艾拉拒絕與他見面而削弱了。

⑩ **wow** [waʊ] v 贏得喝采

Ester wowed the crowds with her acrobatic feats.

艾斯特用他複雜的肢體技藝驚豔了群眾。

PATTERN ♪128-04

❸ **branch out into** 涉足（新領域，尤指工作部分）

Dexter tried to branch out into a new area of studies.

德克斯特嘗試涉足新的學習領域。

❹ **does the talking** 負責談論

Whoever does the talking, I will be there to support him.

無論是誰負責談論這事，我都會在那支持他。

♪128-01 Those who show skill in photography often branch out into ❸ filmmaking. In filmmaking, it is no longer one image that does the talking ❹ . Instead, the filmmaker creates a story through the thought he puts into his filming. He can film a horror story, a comedy, a period piece set at a certain place in time, a sci-fi film, a romance, or a documentary. The **options** ⑧ are limitless and are really up to the director's imagination.

那些擁有攝影技巧的人通常也會涉足電影拍攝。在電影製作中，再也不是單一影像來訴說故事。電影製作人透過他在電影拍攝中投注的想法創造一個故事。他可以拍攝恐怖故事、喜劇、有特定時空背景的故事、科幻電影、愛情電影或者是紀錄片。可以拍攝的主題是無限的，而這都端看導演的想像力來決定。

♪128-02 All of the techniques from photography are still very important as no film that is badly-lighted or out of focus is a **joy** ⑨ to watch. But the challenge now is much like that of a writer –how to win over the audience's hearts. Good filming, dramatic angles, breathtaking backdrop scenery, and amazing action shots can **wow** ⑩ the viewer and make them appreciate the story being told.

攝影中所需要的所有技術於此還是非常的重要，畢竟沒有人會想要看一部光線失敗又失焦的作品。但就目前來說，主要的挑戰就像一個作家會面臨的挑戰一樣——要如何贏得觀眾的心。良好的拍攝技巧、戲劇性的拍攝角度、令人驚豔的拍攝背景以及動人的鏡頭畫面可以讓觀眾感到驚嘆，進而讓他們更重視電影中所要述說的故事。

♪129-01 Sometimes when trying to capture the perfect scene, there is a need for **extra** ⑪ equipment, like a camera on a track so that it moves and films as the actors go by in the image. A camera on a crane can be used to capture midair up-close shots. And then there are drones.

有時候為了捕捉完美的場景，會需要額外的設備來協助，例如使用推軌鏡頭拍攝，所以當演員在移動時也能跟著移動且拍攝；升降鏡頭可以用來捕捉半空中的特寫畫面；也有使用無人攝像機的時候。

♪129-02 Drone photography is developing **rapidly** ⑫ . It has taken over the need for cameramen hanging out of helicopters to capture **panoramic** ⑬ scenery shots. Those shots in the past were quite shaky and hard to focus. Nowadays, a person **on the ground** ❺ can use a drone to capture amazing 4k + sharp imagery and the image stabilizers in professional-grade drone cameras mean ultra-sharp images every time.

無人機攝影正在迅速地發展中。它已經取代了過往需要攝影師懸在直升機上拍攝全景畫面的作法。過去的作法拍攝到的畫面通常很晃也很難聚焦。如今，只需要一個人站在地面操控無人攝影機就可以捕捉到四千以上清晰畫素的驚人影像，專業等級的無人攝影機中內建的防震系統，意味著每次都可以拍攝到極致清晰的畫面。

VOCABULARY ♪129-03

⑪ **extra** [ˋɛkstrə] a 額外的

I'd like to get extra cheese on my pizza.

我的披薩要多加起司。

⑫ **rapidly** [ˋræpɪdlɪ] ad 迅速地

Ice rapidly cooled down the glass of water.

冰塊迅速地讓這杯水降溫。

⑬ **panoramic** [ˏpænəˋræmɪk] a 全景的

I love the panoramic feature on my phone.

我喜歡我手機的全景照相功能。

PATTERN ♪129-04

❺ **on the ground**

Steve has his feet on the ground and his dreams in the clouds.

史蒂芬是個腳踏實地的人，但同時又有許多不切實際的夢想。

VOCABULARY ♪130-03

⑭ **excellent** [ˋɛksḷənt] a 極佳的

Her excellent advice helped Albert win Faith's love.

她極佳的建議幫助艾伯特贏得費絲的愛。

⑮ **motivation** [ˏmotəˋveʃən] n 動機

I wish I had more motivation to lose weight.

希望我有更多動機來減肥。

LEARN MORE! ♪130-04

現在的手機簡直可以取代一般的數位相機，不用買到昂貴單眼相機，用手機就可以玩攝影。

- **front camera** 前置相機
- **rear camera** 後置相機
- **single-camera** 單鏡頭
- **dual-camera** 雙鏡頭
- **wide-angle lens** 廣角鏡頭
- **depth of field** 景深
- **time-lapse** 縮時攝影

♪130-01 Drones can give the audience a true bird's-eye perspective and make it a piece of cake to get **excellent** ⑭ images of city centers or action shots viewed from outside a window. They are just the tool a filmmaker needs to add an additional element of finesse to any film being made.

無人攝影機帶給觀眾一個真正的鳥瞰視角，要捕捉到極佳的鳥瞰市中心畫面或是從窗戶往外看的鏡頭再也不是什麼困難的事。它們只是電影製作人用來在拍攝電影中添加額外精細元素時所使用的工具。

♪130-02 Remember, whatever the **motivation** ⑮ is to capture images and save them in time, photography and filmmaking can both make it possible. Mastering techniques and capturing what you love will help you stand out from a crowd, and incorporating elements like drone footage will make you look like a mastermind to the audiences.

請記得這件事：無論捕捉影像跟及時保存它們的動機是什麼，攝影跟電影製作都讓這件事可行。掌握拍攝技巧跟捕捉你所喜愛的事物可以幫助你從人群中脫穎而出，結合像是無人機鏡頭所拍攝到的畫面在你的作品中更能讓你在觀眾面前顯得技藝超群。

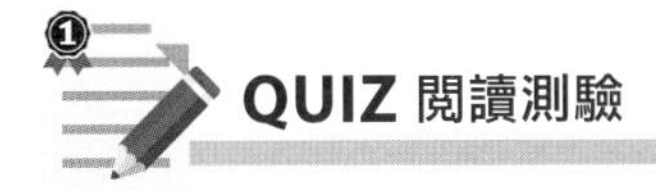

QUIZ 閱讀測驗

1. Which is not mentioned in the piece as a style of photography?
(A) Nature shots (B) Action shots
(C) Portrait photography (D) Underwater photography

2. What is different in filmmaking compared to photography?
(A) Filmmaking is a bunch of photographs connected to tell a story
(B) Photographs tell more of a story
(C) You only need to focus on the lighting in photos
(D) Photos take no time to take

3. What can drone filming replace?
(A) Robot filming (B) Filming from a helicopter
(C) Filming on the ground (D) Filming conversations

4. What does the piece say is the real challenge of filmmaking?
(A) Poor lighting
(B) Out of focus shots
(C) How to win over the audience's hearts
(D) When to film

1. 作為一種攝影風格，文中沒有提及哪一項？
(A) 自然影像 (B) 動作鏡頭
(C) 人像攝影 (D) 水下攝影

2. 與攝影相比，電影製作有何不同？
(A) 電影製作是一堆照片結合在一起後述説一個故事
(B) 照片把故事説得更詳細
(C) 你只需要專注於照片中的光線
(D) 照相不需要什麼時間

3. 無人機拍攝可以用來取代什麼？
(A) 機器人拍攝 (B) 從直升機上拍攝
(C) 在地面上拍攝 (D) 拍攝對話

4. 這篇文章説什麼是電影製作的真正挑戰？
(A) 光線不好 (B) 沒有焦點的鏡頭
(C) 如何贏得觀眾的心 (D) 什麼時候拍攝

ANS: 1. (D) 2. (A) 3. (B) 4.(C)

LEARN MORE! ♪131-01

拍照可以為旅程留下回憶，過了一段時間回頭看看，回憶當時的旅程、了解當時的自己，都是不錯的。

- We should take more pictures here.
  我們應當在這裡多拍幾張照。
- You look so happy in the pictures.
  照片中的你看起來好開心。
- I took many beautiful pictures of scenery.
  我拍了很多美麗的風景照。

aperture 光圈

SD card 記憶卡

film 底片

polaroid 拍立得

tripod 腳架

flashlight 閃光燈

人文

經典建築巡禮

humanities and cultures

Article 4 經典建築巡禮

♪132-01 Buildings are **wonders** ① to behold. To think that ❶ mankind started out in caves and decided that wasn't enough. Man built wood huts and clay huts and a **variety** ② of different housing to keep the elements away. But mankind didn't stop there.

建築物也是可觀賞的奇景。想想看人們最一開始可是從住在洞穴裡開始，但這樣還不夠。人們建造木屋跟泥屋以及各種不同的住屋來保護自己免於惡劣天氣的傷害。但人類沒有在這就止步。

PATTERN ♪132-02

❶ **to think that**
（對某事感到驚訝的）想想看

To think that I almost married you.

想想看我差點就跟你結婚了。

❷ **tie...in with** 與……有關

The kidnapping ties in with the missing woman.

這個綁架案跟那個失蹤的女人有關。

♪133-01 Classical architecture is the point we are getting to. Classical architecture is primarily discussing ancient Greek and Roman architecture. Much of the early architecture is found in Greece and was built mostly during the 7th to 4th centuries BC.

古典建築即是我們要討論的。古典建築主要討論的是古希臘跟羅馬建築。大部分在希臘發現的早期古典建築大約在公元前七到四世紀左右建造。

♪133-02 The focus of these **structures** ③ was on bringing out order, geometry, perspective, and symmetry. The buildings were most often build to **honor** ④ the gods , put statues of the gods on display, and hold grand feasts and celebrations for the gods.

這些建築的結構專注於呈現秩序、幾何學、透視比例跟對稱性。這些建築物通常是被建造來榮耀神明、展示神明們的雕像以及為眾神舉辦盛大的宴會跟慶祝活動。

♪133-03 One of the most **prominent** ⑤ elements of classic architecture is the use of the column. The column is the element that shows the evolution of buildings and that ties new architecture in with ❷ classic. The columns each had unique **specifications** ⑥ and uniform building patterns. In early buildings, the column is very heavy and not very ornate.

古典建築中最著名的元素之一就是使用圓柱。圓柱是展示建築演變的元素，同時也將新的建築跟古典建築牽起連結。每根圓柱都有其獨特的規格與統一的建築模式。在早期的建築物中，圓柱非常的笨重且沒有太多華麗裝飾。

VOCABULARY ♪133-04

① **wonder** [ˋwʌndɚ] n 奇觀、奇跡

The wonders of the world amaze most people.

世界的奇觀驚豔了大部分的人。

② **variety** [vəˋraɪətɪ] n 多樣化、變化

I love the variety of desserts available here.

我喜歡這邊提供的多樣化點心。

③ **structure** [ˋstrʌktʃɚ] n 結構

Those structures don't look very stable.

那些結構看起來沒有很穩定。

④ **honor** [ˋanɚ] v 受到表彰

The students were given awards to honor their hard work.

獎項頒發給這些學生，表彰他們辛苦的付出。

⑤ **prominent** [ˋpramənənt] a 著名的、重要的

The prominent scientist was well respected.

著名的科學家備受敬重。

⑥ **specification** [͵spɛsəfəˋkeʃən] n 規格

Can you tell me the specifications of that machine again?

你可以再跟我說一次那台機器的規格嗎？

♪134-01 The Doric columns, as they are called, are short and heavy and the column has 16 flutes. The top of the column which is called the capital was very **simplistic** ⑦ and was only a circular ring. Buildings that have Doric columns include the most famous Parthenon and the Temple of Zeus at Olympia.

如他們所稱的多利克圓柱，它們較短且笨重，圓柱有 16 個凹槽。稱之為柱頭的圓柱頂端的設計非常簡化，只呈現一個圓環狀。包含多克利圓柱的建築物有最著名的帕德嫩神廟跟奧林匹亞宙斯神廟。

♪134-02 As the architectural skill developed, the desire to make longer columns brought about a new column order, the Ionic column. The column tends to be more **slender** ⑧ and tapered with the fluting still present, but with four more than before. The capital of the column has now become more ornate and has what almost looks like ram's horns at the top. The Temple of Athena Nike and the Athenian Acropolis both have Ionic columns on display.

隨著建築技藝的發展，為了造出更長更高圓柱的渴望帶來了新的柱式：愛奧尼圓柱。這種圓柱較為細長，且隨著高度上升圓周會縮小一些些，仍然有凹槽的設計，比多利克圓柱多了四個凹槽。愛奧尼圓柱的柱頭較為華麗，在頂端有像是公羊角那樣圖案的設計。雅典娜勝利神廟跟雅典衛城中都看得到愛奧尼圓柱的足跡。

♪134-03 The third major Greek column **to surface** ❸ was the Corinthian. The Corinthian is the most ornate of the three. It is normally the tallest, and there are 24 flutes on the columns. However, it is the capital that really stands out. The Corinthian capital is **detail** ⑨ with two rows of acanthus leaves and four scrolls. The Temple of Apollo at Bassae demonstrates this column in Greece and with the crossover into Roman architecture, the Pantheon in Rome has Corinthian columns.

三大希臘圓柱最後一個要出場的是科林斯圓柱。科林斯柱式是三種圓柱中最華麗的，一般來說它也是圓柱中最高的，並且有 24 個凹槽。但最突出的地方莫過於它的柱頭。科林斯圓柱的柱頭有兩排爵床葉紋飾跟四個漩渦形裝飾。巴賽的阿波羅・伊比鳩魯神廟展示了在希臘的這種圓柱，它也跨足影響羅馬建築，例如羅馬的萬神殿就有科林斯圓柱的足跡。

VOCABULARY ♪134-04

⑦ **simplistic** [sɪm`plɪstɪk]
a 過份簡化的

I'm afraid my understanding of this topic is a bit simplistic.
我擔心我對這個主題的了解，有點過份簡化。

⑧ **slender** [`slɛndɚ]
a 苗條的、纖細的

The slender young woman walked across the room.
那苗條的年輕女子穿越了房間。

⑨ **detail** [`ditel] v 詳細說明

The detailed itinerary will be given to you tomorrow.
行程表的細節明天會拿給你。

LEARN MORE!

有機會的話，一定要去的世界知名建築：

- 法國 - 埃菲爾鐵塔（Eiffel Tower）
- 英國 - 大笨鐘（Big Ben）
- 義大利 - 比薩斜塔（Leaning Tower of Pisa）
- 俄羅斯 - 莫斯科紅場（Red Square in Moscow）
- 印度 - 泰姬陵（Taj Mahal）

♪135-01 Roman architecture **popularized** ⑩ another two columns. One was the Tuscan column which was extremely simple and would be compared to the Doric design except the column is not fluted.

羅馬建築也使另外兩種圓柱更為普及，其中一個是有著極簡風格的托斯卡納圓柱，它常被拿來跟多利克圓柱的設計做比較，但托斯卡納圓柱沒有凹槽。

♪135-02 The other major Roman column was a bit more **playful** ⑪ and is called the Composite column. The column took elements from both the Ionic and the Corinthian and married them.

另一種主要的羅馬圓柱則比較有趣一點，它被稱為複合圓柱，它融合了愛奧尼圓柱跟科林斯圓柱的元素。

♪135-03 Just naming the columns so that they can be picked out of a line really **does not do justice to** ❹ the **impact** ⑫ these columns have had on thousands of years of architecture. Combined with the common use of the arch in Roman architecture, an incredible number of modern buildings use these classic columns in their designs to pay homage to classic features and to connect the modern and classic.

如果只是單單在幾行文字間叫出這些圓柱名字就對它們太不公平了，畢竟這些圓柱可是影響了幾千年來的建築。有許多令人驚豔的現代建築結合羅馬建築中常用的拱形結構跟希臘經典圓柱來向經典致敬，同時也連結了古典與現代建築。

VOCABULARY ♪135-04

⑩ **popularize** [ˋpɑpjələˏraɪz]
v 普及、宣傳

Joe popularized the stand-up comedy in his act.

喬透過行動推廣單人喜劇秀。

⑪ **playful** [ˋplefəl] a 有趣的、愛玩的

The playful kitten rolled on the floor.

愛玩的小貓咪在地上滾動。

⑫ **impact** [ˋɪmpækt]
n 巨大影響、衝擊力、撞擊力

The impact of the meteorite was felt miles away.

隕石的撞擊力在幾英里外都感受得到。

PATTERN ♪135-05

❸ **to surface** 浮現、公開

The gambler is going to have to surface at some point to get more money.

賭徒不得不在某些點公開，以賺取更多錢。

❹ **does not do justice to**
不公平地對待、不合理地對待

This painting does not do justice to her beauty.

這幅畫沒有彰顯她的美麗。

VOCABULARY ♪136-03

⑬ **period** [`pɪrɪəd] n 時期

Which periods were most interested in art and music?

什麼時期對於藝術跟音樂是最感興趣的？

⑭ **incorporate** [ɪn`kɔrpə͵ret] v 包含、將……包括在內

We incorporated a lot of old-time music into the performance.

我們在表演中融入了許多舊時代的音樂。

⑮ **front** [frʌnt] v 朝向、面向、（被動用法時的意思為）表面覆蓋著或是鑲以……

The house was fronted with a row of flowering bushes.

這棟房子的表面覆蓋著一整排的花叢。

PATTERN ♪136-04

❺ **suffice it to say that** 無需多說、只要說……就夠了

Suffice it to say that I am done.

簡單地來說我已經做完了。

♪136-01 While it was religious temples to the gods that the buildings were built for in the past, many classic columns show up today in government buildings. Baroque, Neoclassical, and Beaux-Arts **periods** ⑬ of architecture all **incorporated** ⑭ these columns into their designs. The Lincoln Memorial uses Doric columns. The US Capitol and the Supreme Court building have Ionic columns in their designs. And the New York Stock Exchange is **fronted** ⑮ by Corinthian columns.

雖然在過去這些神廟是為了眾神所建造，但有許多經典圓柱在我們現今的政府建築中出現。巴洛克建築、新古典主義建築跟布雜藝術（又稱學院派）時期的建築都融合了這些圓柱在它們的建築設計中。林肯紀念堂使用了多利克圓柱；美國國會大廈跟美國最高法院都使用了愛奧尼圓柱；紐約證券交易所的正面則是嵌入了科林斯圓柱。

♪136-02 **Suffice it to say that** ❺ the classic Greek and Roman architects must have done something right if modern buildings are still choosing to display 2500-year-old columns!

過了兩千五百年，現代建築仍然使用希臘經典圓柱跟羅馬建築的元素，無庸置疑的是這兩者有其無可動搖的價值。

QUIZ 閱讀測驗

1. Which column has a ram's head-like capital?

(A) Doric (B) Ionic (C) Corinthian (D) Tuscan

2. Which column has a simple circular capital?

(A) Doric (B) Ionic (C) Corinthian (D) Tuscan

3. Which column is the longest with acanthus leaves in the capital design?

(A) Doric (B) Ionic (C) Corinthian (D) Tuscan

4. Which is not an element from Roman architecture?

(A) The arch (B) The Tuscan column
(C) The Composite column (D) The Doric column

1. 哪種圓柱有山羊角形狀的柱頭？
(A) 多利克圓柱 (B) 愛奧尼圓柱
(C) 科林斯圓柱 (D) 托斯卡納圓柱

2. 哪種圓柱有簡單的圓環柱頭設計？
(A) 多利克圓柱 (B) 愛奧尼圓柱
(C) 科林斯圓柱 (D) 托斯卡納圓柱

3. 哪一種圓柱最長，且在其柱頭有爵床葉紋飾的設計？
(A) 多利克圓柱 (B) 愛奧尼圓柱
(C) 科林斯圓柱 (D) 托斯卡納圓柱

4. 哪一項不是羅馬建築的元素？
(A) 拱形結構 (B) 托斯卡納圓柱
(C) 複合圓柱 (D) 多利克圓柱

ANS: 1. (B) 2. (A) 3. (C) 4.(A)

希臘神話

Greek myth god

希臘神話反映出古希臘的宗教、政治環境和古希臘文明，它涵蓋許多傳說故事，大多會透過藝術品來表現，故事大多是解釋世界的本源、講述眾神和英雄們的生活與冒險故事等等。

古希臘神話也孕育出歐洲文明，對西方文化、藝術、文學有明顯且深遠的影響，許多詩人和藝術家都是從希臘神話中獲得靈感而進行創作。

比較知名的希臘神明有：

★ 朱比特（Jupiter），又稱「宙斯」，眾神之王，奧林匹斯山的主宰。
★ 阿波羅（Apollo），太陽神，宙斯之子。
★ 馬爾斯（Mars），又稱「阿瑞斯」，為戰神。
★ 密涅瓦（Minerva），又稱「雅典娜」，為女戰神。
★ 維納斯（Venus），又稱「阿芙蘿黛蒂」，是代表美麗、誘惑的女神。
★ 刻瑞斯（Ceres），又稱「狄蜜特」，代表生育、收穫的女神。
★ 涅普頓（Neptunus），又稱「波塞頓」，為海神，手持三叉戟。

運動

健身重訓

exercise & sport

VOCABULARY ♪138-03

① **lightly** [ˋlaɪtlɪ] ad 輕易地、草率地

Do not make the decision to get married lightly.

別輕易地下結婚的決定。

② **build** [bɪld] v 建造

Jasmine loved going to the Build-A-Bear Workshop.

潔絲敏喜歡去 Build-A-Bear Workshop 逛逛。（註：Build-A-Bear Workshop 是美國大型零售店，販賣泰迪熊或是一些填充絨毛玩具。）

③ **plan** [plæn] v / n 計畫

I plan to find a way to drive out to Las Vegas this summer.

這個夏天我計畫找尋一條開車到拉斯維加斯的路線。

PATTERN ♪138-04

❶ **give the all-clear**
得到官方允許開始做某事、發出警報解除信號

Fred was given the all-clear after his knee healed.

弗雷德的膝蓋痊癒後醫生說他的腳沒問題了。

Article 1

健身重訓

♪138-01 Starting a weightlifting program is not something you should do **lightly** ① . Before initiating a program, the first thing you should do is get a checkup with your family physician. If you are given the all-clear ❶ by your doctor, then it is time to decide what your weight training goals are.

開始進行舉重訓練計畫可不是一件你可以草率對待的事。在開始執行舉重計畫之前，第一件你該做的事情就是找你的家庭醫生做個檢查。如果你的醫生說你的狀況沒有問題，那接下來就是決定你重訓目標的時候。

♪138-02 Do you want to **build** ② muscle? Do you want to lose weight? Are you training for a marathon? Or do you just want to stay fit ❷ to look good in a bathing suit? Figuring out your weight training goal will help you stick to your weight training **plan** ③ .

你想要長肌肉嗎？你想要減重嗎？你是要為了跑馬拉松而訓練體能嗎？還是你只是想要保持體態讓你穿泳衣時可以好看？想清楚你的重訓目標將會幫助你堅持執行你的重訓計畫。

♪139-01 Once you know your **reason** ④ for training, it's time to determine how you plan to start. Some people like to watch YouTube videos about workouts to get a grasp on the fundamentals. Others buy magazines or **download** ⑤ exercise apps. Most people will sign up for a gym, and some will hire a personal trainer.

一旦你知道你為何要訓練，接下來你可以決定你要如何開始。有些人喜歡看 YouTube 上面的訓練影片來大概了解一些基礎的內容；也有人是買雜誌或是下載健身的 APP。大部分的人會選擇報名健身房，有些人甚至會聘請私人健身教練。

♪139-02 **Whichever way** ❸ you choose to go about it, there are some common tips to remember. The bulk of weight trainers will ask you to start with **fixed** ⑥ weight machines. These are good for targeting specific muscles. The machines tend to help exercisers get used to proper form so that if they choose to move to free weights at a later date, they know the right positions to get into when lifting.

不論你選擇哪一種方式，有一些基本的要點要記好。大部分的重訓教練會要你先從固定機械式器材開使訓練，它們對於特定肌肉部位的訓練有很好的幫助。機械式器材易於幫助訓練者習慣正確的動作與姿勢，所以他們之後選擇自由重量的訓練時，他們舉重時便會知道該如何做正確的姿勢。

♪139-03 The **benefit** ⑦ of fixed weight machines is that each machine is geared to targeting one set of muscles or one group of muscles. Some pump the quads, some the pecs, others focus on the trapezius, and so on. This enables lifters to decide how they want to train their own body.

固定機械式器材的好處就是每一台重訓機器都有其鎖定的肌肉部位或是肌群。有些人想加強股四頭肌的鍛鍊，有些則強調胸肌，也有些人專注訓練在斜方肌……等等之類。鍛鍊者可以自己決定他們想如何訓練自己的身體。

♪139-04 For example, if you think your legs are naturally strong, but your upper body is **underdeveloped** ⑧ , then you may want to design a top-heavy lifting **schedule** ⑨ . Now that we are on the topic of lifting schedules, it is good to mention that it is not advisable to create a lifting schedule where you are doing the same circuit of machines every day.

舉例來說，如果你認為你的腿部肌肉已經滿強壯，但是你的上半身沒有精實，那麼你可能會想要設計一份針對上半身重訓的計畫。既然我們目前在討論重訓計畫的主題，那就要提醒大家一件事：並不建議大家每天跟著一樣的重訓計畫來訓練。

VOCABULARY ♪139-05

④ **reason** [ˋrizn̩] n 原因

The reason Glen moved to Michigan was to find a new job.

葛蘭搬到密西根的原因是為了找新工作。

⑤ **download** [ˋdaʊn͵lod] v 下載

You need to download this app to be able to play the game.

你要玩這個遊戲的話必須下載這個 APP。

⑥ **fix** [fɪkst] v 固定於

The painting was fixed to the wall.

這幅畫被固定在牆上。

⑦ **benefit** [ˋbɛnəfɪt] n 利益、好處

The party was put on for Todd's benefit.

這場派對是為了陶德才舉辦。

⑧ **underdeveloped** [ˋʌndɚdɪˋvɛləpt] a （尤指國家）不發達的、未發展完全的

The underdeveloped child thrived under careful care.

在細心照料下，這個發展不全的小孩逐漸茁壯。

⑨ **schedule** [ˋskɛdʒul] n 日程表、計劃表

Kris' high school schedule was incredibly challenging.

克里斯就讀的高中的課程表極具有挑戰性。

PATTERN ♪139-06

❷ **to stay fit** 保持體態精實、健壯

Uncle Chris worked out every day to stay fit.

克里斯叔叔每天健身以保持體態。

❸ **whichever way** 任何方式

Whichever way you go, I'm sure it will be all right.

不管你用什麼樣的方式，我很確定都行得通。

VOCABULARY ♪140-04

⑩ **mix** [mɪks] v 混合

You can't mix stripes and dots in an outfit.

你不能混合線條跟原點的元素在成套的服裝中。

⑪ **basic** [ˋbesɪk] a 基本的

Andrew's basic understanding of Mandarin served him well.

安德魯對中文的基本認識已經對他很有幫助。

⑫ **stability** [stəˋbɪlətɪ] n 穩定性

The stability of the table was improved by putting a tissue under the short leg.

藉由在短桌腳的底部墊上衛生紙，桌子有變得比較穩。

⑬ **injury** [ˋɪndʒərɪ] n 受傷

Crystal's injury put her on work leave for two weeks.

克里絲朵受傷的緣故讓她不能上班兩星期。

PATTERN ♪140-05

❹ **give (somebody) time to**
給某人時間做……

Derek gave Jenny time to look for a different job.

德瑞克給珍妮時間尋找一份不同的工作。

❺ **a good rule of thumb is to**
實用的經驗法則是……

It's a good rule of thumb to not forget your girlfriend's birthday.

不要忘記你女朋友的生日是實用的經驗法則。

♪140-01 If your goal is to train five days a week with two days for rest, then you need to **mix** ⑩ things up. One way you can do this is to focus on upper body machines on Monday, Wednesday, and Friday and do leg machines on Tuesday and Thursday. Technically, muscles need about 48 hours after a workout to recover, so that's why this cycle is beneficial.

如果你的計畫是一週訓練五天休息兩天，那麼你需要把訓練的項目混合起來操作。例如你可以星期一三五的時候專注於上半身的機器重訓，星期二四則做腿部的機器重訓。理論上來說，鍛鍊後肌肉需要大概 48 個小時來恢復，這也是為什麼這樣子的循環是有益的。

♪140-02 Remember, during your first training, you have to avoid a couple of **basic** ⑪ mistakes. One is to start out lifting much heavier than you should. Just because you can lift a heavy weight, doesn't mean you should. The best thing you can do is to give your core muscles time to ❹ strengthen naturally. It will give your body the **stability** ⑫ to keep training and keep you from getting hurt.

記好了，當你第一次訓練時，要避免一些基本常犯的錯誤。一個是一開始就舉超過你應該負荷的重量，你可以舉得起來不代表那就是適合你的重量。你的最佳策略是讓你的核心肌群有時間慢慢地自然增強。這也會讓你的身體有持續健身的穩定性，也可以防止你在訓練中受傷。

♪140-03 This means, when you first start out, focus on sets. A good rule of thumb is to ❺ set a weight that you can do 3 sets of 12-15 reps and have soreness but not **injury** ⑬ later. If, after a few days, you notice 3 x15 reps seems easy at the weight you're at, do one of your three sets at a higher weight. If you have no problems, you can gradually move up to that higher weight.

這也代表著，你一開始訓練時，先專注於訓練的組數。經驗法則告訴我們你可以先設定一個你可以重複 12 到 15 下並且做三組的適當重量，訓練後你會感到痠痛但不至於到受傷的程度。如果幾天之後你發現三組重複 15 下的重量開始變得容易，你可以在其中一組中增強重量。如果沒有任何問題，你可以漸漸把全部的組數的重量都增強。

♪141-01 The other main thing to remember is that the first three days are often the **hardest** ⑭ . You are beginning a new routine, and your body will definitely fight you because it likes the energy level it's at. It boosts your energy and helps you gain strength, but you need to not stop when those first three days make you feel like an exhausted **zombie** ⑮ . Stick with it, and it will get better.

另一個要記住的是頭三天通常是最困難的。當你開始了一套新的規律，你的身體肯定會有所反彈，因為它習慣了原本的體能狀態。開始重訓後會增強你的精力跟體能，當你前三天累到像喪屍一樣的時候，也不要停止訓練。堅持下去，你會漸入佳境。

QUIZ 閱讀測驗

1. What is something you should not do when starting an exercise routine?

(A) have a big, last dinner (B) check in with a doctor
(C) decide what kind of program you want to do (D) start slowly

2. What is not mentioned as a way to focus on getting in shape?

(A) watching exercise videos on YouTube (B) signing up at a gym
(C) playing video games (D) downloading fitness apps

3. Which muscle group is not mentioned above?

(A) trapezius (B) quads (C) pecs (D) glutes

4. What is a mistake people make when first lifting?

(A) lifting too light (B) lifting too heavy
(C) lifting all muscles at once (D) lifting without a partner

1. 開始規律運動後你不應該做些什麼？

(A) 吃最後一頓豐盛的晚餐 (B) 給醫生檢查一下
(C) 決定你想要執行怎樣的健身計畫 (D) 慢慢開始

2. 文中沒有提到哪個是專注於保持體態的方式？

(A) 在 YouTube 上觀看運動影片 (B) 報名健身房
(C) 玩電動遊戲 (D) 下載健身 APPs

3. 上述文中沒有提到哪個肌肉群？

(A) 斜方肌 (B) 股四頭肌 (C) 胸肌 (D) 臀肌

4. 人們在第一次舉重時容易犯什麼錯誤？

(A) 舉得太輕 (B) 舉得太重 (C) 一次使用所有的肌群來舉重 (D) 沒有夥伴一起舉重

ANS: 1. (A) 2. (C) 3. (D) 4.(B)

VOCABULARY ♪141-02

⑭ **hardest** [hardɪst] a 最難的

The hardest thing to understand was how the two of them became friends.

最難理解的事情是他們兩個人如何成為朋友的。

⑮ **zombie** [ˋzambɪ] n 殭屍

Grace believes there is a zombies' community at the mountain.

葛雷斯相信山上有個殭屍社區。

LEARN MORE! ♪141-03

weightlifting 舉重

rings 吊環

pommel horse 鞍馬

hurdles 跨欄

horizontal bar 單槓

javelin 標槍

shooting sport 射擊比賽

archery 射箭

運動

籃球比賽（NBA）

exercise & sport

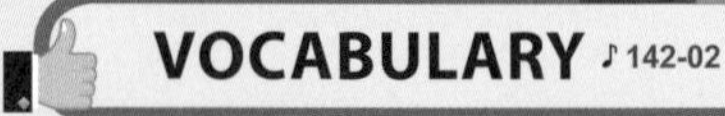

VOCABULARY ♪142-02

① **message** [ˋmɛsɪdʒ] n 訊息

The message was loud and clear.

訊息很清晰易懂。

② **trail** [trel] v 跟在後面

Andre was trailing Robert throughout most of the game.

安德烈在整場比賽中，大部分的時候都落後羅伯特。

PATTERN ♪142-03

❶ **right now it's anyone's game**
（勢均力敵的狀況下）誰都可能贏得比賽

It's a close one folks, and right now, it's anyone's game.

大夥，分數很接近了，現在我們棋逢敵手。

Article 2 籃球比賽（NBA）

♪142-01 That was a **message** ① from our sponsors. Got to remember to "Eat your Wheaties", kids. Now we're back and it's the final four minutes of the fourth quarter of Game Five of the NBA Finals and right now it's anyone's game ❶. The Knicks are **trailing** ② by 6 points, but there's plenty of time left on the clock for them to catch up and take the lead.

這是我們的贊助商發來的消息。孩子們，要記住「吃你的小麥」。我們現在回到 NBA 總決賽第五場第四節的最後四分鐘現場，現在勢均力敵。紐約尼克隊目前落後六分，但現在仍有許多時間讓他們趕緊追上並領先。

♪143-01 Whoa, in fact, Mudiay just pulled up and shot a beautiful three. The Knicks are trailing now by three, and the Golden State Warriors are racing down and, yes, that's a **lay-up** ③. Score is now 85-80 Golden State, the Knicks have the ball and Golden State has a full court press **in effect** ❷. All it takes is one little mistake at this point, and… yep, there it was, DeAndre had the ball **stripped** ④, and the pass down court by Golden State is perfect. DeMarcus powers in and makes the 2.

哇，事實上穆迪埃剛剛跳投一記完美的三分球。現在尼克落後三分，金州勇士隊現在追過來，喔對，那是一記上籃。現在比數 85 比 80，金州勇士領先，現在尼克拿到球，金州勇士採取全場緊逼狀態。現在就只差一分失誤，然後……就是這樣，德安德魯的球被搶了，金州勇士的傳球太漂亮了，德馬庫斯奮力一投得兩分。

♪143-02 We've got 3 minutes left in the game now, and it's going to take everything to win this game. If they lose this game, they'll be down 2-3 in this best of seven NBA Finals. Isiah Hicks for the three and…it's good. Score's now 87-83. Curry is out with an ankle **injury** ⑤, so it's up to the team to keep scoring.

現在我們只剩下三分鐘了，不管怎樣都要想盡辦法贏得比賽。如果他們輸了這場，他們在這次七場 NBA 總決賽最讚的一場球賽中就會用 2-3 的成績收尾。伊塞亞．希克斯現在得三分……很好。比數現在是 87 比 83。柯瑞因為腳踝傷勢離場，現在就要靠整個團隊來得分了。

♪143-03 This is again Game Five with the 2-2-1-1-1 format. The teams are playing tonight in Oakland, and the next game will **definitely** ⑥ be back in New York. Nice shot for Klay Thompson for a quick two. 89-83, but Kadeem has it for a three, and that's **all net** ❸!

再一次地，這是 2-2-1-1-1 模式的第五場比賽。球隊們今晚將在奧克蘭進行比賽，下一場比賽絕對會再回到紐約。克雷．湯普森這兩分得的真是漂亮。現在比數 89 比 83 了，但卡蒂姆剛投出完全沒有擦邊的一顆三分！

♪143-04 89-86 with 2 minutes and 20 seconds to go and this game just doesn't fail to **impress** ⑦. Even though the scores are low, the ball handling has been **exceptional** ⑧, and both sides have been unforgiving for any mistake. Speaking of mistakes, Durant tried to feed the ball to DeMarcus, but he was DENIED. Knicks with the breakaway and…yes, that's DeAndre with the layup.

目前 89 比 86，剩下兩分二十秒結束這場比賽，這場球賽真是精彩啊。雖然得分不高，但控球狀態上極佳，雙方也完全不容忍犯錯餘地。說到失誤，杜蘭特嘗試傳球給德馬庫斯但被攔截了。尼克斯現在衝出來了然後……沒錯，德安德魯一記上籃。

VOCABULARY ♪143-05

③ **lay-up** [ˋleˏʌp] n 上籃

Greg got possession of the ball and broke away for a lay-up.

格雷格拿到球之後殺出一條路上籃。

④ **strip** [strɪp] v 奪走

Fred stripped Carol of the ball.

弗雷德奪走卡羅手中的球。

⑤ **injury** [ˋɪndʒərɪ] n 受傷

The player's injury left her on the sidelines for a month.

這名選手的傷勢讓她一個月不能參賽。

⑥ **definitely** [ˋdɛfənɪtlɪ] ad 絕對

We will definitely have to talk more about this later.

我們等等一定要再多談論此事。

⑦ **impress** [ɪmˋprɛs]
v 使欽佩、留下深刻印象

Everyone was impressed by Theo's resilience after his failure.

每個人都對西奧在失敗後的復原能力感到敬佩。

⑧ **exceptional** [ɪkˋsɛpʃənl̩]
a 卓越的、傑出的

Uma is an exceptional student.

烏瑪是一位傑出的學生。

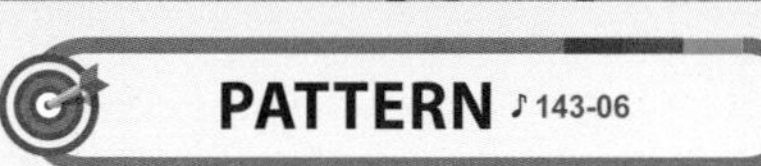

❷ **in effect** 實際上、事實上

There is a storm warning in effect, so please stay indoors until the warning has passed.

實際上有一個暴風雨警報，所以請待在室內直到警報解除。

❸ **all net** 空心進籃

What a beautiful shot; it's all net.

真是漂亮的一球，完全沒有擦到籃框。

♪144-01 Score is now 88-89. DeAndre has had a really **solid** ⑨ game; he has been strong on the boards and tough on defense, and it's really paid off for him. He has a season high of 15 points with 12 rebounds. Fade away jumper and Golden State scores. One minute and 30 seconds left and it looks like the Knicks are taking their last time out.

比數 88 比 89 了，德安德魯真的打得很扎實，他的籃板球很強，在防守方面也很強悍，皇天不負苦心人啊。他有一季的表現，十五得分中有 12 分都是籃板球。仰後式跳投，金州勇士隊再得一分。剩下一分三十秒，看來尼克隊不能再這樣下去了。

♪144-02 Golden State has been the golden team **for years now** ❹ , but the Knicks have really been the team to watch this season. They've fought hard and come back from a few early losses to dominate second part of the season and take over at the Eastern Conference Finals.

金州勇士隊多年來一直是黃金球隊，但本季以來尼克的表現也相當值得注目。他們奮力拼搏，從原本前幾場輸球的狀態回到主導下半季的位置而且也在東部半決賽上拔得頭籌。

♪144-03 And speaking of someone that's been **dominating** ⑩ , Klay Thompson shows that slow and steady wins the race. He might not be the biggest scorer, but he's always powerful and always shooting hot.

說到佔有主導地位的人，我們從克雷．湯普森身上看到不勻不徐跟穩定性是贏得比賽的致勝點。他或許不是最強的得分球員，但他總是表現強大且投入許多好球。

♪144-04 Play's back on, Knicks **possession** ⑪ and, yep, they make quick work of it with a pass inside to Hicks. 91-90, Golden State hanging on by a thread. Will they do it, folks? They do have the home court advantage, but the last minute is our **decider** ⑫ .

回到比賽，尼克現在控球然後……喔沒錯，他們現在合力要把球往內傳給希克斯。91 比 90，金州勇士隊現在岌岌可危，他們會辦到嗎？他們的確有主場優勢，但最後一分鐘才是決定關鍵。

VOCABULARY ♪144-05

⑨ **solid** [ˋsɑlɪd] a 堅固的、扎實的

His solid performance on his exams put him on the honor roll.

考試中他扎實的表現讓他被列入優等生名冊之中。

⑩ **dominating** [ˋdɑmə͵netɪŋ] a 控制的

His dominating personality was the cause for their divorce.

他們離婚的原因是因為他愛控制的人格。

⑪ **possession** [pəˋzɛʃən] n 佔有、擁有、控球

Abel's ball possession helped him win the game.

艾伯的控球幫助他贏了比賽。

⑫ **decider** [dɪˋsaɪdɚ] n 決定性的得分、決勝局

That last three pointer was the game's decider.

最後的三分球是這場比賽的決定性得分。

PATTERN ♪144-06

❹ **for years now** 持續幾年時間了

Elle has had a crush on Tom for years now.

艾拉喜歡湯姆有幾年的時間了。

♪145-01 A feed to Klay and a block by Mudiay…no, wait, there's a **whistle** ⑬ on the play. Thompson is on the free throw line and the first one's good…nothing but net on the second one and the score is now 93-90 in the last twenty seconds.

餵球到內線的克雷然後穆迪埃擋下了……不，等等，裁判吹哨。湯普森現在在罰球線上，第一球投得很好……第二球完全沒有擦邊進球，現在倒數二十秒，比數是 93 比 90。

♪145-02 It's down to the line and it's down the court with 10, 9, 8 is this going to go into **overtime** ⑭ folks? 5,4,3 Kadeem **sends up** ❺ the three, annnnnnnnnd, right with the **buzzer** ⑮ the ball goes in. Game Five is now in overtime!

現在時間迫近，往敵方前進，十、九、八，各位，是否會打延長賽呢？最後五，四，三，卡蒂姆投出一記三分，然後……蜂鳴器響的同時也進球了。第五場現在確定打入延長賽了！

QUIZ 閱讀測驗

1. What part of the game is it at the start of this piece?

(A) 85-80　(B) Game Five of the Finals
(C) the third quarter　(D) overtime

2. What are the names of the two teams playing?

(A) Thompson and Curry　(B) Kadeem and Mudiay
(C) Knicks and Golden State　(D) California and New York

3. How does Thompson do at the free throw line?

(A) He makes one basket.　(B) He misses one basket.
(C) He makes no baskets.　(D) He makes both baskets.

4. Which teams has had a harder time making it to the finals?

(A) Knicks　(B) Golden State　(C) Both teams　(D) Neither team

1. 文章的開頭提到的是比賽的哪部份？
(A) 比數 85-80　(B) 總決賽的第五場　(C) 第三節　(D) 延長賽

2. 比賽的兩個球隊名稱是？
(A) 湯普森跟柯瑞　(B) 卡蒂姆跟穆迪埃　(C) 紐約尼克隊跟金州勇士隊
(D) 加利福尼亞跟紐約

3. 湯普森在罰球線上的表現如何？
(A) 他投進一球。　(B) 他錯失一球。　(C) 他沒有投進。　(D) 他兩球都進。

4. 哪支球隊很辛苦才打進總決賽？
(A) 尼克隊　(B) 金州勇士隊　(C) 兩隊（尼克跟金州勇士）
(D) 兩個球隊都沒有（尼克跟金州勇士）

ANS: 1. (A) 2. (C) 3. (D) 4.(A)

VOCABULARY ♪145-03

⑬ **whistle** [ˋhwɪsl̩] n 哨子

The lifeguard blew his whistle to stop the kids from roughhousing by the pool.

救生員吹哨阻止小孩在游泳池旁邊打鬧。

⑭ **overtime** [ˋovɚˏtaɪm] ad 超時

He worked overtime last week to save enough money to buy Christmas gifts.

他上禮拜超時加班，為了要存足夠的錢買聖誕禮物。

⑮ **buzzer** [ˋbʌzɚ] n 蜂鳴器

The buzzer rang, and the class ended.

蜂鳴器響了，課程也結束了。

PATTERN ♪145-04

❺ **send up** 往上發送

Henry sent up a rescue flare, but no one came to help.

亨利朝天空發送了一顆求救信號彈但是沒人前來救援。

LEARN MORE! ♪145-05

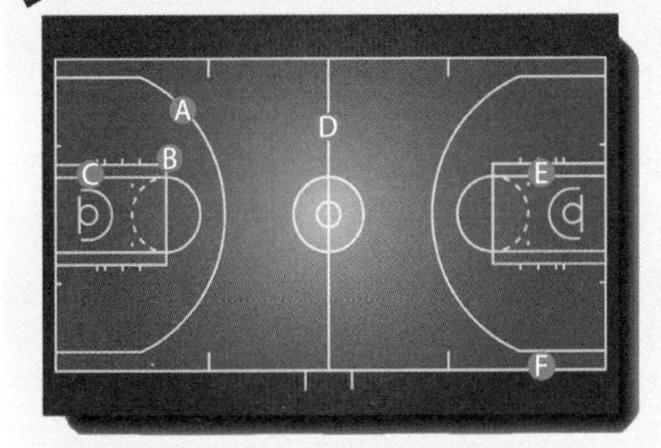

Ⓐ **three-point line / arc** 三分線
Ⓑ **free throw line** 罰球線
Ⓒ **backboard** 籃板
Ⓓ **center** 中間線
Ⓔ **restricted area** 禁區
Ⓕ **side line** 邊線

運動

棒球比賽（MLB）

exercise & sport

VOCABULARY ♪146-03

① **reader** [ˋridɚ] n 讀者

Our readers enjoy receiving the monthly magazine.
我們的讀者喜歡每個月收到雜誌。

② **tier** [tɪr] n 層級

The top tier of the company's management held a meeting.
公司最高階層的管理人員舉辦了一場會議。

③ **fundamental** [ˏfʌndəˋmɛntḷ] a 基本的、根本的

The fundamental reason we broke up was that he was seeing other people.
我們分手的根本原因是他同時跟別人約會。

PATTERN ♪146-04

❶ **are missing out** 錯過

I hope we aren't going to miss out by not going to the party.
希望我們不會因為沒參加派對而錯過什麼。

Article 3 棒球比賽（MLB）

♪146-01 For those **readers** ① out there that have never gotten into Major League Baseball, you **are missing out** ❶ ! Baseball, along with soccer, hockey, and football, is one of the world's most-watched sports. Kids the world over grow up **dreaming of** ❷ playing in the Major Leagues, which is the top **tier** ② of professional baseball.

那些從來沒有參與棒球大聯盟球賽的讀者們，你不知道你錯過了什麼！棒球跟足球、曲棍球還有橄欖球並列為世界最廣受觀看的運用賽事。全世界的小孩在成長過程中都夢想過在棒球大聯盟比賽，棒球大聯盟是專業棒球的最高層級。

♪146-02 More than likely, one of the main reasons you can't get into the game is that you may not know how it is played, and that makes it seem slow moving and boring to watch. Therefore, the best way to up your enjoyment is to get a **fundamental** ③ understanding of the game.

其中一個你無法了解棒球在幹嘛的主要原因很有可能是因為你不知道棒球的規則，所以棒球打起來感覺很慢又很無聊。所以為了讓你有辦法享受觀賽時的樂趣，最好的辦法就是對棒球比賽有基本的了解。

♪147-01 Baseball is a game played between two teams. One is the home team and the other is the visitor. A game is made up of nine **innings** ④ , and one inning is complete when both teams had a chance batted and had gotten three outs on defense. The team that isn't batting first at the top of the inning goes out into the **field** ⑤ . Their job is to get three of the batting team's players out.

棒球比賽是介於兩個球隊之間的比賽。其中一隊是地主隊，另一個則是客隊。一場球賽中有九局，當兩隊都有機會打擊，且有三人出局後結束完整一局。一局中的上半局非進攻的那一隊在場上的守備位置。他們的任務是讓攻擊球隊的三個打擊手出局。

♪147-02 There are nine players in the field with 6 in the infield and three in the outfield. The baseball infield has four bases and a pitcher's **mound** ⑥ (from where the pitcher throws to the batters). The infield positions are first base, second base, third base, Shortstop(between second and third), the pitcher and the catcher (who plays at home plate). The outfield has rightfield, centerfield, and leftfield **positions** ⑦ .

場上有九名球員，六名在內野，三名在外野。球場的內野區域有四個壘包跟一個投手丘（這是投手向打擊手投球的地方）。在內野的位置中，有一壘、二壘、三壘、二壘與三壘之間的位置和投手跟捕手（位於本壘板）的位置。在外野的部分則有右外野手、中外野手跟左外野手的位置。

♪147-03 The pitcher pitches to the batter by throwing the ball to the catcher. He wants to throw it fast or with some **trick** ⑧ styles to it so that it is hard for the batter to ❸ hit. The batter stands in the left or right batter's box to hit. If a pitch is good, the batter should be able to hit it because it's in his strike zone(an area above ❹ the plate between the batter's knees and the **midpoint** ⑨ of his torso).

投手向著打擊手的位置朝捕手投球，投手會想要投出快速球或是有變化的球讓打擊手難以打到。打擊手站在打擊區的左邊或是右邊來打擊。如果是好球，打擊手理當要能夠打到，因為球會落在他的打擊區（在打擊區上介於打擊手膝蓋跟身體中心之間的位置）。

VOCABULARY ♪147-04

④ **inning** [ˋɪnɪŋ] n （棒球中的）局

The top of the inning ended with the team scoring three runs.

上半局在球隊得三分後結束。

⑤ **field** [fild] n 球場

The team in the field worked hard to get the batters out.

球場上的球隊想辦法要讓擊球員出局。

⑥ **mound** [maʊnd] n 土堆、小丘

The burial mound was excavated by the students.

學生把墓塚挖了出來。

⑦ **position** [pəˋzɪʃən] n 位置

The players' positions were decided by the coach.

球員的位置由教練決定。

⑧ **trick** [trɪk] n 把戲

What tricks can we play to pick on my little brother ?

有什麼把戲我們可以用來捉弄我弟弟？

⑨ **midpoint** [ˋmɪd͵pɔɪnt] n 中點

The midpoint of the target is where to aim when you shoot.

目標的中點是你射擊時必須瞄準的地方。

PATTERN ♪147-05

❷ **dreaming of** 夢想、幻想

I've been dreaming all day of eating leftover birthday cake for dessert.

我整天都在幻想吃剩下來的生日蛋糕作為點心。

❸ **it is (+ adj) for (someone)+V** 某事對……是……

It is difficult for the team to find a way to win the game.

對這個團隊來說，要贏得比賽是很難的。

❹ **an area (+ prep)** ……的區域

The treasure chest is hidden in an area near the woods.

藏寶箱被藏在靠近森林的一個區域。

♪148-01 If the batter doesn't hit that good pitch, the Umpire will call it a strike. If the pitch isn't in the strike **zone** ⑩ and the batter doesn't **swing** ⑪ , the Umpire will call this a ball. Each batter gets 3 strikes and 4 balls to try and hit the ball and get on base. If they get 4 balls before they hit, they get to walk to first base. If they get 3 strikes before they hit, they are out. A full count is when you have 3 balls and 2 strikes, and the next pitch will determine whether you're out or on base.

如果打擊手沒有擊中好的投球，裁判會判其為好球。如果投出的球沒有落在打擊區而且打擊手沒有揮棒，裁判會判其為壞球。每個打擊手有三次好球跟四次壞球可以嘗試揮棒跟跑壘，如果他們揮棒前就有四壞球，他們可以移動到一壘；如果揮棒前就有三次好球，他們就三振出局。滿球數指的是你有三壞球跟兩好球，那麼緊接的下一球就會決定你是否出局還是留在壘上。

♪148-02 A batter wants to hit the ball and run around all the bases until they come back home. When they hit the ball, they run like **crazy** ⑫ because they need to get to the base before the base player gets the ball and **tags** ⑬ (touches them with the ball in their glove) them out.

打擊手的目標在於打中球之後跑過每一壘後回到本壘。當他們擊中球時，他們會瘋狂地跑起來，因為他們必須在防守方的球員接到球並把他們觸殺出局（用棒球手套內的棒球觸碰打擊手）之前跑到壘包上。

♪148-03 When a player hits, they are forced to run to first base, and when there is a force, the base player just needs to catch the ball and be on the base to get the batter out instead of needing to tag him. Batters also get out if they hit a fly ball (one in the air) or a line drive and a fielder **catches it before it** ❺ hits the ground.

當打擊手擊中球的時候，他們被迫跑向一壘，而當有封殺的狀況，防守球員只需要接到球並待在壘包上，不用觸碰到打擊手也可以讓他出局。如果打擊手打出了高飛球（球在高空中）或是平飛球，且讓野手在球落地前就接住的話，打擊手也會出局。

♪148-04 When the batting side gets three outs, the teams switch and the fielding team comes in to bat and that's called the bottom of the inning. After nine innings, the team with the highest score wins.

如果進攻方有三次出局，兩隊攻守互換，原本的防守方會變成打擊進攻的一方，下半局也隨之展開。九局比完後，分數最高的隊伍獲勝。

VOCABULARY ♪148-05

⑩ **zone** [zon] n 區域

Stay out of the danger zone to make sure you don't get shot.
遠離危險區域以確保你不會被射到。

⑪ **swing** [swɪŋ] v 揮動（某器具）打擊

The little girl swung a stick at the piñata to make the candy fall out.
小女孩用棍子打擊皮納塔玩具讓糖果掉出來。

⑫ **crazy** [ˋkrezɪ] a 瘋狂的、荒唐的

It's crazy how long we can spend talking on the phone.
我們可以在電話上講這麼久，真的很扯。

⑬ **tag** [tæg]
v 給……貼標籤、（遊戲中）碰觸你在追逐的某人

The boy tagged the girl and ran away because she was it.
男孩碰了女孩一下就跑走了。

PATTERN ♪148-06

❺ **catches it before it**
在它……之前抓住它

Eric caught the ball before it bounced on the ground.
艾瑞克在球彈到地面之前抓住它。

♪149-01 Although these are the **basics** ⑭ , there are so many more interesting elements to baseball such as stealing bases, double plays, home runs and so on that you should learn about. Now, it's time to grab a knowledgeable friend and catch the Cardinals, Orioles, or Cubs as they **knock** ⑮ it out of the park!

這些僅僅只基本規則，還有很多有趣的棒球規則要素，像是盜壘、雙殺、全壘打……等等你應該多學的。現在是時候找個懂棒球的朋友一起去看聖路易紅雀隊、巴爾的摩金鶯隊或是芝加哥小熊隊的比賽了，他們的球賽絕對會驚豔你！

QUIZ 閱讀測驗

1. Which is not mentioned as one of the most-watched sports?
(A) football (B) baseball (C) hockey (D) tennis

2. Why would you probably not like to watch a baseball game?
(A) It's boring. (B) You don't know how it's played.
(C) The players don't sign autographs. (D) It is too long.

3. How many players are there in the infield?
(A) Six (B) Nine (C) 12 (D) Three

4. What is a "full count" ?
(A) Batters on every base (B) Four balls
(C) Three strikes (D) Three balls and two strikes

1. 哪項沒被提及是最廣受觀看的運動之一？
(A) 足球 (B) 棒球 (C) 曲棍球 (D) 網球

2. 你為什麼有可能不喜歡看棒球比賽？
(A) 棒球比賽很無聊。 (B) 你不知道棒球是怎麼玩的。
(C) 球員不幫粉絲簽名。 (D) 比賽時間太長。

3. 內野有多少名球員？
(A) 六名 (B) 九名 (C) 十二名 (D) 三名

4. 什麼是「滿球數」？
(A) 每個壘包上都有打擊手 (B) 四壞球 (C) 三好球 (D) 三壞球兩好球

ANS: 1. (D) 2. (B) 3. (A) 4.(D)

VOCABULARY ♪149-02

⑭ **basic** [ˋbesɪk] n 基本、基礎
We need to get back to the basics in our relationship.
我們必須回歸我們關係中的基礎。

⑮ **knock** [nɑk] v 擊、打
Ellen knocked the eight ball into the corner pocket.
艾倫把八號球打進了底袋。

LEARN MORE! ♪149-03

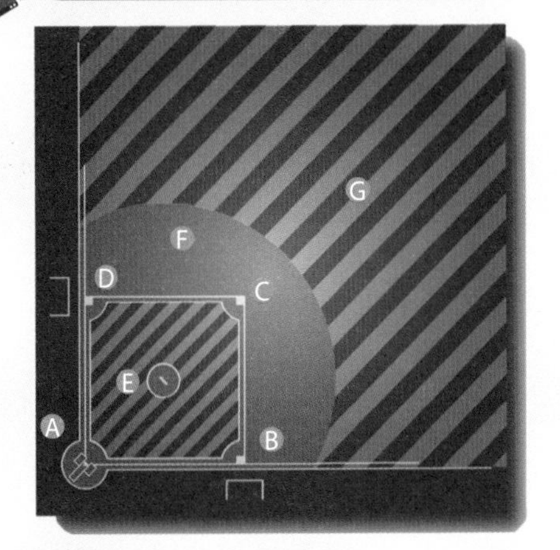

Ⓐ **home base** 本壘
Ⓑ **first base** 一壘
Ⓒ **second base** 二壘
Ⓓ **third base** 三壘
Ⓔ **pitcher's mound** 投手丘
Ⓕ **infield** 內野
Ⓖ **outfield** 外野

- **ROY (Rookie Of the Year)** 年度新人王
- **OBP (on base percentage)** 上壘率
- **PA (plate appearances)** 打席
- **SB (stolen bases)** 盜壘成功
- **SF (sacrifice flies)** 高飛犧牲打數
- **SO (strike outs)** 三振
- **SVOP (save opportunities)** 救援成功率
- **TBF (total batters faced)** 投球人次
- **WP (wild pitches)** 暴投

運動

2020 年奧運

exercise & sport

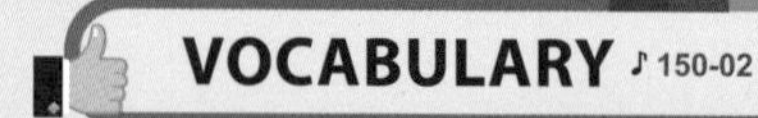

VOCABULARY ♪150-02

① **gather** [ˋgæðɚ] v 聚集

They gathered for the holidays to spend time together.
他們假日時聚集在一起相處。

② **travel** [ˋtrævl̩] v / n 旅行

The couple traveled to Hawaii for a second honeymoon.
這對情侶到夏威夷渡過他們第二次蜜月。

PATTERN ♪150-03

❶ **also known as** 以⋯⋯為人所知

Charles, also known as Charlie, is my best friend.
查理斯，也叫查理，是我最好的朋友。

Article 4 2020 年奧運

♪150-01 From July 24 to August 9 of 2020, the Games of the XXXII Olympiad, **also known as** ❶ the Summer Olympics, will be coming to Tokyo, Japan! During this time, people from all over the world will **gather**① to watch top amateur athletes compete in 339 events in 33 different sports. This is more than double the events held during the Winter Olympic Games. Athletes from 206 different countries will **travel**② to Japan to compete for a chance to "bring home the gold."

第三十二屆奧林匹克運動會（也稱作夏季奧運會），將於 2020 年 7 月 24 日到 8 月 9 日在日本東京舉行！這段期間世界各地的人將會聚集一堂來觀賞專業運動員在 33 項運動項目中的 339 場賽事，這跟冬季奧林匹克的賽事比起來足足多了兩倍之多。來自 206 個不同國家的運動員都會飛到日本來參加奧運，希望把「金牌帶回家」。

♪151-01 Japan won the **ballot** ③ against Turkey and Spain to get the honor of hosting the 2020 event. This will be the forth time Japan has hosted the Olympics and the second time to host the Summer Olympics with the last Summer Olympics held in Tokyo in 1964.

日本在票數上勝過土耳其跟西班牙，贏得 2020 奧運盛事的主辦權，這將會是日本第四次主辦奧林匹克運動會，也是日本第二次主辦夏季奧運會，日本東京上次舉辦夏季奧運會已經是 1964 年的事。

♪151-02 The Olympics **originated** ④ in Greece in 776 BC and **were held** every four years **until** ❷ around 400 AD. In the earliest times, the Games were held for religious celebrations and to gather Greeks from far and wide.

奧林匹克運動會起始於西元前 776 年的希臘，之後就一直每四年舉辦一次直到西元後 400 年。在最一開始的時候，運動比賽是因為宗教慶祝的原因而舉辦，這場盛事聚集各處到來的希臘人。

♪151-03 **Offerings** ⑤ were made to Zeus during the five-day festival, and more than 40,000 people would come to watch each day of the games which include jumping, throwing, running, wrestling, chariot racing and pankration(a mix of wrestling and boxing). All participants competed naked, **were covered in** ❸ oil for some events, and there were no time limits for the boxing.

為期五天的慶祝中，祭品會貢獻給宙斯且會有超過 40,000 人前來觀看每天的競賽，包括跳高、投擲、賽跑、摔角、戰車比賽和潘克拉辛（摔角跟拳擊的結合）。在某些賽事中參賽者是全身抹油且裸體的狀況下跟彼此競爭，拳擊比賽來說的話則沒有時間限制。

VOCABULARY ♪151-04

③ **ballot** [ˋbælət] n 選票 v 投票、選票

The city council's election ballot ended in a tie.

市議會的選舉票數最後打平。

④ **originate** [əˋrɪdʒə͵net] v 起源、開創

The problem originated in the engine but spread to the pistons.

問題來自引擎，但也影響了活塞。

⑤ **offering** [ˋɔfərɪŋ] n 後代

The religious believers left offerings for the gods,

信仰宗教的人把後代交給神明。

PATTERN ♪151-05

❷ **were held (weekly, every year,⋯) until**
舉辦（每週／每年⋯⋯）直到⋯⋯

Classes were held weekly until the end of the semester

課堂會每週舉行直到學期末。

❸ **was covered in** 被⋯⋯覆蓋

The yard was covered in leaves from the maple tree.

花園被楓樹的樹葉覆蓋著。

VOCABULARY ♪152-04

⑥ **element** [ˋɛləmənt]
n 元素、要素、部分

There are elements in his personality that make him so handsome to others.

他的個性中有一些要素，使他對其他人來說非常的帥氣。

⑦ **vastly** [ˋvæstlɪ] ad 大量地

There are vastly different personalities.

人的性格中有大量的差異。

⑧ **cost** [kɔst] v 喪失、付出

Yvonne's dance cost Frieda her chance at the lead.

伊馮娜的舞蹈表演使芙蕾達喪失了她領先的地位。

⑨ **development** [dɪˋvɛləpmənt]
n 發展

The development of the project relies on everyone in the office.

這個計畫的發展倚靠辦公室裡的每一個人。

⑩ **venue** [ˋvɛnju] n 會場

Music venues tend to be great places to meet new friends.

音樂會場是個容易交新朋友的好地方。

⑪ **renovate** [ˋrɛnə͵vet] v 翻新

Grant renovated the old building over the summer.

格蘭特利用夏天時間翻新了舊大樓。

♪152-01 In other words so many **elements** ⑥ from the ancient Games have changed **vastly** ⑦ from those of today. Competitors now do ❹ wear clothes, women compete in the Olympics, and chariot racing is no longer an Olympic sport.

換句話說，古代希臘運動賽事中的元素在現代運動項目中已經大大地轉變。現在的參賽者肯定會穿衣服，女性也在奧林匹克中與他人競賽，而戰車競賽已經不再是比賽項目之一。

♪152-02 Hosting this year's Olympic Games will **cost** ⑧ Japan more than 25 billion dollars. Much of this will be spent on the **development** ⑨ of a better transportation infrastructure, such as a new railway line as well as a significant amount going to venue development.

主辦今年的奧運將會花費日本多於 250 億美元的金額。大部分的金額將花費於開發更好的大眾交通建設，像是新的鐵路路線，也有大筆金額將投入運動會場的準備。

♪152-03 The 2020 Olympic Games will have around 30 **venues** ⑩ for events in and around the Tokyo area–some of which are already built, some are being built, and the rest are being **renovated** ⑪ .

為了 2020 的奧林匹克運動會，東京地區將會有大概 30 個運動會場用來舉辦賽事，有些會場已經蓋好，有些還正在蓋，剩下的則是正在進行翻新的工作。

♪153-01 The efforts made by countries that host the Olympic Games is immense and not always worth the financial investment. One example of this was the recent Rio Games held in Brazil in 2016. The games cost Brazil 50% more than **predicted** ⑫ and attendance was low because of zika fears and warnings of violence barely being kept under control by the military. So, while the Games do give a country a place in history, sometimes it is a great economic **loss** ⑬ .

舉辦奧林匹克運動會的國家耗費巨大心力與財力，而且也不往往值得其財務上的投資。其中一例子是 2016 年在巴西舉辦的里約熱內盧奧運會，舉辦奧運的花費比原本預估的多出了百分之五十，而且因為當時茲卡病毒和軍隊勉強才控制暴力警示消息的關係，參加的人很少。所以說，即使奧林匹克運動會可以為一個國家在歷史上留下足跡，有時候帶來的經濟損失也是很慘重。

♪153-02 One way the games can **counter** ⑭ this is through ticket and memorabilia sales. Tickets to events will start at $70 and will go to $1,300 or more for tickets to the event finals.

一種可以對抗這個問題的方式就是透過賣門票跟紀念商品。賽事門票的價格從 70 美元到 1300 美元，決賽的門票價格甚至會更高。

♪154-03 A mascot has been selected by Japanese schoolchildren. **Adorable** ⑮ mascot Miraitowa looks like a Pokémon and Miraitowa's name is a combination of the Japanese words for future and eternity.

日本的學童們已經票選出了奧運吉祥物，可愛的ミライトワ（Miraitowa）看起來就像寶可夢裡面的神奇寶貝，吉祥物 Miraitowa 的名字是日本語中未來跟永遠這兩個字意的結合。

VOCABULARY ♪153-04

⑫ **predict** [prɪˋdɪkt] v 預測

It was predicted that Carrie would win the race for class president.

據測凱芮會贏得這次班長的競選。

⑬ **loss** [lɔs] n 失去、遺失

The loss of a month's salary because of injury left Craig depressed.

因為受傷的緣故而失去一個月的薪水，讓克雷格很憂鬱。

⑭ **counter** [ˋkaʊntɚ] v 對抗

We need to counter the loss of finances by developing a new merchandise line.

我們必須藉由發展新的商品線來對抗財務損失。

⑮ **adorable** [əˋdorəbḷ] a 可愛宜人的

The adorable stuffed animal was an awesome gift.

這可愛的填充動物娃娃是一個很棒的禮物。

PATTERN ♪153-05

❹ **now do**
現在更……（do 強調後面所接的動詞）

People now do believe in the importance of saving money for retirement.

現在人們更確信為退休存錢的重要性。

♪154-01 Soon copies of Olympic medals, mascot stuffed animals, T-shirts and more will be available for purchase and will surely help to recoup some of the hosting expenses.

不久後奧運獎牌的複製品、吉祥物填充玩具、T 恤跟其他更多商品將會推出，這肯定可以幫助彌補一些主辦奧運的花費。

♪154-02 The Games themselves are always mesmerizing to watch. Athletes that are in peak physical condition and that have dedicated years of their lives to training for their sport will compete to be the best. Softball and baseball will return to the 2020 Games after being removed in 2008.

奧林匹克運動會的賽事一直都是很吸引人觀看的，在最佳體能狀態且投入多年訓練的運動員將齊聚一堂來一較高下。自從 2008 年後被取消的壘球跟棒球將回到 2020 的運動項目中。

♪154-03 And the 2020 Games will introduce four new events—karate, sport climbing, surfing, and skateboarding—to bring the total number of sports that you can feast your eyes on to 33. Now the only thing left to do is go online and get your tickets and plan your Japan getaway!

2020 的奧運會也引進了四種新的運動項目：空手道、運動攀岩、衝浪和滑板運動，總共加起來有 33 個運動項目讓你大飽眼福。現在你要唯一要做的就是趕緊上網買票跟開始計劃日本奧運之旅！

QUIZ 閱讀測驗

1. Where will the XXXII Olympiad be held?

(A) Japan (B) Brazil (C) Turkey (D) Spain

2. Which is not a sport being introduced at the 2020 Olympics?

(A) skateboarding (B) karate (C) sumo wrestling (D) surfing

1. 第三十二屆奧林匹克運動會將在哪裡舉行？

(A) 日本 (B) 巴西 (C) 土耳其 (D) 西班牙

2. 哪一項不是 2020 年奧運會上引進的運動項目？

(A) 滑板運動 (B) 空手道 (C) 相撲 (D) 衝浪

ANS: 1. (A) 2. (C)

Skill!!
撰寫 500 字作文的寫作技巧

500-700 字左右文章通常會含括三到四個段落：前言（introduction）、內文（body）和結論（conclusion）等段落。接下來使用「健康」為主題來做講解。

前言（introduction）

用來吸引讀者、說明主題，必須包含論點（Thesis Statement），告知讀者以及提醒作者文章的內容。例如：

・Health is not the absence of disease. 健康不是不生病而已。

※ 使用反傳統思維的寫作方式吸引讀者的注意力。

・Health is defined by the World Health Organization as "a state of complete physical, mental and social well-being." 世界衛生組織（WHO）定義健康為「完整的身體、心智和社會福祉狀態」。

※ 使用專家機構的定義，增加讀者興趣及可信度。

內文（body）

陳述論點，進一步深入討論。內文依照字數，會涵括幾個支持段落（supporting paragraphs），每個段落一開始就要有主題句（Topic Sentence），摘要說明段落的大意。例如：

・To be healthy, we shall focus on improving well-being rather than treating diseases.
要健康，我們必須提升福祉，而不是治療疾病。

※ 進一步使用反傳統思維概念來做為支持。

・We shall adopt new methods to maintain our health. 我們應該採用新方法來維持健康。

※ 提出建議來說明如何保健。

・Keeping a healthy lifestyle, caring for mental health, and achieving economic harmony in society are ways to ensure our health.
保持健康的生活方式、關注心理健康及實現社會上的經濟和諧是確保我們健康的方法。

※ 實際舉例說明健康的方式。

結論（conclusion）

重複論點或提出解決方式或相關建議做為總結。

・According to WHO, we need to care for our physical, mental, and social welfare if we would like to be healthy. 依據 WHO 的定義，我們如果要健康，就必須照顧我們的身體、心智與社會福祉。

※ 總結與重複論點。

依據以上的論點、主題句和總結句再做論點衍伸就可以完成一篇 500-700 字左右的文章了。

新聞

美國總統大選

news

① **simpler** [ˋsɪmpl̩ɚ] a 更簡單的

Cursive is a simpler way to write quickly.

草寫是讓書寫快速更簡單的方法。

② **recent** [ˋrisn̩t] a 最近的

The recent fight left the couple not on speaking terms.

這對情侶最近的爭吵，讓他們不跟彼此說話。

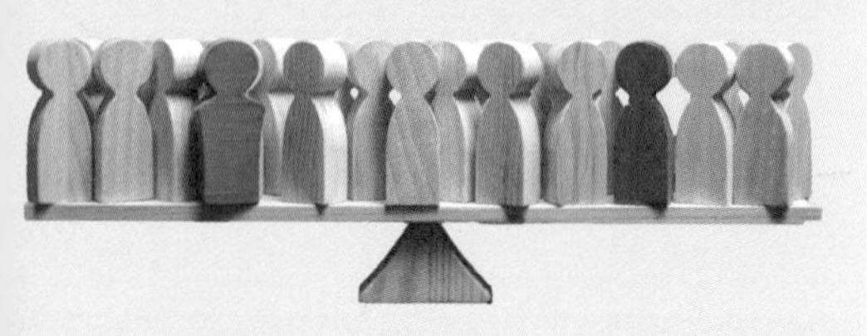

♪002-01

美國總統大選

♪156-01 US Presidential elections of the days of old seem a bit like **simpler** ① things compared to more **recent** ② elections. In the past, the way to win the presidential election was to get out and talk to as many people as possible about your platform and why your platform was better than your opponent's.

跟最近的選舉比起來，過往的美國總統大選看起來似乎是比較簡單的事。在過去要贏得總統選舉的方式，不外乎就是走出來並且跟愈多人講你的政見愈好，以及為什麼你的政見比你的競選對手來得好。

♪157-01 During those days ❶ , a way to get out and talk to the people was to take a train ride across areas of the country and give speeches as you would go ❷ . This was a **method** ③ used effectively by Abraham Lincoln.

在那些過往的日子中，走出來跟人群對話的方式就是搭火車在全國上下走透透並發表演講，亞伯拉罕．林肯就是一個有效使用這個方法的人物例子。

♪157-02 Today, the goal is still to get your platform out to as many people as possible ❸ , but money tends to be a huge **influencer** ④ in determining who wins an election. More times than not, the person that can amass the greatest amount of campaign finances is the one most likely to win the election.

現今的選舉目標一樣是想辦法讓你的政見給愈多人知道愈好，但是財力多寡傾向於變成誰可以贏得選舉的巨大影響關鍵。大多情況上來說，可以募得最高額競選資金的人也是最有可能贏得選舉的人。

♪157-03 This comes in part because the person with more campaign money can use it in many ways to **benefit** ⑤ his campaign. For example, the more money you have available, the larger campaign team you can hire to **oversee** ⑥ the volunteers.

部分原因在於有最多競選資金的人可以多方面運用這些資金使自己的競選造勢活動得利。舉例來說，你如果有愈多可運用的資金，你就可以雇用更大的競選團隊來監督自願者。

VOCABULARY ♪157-04

③ **method** [ˋmɛθəd] n 方法

One method to clean is to just thrown everything away.

清理的一種方式就是把全部的東西都丟掉。

④ **influencer** [ˋɪnfluənsɚ] n 影響者、有影響力的人

The stances on the environment will be a big influencer in this election.

對環境議題的態度，將會是影響這場選舉的關鍵。

⑤ **benefit** [ˋbɛnəfɪt] n 利益、好處

The benefit of makeup is that it can hide wrinkle.

化妝的好處是可以遮蓋住皺紋。

⑥ **oversee** [ˋovɚˋsi] v 監督、監察

We need a supervisor to oversee the process.

我們需要一名主管來監看過程。

PATTERN ♪157-05

❶ **during those days** 在那些日子中

During those days when we were young, we spent our days outside.

那些我們還年輕的日子中，我們都待在外頭。

❷ **as you go** 當你走……

As you go down the hall, please turn out the lights.

當你走過走廊，請把燈都關掉。

❸ **as many (N) as possible** 愈多愈好

We need to gather as many lightning bugs as possible.

我們需要捕捉到愈多螢火蟲愈好。

VOCABULARY ♪158-04

⑦ **gathering** [ˋgæðərɪŋ]
n 聚會、聚集

Town hall gatherings are a great place for people to express themselves.

市政廳的聚會是一個讓人們發表意見的好地方。

⑧ **cynical** [ˋsɪnɪk!] a 憤世嫉俗的

A cynical person rarely sees the good in people.

一個憤世嫉俗的人，很難相信人有好的一面。

⑨ **mantra** [ˋmʌntrə]
n 口號、（冥想或祈禱時反覆說的）咒語

My mantra is to chill out and take life easy.

我的咒語是放輕鬆跟輕鬆看待一切。

⑩ **term** [tɝm] n 任期

The president's term in office lasts four years.

總統的任期有四年。

⑪ **element** [ˋɛləmənt] n 元素、要素

One element of the problem is your inability to listen.

問題因素在於你缺乏聆聽的能力。

♪158-01 The more money, the more campaign fliers, posters, banners, buttons and whatnot you can buy. The more money, the bigger speech **gatherings** ⑦ you can throw to reach out to more voters. And the more money, the bigger parties you can throw to attract the big money and powerful people to vote for you.

愈多資金就代表著愈多競選單、海報、旗幟、胸章跟諸如此類可買的東西；愈多資金就代表著你可以舉辦更大的演説活動，把觸角深入更多選民；愈多資金就代表著你可以組織更大的造勢活動，來吸引更多資金以及有權勢的人投票給你。

♪158-02 It would be **cynical** ⑧ to say that elections are only about money because they are also definitely about the platforms you choose, too. A very wealthy candidate that doesn't know what the citizens of the country want and worry about will not be a likely winner.

如果説選舉就真的只是跟錢有關就有點太憤世嫉俗，因為要贏得選舉絕對也跟你選擇的政見立場有關。一個很有錢的競選人，如果不知道國家市民想要什麼，跟擔心什麼的話，也不太可能會是贏家。

♪158-03 But a candidate that has understood what the public is interested in and tells the people that he will fight for these things is going to be a very strong candidate.

但如果是一個了解大眾關注的利益在哪裡，且告訴人民他會奮力為大家博取這些權利的候選人，就會是很有希望的候選人。

♪159-01 **Whether the focus is on** ❹ bringing jobs back to America from overseas, raising the minimum wage, improving gun laws, a candidate is doing best when his **mantra** ⑨ is, "what the people want, the people get." These promises to the people are called campaign promises, and that's all they really are, promises.

無論政見重心是在於把工作機會帶回美國本土、提高最低薪資還是改善槍枝管制法，一個候選人最佳的競選策略就是當他奉行的口號是「人們要什麼，就可以得到什麼」。這些給選民的承諾被稱作為競選時的承諾，這也說明了一切，就只是承諾。

♪159-02 The elected president is not required by law to fulfill all of his campaign promises but often, if he wants to get reelected and have a second **term** ⑩ in office, he will need to show that he is **making an effort to** ❺ make those promises a reality.

勝選的總統在法律約束上是不用兌現他當初承諾的競選政見，但大多時候如果他想要再次獲選且有第二次總統任期，他必須展現他有努力要兌現這些承諾。

♪159-03 One other **element** ⑪ that has not really changed in campaigns but has for sure been more in the spotlight with the 2016 US Presidential Election is that of talking down about your opponents. Political mudslinging as it is often known as is a method of saying your opponent is all sorts of terrible, negative, unsafe things that would be bad for the country.

還有一項在競選活動中沒有真的改變過，但反而在 2016 總統大選中被更加受到注目的是貶低你的對手。政治毀謗最為人所知的就是盡說你的對手是那些糟糕、負面且證據不足的事，說服大家這些事會對國家造成負面影響。

PATTERN ♪159-04

❹ **whether the focus is on**
是否重點在於……

Ask yourself whether the focus is on the right problem.

你要問問自己是否有把重點放在對的問題上。

❺ **making an effort to**
努力做……

I'm making an effort to help him with his homework.

我正在努力幫他用他作業的東西。

LEARN MORE! ♪159-05

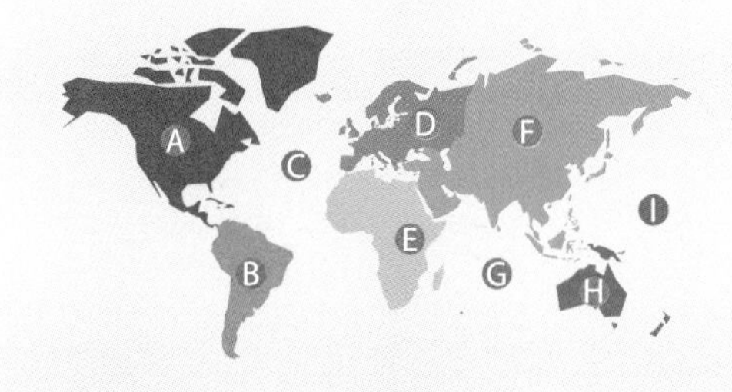

- Ⓐ **North America** 北美洲
- Ⓑ **South America** 南美洲
- Ⓒ **Atlantic Ocean** 大西洋
- Ⓓ **Europe** 歐洲
- Ⓔ **Africa** 非洲
- Ⓕ **Asia** 亞洲
- Ⓖ **Indian Ocean** 印度洋
- Ⓗ **Oceania** 大洋洲
- Ⓘ **Pacific Ocean** 太平洋

美國政治 U.S.A politics

美國是個聯邦制的共和國家，依據美國憲法，總統、國會、法院共同擁有聯邦政府的權力。而美國的兩大政黨分別為共和黨（Republican Party）、民主黨（Democratic Party），從美國內戰之後，這兩黨便一直主導與控制美國的政治。

♪160-01 Great politicians try to steer away from this very low level of engagement because the character assassination just makes the campaign very base and **pathetic** ⑫ . However, sadly, the problem is that this negative campaigning often works.

好的政治人物會試著遠離這種很低級的活動，因為這種詆毀他人人格的作法只會讓競選活動變得很粗糙且可悲。然而，令人難過的是這樣子負面的競選手段通常會奏效。

♪160-02 Such was the case with Trump in his **tirades** ⑬ against Hillary Clinton in the 2016 elections. He cut and cut and cut, and left many people believing that Hillary was a dangerous **option** ⑭. Hillary tried to follow Michelle Obama's tenet of "when they go low, we go high" but sadly, the pettier style got more attention and votes.

例如在 2016 年的選舉中，川普就是用他的長篇抨擊演說對付希拉蕊．克林頓。他滔滔不絕地一直說，進而讓許多人相信希拉蕊真的是一個危險的候選人。希拉蕊嘗試遵循蜜雪兒的信條：「他們往低處走的話，我們就往高處前進」。但很遺憾的，這種小心眼的手段得到更多注目跟選票。

♪160-03 The hope in the end is for a **fair** ⑮ election, with no meddling from other world governments and with candidates focusing on the platform and not the denigration of the competition. Whether this will be possible during the 2020 election process remains to be seen.

最後我們希望的是一場公平的選舉，沒有其他國家政府的干預，且候選人可以專注於他們的政見而非比賽誰更會詆毀他人。我們就看看這是否可以在 2020 年的選舉中實現了。

VOCABULARY ♪160-04

⑫ **pathetic** [pə`θɛtɪk] a 可悲的、可憐的、差勁的

It is pathetic to not bring a gift to a party.

沒有帶禮物到派對上是很差勁的。

⑬ **tirade** [`taɪˏred] n 長篇抨擊性演說

His tirades left his employees in fear.

他長篇大論的抨擊使他的員工們處於恐懼。

⑭ **option** [`ɑpʃən] n 選擇、選項

One option we could consider is moving.

我們可以考慮的一個選項是搬走。

⑮ **fair** [fɛr] a 公平的

It's not fair to leave Alan here alone.

讓艾倫一個人待在這是不公平的。

美國國旗由紅、白、藍三色組成，分別表示勇氣、真理、正義。

- 13 條紅白間紋：表示美國最早建國時的 13 個殖民地。
- 50個白色五角星：代表美國的50個洲。

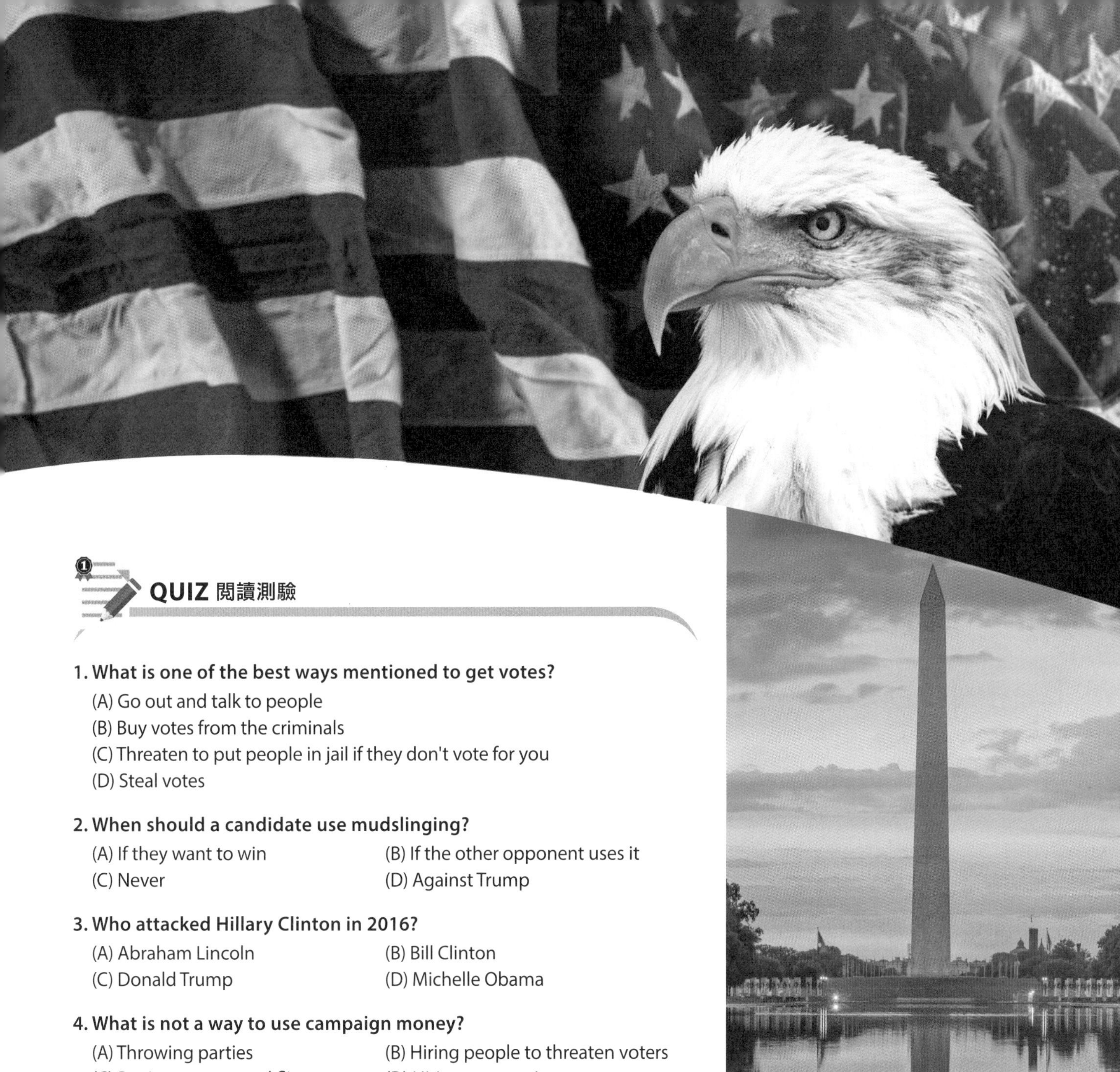

QUIZ 閱讀測驗

1. What is one of the best ways mentioned to get votes?

(A) Go out and talk to people
(B) Buy votes from the criminals
(C) Threaten to put people in jail if they don't vote for you
(D) Steal votes

2. When should a candidate use mudslinging?

(A) If they want to win
(B) If the other opponent uses it
(C) Never
(D) Against Trump

3. Who attacked Hillary Clinton in 2016?

(A) Abraham Lincoln
(B) Bill Clinton
(C) Donald Trump
(D) Michelle Obama

4. What is not a way to use campaign money?

(A) Throwing parties
(B) Hiring people to threaten voters
(C) Buying posters and fliers
(D) Hiring a campaign team

1. 文中提及獲得選票的最佳方法之一是什麼？

(A) 出去和人交談
(B) 收買犯罪分子的選票
(C) 如果他們不投票給你，就威脅把人關進監獄
(D) 偷選票

2. 候選人何時應該使用政治誹謗？

(A) 如果他們想贏
(B) 如果其他對手使用此方法
(C) 決不使用
(D) 反對川普

3. 誰在 2016 年總統競選活動中抨擊希拉蕊．柯林頓？

(A) 亞伯拉罕．林肯
(B) 比爾．柯林頓
(C) 唐納．川普
(D) 蜜雪兒．歐巴馬

4. 什麼不是使用競選資金的方式？

(A) 舉辦造勢活動
(B) 僱用人來威脅選民
(C) 購買海報和傳單
(D) 聘請競選團隊

ANS: 1. (A) 2. (C) 3. (C) 4.(B)

新聞

news

全球暖化

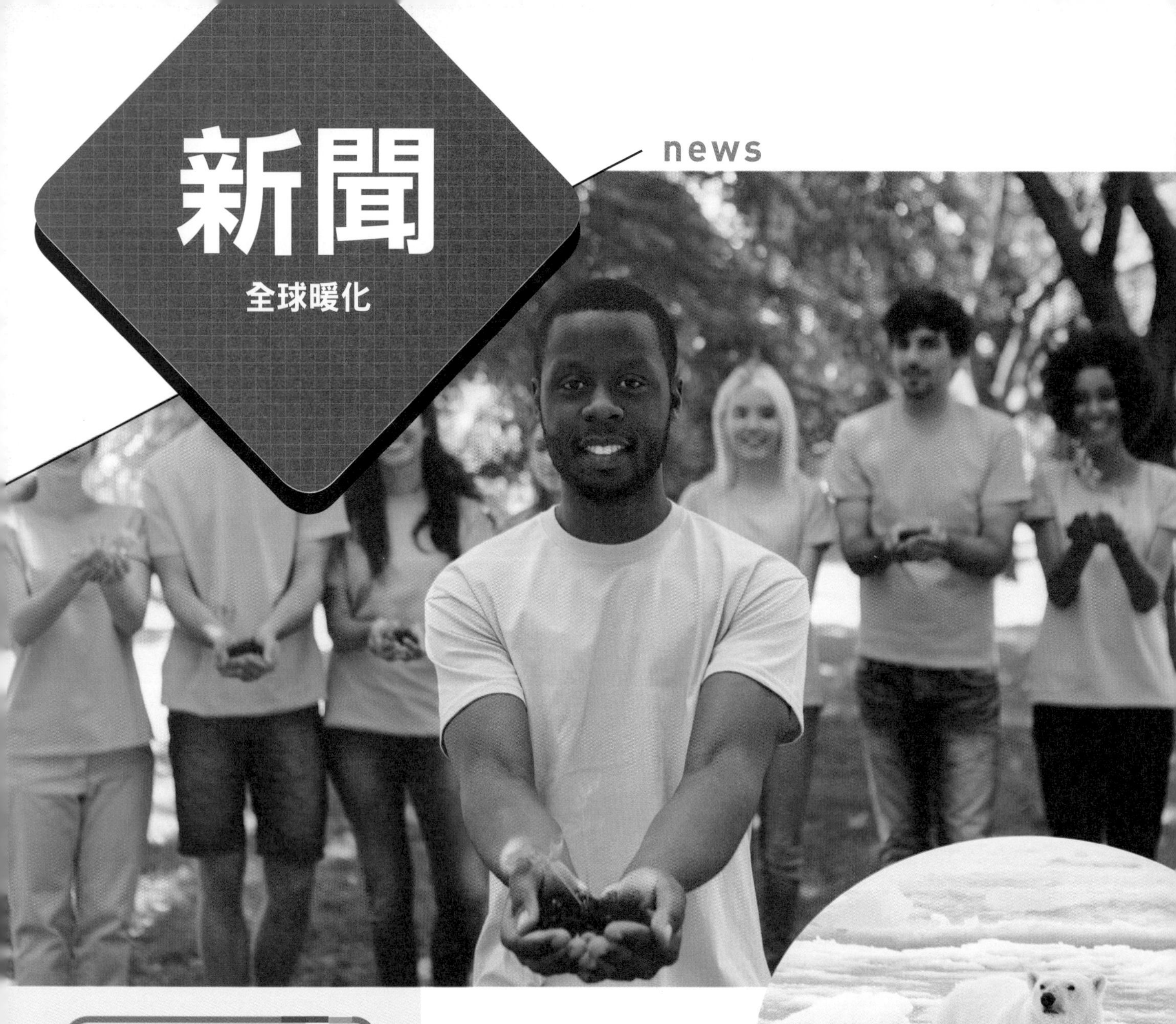

VOCABULARY ♪162-02

① **heating** [ˋhitɪŋ] n 暖氣設備

The heating in this car isn't great.

這台車的暖氣設備不好。

② **primarily** [praɪˋmɛrəlɪ] ad 主要

He is primarily at home during the day.

他白天主要待在家裡。

PATTERN ♪162-03

❶ **that's for sure** 那是當然的

I have a huge headache, that's for sure.

我的頭真的是很痛。

Article 2 全球暖化

♪162-01 The world is **heating** ① up, that's for sure ❶ . And scientists believe the reason behind it is **primarily** ② related to human activities. Humans driving cars and scooters; humans taking planes, trains, and buses; humans using air conditioners and burning fossil fuels increase greenhouse gases.

可以很確定的是這個世界燒起來了。而科學家相信這背後的原因主要是跟人類活動有關。人們開車跟騎摩托車；人們搭飛機、火車跟公車；人們使用冷氣跟燃燒化石燃料，這些行為都增加了溫室氣體。

♪163-01 Global warming is primarily a problem of there being too much carbon dioxide in the **atmosphere** ③ . This CO2 stays for a long time without **dissipating** ④ , and that creates something like a **blanket** ⑤ effect, where heat is trapped in, and it heats up the planet. If this situation isn't addressed seriously and immediately, the world as we know it is going to go through some **drastic** ⑥ changes.

全球暖化基本上就是有太多的二氧化碳在大氣層中的問題。二氧化碳會在大氣層中停留很長一段時間且不會自行消散，導致一種像是雲毯效應的結果，指當熱能被保存在雲朵中進而升溫地球的現象。如果沒有馬上嚴肅認真地看待此問題，我們所熟悉的世界將會經歷劇烈的改變。

♪163-02 **Evidence** ⑦ exists that just a 2 degree Celsius increase from our current temperature will start to manifest in serious issues. Those 2-degrees would cause a sea level rise of at least 1.8 feet. This might not seem like much, but for many **coastal** ⑧ regions, this will spell disaster.

證據指出現有氣溫只單單升高攝氏兩度，一些嚴重的問題就會開始顯現出來。這兩度會導致海平面上升至少 1.8 英尺，感覺起來不多，但其實對許多沿岸地區，這意味著巨大災難。

VOCABULARY ♪163-03

③ **atmosphere** [ˋætməsˏfɪr] n 氣氛

The atmosphere in this room seems a little off.

這房間的氣氛似乎有點不對。

④ **dissipate** [ˋdɪsəˏpet] v （使）逐漸消失

I hope his anger will dissipate some soon.

我希望他會快點消氣。

⑤ **blanket** [ˋblæŋkɪt] n 毯子

The blanket felt perfect wrapped around her legs.

包覆在她腳上的毯子感覺很棒。

⑥ **drastic** [ˋdræstɪk] a 嚴厲的、猛烈的、激烈的

This is a drastic decision you've made.

你做的這個決定很嚴重。

⑦ **evidence** [ˋɛvədəns] n 證據

The evidence points to Alexander being a thief.

證據指出亞歷山大是個小偷。

⑧ **coastal** [ˋkostḷ] a 海岸的、沿海的

I am always drawn to coastal locations.

我總是被沿岸的地點吸引。

♪164-01 Coral bleaching, the removal of algae from coral and leaving them **vulnerable** ⑨ will happen **to virtually all** ❷ coral with a 2-degree temperature increase. Two degrees will cause there to be an ice-free Arctic summer at least once a decade. 2.7 billion people will be affected by **extreme** ⑩ heat waves once every five years with a 2-degree increase, and there will be a 170% increase in flood risk and an increase in the spread of disease.

珊瑚白化（共生海藻的離開或死亡）的現象隨著攝氏兩度的上升，幾乎會讓所有的珊瑚變得脆弱不堪一擊。這兩度也會導致至少十年一次的夏天北極是無冰狀態。這兩度也將讓全球 27 億人至少每五年一次受到極端熱浪的影響，同時也會提升洪水災難的風險到百分之一百七十以及提升疾病傳染的機會。

♪164-02 Our planet's **wildlife** ⑪ habitat will also suffer with 18% of insects, 16% of plants, and 8% of vertebrates at risk of losing more than 50% of their habitats. To put it **mildly** ⑫, the 2-degree increase will cause disaster.

我們地球野生動物的棲息地也會受到影響，百分之十八的昆蟲、百分之十六的植物跟百分之八的脊椎動物都將面臨損失至少一半以上棲息地的風險。保守地說，這兩度的上升將會造成災難。

♪164-03 Places like Venice and areas that are low lying like Singapore are going to be significantly affected. The distressing part of it is that many people don't seem to **be willing to believe** ❸ those two measly degrees can do so much damage. **Most likely, it will** ❹ take people feeling it on a local level to comprehend the gravity, and the worry is that then it might be too late.

像是威尼斯或是跟新加坡一樣低窪的地區將會嚴重地被影響。感到挫折的是大部分的人似乎不願意相信這僅僅兩度可以造成如此巨大傷害。當這兩度的上升影響到人們的生活，他們可能才會意識到這兩度的嚴重性，但令人擔憂的是到時候才意識到已經太晚了。

VOCABULARY ♪164-04

⑨ **vulnerable** [ˋvʌlnərəbl̩] a 脆弱的

His deceit left me feeling vulnerable.

他的欺騙讓我感到很受傷。

⑩ **extreme** [ɪkˋstrim] a 極端的

The extreme weather this year has been distressing to see.

今年極端的氣候讓我很煩。

⑪ **wildlife** [ˋwaɪld͵laɪf] n 野生動植物

Wildlife parks are good in theory but usually terrible in practice.

野生動物園這樣的地方理論上是好的，但通常實際上很糟糕。

⑫ **mildly** [ˋmaɪldlɪ] ad 略微地、溫和地

I am annoyed, to put it mildly.

講好聽一點就是我有點惱怒。

PATTERN ♪164-05

❷ **to virtually all** 實際上全部

I sent out Christmas cards to virtually all of my friends.

我寄聖誕卡片給幾乎我全部的朋友。

❸ **be willing to believe** 願意相信

I am willing to believe that the Earth is round.

我願意相信地球是圓的。

❹ **most likely, it will** 很有可能，某事將會……

Most likely, it will take several weeks to clean this place up.

要完全清理這個地方，很有可能要花幾週的時間。

♪165-01 So, what can be done? People in developing countries tend to have a lower carbon footprint overall than people in places like the US, but that doesn't mean it's not important to change your lifestyle anyway.

那麼，可以做些什麼？住在開發中國家的人跟其他國家的人比起來（例如美國）整體上傾向於製造較少的碳足跡，但這也不代表對他們來說改變生活型態不是件重要的事。

♪165-02 So, if you are living in the US (or elsewhere in the world), there are some things you can do to improve your carbon footprint. **Your** carbon footprint **means** ⑤ the amount of carbon dioxide **released** ⑬ into the atmosphere because of person's or community's actions. So, the most elemental fix-it is to focus on reducing your individual carbon footprint.

所以說，如果你是住在美國（或是世界上其他地方），你可以藉由付出一些行動來減少你的碳足跡。你的碳足跡指的就是因為個人或是社群活動所製造且排放進入大氣層的二氧化碳含量。因此最基本該做的事就是專注於減少你個人的碳足跡。

♪165-03 You can start by driving a low carbon vehicle, like an electric car. When driving, unnecessary acceleration ups your gas consumption and therefore, your carbon footprint, so slow down and take it easy.

你可以從開低碳排放的汽車開始，像是電動車。開車時那些沒有必要的加速都會增加汽油消耗，這也意味著你的碳足跡將會上升，所以請慢下來且輕鬆開。

VOCABULARY ♪165-04

⑬ **release** [rɪˋlis] v 發布、公開

The director released an uncut version of the film.

導演公布了一刀未剪版本的電影。

PATTERN ♪165-05

⑤ **your (N / V) means**
你的……代表……

Your silence means you are angry at me.

你的沈默代表你正在對我生氣。

LEARN MORE! ♪165-06

solar panel
太陽能

electric tower
電塔

electricity
電力

wind power
風力發電

drilling well
鑽井

oil
石油

VOCABULARY ♪166-04

⑭ **avoid** [əˋvɔɪd] v 避免

I want to avoid getting in her way.

我想要避免阻擋她的去路。

⑮ **appliance** [əˋplaɪəns] n 電器用品

These appliances make life a lot easier.

這些電器用品讓生活更簡單便利。

LEARN MORE! ♪166-05

現在全球暖化的情形愈來愈嚴重，有時候冬天也過得像夏天，冷氣都快要變成珍品了呢！值得注意的是，air conditioner 指的是一台冷氣的機器，而 air conditioning 指的是空調的系統喔！

- Would you mind if I turn on the air conditioner?

  你介意我開冷氣嗎？
- The air conditioning has broken down.

  空調壞了。
- The air conditioning is not working!

  空調無法運作！
- We have central air conditioning.

  我們有中央空調。
- The office includes air-conditioning.

  這間辦公室有附空調。
- Since she felt cold, she turned off the air conditioner.

  她覺得冷，所以把冷氣關掉了。

♪166-01 **Avoid** ⑭ traffic to not waste gas and produce fumes. Combine errands so that you go on one trip out to do six things instead of six trips to do one thing. Stop work air travel and substitute it with video conferencing. Take fewer long vacations and don't fly on private jets.

你也可以避免交通阻塞時減少汽油浪費跟製造少一點廢氣。把要做的雜事集中起來，這樣你出門時可以用一趟車程完成六件事，而不是開車出門六次做一件事。用視訊會議取代飛機出差。少放一些坐飛機出遠門的長假，也不要用私人專機飛行。

♪166-02 Buy energy-efficient **appliances** ⑮ and insulate your home to make it energy efficient. Turn off the lights you're not using and think about installing solar panels. Eat locally produced organic food and cut out the beef and dairy. The bottom line is to reduce, reuse and recycle.

買省電型電器用品且把你的家做隔熱處理以達到節能功效。沒用的時候就把燈關掉且考慮安裝太陽能板。吃當地產的有機食物並且不要吃牛肉跟奶製品。基本上來說就是降低能源使用、重複利用現有資源跟做好回收這三個原則。

♪166-03 There are so many ways in which we can help our world and ensure that it is doing its job for our future generations. The beginning is to believe your actions make a difference and then step up and take the actions to make a difference.

有很多方式我們可以用來幫助我們的地球且確保我們的努力可以幫助下一代。首要之務就是相信你的行動可以做出改變，現在就站出來開始行動為實質改善做出努力吧！

QUIZ 閱讀測驗

1. What is not a human action that is causing the world to heat up?

(A) Humans riding bicycles.
(B) Humans driving cars.
(C) Humans cooling houses.
(D) Humans flying to Hawaii.

2. What needs to happen to CO2 in the atmosphere?

(A) There needs to be more.
(B) It needs to break down into H2O.
(C) It needs to not continue to build up so much.
(D) It needs to create a blanket effect.

3. What is your carbon footprint?

(A) The wet footprint left on the floor.
(B) The way carbon is released from our bodies.
(C) The way our actions create carbon emissions.
(D) The footprint left behind when animals die.

4. What is not a way to lower your carbon footprint?

(A) Ride a bike to work
(B) Carpool with friends
(C) Leave the refrigerator open overnight
(D) Turn off the lights

1. 什麼不是導致地球溫度升高的人類行為？

(A) 人騎自行車。 (B) 人駕駛汽車。 (C) 人開冷氣。 (D) 人坐飛機飛往夏威夷。

2. 大氣中的二氧化碳需要什麼處置？

(A) 需要更多二氧化碳。
(B) 它需要分解為 H2O。
(C) 它不需要繼續大量積累下去。
(D) 它需要創造雲毯效應。

3. 你的碳足跡是什麼？

(A) 留在地板上的濕足印。
(B) 碳從我們的身體釋放的方式。
(C) 我們的行為所導致的碳排放。
(D) 動物死亡時留下的足跡。

4. 什麼不是降低碳足跡的方法？

(A) 騎自行車上班
(B) 與朋友共乘
(C) 將冰箱門整晚開著
(D) 把燈關掉

ANS: 1. (A) 2. (C) 3. (C) 4.(C)

① **chase** [tʃes] v 追逐

The player chased the ball after it was hit into the outfield.

球被打出外野後，球員追著球跑。

② **adopt** [əˋdɑpt] v 採用

The government was looking to adopt a new method to ticket speeders.

政府現在正在尋求採用新做法，來對超速駕駛者開罰。

③ **apprehend** [ˏæprɪˋhɛnd] v 逮捕、拘捕

The police worked hard to apprehend the robber.

警察很努力要抓到那個強盜。

人臉辨識科技

♪168-01 So you're standing on a street corner when someone walks up to you and steals your brand-new Gucci bag. You let out a scream ❶ and start to **chase** ① after the guy, but then you stop. You remember that China's facial recognition technology has been **adopted** ② and is now in full swing. The police will be **apprehending** ③ the fellow any time now, and you'll probably have your bag back in your hot little hands by nightfall.

想像你現在站在街角上，之後有一個人向你走來且搶走了你全新的 GUCCI 包包，你大聲尖叫後開始追逐那個人，但你突然停了下來，因為你想起中國已經採用人臉辨識科技而且已全面上線。警方隨時都能將那個人逮捕，你可以在傍晚之前就把包包找回來。

♪169-01 While this scenario is not yet completely reality, for China it's definitely coming. The goal for the use of facial recognition technology is that it is supposed to **dissuade** ④ people from doing bad things. **In combination with** ❷ a social point system that will also go into effect, Big Brother is really watching.

雖然這樣的景象不全然是現實狀況，但在中國已經正在發生。使用人臉辨識科技的目標在於勸阻人們做壞事，再加上之後會啟用的社會信用系統，老大哥真的關注你的一舉一動了。

♪169-02 In fact, it sounds like the Netflix show *Black Mirror* episode *Nosedive* actuated in the real world. *Black Mirror* is a sci-fi series that includes a lot of technology **paranoia** ⑤ and throwbacks to *The Twilight Zone* TV show.

這實際上聽起來就像 Netflix 影集《黑鏡》其中一集《急轉直下》的場景實際在現實世界中發生。《黑鏡》是一部科幻影集，它包括了許多跟科技恐慌有關的主題，類似《陰陽魔界》這部電視劇。

♪169-03 In *Nosedive*, a young woman wants to **move up** ❸ in a world where coworkers, casual acquaintances and friends **determine** ⑥ your social rank. If you are nice, people should rate you high and when you do something bad, people should rate you low. Trying to reach for a higher social ranking, the woman meets with a **terrifying** ⑦ array of misfortune. Watch the show to see something very entertaining to imagine on the video screen but disturbing to consider in real life.

在《急轉直下》中，一個年輕女子想要在一個你的同事、點頭之交跟朋友可以決定你社會地位的世界往上爬。如果你人好，人們就會給你高分；如果你做了些壞事，人們就給你低分。當這名年輕女子想辦法追求更高的社會地位時，她也遭遇一連串糟糕不幸的事件。看這部影集時，你可以在螢幕上看到一些有趣的東西來設想這樣的生活，但如果真的在現實生活中發生的話，那可不是這麼好玩的事了。

VOCABULARY ♪169-04

④ **dissuade** [dɪˋswed] v 勸阻

We need to dissuade Karl from moving in with Angel.

我們需要勸阻卡爾不要跟安琪一起搬進來。

⑤ **paranoia** [ˌpærəˋnɔɪə] n 偏執、多疑

The man's paranoia made it difficult for him to sleep at night.

那名男子疑神疑鬼的，讓他晚上很難睡覺。

⑥ **determine** [dɪˋtɝmɪn] v 確定、決定、影響

Who can determine what caused the engine to freeze up?

誰可以確定是什麼讓引擎堵塞的？

⑦ **terrifying** [ˋtɛrəfaɪɪŋ] a 可怕的

My goodness, that *Annabelle* is terrifying.

我的老天啊，《安娜貝爾》真是可怕。

PATTERN ♪169-05

❶ **let out a scream** 尖叫出聲

Yolanda let out a scream when the snake bit her.

當蛇咬到尤蘭達的時候，她尖叫出聲。

❷ **in combination with ……** 和……結合

Exercise, in combination with good nutrition, is the best way to get in shape.

保持體態的最好方法，就是結合運動跟好的營養。

❸ **move up** 升職、升官

Ella wanted to move up in the company, so she worked hard every day.

艾拉想要在公司中升職，所以她每天都很努力工作。

VOCABULARY ♪170-04

⑧ **observe** [əbˋzɝv] v 觀察、監視

The nurse observed the patient to make sure his symptoms didn't worsen.

護士觀察病人以確保他的症狀沒有變更糟。

⑨ **surprise** [sɚˋpraɪz] v 驚訝

Everyone was surprised to hear that Jane was getting married.

每個人聽到珍要結婚了都感到很驚訝。

⑩ **detain** [dɪˋten] v 拘留、扣留

The policeman detained the fighter after his opponent died.

警察拘留了這個打死敵人的鬥毆者。

⑪ **disturbing** [dɪsˋtɝbɪŋ] a 令人心煩的、令人焦慮的

It is disturbing to find out that someone has been stalking her.

發現有人一直在跟蹤她很令人感到焦慮。

⑫ **originally** [əˋrɪdʒənl̩ɪ] ad 原本

Originally, we were going to the beach, but it's raining.

我們原本要去海邊，但正在下雨。

⑬ **condemnation** [ˌkandɛmˋneʃən] n 責備

The coworker's condemnation made Erwin very sad.

同事的責備讓艾爾溫很難過。

♪170-01 Privacy is not something we think of as being a luxury. People talk about the things we do in the "privacy of our own home" being our own business. But when every step you make is being **observed** ⑧ and analyzed, this is when there is a loss of ❹ a sense of autonomy.

隱私不是我們想的那樣奢侈的事了，人們在「保有隱私的自家」談論不同的事，管好自己的事，但是當每一件你做的事都被觀察且分析，那就失去了一個人保有自主的感受。

♪170-02 Privacy comes from the freedom from ❺ been observed 24-7, and that's why cities like San Francisco are banning the implementation of facial recognition technology. Yet in places like China, facial recognition technology is becoming a reality that citizens give no second thought.

隱私代表的是你免於一天到晚受到監視，這也是為什麼有些城市，例如舊金山，禁止人臉辨識科技的使用。但像是在中國這樣的地方，人臉辨識科技已經成為人們現實人生中的一部分，而且人民是沒有考慮餘地的。

♪170-03 A road crossing in Shenzhen is a great example of the use of this technology. There, pedestrians that jaywalk when they think no one is watching are **surprised** ⑨ to see their faces up on screens to shame them for their misbehavior.

在深圳過馬路展現了此科技使用上的絕佳例子。在深圳，亂闖馬路且以為沒人在看的行人，會很驚訝地發現自己的臉出現在大屏幕上，使他們為自己不端正的行為感到羞愧。

♪170-01 Companies with A.I-powered facial recognition like Intellifusion that is behind this Shenzhen example and SenseTime, which is the world's most valuable A.I. startup, are honing in on the surveillance market.

有人工智慧驅動的人臉辨識科技的公司，像是深圳例子背後操手的雲天勵飛（Intellifusion）公司跟世界上市值最高的人工智慧新創公司商湯（SenseTime），都正在進攻監控系統的市場。

♪171-02 And an eerie surveillance it is. Police are being equipped with A.I. powered sunglasses to single out the baddies. Outside observers have noted the concerning side of this in connection with China's minority population, especially with the use of facial recognition in tracking the comings and goings of members of the Uighur population in China.

就是這樣子令人感到毛骨悚然的監控，中國的警察們現在可以配備具有人工智慧的太陽眼鏡來偵測出壞蛋。外界已經注意到這樣的科技在控管中國少數民族上有其隱憂，尤其是當中國政府利用人臉辨識科技來追蹤中國維吾爾族人民的去向時。

♪171-03 It is especially distressing that this could be used to **detain** ⑩ Uighurs perhaps for just running a red light on a bicycle. The **disturbing** ⑪ element is that the recognition technology was **originally** ⑫ mainly being used to observe Uighurs in western China, but there is some evidence that now Uighurs in cities like Wenzhou and Hangzhou are being singled out from a crowd. That has led to wide international **condemnation** ⑬ .

尤其讓人煩憂的就是中國政府用這個方式來拘留維吾爾族人，即使他們只是騎著腳踏車闖了紅燈。最讓人不能接受的是人臉辨識科技當初主要就是用於監察中國西部的維吾爾族人，但現在也有證據指出住在像是溫洲跟杭州等城市的維吾爾族人，也會從人群中被特別辨識出來。這樣子的做法已經掀起廣泛的國際撻伐。

PATTERN ♪171-04

④ there is a loss of ……的遺失

There is a loss of innocence when good people dies.

當好人死的時候我們失去了純真。

⑤ freedom from 免於……

Shaun has been looking forward to freedom from pain.

尚恩已經期許遠離痛苦很久了。

人臉辨識 Facial Technology

臉部辨識科技是只比較臉部的視覺特徵資訊，進行身分鑑別的電腦技術，它屬於生物特徵的辨識技術，是近期非常熱門的研究領域。在應用上，使用者可以透過臉部進行身分辨識、身分尋找等，可以進行公司或學校的點名報到、商店的行動支付……等等。

但發展至今，在法律面、隱私權等面向中，引起的爭議也愈來愈多，微軟甚至刪除了全球最大的開放臉部辨識資料庫——MS-Celeb-1M。然而即使目前爭議不多，相關科技的研究與發展仍是如火如荼地展開。

♪172-01 This extreme and extensive method of surveillance is **perfect** ⑭ for a country with a 1.4 billion population that needs to successfully keep an eye on its citizens and try to prevent someone from doing something dangerous by using the A.I. technology to single out those displaying dangerous behavior **patterns** ⑮ .

藉由人工智慧科技挑出那些顯現危險行為模式的人，這種極端且全面監控的方式對一個有 14 億人口的國家來說是個絕佳的辦法，他們要確保看緊每一個市民並預防有人做出危險的事。

♪172-02 With the realization that the police could be watching you at all times to see if you are a threat, who knew jaywalking could be so dangerous?

現在警察可以隨時監視你，以確保你不是一個潛在威脅已經是既定事實，誰知道連闖個馬路都會是件危險的事呢？

VOCABULARY ♪172-03

⑭ **perfect** [ˋpɝfɪkt] a 完美的

Sickness is the perfect excuse for missing school.

生病是不去上課的完美藉口。

⑮ **pattern** [ˋpætɚn]
n 方式、模式、花樣

I love the tile patterns on this entry area floor.

我喜歡入口處地板上的磁磚花樣。

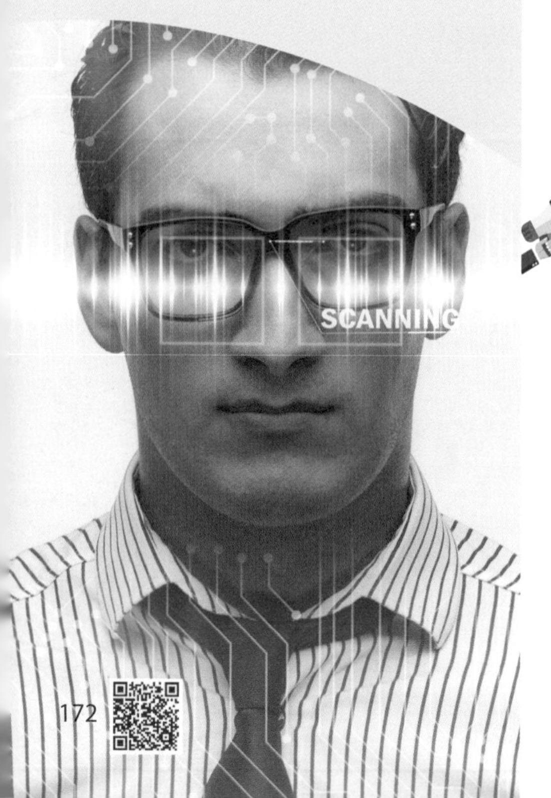

LEARN MORE!

♪172-04 ❶ **Is there any misunderstanding?** 有什麼誤會嗎？

A: You haven't played basketball with me for a long time. Is there any misunderstanding?
你們好久沒找我打籃球了。有什麼誤會嗎？

B: We heard that you spoke ill of Gary.
我們聽說你說了蓋瑞的壞話。

♪172-05 ❷ **What's going on here?** 怎麼回事？

A: What's going on here? Why is everyone lying on the ground?
怎麼回事？為什麼每個人都趴在地上呢？

B: There was a robbery just now. 剛剛發生搶劫了。

QUIZ 閱讀測驗

1. What does the word "apprehending" mean when used here?
(A) following
(B) chasing
(C) catching
(D) torturing

2. What is mentioned as the focus of facial recognition technology?
(A) to create a database of everyone
(B) to stop people from wanting to do bad things
(C) to help people find their friends
(D) to hurt people that lie

3. How do many citizens in China feel about the use of facial recognition technology?
(A) They are excited to use it.
(B) They would like to wait and see.
(C) They give it no second thought.
(D) They want everybody to have it.

4. What did people do to get their faces up on screens in Shenzhen?
(A) They smiled at the camera.
(B) They were publicly intoxicated.
(C) They stole something.
(D) They jaywalked.

1. 文中使用的「apprehending」是什麼意思？
(A) 追蹤 (B) 追逐 (C) 捕捉 (D) 折磨

2. 什麼被提及是臉部識別科技的重點？
(A) 創建每個人的資料庫 (B) 阻止人們做壞事
(C) 幫助人們找到他們的朋友 (D) 傷害說謊的人

3. 中國的許多公民們如何看待臉部識別科技的使用？
(A) 他們很高興使用它。 (B) 他們想拭目以待。
(C) 他們沒有考慮的餘地。 (D) 他們希望每個人都擁有它。

4. 人們做了什麼會讓自己的臉出現在深圳的屏幕上？
(A) 他們對著鏡頭微笑。 (B) 他們光天化之下喝醉酒。
(C) 他們偷了東西。 (D) 他們亂闖馬路。

ANS: 1. (C) 2. (B) 3. (C) 4.(D)

LEARN MORE!

♪173-01 ❶ **...ought to...** ……應該要……

A: Did you see the video? Many people left comments below.
你有看這個視頻嗎？好多人都在下方留言。

B: Yes, I did. He ought to examine his mistakes and stop letting his child smoke.
有，他應該要檢討自己的錯誤並停止讓孩子吸菸。

♪173-02 ❷ **I'm glad to...** 我很樂於……

A: I'm glad to see your improvement.
我很高興看到你的進展。

B: I owe it all to you.
這一切都要感謝你。

♪173-03 ❸ **What type of...?** ……是什麼類型呢？

A: What type of project are you working on?
你在做的專案是什麼類型呢？

B: I'm working on a project about information technology.
我在做有關資訊科技的專案。

Technology 生物辨識技術

生物特徵辨識技術，是透過生物特徵進行辨識，例如：臉部、指紋、掌紋、虹膜、視網膜、聲音、體型……等等，甚至可以透過簽名方式、敲擊鍵盤的力度和頻率進行辨識。

在許多電影中都會看到這類技術的應用，例如：《天使與魔鬼（Angels and Demons）》裡的眼睛辨識、《鷹眼（Eagle Eye）》裡的聲音辨識、《不可能的任務：失控國度（Mission: Impossible – Rogue Nation）》裡透過走路的儀態等進行辨識。

新聞

news

股票趨勢

VOCABULARY ♪174-02

① **income** [ˋɪn͵kʌm] n 收入

The woman's income was spent every month on housing and food.

這個女人的收入每個月都花在房租跟食物上。

② **liquid** [ˋlɪkwɪd] n 液體

The liquid in the glass was not water but alcohol.

玻璃杯裡的液體不是水，是酒。

PATTERN ♪174-03

❶ **the rule of thumb** 經驗法則

Friends help each other as a rule of thumb.

經驗法則來說朋友會幫助彼此。

Article 4 股票趨勢

♪174-01 Investing some of your **income** ① in stocks can be a great way to diversify your portfolio. Most wealth advisors would recommend that you keep some **liquid** ② funds, or cash, available in case of an emergency such as loss of job, accident, or major health issues. In general, the rule of thumb ❶ is to keep about two months' worth of salary on the side as cash.

把你的一些收入投資在股票可以是一個好方法來讓你的投資組合更多樣化。大部分的財富管理顧問，都會推薦你存有可運用的流動資金或是現金，預防緊急狀況的不時之需，像是失去工作、意外或是一些健康問題發生的時候。一般來説，經驗法則告訴我們至少保有兩個月薪水的錢在身邊。

♪175-01 After that, if you still have money left over, buying **property** ③, investing in mutual funds, and investing in stocks tend to be the next **recommendations** ④. Buying property is a good idea ❷ because most of the time it is a very safe investment. The value of houses tends to always be on the rise, so you are not very likely to lose money. After that, the next good **area** ⑤ to try to make your money work for you is in the stock market.

如果之後你還有多餘的錢，才會建議你買房產、投資共同資金跟股票。買房子會是一個好主意，因為大部分的情況上來說這是一個安全的投資，房價也傾向於愈漲愈高，所以你不太可能會賠錢。下一個可以嘗試用錢賺錢的好投資領域就是股票市場。

♪175-02 Most advisors would tell you that the best place for **beginning** ⑥ investors to start is by investing in index funds or in mutual funds. An index fund is one type of mutual fund. An index fund creates its portfolio based on what is on a popular trading forum, like the S&P 500 (Standard and Poor's 500) or the Dow.

大部分的顧問會跟你説對投資新手來説，最好著手開始的就是投資指數基金或是共同基金。指數基金是其中一種共同基金。指數資金創造投資組合的內容是根據受歡迎的股票市場指數公司所選，像是標準普爾 500 指數或是道瓊工業平均指數。

♪175-03 By **holding** ⑦ stocks that are the same as on a market index, the buyer is able to invest broadly in the market for not too much expense and little need to constantly buy and sell stocks. And if the index is doing well, then the fund will also be doing well. While there is not always a huge percentage of annual profit, index funds tend to be steady and less **volatile** ⑧ than other investment options.

如果所持有的股票跟在股市指數上是一樣的，買家可以小額且廣泛地在股票市場投資而且不用一直買進跟賣出。如果指數運作的不錯，那麼基金也會跟著好。因為每年利潤的百分比並不總是很高，跟其他投資選項比起來指數資金傾向於較穩定跟不容易波動。

♪175-04 Index funds are great supplements to retirement accounts, and Warren Buffett says they are a great safe investment for your sunset years.

投資指數基金是補充退休帳戶基金的好方法，沃倫．巴菲特就曾説過指數基金是一個幫助你晚年生活的安全好投資。

VOCABULARY ♪175-05

③ **property** [ˋprapɚtɪ]
n 房地產、財產

The beachfront property was an incredible place for the tourists to stay.

面朝海的這棟建築物，對觀光客來説，是一個極佳的留宿地點。

④ **recommendation** [͵rɛkəmɛnˋdeʃən] n 推薦

The teacher's recommendation was that the boy be the class leader.

老師推薦的是讓那個男孩當班長。

⑤ **area** [ˋɛrɪə] n 區域

The area next to the wall has been planted with beautiful flowers.

這面牆隔壁的區域種滿了美麗的花朵。

⑥ **beginning** [bɪˋgɪnɪŋ] n 開始

The beginning of this discussion was a bit aggressive.

這討論的開端有一點挑釁。

⑦ **hold** [hold] v 抑制、抓住

Holding in your emotions can cause you to get very angry.

憋著你的情緒可能導致你更生氣。

⑧ **volatile** [ˋvalətl̩]
a 不穩定的、喜怒無常的、易揮發的

The volatile ups and downs in the market left investors concerned.

股票市場不穩定的高低走勢，讓投資者很擔心。

PATTERN ♪175-06

❷ **(V+ing + N) is a good idea**
……是好主意

Buying a rental property is a good idea if you have some extra money.

如果你有多餘的錢，購買出租物業是個好主意。

VOCABULARY ♪176-05

⑨ **broader** [brɔdɚ] a 更寬廣的

Sometimes it takes a broader view on a problem to find a solution.

有時候要找到問題的解決辦法需要用更寬廣的視野來看待問題。

⑩ **unit** [ˋjunɪt] n 單元

The gram is a great unit of measurement.

克是一個很棒的測量單位。

⑪ **risk** [rɪsk] n 風險

The risk involved in hunting for buried treasure is worth the gain.

尋找埋藏寶藏的風險是值得的。

⑫ **prefer** [prɪˋfɝ] v 偏好

James would prefer to find the missing watch himself.

詹姆士偏好自己找到遺失的手錶。

⑬ **point** [pɔɪnt] v 指出

All information points to Eric being the one that stole the test.

全部的訊息都指出艾瑞克是偷考試卷的人。

⑭ **questionable** [ˋkwɛstʃənəbl̩] a 可質疑的、不確定的

I find your reasons for being here very questionable.

我覺得你在這邊的理由很可疑。

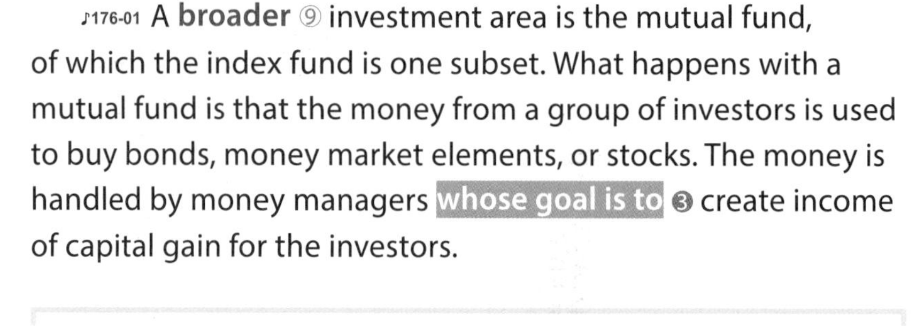

♪176-01 A **broader** ⑨ investment area is the mutual fund, of which the index fund is one subset. What happens with a mutual fund is that the money from a group of investors is used to buy bonds, money market elements, or stocks. The money is handled by money managers **whose goal is to** ❸ create income of capital gain for the investors.

更廣的投資領域則是共同基金，上述的指數基金是它的其中一個子集。共同基金的運作方式在於它使用投資人的錢去購買債券、貨幣市場的投資商品或是股票。這些錢由資金管理人來管理，而他的主要目標就是為投資人創造資本利得（即錢滾錢、買賣中的價差）。

♪176-02 The investors usually buy a **unit** ⑩ of the fund, and the thing you are buying is its performance. Some funds are considered to be good earners, but because of that, they are often more volatile. Some are lower earners, but also tend to carry less of a **risk** ⑪ for investors to lose money.

投資人通常買的是基金單位，買的東西則是他的實質表現。有些基金被視為賺錢好手，但也因為這樣它們更容易波動。有些賺得比較少，但同時也讓投資人賠錢的風險降低。

♪176-03 People that have a good understanding of the stock market or that **prefer** ⑫ to be in direct control of their investments instead of having money managers do their work for them are likely to invest directly in the stock market. **Knowing what to buy when** ❹ and when to sell can be the greatest challenge for an individual investor.

對股票市場有所了解或是偏好自己掌控投資，而非透過資金管理人來處理的人，就是有可能會自己直接在股票市場投資。知道什麼時候買哪支股票跟什麼時候該賣出，對個人投資者來說會是一個最困難的挑戰。

♪176-04 The best way to know this sort of information is to read the market trends. That means you need to take at least three **points** ⑬ from a stock graph of a stock, then you need to determine which direction the points are showing the stock heading, whether it's up, down or horizontal.

要知道這樣資訊的最好作法就是觀察股票趨勢，這代表你必須在股市圖中看三個點，然後判斷這些點呈現的股票走向趨勢是什麼，是高還是低，還是維持水平呢。

♪177-01 Next, it's important to watch the slope that the points when formed into a line create. If the slope is too steep, then the stock value will need to correct itself because a steep slope is unsustainable for healthy market growth or decline. If the slope is too flat, then the trend is **questionable** ⑭ .

下一步就是觀察點跟點間連成的斜線。如果坡度太陡，那麼股票價值就會需要自我修正，因為太陡的斜線走勢對健康市場的成長或下滑是沒有持續性的。如果斜線太水平，那麼走向趨勢則是可疑的。

♪177-02 Also time is important when looking for trends, so look at weekly or monthly trends as opposed to daily ones. And the longer a trend lasts, the more likely it will continue. And in knowing this, you know ❺ the best stocks to consider investing in for the long or short term.

時間也是觀察股票走向的重要考量，所以比起每天看股票走向，觀察每週跟每月的整體走勢更為重要。走向趨勢維持較長時間，也代表更有可能會持續下去。知道這點的話，你就知道哪支股票是你考慮長期或是短期投資的好選擇。

PATTERN ♪177-03

❸ N whose goal is to
某人的目標是……

Climbers whose goal is to search out adventure, find new places to climb.

目標是找到新冒險的攀登者尋找新的地點來攀爬。

❹ knowing what to (V) when
當……知道要做……

Knowing what to eat when you are trying to lose weight is a big help.

當你嘗試減肥的時候，知道該吃什麼是很大的幫助。

❺ in knowing this, you know
在這部分的理解，你知道……

I feel that in knowing this, you know more than most people.

我感覺在這方面你比大部分的人都懂。

QUIZ 閱讀測驗

1. What is not mentioned as a way to diversify your portfolio?
(A) keeping cash (B) buying stocks (C) buying property (D) buying a car

2. How does an index fund determine the stocks it has?
(A) It picks what the customers want.
(B) It finds the best-performing stocks.
(C) It decides based on the stock index it is based on.
(D) It lets the money managers decide.

3. What is a reason mentioned for why index funds are good investments?
(A) You are just like a real stock broker.
(B) They are not as volatile as other funds.
(C) They give great dividends.
(D) They are free to buy.

1. 文中沒有提到什麼是使你的投資組合多樣化的方法？
(A) 保留現金 (B) 買股票 (C) 購買房產 (D) 買車

2. 指數基金如何決定其所持有的股票？
(A) 它挑選客戶想要的東西。 (B) 它找表現最好的股票。 (C) 它根據它所依據的股票指數來決定。 (D) 它讓資金管理人決定。

3. 文中提到什麼是指數基金是個好投資的原因？
(A) 你就像一個真正的股票經紀人。 (B) 它們不像其他基金那樣不穩定。 (C) 它們回饋許多紅利。 (D) 它們可以自由購買。

ANS: 1. (D) 2. (C) 3. (B)

買演唱會票

concert

VOCABULARY ♪178-01

① **access** [ˋæksɛs]
n 通道、途徑、使用或是看某物的機會

Access to this room is only possible with an ID.
進入這個房間的唯一可能性是使用身分證。

② **easy** [ˋizɪ] a 簡單的

The easy test was quickly completed by the entire class.
整個班級很快地就把這份簡單的考試完成。

③ **verification** [͵vɛrɪfɪˋkeʃən]
n 驗證

You need to bring a passport with you for verification.
你需要帶護照驗證你的身份。

④ **submit** [səbˋmɪt] v 呈交

We are submitting the adoption papers today.
我們今天會交出領養文件。

Article 1 加入會員

Sign up to access ① tickets for concerts. Check out will be easy ② once you're a member!

First Name: **Last Name:**

email address:

Confirm email address:

Phone number: (all phone numbers require verification ③)

Password: (must be ❶ at least 8 digits long, include one capital letter and one number)

Postal/zip code: **Country of residence:**

＊ By submitting ④, you agree to our Terms and Purchase Policy and understand your information will be used as described in our Privacy Policy.

註冊以取得演唱會門票。 一但成為會員，結帳手續上會更簡單！

名字： **姓：**

電子郵件地址：

再次書寫確認電郵地址：

電話號碼：（所有電話號碼都需要驗證）

密碼：（必須至少含有 8 位數，包括一個大寫字母和一個數字）

郵政編碼： **居住國家：**

＊ 提交即表示您同意我們的條款和購買政策，並了解您的信息將按照我們的隱私政策中的說明使用。

選擇時間場次

All Events		Sort By ❷: Date
Jun 14 Fri • 6:30 pm	Xfinity Center-Mansfield, MA Kiss 108's KISS CONCERT 2019	See Tickets
Jun 16 Sun • 4:30 pm	Jones Beach Theater-Wantagh, NY BLI Summer Jam ⑤ 2019	See Tickets
Aug 7 Wed • 7:30 pm	Honda Center-Anaheim, CA KBRO SUMMER TOUR 2019 ADD-ONS AVAILABLE ⑥	See Tickets
Aug 9 Fri • 7:30 pm	Enterprise Center-St. Louis, MO Summerfest 2019	See Tickets

所有活動		排序依據：日期
6 月 14 日 星期五 ・ 下午 6:30	Xfinity 中心 - 麻薩諸塞州曼斯菲爾德 Kiss 108 的 KISS 2019 演唱會	查看門票
6 月 16 日 星期日 ・下午 4:30	瓊斯海灘圓形劇場 - 紐約州旺托 BLI 2019 夏天爵士音樂會	查看門票
8 月 7 日 星期三・下午 7:30	本田中心 - 加利福尼亞州安那翰 KBRO 2019 夏日巡迴演唱會 可選擇附加選項	查看門票
8 月 9 日 星期五・下午 7:30	企業中心體育場 - 密蘇里州聖路易斯 2019 夏日盛宴	查看門票

VOCABULARY ♪179-01

⑤ **jam** [dʒæm]
n （爵士樂的）即興演奏

Five thousand people attended the music jam.
五千人參加了這場即興演奏的音樂會。

⑥ **available** [əˋveləbḷ]
a 可獲得的、可用的、有空的
Are you available tomorrow morning at 10?
明天早上十點你有空嗎？

⑦ **resale** [ˋri͵sel]
n 轉售、再次售出

The resale outfit is 30% cheaper than a new one.
轉售的套裝比全新的便宜百分之三十。

選擇票價

Select your Ticket		選擇你的門票	
Sec 427, Row S	$75.00 ea	427 區，S 排	總票價 $75.00
Sec 230, Row N Verified Resale ⑦ Ticket	$80.00 ea	230 區，N 排 已驗證的轉售票	總票價 $80.00
Sec 123, Row T	$92.00 ea	123 區，T 排	總票價 $92.00
Sec 325, Row T	$103.00 ea	325 區，T 排	總票價 $103.00
Sec 228, Row K	$132.00 ea	228 區，K 排	總票價 $132.00

Article

4 注意事項

Customers may pick up ❸ tickets beginning 90 minutes prior to event time at the Ticket Office. Customer must have photo ID, but should also bring an actual credit card and confirmation number.

- **Parking**

  The center features 5,000 parking spaces on-site. Charge for parking varies by event. An additional 10,000 parking spaces are available within a short walk. Pick-up after the event is at the NE Rotunda. The service is typically ⑧ available one hour before doors open until approximately ⑨ 90 minutes after the event.

- **Accessible Seating**

  Special seating is available for guests ⑩ with disabilities.

- **General Rules**

  Video cameras, monopods, tripods, audio recording devices, and cameras with telephoto or zoom ⑪ lenses are not permitted. The standard policy for most events allows still cameras with a lens no greater than 100mm without flash. Special Events may have their own tour policy.

消費者可以在活動時間前 90 分鐘從售票處領取門票。 消費者必須出示附有照片的身份證件，且同時需要攜帶使用的信用卡跟確認號碼。

・ **停車**

該中心設有 5,000 個停車位。停車費用因活動而異。短距離腳程可達處另額外設有 10,000 個停車位。活動後要取車請至圓形建築的東北門。停車場的服務時間基本上是開門前一小時直到活動結束後九十分鐘。

・ **無障礙座位**

殘障人士可使用特殊座位。

・ **一般規則**

不允許使用攝影機、獨腳架、三腳架、錄音設備和遠攝或變焦鏡頭的相機。標準政策規定大部分的活動演出允許使用不超過 100mm 鏡頭的相機且不能開閃光燈。特殊活動可能會有自己另設的巡迴政策。

VOCABULARY ♪180-01

⑧ **typically** [ˋtɪpɪklɪ]
ad 典型地、通常、一般

I typically spend three to four hours a day using a computer.
我一天通常用電腦三到四個小時。

⑨ **approximately** [əˋprɑksəmɪtlɪ]
ad 大概

This box is approximately 90 cm wide.
這個箱子大概 90 公分寬。

⑩ **guest** [gɛst] n 客人

The guests at the hotel are lounging by the swimming pool.
飯店的客人在游泳池旁消磨時間。

⑪ **zoom** [zum]
n 可變焦距鏡頭（同 zoom lens）

The zoom lens is amazing for taking photos of wildlife.
可變焦距鏡頭對拍野生動物來說很棒。

Ⓐ **drum set** 爵士套鼓
Ⓑ **bass drum** 大鼓
Ⓒ **snare** 小鼓
Ⓓ **hi-hats** 踏拔

訂購結帳

Payment	付款
Pay With Discover, MasterCard, Visa, American Express, PayPal	使用 Discover、MasterCard、Visa、American Express 或是 PayPal 付款
Name on Card	持卡人姓名
Card Number	卡號
Expiration ⑫ Date	過期日
Security Code	安全碼
Address	地址
Postal Code	郵政編碼
City	城市
Phone Number	電話號碼
State	州
Save this card for future ⑬ purchases Or check out with PayPal	保存卡片資訊以利下次購買時使用，或者，使用 PayPal 付款

收到取票條碼

A confirmation mail will be sent to your email.

Your booking reference number is: RF4XQZ79

If for any reason ❹ you don't receive an email confirming ⑭ your ticket purchase, you can go to this link to print out ❺ a copy of your tickets:

https://www.kbroshows.com/RFXQZ79

We hope you enjoy ⑮ the show and come to us again the next time you need tickets!

確認郵件將發送到您的電子郵箱。

您的訂購編號是：RF4XQZ79

如果由於任何原因您沒有收到確認購票的電子郵件，您可以使用此連結來影印您的門票複本：https://www.kbroshows.com/RFXQZ79

我們希望您喜歡這個節目，下次需要購票時請再次蒞臨！

VOCABULARY ♪181-01

⑫ **expiration** [ˌɛkspəˋreʃən] n 到期、結束

The expiration date on the milk was yesterday.

牛奶的到期日是昨天。

⑬ **future** [ˋfjutʃɚ] n 未來

My future is hanging by a thread.

我的未來危在旦夕。

⑭ **confirm** [kənˋfɝm] v 確認

We will be confirming the date of the party by Friday.

我們星期五前會確認派對的日期。

⑮ **enjoy** [ɪnˋdʒɔɪ] v 享受

I enjoy spending my days gardening.

我很享受我的園藝時光。

PATTERN ♪181-02

❶ **must be** 必須在……

You must be at the performance by 6 P.M. tomorrow.

明天下午六點前你必須出現在演出中。

❷ **sort by** 用……分類

Let's sort these clothes by color.

讓我們用顏色幫這些衣服分類。

❸ **may pick up** 可以取拿

You may pick up your tickets on May 3.

你可以在五月三日拿票。

❹ **if for any reason** 不管什麼原因，如果……

If for any reason you want to go to the movies with me, just let me know.

不管什麼原因，如果你想要跟我去看電影，就跟我說。

❺ **to print out** 印出

I need to print out my homework to hand in.

我需要把作業印出來繳交。

① **avoid** [ə`vɔɪd] v 避免

You can't avoid me forever; we need to talk about this.

你不能永遠避開我，我們需要談論這件事。

② **leak** [lik] v 漏、洩漏

There is jelly leaking out of that doughnut.

甜甜圈的果醬餡漏出來了。

③ **include** [ɪn`klud] v 包括

There are twelve books here including those two over there.

總共有十二本書，也包括那邊那兩本。

④ **choose** [tʃuz] v 選擇

You need to choose your favorite colors from these five.

你要從這五個顏色中，選出你最喜歡的顏色。

⑤ **standard** [`stændɚd] n 標準

A standard size is probably all we need for the living room.

我們需要的客廳大小，大概就是標準規格那樣。

加入會員

New Member Registration **Title:** Mr. / Mrs. / Miss

First Name: **Last Name:**

email: (please use an email other than ❶ Yahoo or Hotmail to avoid ① loss due to blocking or leaking ② of emails)

Confirm email:

Password: (must be 8-20 digits, including ③ one uppercase letter, a number and a symbol)

Confirm Password: **Date of Birth:**

Shipping Address: **Street:**

City: **State:** **Zip Code:** **Country:**

Mobile Number:

☐ **I have already read the Terms of Service**

Cancel **Confirm Registration**

新會員註冊 稱呼： 先生／夫人／小姐

名字： 姓：

電子郵件：（請使用除了 Yahoo 跟 Hotmail 以外的電子郵件信箱，以避免因擋信或電子郵件外流而造成的損失）

確認郵件：

密碼：（必須是 8-20 位數字，包括一個大寫字母，一個數字和一個符號）

確認密碼： 出生日期：

收件地址： 街： 市： 州：

郵政編碼： 國家： 手機號碼：

☐ 我已經閱讀了服務條款

取消 確定註冊

2 寄送方式與運費計算

Billing Address: **Name:**
Shipping Address: **Street:**
City: **State:**
Zip Code: **Country:**
Shipping Address : (if different from ❷ the Billing Address)
Shipping Address: **Street:**
City: **State:**
Zip Code: **Country:**
Choose ④ **your Shipping Method:**
Free standard shipping: (for orders of $50 or more)
(takes 5-10 business days)
Express standard ⑤**:** (takes 3-5 business days)
Express: (takes 2-3 business days)
Overnight:

帳單寄送地址： **姓名：**
收件地址： **街：**
市： **州：**
郵政編碼： **國家：**
收件地址：（如果與帳單寄送地址不同）
收件地址： **街：**
市： **州：**
郵政編碼： **國家：**
選擇您的運送方式：
免費標準運送：（訂單滿 $50）（需要 5-10 個工作天）
標準快遞：（需要 3-5 個工作天）
快遞：（需要 2-3 個工作天）
隔日送達：

PATTERN ♪183-01

❶ **other than** 除了

Someone other than Jane should come to pick up her last check.

除了珍之外，要有其他人來取她的支票。

❷ **if different from**
如果跟……不一樣

Please write down the new address if different from the current one on file.

如果地址跟現在檔案中的資訊不同，請寫下新的地址。

郵遞區號 Postal Code

郵遞區號（Postal Code）最早是由烏克蘭發明，於 1932 年 12 月啟用，是國家或是地區，為了方便郵件分撿、加快郵件傳遞速度，將全國劃分的編碼方式。

大多數國家或地區的郵遞區號是用數字標示，例如美國使用 5 或 9 位數字、墨西哥使用 5 位數、澳洲使用 4 位數、印度使用 6 位數，而在英國和加拿大也有羅馬字、數字混用的情況。

VOCABULARY ♪184-01

⑥ **punk** [pʌŋk] n 龐克

The punk outfit the girl wore for Halloween was outstanding.
這女孩為了萬聖節穿的龐克裝特別突出耀眼。

⑦ **dusky** [ˋdʌskɪ] a 黑色的、暗的

The dusky eyeshadow brought out the young lady's eyes.
暗色眼影更襯托出這個年輕女子的眼睛。

⑧ **sunshine** [ˋsʌn͵ʃaɪn] n 陽光

The sunshine in her eyes brought out a lovely glow.
她眸中的陽光流溢出美好光芒。

LEARN MORE! ♪184-02

在網路上購物，除了滿額可以免運費之外，有時候也會有滿額贈的活動，也是吸引人購物的行銷方式。

- **ceramic cup** 陶瓷杯
- **parasol** 陽傘
- **perfume** 香水
- **electric razor** 電動刮鬍刀
- **suitcase** 小型旅行箱
- **essential oil** 精油

Article 3 選購衣物

Women's **Punk** ⑥ Tee

(sizes XS-XL) Select size___

$19.95

Summer Dress

(sizes 6-18) Select size_____

$35.99

Select color: (white with coral pink print, coral pink with white print, **dusky** ⑦ blue with brown print, forest green with **sunshine** ⑧ yellow print)

女版龐克 T 恤（尺寸 XS-XL）

選擇尺寸 ___ $19.95

夏季連身裙（尺寸 6-18）

選擇尺寸 _____ $35.99

選擇顏色：（白色搭配珊瑚粉色印花、珊瑚粉色搭配白色印花、深藍色搭配棕色印花、森林綠搭配陽光黃印花）

結帳

	Item	Size	Quantity	Price
	Women's Punk Tee	M	1	$19.95
	Summer Dress white / coral pink	10	1	$35.99
	Summer Dress dusky blue/ brown	10	1	$35.99
			Subtotal:	$91.93
			Sales tax: (8%)	$ 7.35
			Total:	$99.28

	項目	尺寸	數量	價格
	女版龐克 T 恤	M	1	$19.95
	夏日連身裙 白色／珊瑚粉色印花	10	1	$35.99
	夏日連身裙 深藍色／棕色印花	10	1	$35.99
		小計：		$91.93
		消費稅：：(8%)		$ 7.35
		總計：		$99.28

LEARN MORE!

♪185-01 ❶ **I'd like to exchange...for...**
我想將……換成……

A: I'd like to exchange my refills for your Barbie doll.
我想用筆芯跟妳的芭比娃娃交換。

B: Nope. That doesn't make sense to me.
不要，那對我來說不合理。

♪185-02 ❷ **to be honest,...**
老實說，……

A: To be honest, what you said just hurt me.
老實說，你說的話傷到我了。

B: I didn't mean it.
我不是故意的。

♪185-03 ❸ **How short...?** ……多短呢？

A: How short should I cut the cloth?
我該剪這塊布多短呢？

B: Please cut off the length of ten centimeters.
請剪下十公分的長度。

VOCABULARY ♪186-01

⑨ **progress** [ˋprɑgrɛs] n 進步、進展

The progress on this project has been slowly coming.

這個計畫的進度慢慢進行中。

⑩ **transit** [ˋtrænsɪt] n / v 運輸、運送

The package is in transit and should be here by Thursday.

包裹正在運輸中，星期四前應該就會到了。

⑪ **process** [ˋprɑsɛs] v 處理、辦理

This criminal case needs to be processed very carefully.

這個刑事案件必須小心處理。

⑫ **estimate** [ˋɛstə͵met] v 估測、預測

We estimated that it would take us five hours to get home again.

我們預估大概會花我們五小時到家。

⑬ **pickup** [ˋpɪk͵ʌp] n 取拿

The pickup of the items should be made within 48 hours.

取貨時間要在 48 小時內完成。

⑭ **package** [ˋpækɪdʒ] n 包裹

A package with Carlos' name on it was delivered today.

寫著卡洛斯名字的包裹今天送到了。

⑮ **return** [rɪˋtɝn] v 帶回、歸還

If something is returned unopened, you can receive a full refund.

如果歸還時原封不動，你可以拿到全額退款。

PATTERN ♪186-02

❸ **by the end of the day**
在一天結束前

The teacher should be here by the end of the day.

今天結束前老師應該要出現在這。

❹ **has been delivered** 已經被遞交

Crystal's package has been delivered to the wrong address.

克里斯蒂的包裹被送去錯的地址。

Article 5 查詢寄件狀況

Shipping Progress ⑨: **Order Reference Number:**

Shipping currently: In transit ⑩ **Mailed on:** 5/18/2019

5/19/2019 Processed ⑪ through Georgia Distribution Center

5/20/2019 Processed through Atlanta Regional Distribution

Estimated ⑫ date of delivery: 5/21/2019 by the end of the day ❸

運送進度： **訂單編號：**

目前運送進度：運送中

寄送日期：2019 年 5 月 18 日

2019 年 5 月 19 日通過喬治亞配送中心處理

2019 年 5 月 20 日通過亞特蘭大地區配送中心處理

預計交貨日期：2019 年 5 月 21 日當天

Article 6 收到取貨信

Dear customer:

Your order QR560BT has been delivered ❹. Please pickup ⑬ your order at your selected location:

Atlanta District 2390 Post Office

2970 Alabama St

Atlanta, GA 30543

USA

Please pick up your package ⑭ within 7 days, or it will be returned ⑮.

親愛的客戶：

您的訂單 QR560BT 已發貨。 請在您選擇的地點領取您的貨品：

亞特蘭大地區 2390 郵局

2970 阿拉巴馬街

亞特蘭大，GA 30543

美國

請在 7 天內領取您的包裹，否則將會被退回。

Skill!!

網路消費需要注意的事項與訊息

一週七天、一天 24 小時全年無休的網路購物，因為方便性，吸引了許許多多的消費者。在網路上消費，必須要注意什麼呢？

Point 1 建立帳號

首先是網站上應該了解的使用功能。一般而言，user（使用者）必須要 register（註冊），必須建立 account name（戶名）及 password（密碼）。

建議帳號的時候，需要輸入 personal information（個人資料），包括 name （姓名）、Mr. Mrs./Ms（先生、女士或小姐）、date of birth（出生年月日） 、nationality（國籍）、address（地址）等。

有時候密碼的設立會依網站有不同的要求，例如：
Your password shall be between 8 - 32 characters long and include at least 3 of the following character types: English alphabet uppercase letter(A-Z) English alphabet lowercase letter(a-z), and Decimal digit number(0-9).
您的密碼應該為 8-32 個字元長度，並且包括至少以下的三種字元種類：大寫字母 A-Z、小寫字母 a-z 及數字 0-9。

Point 2 關鍵字搜尋

再來使用關鍵字，把你想要購買的，不管是產品或服務，當成關鍵字來搜尋。

例如訂房時，使用 destination （目的地）、type of room （房型）、number of occupant （住房人數）、type of travel （旅遊類別）、duration of stay （住房時間）等關鍵字來搜尋。如果是購買有形產品時，雖然有圖片可以看，要特別注意 size（尺寸）、specification （規格）及 availability（有無現貨）等。

Point 3 付款與取貨

一般網路消費會有幾種付費與取貨的方式：

付費方式：信用卡刷卡、郵局劃撥或轉帳、行動支付、超商取貨付款

取貨方式：宅配、郵局寄送、便利商店取貨、自取

而在信用卡付款時會使用到的英文單字有 credit card / debit card（信用卡、金融卡）、coupon code （折價碼）、name of card holder （持卡人姓名）、card number （卡號）、the expiry （到期日期）、the three-digit security code （三位數的安全碼）等。

Point 4 退換貨

收到貨品後，如果不滿意的話可以進行退換貨，但由於每間店家的規定都不大一樣，所以在付款前要記得先確認取消與退貨政策（cancellation and refund policy），避免產生消費糾紛。

- Some tickets cannot be changed or cancelled.
  有些票不得變更或取消。
- You can get all your money back if not satisfied with services.
  如果對服務不滿意，您可以獲得全額退費。
- "No Shows" will be charged 100% of the quoted tour price. 未出現會被收取 100% 的團費報價。

① **organizer** [ˋɔrgə͵naɪzɚ]
n（指放在書桌上的）文具收納盒

A desk organizer is a necessity to take care of this mess.
要處理這樣凌亂的書桌必定要買一個文具收納盒。

② **ebony** [ˋɛbənɪ] n 黑檀木

An ebony opal makes an exquisite jewel in a necklace.
鑲有貓眼石的黑檀木墜飾讓項鍊更精緻優雅。

③ **cedar** [ˋsidɚ] n 雪松木

The cedar trees in the woods are extremely fragrant.
樹林中的雪松木有很濃郁的芬芳。

訂購

	Organizer ① 5-in-1 ❶ 整合式五合一衣物儲藏櫃	ebony ② 黑檀木	1	$329.99
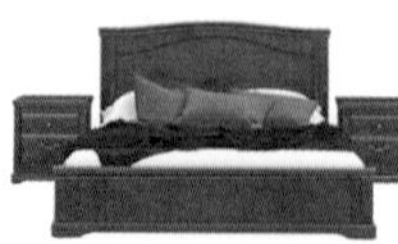	Bed frame California king 床架 加州特大尺寸	ebony 黑檀木	1	$579.99
	Highboy 抽屜收納櫃	dark cedar③ 黑雪松木	1	$300.00

Article 2 結帳

Organizer 5-in-1 整合式五合一衣物儲藏櫃	ebony 黑檀木	1	$329.99
Bed frame ④ California king 床架 加州特大尺寸	ebony 黑檀木	1	$579.99
Highboy 抽屜收納櫃	dark cedar 黑雪松木	1	$300.00

Subtotal ⑤ ／小計：	$1,209.98
Sales tax (7%) ／消費稅：(7%)	$ 84.70
Shipping ／運費：	$129.00
Total Due ⑥ ／總金額：	$1,423.68

Article 3 收到缺貨通知

Dear customer ⑦,

At the moment ❷, our dark cedar Highboy Item number 23432 is out of stock ⑧. We can let you know when ❸ the item is available. For now, we will refund the amount for this item. If at the time when our product ⑨ is back in stock ❹, you would still like to purchase ⑩ the item, please go through the purchasing process ⑪ again.

We apologize ⑫ for the inconvenience ⑬.

Carton Furniture and More

親愛的顧客：

目前，我們的黑雪松抽屜收納櫃，產品編號 23432，缺貨中。我們可以在此商品可購買時通知您。目前我們將先退還給您此商品的金額。若此商品到貨時您仍想購買，請再次照訂購流程下單。

我們對此造成的不便深感抱歉。

紙箱傢俱公司

VOCABULARY ♪189-01

④ **frame** [frem] n 框架

The frame of these sunglasses could use a polish.

這些太陽眼鏡的框架需要擦亮。

⑤ **subtotal** [sʌb`totḷ] n / v 小計

The subtotal of your order is just under $200.

你的訂單小計低於兩百美元。

⑥ **due** [dju] a 到期的

The books are due this weekend.

這個週末這些書就到期了。

⑦ **customer** [`kʌstəmɚ] n 客人

A customer at the shop asked Anthony where to find printer paper.

商店裡的客人問安東尼哪裡可以找到影印紙。

⑧ **stock** [stɑk] n 存貨、庫存

The storage cabinet is in stock.

儲物櫃還有庫存。

⑨ **product** [`prɑdəkt] n 商品

Which product were you looking for?

你在找的商品是哪個？

⑩ **purchase** [`pɝtʃəs] v / n 購買

If you purchase 10, we can give you one for free.

如果你買十個，我們可以一個算你免費。

⑪ **process** [`prɑsɛs] v 處理

Our company will process the order first thing in the morning.

我們公司早上第一件事就是處理訂單。

⑫ **apologize** [ə`pɑlə͵dʒaɪz] v 道歉

I'm sure Willy will forgive you if you apologize.

如果你道歉的話，我確定威利會原諒你的。

⑬ **inconvenience** [͵ɪnkən`vinjəns] n 不方便、麻煩

This meeting is a real inconvenience, but it is mandatory.

參加這個會議真的很煩人，但規定一定要去。

VOCABULARY ♪190-01

⑭ **item** [ˋaɪtəm] n 項目

Every item in our store is currently on sale.

我們店裡的每項商品目前都特價中。

⑮ **discount** [ˋdɪskaʊnt] n 折扣

This coupon is for a 10% discount.

這張折價卷可以打九折。

PATTERN ♪190-02

❶ **5-in-1** 五合一

Our 5-in-1 cabinet can do some cool things.

我們的五合一儲物櫃可以做很多很酷的利用。

❷ **at the moment** 目前

At the moment, Ashley needs to find a way to call her dad.

現在艾希莉需要找個方法打給她爸。

❸ **let you know when** 當……會讓你知道

Chris, I'll let you know when we can meet next week.

克里斯，我會再跟你說下星期我們何時可以見面。

❹ **back in stock** 到貨

These shoes will be back in stock on Friday.

星期五這些鞋子會到貨。

❺ **reason for** ……的原因

The reason for James's anger was difficult to understand.

詹姆士生氣的原因很難理解。

Article 4 退貨

Refund

Reason for ❺ refund: Item Out of Stock

Item ⑭ Number 23432:

Highboy	dark cedar	1	$300.00
		Tax refund: (7%)	$ 21.00
		Discount ⑮ on Shipping:	$ 29.00
		Total Refund Credited:	$350.00

退款

退款原因：品項缺貨

產品編號 23432：

抽屜收納櫃	黑雪松木	1	$300.00
		消費稅退款：(7%)	$ 21.00
		運費折扣：	$ 29.00
		退款總金額：	$350.00

MORE VOCABULARY ♪191-01

carpenter [ˋkarpəntɚ] n 木匠
bricklayer [ˋbrɪk͵leɚ] n 磚匠
plumber [ˋplʌmɚ] n 水電工
painter [ˋpentɚ] n 油漆工
architect [ˋarkə͵tɛkt] n 建築師
technician [tɛkˋnɪʃən] n 技師
mechanic [məˋkænɪk] n 修理工

LEARN MORE!

♪191-02 ❶ **Can I speak to someone in charge of…?**
我可以和負責……的人員通話嗎？

A: Can I speak to someone in charge of this matter?
我可以和負責這件事的人員通話嗎？

B: Just a moment, please. I'll put you through.
請稍等一下，我幫你轉接。

♪191-03 ❷ **there's something wrong with…** ……有問題

A: There's something wrong with the printer. It doesn't work.
印表機有問題，無法使用。

B: The general affairs personnel will fix it later.
總務人員等一下會來修理。

LEARN MORE! ♪191-04

有了自己的家之後，每個人對於居家裝潢的風格都有些想法，來看看有那些裝潢風格：

Ⓐ **Japanese** [͵dʒæpəˋniz] a 日式的
Ⓑ **Scandinavian** [͵skændəˋnevɪən] a 北歐風的
Ⓒ **Baroque** [bəˋrok] a 巴洛克的
Ⓓ **country** [ˋkʌntrɪ] a 鄉村風的
Ⓔ **contemporary** [kənˋtɛmpə͵rɛrɪ] a 現代風的
Ⓕ **classical** [ˋklæsɪkl̩] a 古典的

預約居家清潔服務

house clean

① **book** [bʊk] v 預約、預定

I am going to book a trip to New Orleans.

我要預定去新紐奧良的旅行。

② **date** [det] n 日期

My date of departure is May 13.

我的出發日期是五月十三日。

③ **recommend** [ˌrɛkəˋmɛnd] v 推薦

I recommend that we go for lunch.

我建議我們一起吃中餐。

預約服務

Book ① a House Cleaning	預訂房屋清潔
Zip Code (for location to be cleaned):	**郵政編碼**（適用於清潔地點）：
Number of bedrooms to be Cleaned:	**要清理的臥室數量**：
Number of bathrooms to be Cleaned:	**要清潔的浴室數量**：
Date ② of Cleaning:	**清潔日期**：
Time of Cleaning:	**清潔時間**：
Phone Number:	**電話號碼**：
email:	**電子郵件**：

For your home size, we recommend ③ : _____ hours

對於您住家的大小，我們建議：____ 小時

Get a Price　　取得報價

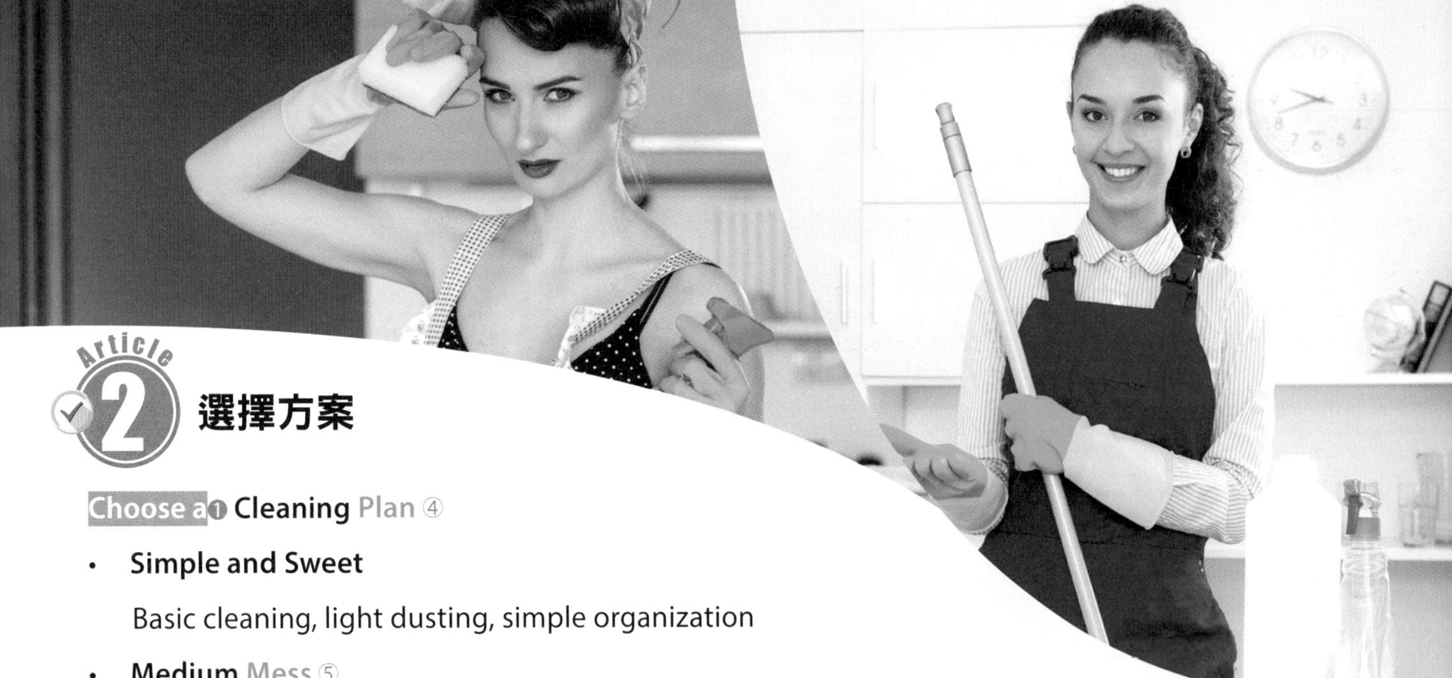

Article 2 選擇方案

Choose a❶ Cleaning Plan ④

- **Simple and Sweet**

  Basic cleaning, light dusting, simple organization

- **Medium Mess ⑤**

  Got a mess? We can clean and organize. Kitchens and bathrooms will receive ❷ a deep clean

- **Deep ⑥ Clean for Big Dirt**

  Deep clean and organizing ⑦, dusting, vacuuming, mopping

選擇清潔計劃

- 簡單輕鬆掃：基本清潔、輕度除塵、簡單收納。
- 中等混亂：家裡一團糟嗎？ 我們可以清潔和收納。進行廚房和浴室的深度清潔。
- 髒污深度大掃除：深度清潔和收納、除塵、吸塵器清掃，拖地。

Article 3 選擇時間

For your cleaning needs, we recommend 4.5 hours of cleaning time.

Date selected: 7/24/2019

Please select from the following available times:

Times: ☐ 8 A.M. ☐ 8:30 A.M ☐ 9 A.M. ☐ 9:30 A.M. ☐ 1 P.M.

為了滿足您的清潔需求，我們建議您選擇 4.5 小時的清潔時間。

選擇日期： 2019 年 7 月 24 日

請從以下時段中選擇：

時段： ☐早上 8 點 ☐早上 8 點 30 分 ☐早上 9 點 ☐早上 9 點 30 分 ☐下午 1 點

VOCABULARY ♪193-01

④ **plan** [plæn] n / v 計畫

The plan is to go to the movies on Friday.

計畫是星期五去看電影。

⑤ **mess** [mɛs] n 骯髒、雜亂

The mess in this room is insane.

這房間的髒亂程度真的很扯。

⑥ **deep** [dip] a 深度的

We need to do a deep cleaning to make up for not doing anything lately.

我們必須做個深度大掃除彌補近日來的無所事事。

⑦ **organize** [ˋɔrgəˏnaɪz] v 組織

I am organizing a little party here tonight.

今晚我將在這辦一個小型派對。

PATTERN ♪193-02

❶ **choose a** 選擇一個……

We want to choose a good location for the celebration.

我們想要選一個好地點來慶祝。

❷ **will receive** 將會接收、得到……

The building will receive a makeover during the break.

這棟建築物在放假期間會進行翻修。

VOCABULARY ♪194-01

⑧ **select** [sə`lɛkt] v 選擇

You need to select the kind of car you want to drive.

你必須選擇你要開的車的種類。

⑨ **cleaner** [`klinɚ] n 清潔工

A cleaner found a left airpod in the library today.

清潔員今天在圖書館發現一只左邊的藍牙無線耳機。

PATTERN ♪194-02

❸ **help us to** 幫助我們……

You can help us to find names for new stars.

你可以幫我們找給新恆星的名字。

❹ **tell us what you think** 告訴我們你怎麼想……

If you tell us what you think, maybe we can find you help.

如果你跟我們說你怎麼想的，或許我們可以幫你找到幫助。

❺ **how did you hear about** 你如何得知……

Could you tell us how you heard about us?

你可以跟我們說你如何得知我們的嗎？

Article 4 選擇清掃人員

Select ⑧ an available cleaner ⑨:

Stacey Johnsen	rated 4.9 stars
Alenna Andrews	rated 4.9 stars
Marla Hernandez	rated 4.9 stars
George Garris	rated 4.8 stars
Brenda Barlows	rated 4.6 stars

選擇可提供服務的清潔人員：

斯泰西・約翰森	評價 4.9 顆星
愛蓮娜・安德魯	評價 4.9 顆星
瑪拉・荷娜黛茲	評價 4.9 顆星
喬治・加里斯	評價 4.8 顆星
布蘭達・巴洛斯	評價 4.6 顆星

撰寫意見調查表

Please rate ⑩ our service!

Your comments help us to ❸ improve. Please tell us what you think ❹!

- **Date of Cleaning:**
- **Name of Cleaner:**
- **Rate your Cleaner:**
- **Comments on satisfaction ⑪ or areas for improvement:**
- **Rate our website ⑫ ease of use:**
- **Would you recommend our services ⑬ to others?**
- **How did you hear about ❺ us?**
- **Additional ⑭ Comments:**

Thank you very much for your input ⑮. We hope to hear from you again!

請評價我們的服務！

您的意見有助於我們改進，請告訴我們你的意見！

- 清潔日期：
- 清潔人員名稱：
- 為您的清潔人員評分：
- 關於滿意度或改進領域的意見：
- 評價我們網站的易用性：
- 您會向他人推薦我們的服務嗎？
- 您是怎麼知道我們的？
- 其他意見：

非常感謝您的寶貴意見。 盼望再次收到您的消息！

VOCABULARY ♪195-01

⑩ **rate** [ret] v 評分

If you rate your service, we will give you a discount on your next purchase.

如果你幫我們的服務評分，我們會給你下次的購物折扣。

⑪ **satisfaction** [͵sætɪsˋfækʃən] n 滿足、滿意

The satisfaction of our customers is our top concern.

我們最主要的考量，就是我們客戶的滿意程度。

⑫ **website** [ˋwɛb͵saɪt] n 網站

The client's website is up and running.

客人的網站已經上線開始經營了。

⑬ **service** [ˋsɝvɪs] n 服務

Our car wash has additional services available.

我們的洗車服務有附加的服務可提供。

⑭ **additional** [əˋdɪʃənḷ] a 外加的、額外的

There will be an additional charge to check out of the hotel later.

等一下才辦理退房手續的話，會有額外的費用產生。

⑮ **input** [ˋɪn͵put] n 投入、輸入

Your input will help us with our development.

你的投入會幫助我們的發展。

預約搬家服務

moving house

① **need** [nid] n 需求

The needs of our patients are our greatest concern.
我們最主要關心的就是我們病人的需求。

② **move** [muv] n 移動、行動、措施

A move can be a good thing to give a person a change of scenery.
移動一下（換個地方）可以幫人改變心境。

③ **residential** [ˏrɛzəˋdɛnʃəl] a 居住的

The residential building was filled with luxury apartments.
這些住宅建築內有許多奢華的公寓。

④ **delivery** [dɪˋlɪvərɪ] n 運送、遞送

The delivery of goods will be completed on Tuesday by noon.
貨物的運送將在星期二中午前完成。

預約服務

Time to Move? 何時要搬家？

We've can take care of all your moving needs ①.
我們可以滿足您所有搬運上的需求。

Let's start with ❶ you telling us a little bit about ❷ what you need.
讓我們先了解一下你需要什麼服務。

State of move ②:	搬運狀態：
Address at location:	所在地地址：
Business or residential ③?	商業或住宅？
Moving in-state?	州內搬運？
Address for delivery ④:	目的地地址：
Moving date:	搬運日期：
Name:	名稱：
Phone number:	電話號碼：
email:	電子郵件：

Article 2 選擇方案與時間

Choose your package

☐ **Large Furniture** **$150/hr**

For local ⑤ moves only. We take care of your large furniture. Sofas, beds, cabinets, refrigerators, washers and dryers. You take care of the rest!

☐ **Full House** **price varies**

You prepack ⑥. We move it. We will price out the move based on the size of the house, the truck size necessary, and the number of movers needed.

☐ **Total Package** **price varies**

We box and pack up everything.

Choose a starting time to move: ☐ 8:00 A.M. ☐ 12:30 P.M.

選擇您的方案

☐ **大型家具** **150 美元／小時**

僅限本地移動。我們會照料好您的大型傢俱。沙發、床、儲藏櫃、冰箱、洗衣機和烘乾機。剩下的由您處理！

☐ **全屋搬運** **價格視情況而異**

你預先打包好。我們負責移動搬運它們。我們會根據房子大小、需要的貨車大小跟搬運工人數來決定報價。

☐ **全套服務** **價格視情況而異**

我們裝箱並打包全部房內的傢俱物品。

選擇搬運開始的時間：☐上午 8 點 ☐下午 12 點 30 分

VOCABULARY ♪197-01

⑤ **local** [ˋlokḷ] a 當地的

Our local park got a recent renovation.

我們當地的公園最近才翻新。

⑥ **prepack** [priˋpæk] v 事先包裝、事先打包

We need to prepack before the moving company arrives.

我們要在搬家公司抵達之前事先打包好。

PATTERN ♪197-02

❶ **let's start with** 讓我們從……開始

Let's start with a conversation about when we should take a trip.

讓我們先從討論我們何時要旅行開始。

❷ **tell us a little bit (about)** 簡單說關於……

Tell us a little bit about your favorite hobbies.

跟我們說一點你最喜歡的興趣。

VOCABULARY ♪198-01

⑦ **reassemble** [riə`sɛmbḷ] v 組裝

It took me 2 hours to reassemble the desk.

我花了兩小時組裝這張桌子。

⑧ **destination** [ˌdɛstə`neʃən] n 目的地

How long will it take us to get to our destination?

要花多久時間，我們才可以抵達目的地？

⑨ **quote** [kwot] v 引用、引述

The newspaper quoted the musician in the article.

這個報社在這篇文章中引述了這個音樂家。

PATTERN ♪198-02

❸ **hired you for** 雇用你來……

We hired you for the evening to serve drinks and snacks.

我們今晚雇用你來招待點心跟酒水。

❹ **arrived on time** 準時抵達

Jasi arrived on time, but she was very tired.

賈西準時抵達，但她非常的累。

❺ **was supposed to be** ……應該要是……

This was supposed to be a quick job to finish.

這照理說應該是可以很快完成的工作。

Article 3 追加服務

Additional Services

- **Boxing up Kitchen**
- **Box up Rooms**
- **Out-of-State Move**
- **The Works**

We unpack, place, and **reassemble** ⑦ everything in your delivery **destination** ⑧.

Call us as 1-612-555-9022 for a **quote** ⑨ today!

額外服務

- **裝箱廚房用品**
- **裝箱房間內物品**
- **州外搬運**
- **全套服務**

到達您指定的運送目的地後，我們會進行拆箱、安置傢俱與物品，並重新組裝全部的東西。

今日就致電 1-612-555-9022 拿取報價！

Article 4 撰寫意見調查表

Dear Moving Masters,

We hired you for ❸ our move to Daytona, Florida in June.

Overall, we were wonderfully pleased with the service we received. We purchased ⑩ The Works. The movers arrived on time ❹ on the day of the move and very professional in the handling ⑪ of our moving needs.

The transit time was speedy, and when we arrived in Daytona a week later, everything had been unpacked ⑫ and reassembled as requested ⑬.

In fact, the only issue ⑭ we had was that the set-up in two of the rooms seemed to have gotten mixed up. Our study was set up where our son's bedroom was supposed to be ❺. Ironically, we prefer that set up and have chosen to keep it this way. We are merely ⑮ informing you to help with future moves.

Thank you again for the wonderful moving service.

The Kerry Family

親愛的移動大師：

我們於今年六月雇請貴司提供搬運服務至佛羅里達州的代托納。

整體來說，我們對於此次服務感到非常滿意。我們購買了「全套服務」。搬家公司在搬家當天準時到達，非常專業地處理我們的搬家需求。

運送時間很快，當一周後我們到達代托納時，所有東西都已拆封並按我們的要求重新組裝好了。

事實上，我們唯一的問題是有兩個房間的傢俱跟物品擺放似乎被搞混了。我們書房的東西被安置在原本應該是我們兒子的房間裡。但好玩的是我們其實比較喜歡搞混的版本，也決定不再更動。我們寫信只是想通知貴司這件事，以幫助貴司未來的搬運服務。

再次感謝貴司提供的完美搬運服務。

凱瑞家

VOCABULARY ♪199-01

⑩ **purchase** [ˋpɝtʃəs] v 購買

We purchased an electric toothbrush, but it wouldn't charge.

我們買了一個電動牙刷，但沒有辦法充電。

⑪ **handling** [ˋhændlɪŋ] n 處理

The shipping and handling will be covered by the customer.

運費費跟處理費將由客人負擔。

⑫ **unpack** [ʌnˋpæk] v 拆封

I unpacked the box and was surprised to find nothing inside.

我拆開了箱子之後很意外地發現裡面沒有東西。

⑬ **request** [rɪˋkwɛst] n / v 要求

I wrote the letter as you requested.

我應你的要求寫了一封信。

⑭ **issue** [ˋɪʃjʊ] n 議題、問題

The issue with the bed was that there was a crack in the frame.

這個床的問題是床架有一個裂縫。

⑮ **merely** [ˋmɪrlɪ] ad 僅僅、只

Ian is merely trying to find a new way to fix the problem.

伊恩只是嘗試找新方法來解決這問題。

LEARN MORE! ♪199-02

運輸方式和工具有很多種，帶給人類很大的便利呢！

- **freight transport** 貨物運輸
- **ferry** 渡輪
- **subway** 地鐵
- **high speed rail** 高鐵
- **airplane** 飛機

旅遊

travel

VOCABULARY ♪200-01

① **garden** [ˋgardn̩] n 花園

The garden is overrun with weeds.

這花園長滿了雜草。

② **wander** [ˋwandɚ] v 漫步、閒逛

We went wandering around the town.

我們在小鎮上閒晃。

③ **fill** [fɪl] v 填滿

Fill your time with hobbies and classes if you want.

如果你想要，就把你的時間填滿要上的課跟興趣。

④ **session** [ˋsɛʃən] n 一場、一節

The music sessions are forty-five minutes long.

每一場音樂會的長度是 45 分鐘。

Article 1 查找資料

Budapest in the early summer is delightful! Garden ① bars in the evening, wandering the Central Market, and wandering ② the streets of Budapest will fill ③ your days. You can round things up by taking a ferry ride on the Danube and joining traditional Hungarian music and dance sessions ④!

初夏的布達佩斯是很吸引人的！晚上的花園酒吧、在中央市集逛逛以及在布達佩斯的街道上漫遊將充實你的每一天。您可以乘坐遊多瑙河的渡輪前往參加傳統匈牙利音樂和舞蹈表演來結束美好一天！

Article 2 訂機票

Book ⑤ your Tickets

One Way Trip　　Round Trip　　Multicity Trip

Takeoff Location:　　Destination:

Start Date:　　Return Date:

訂購您的機票

單程　　來回　　多個目的地停留

起飛地點：　　目的地：

出發日期：　　回程日期：

VOCABULARY ♪201-01

⑤ **book** [buk] v 預定

We desperately need to book a hotel.

我們迫切地需要訂旅館。

LEARN MORE! ♪201-02

❶ **wrap things up by**
藉由……概述某事

I want to wrap things up by talking about our meeting next week.

我想要藉由討論我們下星期的會議來把事情做個概述。

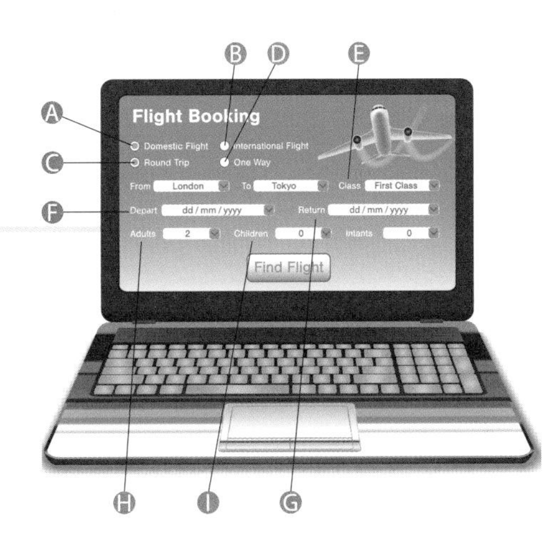

♪201-03

Ⓐ **domestic flight** 國內班機
Ⓑ **international flight** 國際班機
Ⓒ **round trip** 來回票
Ⓓ **one way** 單程票
Ⓔ **class** 艙等
Ⓕ **depart** 出發日
Ⓖ **return** 回程日
Ⓗ **adult** 成人
Ⓘ **children** 小孩

廉價航空機票

廉價航空的機票雖然票價較為便宜，但相關規定也較多，例如：不可退票或退費、更改日期需要支付手續費……等等，若要挑選座位、托運行李、購買餐點也都需要另外付費，在訂購前要特別留意。

Article 3 訂飯店

Book your stay with us! Let us know when you want to stay.
預訂我們的住宿！如果您想留宿，請告訴我們。

Name:	名稱：
email:	電子郵件：
Arrival ⑥ date:	到達日期：
Departure date:	離開日期：
Number of guests:	人數：
Number of rooms:	房間數量：
Standard room	標準間
Executive ⑦ suite	行政套房
Breakfast included ☐ Yes ☐ No	含早餐 ☐ 是 ☐ 否
Wi-fi access ☐ Yes ☐ No	含無線網絡連線 ☐ 是 ☐ 否
Gym access ☐ Yes ☐ No	含健身房使用服務 ☐ 是 ☐ 否

LEARN MORE! ♪ 202-01

24 HRs security
24 小時保全

vending machine
販賣機

laundry service
洗衣服務

room service
客房服務

luggage storage
行李寄放

airport shuttle
機場接送

pet allowed
可攜帶寵物

free wifi
免費 wifi

jacuzzi bath
按摩浴缸

breakfast
早餐

wake up call
晨喚服務

online reservation
線上預約

Article 4

填寫簽證申請表

Visa Application

Given ⑧ Name(s): **Surname:**
D.O.B.:

Place of Birth:

Passport Number:

Place of Issue:

Date of Issue:

Date of Expiration ⑨:

Reason for Visit:

Places planning to visit:

Address during stay ⑩:

Signature:

* Please complete the form and submit with a copy of Passport and 2 2-inch passport photos.

簽證申請

名字： 姓： 出生日期：

出生地： 護照號碼： 簽發地點：

發行日期： 到期日期： 拜訪原因：

計劃拜訪的地方：

停留期間的地址：

簽名：

※ 請填寫表格並提交一份護照副本和兩張 2 英寸的護照大頭照。

VOCABULARY ♪203-01

⑥ **arrival** [əˋraɪvḷ] n 抵達

The arrival date is later than we expected.

抵達日期比我們設想的還晚。

⑦ **executive** [ɪgˋzɛkjʊtɪv] a 決策的、管理的

The executive package is difficult to afford.

管理職的待遇很難負擔。

⑧ **given** [ˋgɪvən] a 規定的、特定的

Your given name is also known as your first name.

你出生時取的名字就是你姓氏前面的名字。

⑨ **expiration** [ˏɛkspəˋreʃən] n 過期

The expiration date on the cheese was two weeks ago.

起司的過期日是兩個禮拜之前。

⑩ **stay** [ste] n / v 留下、停留

We have a week-long stay in New York.

我們會在紐約待一星期。

VOCABULARY ♪204-01

⑪ **location** [lo`keʃən] n 位置

Dean's location was easy to find using GPS.

迪恩的位置透過 GPS 很好找到。

⑫ **international** [ˌɪntɚ`næʃənḷ] a 國際的

This year's international competition was larger than last year's.

今年的國際競賽比去年的大。

Article 5 租車

Car Rental	汽車出租
Pickup Location:	取車地點：
Drop off Location:	還車地點：
(if at a different location ⑪)	（如果不同於取車地點）
Date of Pickup:	取車日期：
Date of Return:	還車日期：
Name:	名稱：
email:	電子郵件：
Contact Number:	聯繫電話：
☐ I am 25+ years old.	☐ 我 25 歲以上。
☐ I have an international ⑫ driver's license.	☐ 我有國際駕駛執照。

購買交通票券

Purchase ⑬ a city transportation Day-Pass

Passes are for use on all forms of ❶ Public Transportation. Included in the transportations allowed are the metro, public buses, hop-on hop-off buses, public ferries ⑭, and rental bikes.

	Adult	Child
Half-day Pass	$7.99	$5.99
24-hour Pass	$11.99	$9.99

Number of adult passes:

Number of child passes:

購買城市大眾交通工具的日通行票

通行票適用於所有形式的大眾交通工具服務，其中包括地鐵、公共巴士、觀光巴士、公共渡輪和自行車出租服務。

	成人	兒童
半日通行票	$7.99	$5.99
24 小時通行票	$11.99	$9.99

成人通行票數量：

子女通行票數量：

VOCABULARY ♪ 205-01

⑬ **purchase** [ˋpɝtʃəs] v 購買

When you purchase three, you get one for free.

你買三個的話可以一個免費。

⑭ **ferry** [ˋfɛrɪ] n 渡輪、渡船

We took ferries all over Venice.

我們坐渡船遊了整個威尼斯。

⑮ **entry** [ˋɛntrɪ] n 進入

The entry cost to the museum is only $5.

博物館入場費只要五美金。

PATTERN ♪ 205-02

❶ **for use on all forms of**
可用在……的任何形式

This ointment is for use on all forms of skin fungus.

這個藥膏可用於任何皮膚真菌感染。

PATTERN ♪206-01

❷ **children under 12**
十二歲以下的孩童

Children under 12 eat free with a parent.

十二歲以下由父母其中一方陪伴的孩童可以免費用餐。

❸ **travel free on** 在……免費搭乘

You can travel free on the metro if an elementary school-age child is with you.

如果你陪同小學生年紀的小孩，可以免費搭乘地鐵。

❹ **we will definitely**
我們肯定會……

We will definitely be seeing you again.

我們肯定會再跟你見面的。

Article 7 購買觀光票券

Tourist Pass

This 2-day pass includes public transportation, choice of museum entry (Natural History Museum, Astronomy Museum, Museum of Contemporary Art, Museum of Art, Museum of Science), entry to the City Zoo.

Choice of 2 museum entries: $29.99
Choice of 3 museum entries: $32.99
Choice of 4 museum entries: $35.99
Date of Pass Start:
Number of Adult Tickets:

Children under 12 ❷ receive free museum **entry** ⑮ with included Family Pass and **travel free on** ❸ public transportation.

旅遊通行證

這個為期 2 天的通行證包括可使用大眾交通工具、選擇想參觀的博物館（自然歷史博物館、天文博物館、當代藝術博物館、藝術博物館和科學博物館）以及參觀城市動物園。

可入場兩個博物館：$29.99

可入場三個博物館：$32.99

可入場四個博物館：$35.99

通行證開始日期：

成人票數：

使用家庭通行證的 12 歲以下的兒童可免費參觀博物，以及免費乘坐公共交通工具。

一生必去的博物館

★ 法國羅浮宮
（Musée du Louvre）

★ 美國大都會藝術博物館
（Metropolitan Museum of Art）

★ 法國龐畢度中心
（Centre Georges-Pompidou）

★ 英國大英博物館
（British Museum）

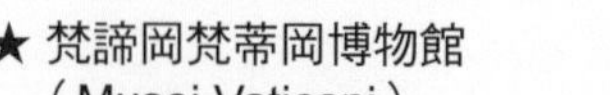

★ 梵諦岡梵蒂岡博物館
（Musei Vaticani）

Article 8 發布貼文

We loved our trip to Budapest! Beautiful churches and great walks! We got a 2-day pass for public transportation and museums, and our kids enjoyed travelling around. **We will definitely** ④ go back!

我們喜歡我們的布達佩斯之旅！參觀美麗的教堂和很棒的散步！我們買了為期兩天的公共交通和博物館通行證，我們的孩子很享受一起旅行。我們一定會再次造訪！

Keyword Search 網路關鍵字搜尋

網路上的資訊沒有經過系統整理，比較雜亂無章，有時候可信度也不夠。在搜尋的時候適時使用關鍵字將範圍縮小。而閱讀網路文章的時候，注意以下幾點，將有助於透過以上幾點，可以幫助我們判斷網路資訊的可靠性和正確性。

1. 作者（author）
   身分、學術背景、專業背景……等。
2. 贊助商（sponsor）
   是否為業配文（sponsored post），有沒有置入性行銷（embedded advertising / product placement）。
3. 時效性（currency）
   文章或資訊來源的張貼、刊登時間。
   例如：Posted: January 19, 2019 張貼時間：2019 年 1 月 19 日
   Updated: April 12, 2019 更新時間：2019 年 4 月 12 日

午休5分鐘的英文閱讀：利用「零碎時間」，學習最有效率！ / 不求人文化編輯群著. -- 初版. -- 臺北市：不求人文化, 2019.08
面； 公分
ISBN 978-986-97517-4-2（平裝）
1.英語 2.讀本
805.18 108009226

午休5分鐘的英文閱讀 Spending Five Minutes in Lunch Break to Learn English Reading

書名 / 午休 5 分鐘的英文閱讀：利用「零碎時間」，學習最有效率！
作者 / 不求人文化編輯群
發行人 / 蔣敬祖
出版事業群總經理 / 廖晏婕
銷售暨流通事業群總經理 / 施宏
總編輯 / 劉俐伶
校對 / 楊易、劉婉瑀
視覺指導 / 姜孟傑、鍾維恩
排版 / 菩薩蠻電腦科技有限公司
封面圖片 / www.shutterstock.com
內文圖片 / tw.pixtastock.com
法律顧問 / 北辰著作權事務所蕭雄淋律師
印製 / 皇甫彩藝印刷股份有限公司
初版 / 2019 年 8 月
初版五刷 / 2022 年 8 月
出版 / 我識出版教育集團——不求人文化
電話 / (02) 2345-7222
傳真 / (02) 2345-5758
地址 / 台北市忠孝東路五段 372 巷 27 弄 78 之 1 號 1 樓
網址 / www.17buy.com.tw
E-mail / iam.group@17buy.com.tw
定價 / 新台幣 349 元 / 港幣 116 元
facebook 網址 / www.facebook.com/ImPublishing

總經銷 / 我識出版社有限公司出版發行部
地址 / 新北市汐止區新台五路一段 114 號 12 樓
電話 / (02) 2696-1357 傳真 / (02) 2696-1359

港澳總經銷 / 和平圖書有限公司
地址 / 香港柴灣嘉業街 12 號百樂門大廈 17 樓
電話 / (852) 2804-6687 傳真 / (852) 2804-6409

2011 不求人文化
2009 懶鬼子英日語
2005 意識文化
2005 易富文化
2003 我識地球村
2001 我識出版社

I'm 我識出版集團
I'm Publishing Group
www.17buy.com.tw

2011 不求人文化

2009 懶鬼子英日語

2005 意識文化

2005 易富文化

2003 我識地球村

2001 我識出版社